THE
AGE
OF
DESIRE

THE Age OF Desire

A Novel

JENNIE FIELDS

PAMELA DORMAN BOOKS/VIKING

VIKING

Published by the Penguin Group

Penguin Group (USA) Inc., 375 Hudson Street, New York, New York 10014, U.S.A.

Penguin Group (Canada), 90 Eglinton Avenue East, Suite 700, Toronto, Ontario, Canada M4P 2Y3
(a division of Pearson Penguin Canada Inc.)

Penguin Books Ltd, 80 Strand, London WC2R 0RL, England

Penguin Ireland, 25 St. Stephen's Green, Dublin 2, Ireland (a division of Penguin Books Ltd)

Penguin Books Australia Ltd, 250 Camberwell Road, Camberwell, Victoria 3124, Australia
(a division of Pearson Australia Group Pty Ltd)

Penguin Books India Pvt Ltd, 11 Community Centre, Panchsheel Park, New Delhi – 110 017, India

Penguin Group (NZ), 67 Apollo Drive, Rosedale, Auckland 0632, New Zealand
(a division of Pearson New Zealand Ltd)

Penguin Books (South Africa) (Pty) Ltd, 24 Sturdee Avenue,
Rosebank, Johannesburg 2196, South Africa

Penguin Books Ltd, Registered Offices: 80 Strand, London WC2R 0RL, England

First published in 2012 by Viking Penguin, a member of Penguin Group (USA) Inc.

A Pamela Dorman Book / Viking

This a work of fiction based on real events.

Excerpts from the letters and diary of Edith Wharton are reprinted by permission of the estate of Edith Wharton and the Watkins/Loomis Agency. The letters are from the collection of Harry Ransom Center, the University of Texas at Austin. The diary is from the collection of Lilly Library, Indiana University, Bloomington, Indiana.

Excerpt from "The Imprint" by Anna de Noailles, translated by Catherine Perry. By permission of Catherine Perry.

ISBN 978-1-62490-005-1

Printed in the United States of America
Designed by Nancy Resnick

In memory of my parents, Belle and Ira Fields,
who taught me the power of words, books and ideas

ACKNOWLEDGMENTS

The first person I must thank is my wonderful agent, Lisa Bankoff. I was struggling to find direction for a new novel when an e-mail from Lisa asked me to call her. That very day, for the first time, I had walked through the Paris neighborhood of my favorite author, Edith Wharton. Unaware that I was in Paris, she said, "Why don't you write about Edith Wharton?" What beautiful serendipity! Because of Lisa, I entered a special and rarefied world that captivated me as no subject ever has. I will forever be in her debt.

I also want to thank my editors, Pamela Dorman and Julie Miesionczek, for their enthusiasm for the book and insightful editing. I am grateful for my patient and thoughtful first readers: Kare Godsell, Irene Goldman-Price (my favorite Wharton scholar), Lindy DeKoven and Susan Spano. Thanks also go to Chris Coover at Christie's, who graciously allowed me access to the Wharton/Bahlmann correspondence before it came up for auction. (What a tremendous surprise and pleasure it was when those letters came to light just months after I focused on Anna as my secondary point of view.) And I want to warmly thank Laura Shoffner, Anna's great-grandniece, who painstakingly transcribed Edith's letters to Anna, put those letters up for auction so scholars could have access to them and very kindly answered my impertinent questions, telling me all she knew of her very special relative.

Thanks also go to the Beinecke Rare Book and Manuscript Library at Yale University; the Lilly Library at Indiana University; and Harry

Ransom Center, the University of Texas at Austin. And I am also indebted to two talented and painstaking biographers: Shari Benstock and Hermione Lee, whose years of thoughtful research helped to guide me along the way.

I am sure that I will step on some academic toes. I have attempted as much as possible to be accurate, and true to Edith Wharton's story. But it is, alas, a novel, with dialogue and scenes that may never have happened. I hope that, as a novelist, the very private and proud Edith looks down on me with indulgence and does not rebuke me for telling her story in the best way I know how.

THE
AGE
OF
DESIRE

ONE

He stands at the edge of the salon, and Edith has the uncomfortable feeling he's staring. A dark-haired man. Formal. Self-certain. There are ten roués like him in every café in Paris. But his sapphire eyes glimmer with a discernible intelligence. His coal black lashes are as long as a giraffe's. Men should not be allowed to have lashes so seductive. He leans on one leg, observing the room, calculating. How hard he seems to work at doing nothing!

Though Edith has been attending Comtesse Rosa de Fitz-James's Paris salons for just over a month, she already knows most everyone in attendance. The Abbé Mugnier, with his comical fountain of white hair and bawdy sense of humor. ("*And there she was, wearing nothing but . . .*") Playwright Paul Hervieu and poet Abel Bonnard arguing in the corner about what makes a human being beautiful. Russian ballet dancer Alexi Toplar with maestro Emmet de Carlo, who leans his head toward him too affectionately while Toplar's wife stands sulkily watching. And their hostess, Comtesse Rosa, enthroned by the fire, her crippled leg propped on an orange velvet hassock. They say the late Count beat her and broke her leg on purpose. The fact that she is an Austrian Jewess did not stop the denizens of this bohemia from taking her long ago to their hearts. The French love nothing better than a female martyr.

Clotting together at the side of the room are the table-enders, hardly older than students, each waiting for a chance to say the witty thing that will make his mark. Ah, to be a young man, with the world laid before one! All a man needs is to be clever, and have some access to money, or a profession. When Edith was a girl, her only option was to marry Teddy Wharton. Now, she has managed to make a name for herself with her books. How gratifying that her most recent one has drawn such a reaction! No one paid the least attention to the others.

The nameless man glances up again through those absurd lashes and smiles vaguely as though he thinks he knows her. She refuses to walk over and speak to him and is relieved when Rosa beckons.

"Dear Edith, listen to that downpour." Rain sheets the windows and the weak fire barely alleviates the damp chill. Rosa leans in and drops her voice. "The Bourgets usually arrive with you. Aren't they coming?" Her eyebrows meet in the middle with disappointment. "And I've invited someone *very* special who's failed to arrive as well. It must be the weather!"

Edith pats Rosa's thin shoulder. "Well, I can't speak for your 'someone special' but the Bourgets always come." The Bourgets are Edith's closest friends in France—and the ones who introduced her to the Comtesse.

"But the Bourgets are usually first," Rosa says. "I'm worried."

Reaching for the fire poker, Edith begins to nudge the guttering flames. Before she knows what's happening, a man's hand wrests the metal spear from her grip. Turning, irritated, she sees that the poker thief is her roué. Leaning across her, he jabs at the fire so fiercely it coughs up a constellation of sparks.

"Dear Rosa, I can't remember the last time you weren't worried about something," he says in perfect French.

"Have you met Mr. Fullerton?" Rosa asks. She speaks his name tenderly, and with a French accent: Full-air-tawn. "Monsieur Morton Fullerton, Madame Edward Wharton. Edith."

The man turns to Edith, sets the poker back in its stand and—his eyes filling with light—takes her hand. "Edith Wharton? So that's who you are!" He pronounces "are" as "ah." His accent is as broad and Bostonian as Teddy's. He's an American! In that perfect French suit. She never dreamed. "I've just finished *The House of Mirth*! What an extraordinary book, Mrs. Wharton! The best I've read since . . ." He shakes his head.

"Thank you." She hears a flutter in her voice. She still has not gotten used to the discomfort and thrill of hearing people she's never met say they've read *The House of Mirth*. As he lets go of her hand, she looks to see that her palm is sooty. Was it from the poker? He takes out a handkerchief, crisp white and embroidered, and gently wipes her fingers. She is astonished, as he seems to think it's his right to take her hands in his. "I have to ask . . . did that lovely creature Lily Bart plan to . . . did she mean to . . . well, I nearly wept and it was quite a knock to my manhood." Wiping his own hands, then folding the handkerchief neatly inward, he tucks it in his pocket, leans over and, nearly touching his lips to her ear, says, "Did she mean to end it all?"

Edith lowers her voice too, as though they are sharing the darkest of secrets. "I only tell my closest friends."

"So hah! You don't know yourself?"

She looks him in the eye. "Well, I didn't say that."

"No, I believe you *don't know*. It would be very French of you not to know. To let your characters carry their secrets to their graves." He glances away, but she sees that his mouth sucks on his mischievousness as one might savor a hard candy.

Edith smiles. "It looks to me as though you've managed to hold on to your manhood quite well, Mr. Fullerton. Only a man could look so pleased with himself."

His blue eyes flash and he laughs. She didn't expect he could laugh at himself.

"So," she says, crossing her arms, thinking that perhaps she will not dislike him after all. "What do you do?"

"I'm a journalist for the *Times* of London."

"An American at the *Times* of London?"

There is a sweet shyness when he nods. She did not expect that either.

"I'm impressed." She notes his lustrous aubergine cravat stuck through with a perfect pearl. His starched shirt with its separate *plastron*. She was so certain he was French!

"How long have you been in France?" she asks.

"Sixteen years . . ."

"You've become a Frenchman, then?"

"Oh no. I'm an American through and through."

"Even after sixteen years? France doesn't feel like home?"

He shakes his head. "The French are a constant source of *surprise*, you see." He speaks the word with a French flair (soo-preeeez). "Of course, New England can be a bit of *soo-preeeez* as well. Going home feels like being dunked in ice water."

"Yes, I've had a similar experience," she says.

"We have a friend in common, you know."

"Do we?"

"A certain Mr. James."

Edith raises her brows. "You know Henry?"

"Intimately." He smiles a devilish smile. "He tells me that you are great friends, which impressed me. He is very choosy about his friends."

Henry James loves the company of stylish, attractive young men, whom he fawns over and to whom he imparts his wisdom. Edith isn't blind to this. She enjoys the company of Henry's fair friends as well. But there is a softness about the majority of Henry's male entourage. A sense that they'd be more comfortable staying home embroidering. Mr. Fullerton seems uniquely brazen and masculine.

"Mr. James is coming to visit me this month," Edith says. "We're going on a motor trip."

"So he wrote. He says motorcars have put the romance back into travel."

Edith smiles. Those were the exact words she'd written to Henry to entice him to come! So Henry's quoting Edith now!

She feels Mr. Fullerton appraising her, and it makes her self-conscious. While Edith Jones Wharton isn't young anymore, she's kept her youthful figure, her litheness. But lately, she's seen signs of growing older. Her neck has subtly smocked with age. She hides it with fashionable high collars, or lace jabots. The crescents beneath her eyes, from years of breathing problems and intermittent nausea, have grown hollow and her cheeks gaunt, making her hazel eyes look larger, sadder. Orphan eyes, she tells herself. She still has a pile of lush auburn hair. It's certainly more beautiful now than in her carrot-topped youth (the cause of much teasing from her brothers). But it has recently been reinforced with threads of silver.

"Listen," Mr. Fullerton says, his voice very intimate, his face very close to hers. "Mrs. Wharton . . ." She feels a salty burn at the base of her throat as he touches her arm. "Do you think that we might . . ."

"The Bourgets at last!" Rosa crows, breaking the spell. Edith looks up to see Paul and Minnie step into the room, the crowd scattering to make way for them. Minnie shakes out her damp skirts. Paul greets everyone with bright eyes.

"My dearest dear," Minnie says, coming directly toward Edith and, stepping in front of Fullerton, kissing her on both cheeks. "Sorry we're so late. Paul needed to *gather* himself." She rolls her eyes sweetly and squeezes Edith's hands.

"A man's toilette is so much more complicated than a woman's," Edith says with a wry smile, assuming she has an audience. "By the way, have you met Mr. Fullerton?" Edith turns, but he is already gone. How had he slipped away so quickly? What had he meant to say?

"Oh, I've met him many times. Perhaps *too* many." Minnie flashes an inscrutable smile. Edith is about to ask her what she meant when Rosa summons the guests with her chalk-squeak voice to join her in the dining room.

But before the party can move toward the elaborately set table, the drawing room doors fly open and a languid figure steps forth: a woman in a gossamer gown with parrot green feathers at the shoulders, dark, heavy hair piled on her head and eyes so large and fiery they could melt the room.

"Madame la Comtesse de Noailles," someone whispers. It's as though the heartbeat of the party stops for a lurching moment.

"Anna," Rosa beams with pleasure. "You've come."

Edith is stunned. All of Paris has whispered of Anna de Noailles, the young poetess whose daring, sensual poems have thrilled every true reader in France, whom painters are lining up to paint. She has never before come to Rosa's. In fact, she has her own selective salon that not one of Edith's friends has been invited to. Paul Bourget had shown Edith her most recent book of poetry with admiration and envy. The earthiness of the poems fascinated Edith and made her blush to her ears.

"Forgive me for being late," Comtesse de Noailles says, taking Rosa's arm and escorting her into the dining room. "It completely slipped my mind that tonight is Tuesday."

Edith sees that Fullerton, now on the other side of the room, is watching de Noailles with interest, but then his gaze shifts to Edith and he flashes her a sweet, bemused grin.

The dining room is hung with finely woven tapestries the color of spices and priceless, delightful paintings. A David of a languorous, round-faced woman lounges over the fireplace. Anna de Noailles, with her peach like breasts, could have modeled for it. How plain and unworthy de Noailles makes Edith feel!

In the tradition of fashionable French dinner parties, Rosa sits in the middle of one side of the table, where she is in contact with the most possible guests. In very purposeful order, the diners fan out from her nucleus, seated on a spectrum from most to least important according to ancient and inflexible French traditions. Anna de Noailles, a comtesse by marriage, a Romanian princess by birth, is placed beside Rosa. Edith finds herself somewhere in the middle with Fullerton just opposite. Napkins are unfolded onto laps. Wine is poured. Edith glances across at Fullerton, who is no longer watching Anna de Noailles like everyone else, but Edith. Every time she looks up, his eyes are fixed on her face. She is praying her face won't redden. How absurd for a woman over forty to blush!

Paul Hervieu says, "Did you read that Giosuè Carducci died?"

Abel Bonnard nods. "They gave him the Nobel Prize just in time."

Edith herself wrote a poem "in the manner of Giosuè Carducci" a few years earlier. She's sad to hear he's died.

"Why do they give Nobels only to dying old men?" one of the table-enders asks.

L'Abbé Mugnier sips his wine and sets his glass down with a smile. "It takes a lifetime to be worthy of such a prize, young man." He nods to himself, pleased he's answered the challenge so neatly.

Anna de Noailles's black eyes sparkle with mischief. "Since you are so wise, Monsieur Abbé, perhaps you can answer this question." She drops her voice so that everyone must lean forward. "Why do they never give the Nobel Prize to a woman?"

"Ah . . ." The Abbé raises a finger. "You are mistaken, Comtesse. They gave the Nobel Peace Prize to a woman just the year before last. Can anyone remember her name?" There is an extended silence.

"Well, that makes the point!" Minnie says. "No one can recall her name."

"What do I care for the Peace Prize?" de Noailles says. "I ask you . . ." She looks back and forth along the table so that each and every guest is graced by her gaze, then drops her voice to a near whisper. "Is there peace in the world? Not a shred. So why give a prize for something incomplete?" There is laughter all around. Even Edith can't help but smile. "It's the literature prize I'm speaking of. At least writers are required to finish *their* work."

"Are you planning to win someday, Comtesse?" Minnie Bourget says.

"And why not, Madame Bourget? Am I less worthy than dusty old Giosuè Carducci because I have bosoms? I predict a woman will win very soon."

Edith looks at Anna de Noailles and sees the world altering before her eyes. Her ease, her acceptance here are thrilling and disconcerting. She clearly wears no corset beneath the diaphanous gown. She is not afraid to show off those luminous bosoms to which she has called attention. Her glossy hair is dark and uncontrolled. Insubordinate hair, Edith thinks with amusement. Everything about de Noailles is made to seduce. There isn't a man at the table who isn't stirred by her. Even those who aren't the least interested in women. She can see it in their rosy cheeks and burning eyes, as though just glancing intoxicates.

Edith peers down at her own frilly bodice, heavy pearls, and layers of boning and muslin and silk and wool with new dissatisfaction. It seems more like upholstery than clothing. She is old-fashioned and less than beautiful. Proper and stiff. She cannot imagine having the physical self-confidence that de Noailles projects. And then there is this: Anna de Noailles is a woman who knows the pleasures of the body—something Edith, encased in her sexless, empty marriage will never know. Edith was raised to be a lady, not a woman.

"What I think," Comtesse de Noailles says, "is that talent and gender are completely independent. You do not judge a racehorse by the barn it is housed in. You judge it by how swiftly and beautifully it runs, do you not? If exquisite talent is housed in a woman, do we dismiss it?"

Edith is struck by her words. Should she despise this woman for her defiance, or see her as Jeanne d'Arc, leading feminine legions to victory? Up until now suffragists have annoyed Edith. Man hating. Angry. Edith loves the company of men and is proud to have been included in their inner circles. Most women don't deserve a place at the table, in her opinion. But de Noailles—she celebrates womanhood, creates her own intellectual circle and deigns to let men in! Edith is stunned when Morton Fullerton leans forward and gestures to Edith. "Mrs. Wharton here has proven that talent wins out, Comtesse," he says. "All of New York is talking about her latest book. I've never heard a woman's work so lauded. Some reviewers have called her the greatest living American writer."

Edith feels the blood rising to her temples. "That's very kind of you, Mr. Fullerton," she says. "Far too kind."

"What do you write, Mrs. Wharton?"

"Novels, short stories, some poetry."

"Do you write as a woman, about women, for women?"

Edith wants the Comtesse to applaud her. And yet, she is a stickler for honesty. Has she ever written *for women*?

"I write about how in certain strata of American society, there are different rules for men and women. And different consequences. And there is nothing"—she struggles to find the perfect word in French—"*just* about it."

Edith feels surprisingly exposed. *The House of Mirth* said all this and more. But she has never openly spoken of it. And part of her— the part that is disdainful of sudden change—knows her book has pointed out the misfortune of women in this world, yet cannot envision a society without such poorly weighted rules. She questions her own words.

And yet de Noailles seems galvanized by them. "Bravo, my friend. I would very much like to read your book. Sadly, my English is like lace. There are holes in it. Has it been translated into French?"

"I'm hoping it will be soon."

"I'll read it the moment it comes out." Her smile is like morning sun.

Edith feels the magnificence of its heat and the shame that perhaps she does not deserve it.

When the dinner is over, topics volleyed and returned, and cigarettes and cigars smoked, Edith kisses Rosa good-bye, and then Anna de Noailles steps around Hervieu and the Abbé to take her hand.

"Madame Wharton, I wish to know you better. You will come have tea with me, won't you? Of everyone here, you are the fish I would like to catch." Edith breathes in the musky Oriental perfume which rises from the Comtesse's unearthly smooth skin.

"I'd be honored," Edith says.

And then Edith is ruffled by her very breeze as de Noailles flicks her wrap over her shoulders and glides out into the night. Edith looks around for Mr. Fullerton, to thank him for his kind words at dinner, but it's as though he vanished into the cigar smoke at the end of the evening. She searches every open room until she's satisfied he's truly gone.

Paul and Minnie offer to walk Edith home since their flat is just around the corner on the Rue Barbet de Jouy. Minnie takes one arm, Paul the other. They walk hip to hip, as the sidewalk is narrow. It's late, the rain has stopped, and the air is now perfectly icy. The grand and glittering buildings seem to lean over the narrow street like a bower of trees. Oh, how Paris has thrilled Edith. Its beauty never fails to rouse her. And the company. What fine company she has found here!

"Well," Minnie says. "Anna de Noailles doesn't let another soul get a word in, does she?"

"Did you feel that?"

"Didn't you? She monopolized the entire conversation. You barely said a word, Edith. And that's not like you."

"I must admit, I was rapt. The things she said . . . did you not feel she was . . . stirring? Her point of view. I found it so modern. I fear I'm lagging behind in that thinking."

"It's all about *her*. She speaks only of herself. She sets herself up as a deity."

"And what do you think, Paul?" Edith asks.

"I'm a man. I am blinded by her. But of course, I can't hear a word she says."

Minnie shoves him with annoyance. "It was nice of Mr. Fullerton to speak of your book, though, I must say," Minnie adds turning to Edith.

"You said something earlier about Mr. Fullerton," Edith says. "Something not entirely flattering."

"I have nothing against him . . . exactly," she says.

"Fullerton's a decent enough fellow," Paul says.

"But I don't care to know him better," Minnie says.

"Why?"

She shrugs. "One hears things."

"What sorts of things?"

"I don't repeat gossip." It was true: it was one of Minnie's most admirable and irritating traits. She too often hinted at hearsay she wouldn't clarify.

"Besides, even if he is handsome, I don't find him quite appealing."

"Minnie only has eyes for me," Paul says.

Edith squeezes her dapper friend's arm.

"As she should, Paul. As she should."

"While Paul only has eyes for Anna de Noailles," Minnie says with an exaggerated pout.

"Tell Minnie I'll wear a blindfold next time I see Madame la Comtesse."

"Please inform Paul that I will be the one that ties on the blindfold."

"And now," Edith says, reaching 58, rue de Varenne, "I have to appease Teddy, who is no doubt staring at the wall."

"Why don't you bring him next time?"

"Because he wouldn't comprehend a word that's spoken. He refuses to learn French. He can't even pronounce *merci* or *s'il vous plaît* properly!"

"Well, say hello for us," Minnie grips her husband's arm. "In English, of course." Edith can tell she is looking forward to being alone with Paul. Either to scold him or flirt with him. Minnie and Paul are a love match, something as foreign to Edith as French is to the man she married.

The ancient apartment that the Whartons are renting this winter belongs to their friend George Vanderbilt. Edith was enamored the moment she stepped in to visit George a few seasons ago. It boasts all the Faubourg's most ravishing touches: high ceilings, exquisite boiseries and elegant moldings. George's oriental vases and lush Aubusson carpets only make it more elegant.

Marthe, the young *bonne* they've hired locally, sleepily greets Edith at the door, pleased she's come at last. Edith hands over her furs and wraps. Mitou, one of the Pekinese, comes skidding up the hall with little yips of glee and jumps at Edith's skirts. Edith lifts him for a kiss. Jules the bearded collie follows, with a comic, lugubrious gait. He looks away as Edith squats down to pat his head, as though saying, "I didn't ask for this attention." They are her babies. Both so different. Both so lovable. When Edith looks into the eyes of her dogs, she feels an abiding love she feels for no one else—has never felt for anyone else. Sometimes she is sad to recognize this. Other times she knows she is blessed to at least have her pets.

"My angels," she says. "Are you glad Maman is home? Where's Nicette?" She glances about for the other Pekinese.

A whispery voice answers. "Nicette is with Mr. Wharton."

Edith stands to greet Anna Bahlmann with a smile. She never hears her secretary arriving. Dressed in gray wool as always, Anna is a little sparrow, and alights in a room as silently.

"A nice evening?" Anna asks. Her American accent has melted into a sort of elegance over the years, modeled perhaps on Edith's own. When Anna speaks, she is as quiet as a librarian. And as she ages, as her hair mottles from golden to silver, her voice grows softer and more airy.

"Oh, Tonni, it was wonderful. Anna de Noailles was at the salon tonight!" Edith says.

"Was she? Is she all they say she is?"

Edith has shown Anna Bahlmann some of de Noailles's poems and, as expected, they made Miss Bahlmann grow pale and tongue-tied. How different these two Annas are!

"She's even more extraordinary than I imagined," Edith tells Anna. "She rivets a room even when she whispers. Men can't stop looking at her. And . . ." Edith pauses, wondering how to explain. "I doubt she was wearing a single undergarment under her dress."

Her eyebrows raised, Anna says, "It's probably best if I don't hear more!"

Edith laughs and gives her a hug. Anna Bahlmann's sweet countenance and maidenly modesty are unchanged since the day over thirty years ago when she arrived on the Jones's doorstep with an armful of weighty leather books and a brown paper sack of taffy apples, ready to introduce ten-year-old Edith to German poetry. Tiny and slender, with dark golden hair, Anna sat on the sofa in Edith's nursery and brought out a glistening caramel apple on a stick. "Shall we start with one of these?" she asked, passing it to Edith. "In German this is called *ein Apfel*."

Just a few months later, she moved in with the Joneses to become Edith's "finishing" governess. She was barely taller than her charge. And though Mrs. Jones pronounced this tiny German American girl no match for her impossibly headstrong daughter, Anna has matched Edith infinitely well for years and years. Dear Tonni (the Rutherford boys next door, who employed her first, gave her the name, a childish twist on *tante*, or aunt) has slipped in and out of Edith's world, spending entire summers teaching other children, or seasons in Virginia visiting relatives while Edith's family toured abroad, or even a full year in Cuba with another family, but whatever paths they've taken, their lives have become inextricably tied. She is more than an aunt to Edith. A friend, a substitute mother, a conscience. When they're apart, there are always letters. Anna is the first to read Edith's written words and comment, the first to guess when she is happy or unwell. She accompanies the Whartons to dinners, to the theatre sometimes. She is even willing right now to sleep upstairs in a servant's room to be of service. Edith has promised she will find her a flat nearby, but hasn't had the time, and Anna hasn't complained. There is probably no one who knows Edith better than Anna.

"Teddy's still up?" Edith asks, yawning.

"In the library." Anna colors and looks down at her hands. "He was agitated for a while after you left, Herz. I heard him speaking to himself. I don't like to say it . . . but . . . he isn't happy when you leave . . ."

"He tries to start a fight with me every Tuesday evening. As though he can stop me from going to Rosa's! And he manages to be perfectly miserable the rest of the night. We've trained the dogs. How can we train Teddy to stop doing that?"

"He enjoys your company, Edith. He's sorry when you're not around."

From the moment she met him, Anna thought Teddy a fine match for Edith. "He's a good man," she told Edith. "Generous and kind. Even if he doesn't read literature, is that so important in a man? One can't expect men to appreciate what we appreciate." When it comes to men, Anna knows very little.

Leaving Anna in the foyer, Edith strides down the hall to the library. She was hoping Teddy would have gone to bed, but she finds him, as usual, in the tall leather chair he wed the day they moved into the apartment. Nicette is lounging contentedly in his lap. Teddy certainly doesn't look cheerful; he appears lost.

"Dear?" she says.

It's as though he's been on a long journey and has just now arrived back in the room. "Oh, Pussy. You're back."

Edith's mother's nickname for her feels as ridiculous and coquettish as a ruffled dress on a middle-aged woman. Unseemly. Still, Teddy can't outgrow calling her Pussy, and speaks of her to everyone as Puss. She's asked him not to, but to no avail.

He looks down at Nicette as though surprised she's there. Edith struggles as she observes him. In so many ways, Teddy is like a child. He simply wants her attention, to hear that he matters. Surely she can find some patience in herself? She has never thought of herself as vindictive, but lately she has found that puzzle piece of her mother's snapping into place when she is near her husband. How her mother punished her father when he annoyed her or didn't give her what she wanted!

Edith knows Teddy dislikes Paris and misses The Mount, the house they've built in Lenox, Massachusetts, with its horses and pigs and chickens. He seems happiest where there's land and animals, and mud on his boots. And unlike Edith, he wouldn't even have minded spending the winter at their house on Park Avenue, where he could have at least found solace at his Knickerbocker Club just downtown.

"Are you all right?" she asks him.

"I'm fine." His receding hair is a faded gold, as is his thick, bristly mustache. His eyes are an empty sort of blue. A jolly man, she once thought him. A good enough sort of fellow. When he's in fine form, he can tell a rousing story. But on the table by the chair, there's the brandy—which always has a place on that table these days. It's changed him. Edith has noted his face has become coarser and more red lately, the heavy pouches beneath his eyes weightier; his hands have grown shaky. He's twelve years her senior and every year shows on his face. The brandy has done him no favors.

"Did the cook feed you?"

"I think she's attempting to poison us," he says. "I don't know what it was she gave me."

"Did you eat any of it?"

"Not much."

The cook, like the *bonne*, was hired locally, the recommendation of a friend of a friend, but so far she's been a disappointment. Shouldn't French food be delectable, delicate, digestible?

"Well, she's not the best *cuisinière* we've had," Edith says, sighing. Still, Edith doesn't think Teddy's trouble is the dinner. She can't help feeling the burden of his melancholia more and more. A dark sail coming closer and closer to shore. It's even harder to bear because she herself has lately been so happy. But after what Teddy's father did to himself, well, she knows she has to watch him. She hates the thought that maybe she shouldn't have insisted they spend the winter in Paris.

"HJ's coming next week," she says in her most cheerful voice. "And we're going on that motor trip. You'll enjoy that."

Teddy always perks up when they travel. When the Whartons experience new things together, they feel harmony, become suddenly suited to each other. Teddy's a "game" man. He likes new things, new places, and lights up when Edith is delighted. But after a trip, the dullness separates them once more and they simply tolerate each other.

"Henry's such an old lady," Teddy declared after their last trip together. And Edith recognizes that Teddy and Henry haven't a single thing in common except perhaps an interest in whatever touring cars the Whartons employ.

"I walked down to the water today," Teddy says, dreamily.

When she looks at him, her heart prickles as limbs sometimes do when too much has weighed on them for too long.

"Well, that's good. At least you got out," she says.

"Do you think, Puss, we might take a boat ride down the Seine sometime? There are those big public boats. It might be nice."

"Those boats are so vulgar, though." Edith is surprised to hear these words coming from her mouth. She had intended to be gentle with him. "Isn't it too early in the season? I mean, dear, wouldn't it be cold?" How hard she tries to soften her tone.

He closes his eyes sadly. "I suppose you're right."

Yet she feels regretful. She could have been kinder, could have imagined how sparkling Paris would look from the water. Dusk. The fairy-tale turnings of the Beaux Arts buildings. Mansard roofs, glass doors reflecting the plashing of river water, graceful vinelike balconies. Why has she lost all patience with him? She struggles harder and harder to find it.

"I'm getting ready for bed," she says.

He sits there, watching her, not moving. "Go on then." She sees something in his eyes that throws her.

"Are you all right?" she asks again.

"Don't fuss," he says. "You know I don't like it when you fuss."

TWO

Edith Jones married Teddy Wharton for all the wrong reasons. She was spending the summer in Bar Harbor the year she turned twenty-one, getting over an unhappy, mistaken engagement to Harry Stevens. And she was "seeing" Walter Berry, a lawyer. Walter seemed like Edith's mirror image: sprung from the same New York society, having spent much of his childhood in Europe. All through the cool blueberry-graced summer of 1883, she and Walter walked side by side, poetry books in hand. They paddled in canoes. They sat on the Jones's rented porch overlooking the ocean and talked and talked.

Unfortunately, even their most placid discussions turned into shouting matches. Once he took her out in a canoe, and they argued so vociferously that a flock of birds rose from the water, spattering silver drops on them, so they had to laugh at themselves. But soon enough, they were at it again.

The reason Edith didn't fall in love with Walter then, and she's somewhat ashamed of this now: he intimidated her. He was so bright, so sharp, he made her feel small. He challenged her too well. He made her see herself as less than the person she wanted to be.

She couldn't help wishing for someone like her father instead, someone kindly and unchallenging who thought she made the world spin. Walter would never think this. He would make her feel too often like a fool. And then, Walter didn't really declare himself. Maybe it was

because back then he was a penniless lawyer. And proud. Not the sort
of man who would take money or rely on his bride's.

Teddy Wharton, her brother Harry's friend, was also in Bar Harbor
that summer. She had known him for a good decade since she was just
a little girl tagging along. He was older, in his thirties, an easygoing fellow with golden hair and a mischievous smile. He often led Bar Harbor's
young elite on adventures: the scavenger hunt everyone talked about for
the rest of the summer, the cake-eating contest on the Van Degan's
whitewashed veranda. She was just Harry's little sister. She didn't expect
him to pay any attention to her. In fact, she was not the sort of girl who
participated in his variety of escapades. But he looked charming and
funny in his straw boater. He smelled good, like cinnamon and lime
(cologne, she suspected). And she did enjoy the times he insisted she
join them in their mad schemes. He told her once when she arrived on
her brother Harry's arm to a shoreside dinner at Eleanor Allen's house
that she looked "somewhere beyond beautiful" in her kelly green dress.
She could feel his sincerity, his admiration. It was as palpable as the spicy
scent that rose from his skin whenever she came near.

She was not used to people telling her she was beautiful. Her mother
made a point of saying she was a disappointment, in need of constant
improvement. The night of the dinner at Eleanor Allen's, Edith looked
in the mirror as she removed her pearls, and—staring as dispassionately
as she could at her too square, too masculine jaw, her heavy brow, her
thin lips—she felt blessed that Teddy Wharton could see beauty in her.

When, at the end of the summer, Walter Berry went back to
Washington to pursue his law, Teddy Wharton came to New York and
started paying attention to Edith. She thought him kindly, and being
older, he gave her a sense of safety, ease. That winter, he escorted her to
the Patriarch's Ball at Delmonico's, where he proved himself a fine
dancer. He told her that her tiny waist was perfect in her lavender taffeta
as he held his hands around it, his large fingers nearly meeting, his eyes
lit with pleasure.

Months later, when they became engaged, word came to Edith that
Walter Berry was "heartsick" and literally got right into bed with the flu
and would not get out for a week. Eventually, she received a letter from
him in a thick cream envelope: "I wish you all the best, my dearest dear.

Teddy is a fine fellow, and I know he will treat you handsomely. Yrs. W."
The letter made Edith furious, somehow. Even in his magnanimous
note, he was attempting to get the upper hand. Calling her his dearest
dear! The nerve. She would never win when it came to Walter Berry!

And then there was the business of being married. Her mother felt it was
her duty—no, her *right*—to choose where and when the wedding would
take place, what the guests were to eat, and how Edith herself should
dress. Edith let her. There was no winning over Lucretia. She was even
more formidable than Walter Berry!

Three days before the wedding, as the dressmaker placed the finishing touches on a high-collared elaborately pleated gown, as the cooks
gathered provisions for Lobster Newburg and Cherries Jubilee, as the
diamond tiara that Lucretia had worn for her own wedding already sat
aglint on Edith's dressing table, Edith simply needed to speak to her
mother.

"I wouldn't go in there right now," Anna Bahlmann said, standing
by the door of Lucretia's boudoir. "I believe she would not be good
company."

"But I *have* to see her, Tonni."

"You know as well as I do, Edith, that one must pick one's times with
your mother."

Anna often gave sage advice when it came to Lucretia's unpredictability. But Edith couldn't heed her today. She was about to vow to love,
honor and obey Teddy Wharton and she had no idea what that meant.
She knew *something* would take place in the marriage bed, but what?
She had asked her mother vaguely in the past and had been told it was
unseemly to bring up the topic. Now it was imperative.

Edith stepped quietly past Anna and knocked on the mahogany
door.

"Come in if you must," Lucretia said. She was sitting ruler-straight at
her silk-skirted dressing table, pinning up her graying hair. Lucretia had
a maid, but she always took her hair down as soon as the maid left the
room and redid it.

"Mama. Do you have a moment to speak with me?" The pounding of Edith's own heart deafened her.

Lucretia spun around and her slate eyes flashed with annoyance. "You can see I'm dressing to go out."

"It's important."

"And what's your idea of important?" Lucretia asked. Her voice sounded to Edith like the snap of dried twigs in a frosty forest.

"The wedding. I need to know . . . what's expected of me. . . ."

"What's expected of you?"

"I need to know . . ."

"You're expected to keep your head high and say as little as possible. Your role as bride will say enough. Chatty brides are intolerable."

"I mean after the wedding. I mean . . . on my wedding night. I need to know . . . what will . . . happen to me!"

"I never heard such a ridiculous question!" The icy shatter of her words fell as she turned her back on her daughter and continued stuffing pins into her silver hair.

"But I don't know what will happen, Mama. I'm afraid!"

Her mother made a noise that could have been a sigh, except it came from the vicinity of her nose and sounded irritated and damning. She did not speak for a long while, and Edith had to stand and listen to the pump of blood in her ears. "You've seen enough pictures and statues in your life, Puss. Haven't you noticed that men are—made differently from women?"

"Yes." Of course she'd noticed. She'd stared at Michelangelo's *David* when she was twelve. She'd seen paintings of naked men. And she had brothers who didn't always lock the bathroom door, much to her mortification and their amusement. But what did it mean? So what if they were made differently?

"Well, then," Lucretia said, as though that settled everything.

Edith was speechless. She fished hard for a question that would not make her a fool. "But . . ."

"For heaven's sake, don't ask me any more silly questions, Edith. You can't possibly be as stupid as you pretend! I never had to tell the boys a thing. Hand me that hat." Edith lifted a beautiful black hat off the hat stand, fluffing the osprey feathers before she passed it to her mother. "And now leave me alone," Lucretia said, pinning the hat to her just refined hair. "You're tiring me out."

❀

The wedding reception was held at the house on Twenty-fifth Street. Through it all, Edith felt as though there were a pane of glass between her and the festivities. She did not take well to champagne, or to any wine for that matter. And her discomfort was heightened because the maid had winched in her corset even more firmly than usual to make her look sylphlike in her gown. She could barely take a breath. By the second hour of the reception, Teddy was not himself either. He had drunk too much, and was loud and clownish. This from a man who could normally drink to excess without evident behavior. He was showing Edith off as though she were a new toy, or a possession. "My wife, Edith. Have you met my new wife, Mrs. Edward Wharton?" he asked the guests, one after the other. Before everyone fled out of sheer annoyance, the newlyweds were tucked into a carriage to wave good-bye and head for their "secret" destination, Pen Craig Cottage, the musty little house that sat across the street from Pen Craig, her mother's manse in Newport—an endless journey by carriage. There was no money after the extravagance of the reception for a night at a fine Manhattan hotel.

It was late April, so not yet warm, but with the rocking of the carriage and the bumpy roads, they were soon both asleep. When Edith woke, it was dusk outside and she felt sick to her stomach. Her throat nearly closed with panic. She was alone in the carriage with Teddy Wharton, who was still fast asleep, his mouth agape, looking perfectly absurd. And she was terrified.

She scanned the landscape out the window, and though she couldn't tell where they were, she knew they had a long way to go. It would be nearly morning before they'd arrive at Pen Craig. The little cottage would be theirs as long as she wanted, her mother had said, because, frankly, she and Teddy had no money for a place of their own. Edith had never loved Newport. Year after year, she fell ill there. The moldy sea air exacerbated her breathing problems. But worse, at this moment, observing the slack face of the man she'd just married, she was uncertain about whether she loved him. When she'd agreed to marry him, she had imagined a grand life together: travel and beautiful houses and teas with the two of them gazing adoringly. Now he felt like a stranger. And she had no idea what was expected of her . . . intimately. Teddy woke to a weeping wife.

"Puss, what is it?" he asked. Edith, who often translated for others, could suddenly find no words for herself.

"A little of the wedding nerves?" he asked. He seemed kindly but foolish to her, with his reddish-gold mustache, his glazed blue eyes. She wished she could go home. Even if it meant going back to Lucretia and the house on Twenty-fifth Street.

"I don't feel very well," she said softly.

"You just settle back and enjoy the ride," Teddy said, patting her hand. After a while he added, "You needn't worry about me, dear," he said. "You're lucky, because you've married a patient man." She was stunned he had read her fears without her bringing them up, but also mortified that he was even speaking about it—what she feared, what she didn't know.

When they arrived, right before the sun rose, Teddy tucked her into her bed with a pristine kiss.

"You see, I'm not going to do anything but give you a kiss. Tomorrow night, we'll see what happens." She slept with utter relief.

It was two weeks before Teddy Wharton finally gave up waiting for Edith to give him the signal that she was ready for him. Nearly every night she'd have a full-fledged asthma attack and push him right out of her bed. She'd flail. She'd even slap him. She was mortified by her own behavior but equally outraged by his. She would apologize in the morning. She would say it was the overripe air, or the cottage at Pen Craig; that Newport was anathema to her and she had often had breathing issues in the past. But after days and days of this, which he had come to call her "histrionics," he'd found it was better to call her maid and go back to his own room. And then one night, after three glasses of brandy, he came into her bed in the middle of the night.

"No, Teddy, it's late," she told him. "I was sleeping."

"I don't care, Puss. A married man has his rights. This has to end."

"You said you'd be patient," she said.

"No one is this patient. Not even me."

"You've been drinking."

"Of course I've been drinking. It's the only way I've been able to bear this nonsense." Tonight, he didn't even kiss her, he merely climbed atop her, as though she were a mountain he must conquer and he had a flag to thrust into her soil. She cried out at the pain. There was no touching, no caressing. It was more awful than she'd imagined: the bucking, the sharpness, the grunting. No wonder Lucretia couldn't even speak of it! The searing pain served one good purpose: it did distract her from the fact that she couldn't breathe. When he was done, which was in very short order, he pulled himself off her and lay on his stomach on the bed, his head away from her, and was very silent.

"How could you?" she said, her voice as marring as a nail on glass. "Don't *ever* do that to me again!"

He muttered something in a crushed, angry voice, which took her ears a moment to interpret. "It wasn't even worth it," is what he said, and he began to cry. Truly cry. She didn't know if he was lachrymose from the liquor, or hurt, or angry. But she was horrified. She would have apologized to him if she hadn't been so miserable, still throbbing with pain, still in shock. Teddy got up from her bed. And in all these twenty-two years, he has rarely returned. When he has, her head has been turned, her eyes squeezed shut. It's been miserable for both of them. It's become their silent truce to leave each other alone, to sleep apart. It's the marriage they've made together. She doesn't know whether he sees other women. She imagines he must have at one time. As long as it is done very quietly, she hasn't wanted to hear about it. She is only too happy to give him a wide berth.

For years, Edith has wondered how other women seemed to *long* for this shattering intimacy that feels more like injury than love. Why should the Comtesse de Noailles find blissful pleasure where she finds pain? Maybe Teddy did it wrong. More likely, she is a woman not made for love. This, in the end, is what she's come to believe. That she is mis-made. A woman unlike other women. A freak of nature.

For the first years of her marriage she was miserable, nauseated at least once a day, sometimes even unable to get out of bed. Her great friend through everything has been her old beau, Walter Berry. He writes her often, visits when he can. Having suffered childhood malaria, he's been ill much of his life. He understands her almost as well as Anna does. Once, a few years into the marriage, when Edith was particularly ill and Teddy his jolly joking self, Walter walked her to her room to lie down.

Tucking her tenderly into bed, he said, "Dear Edith, I have to ask . . ."

"What? Ask me. I don't keep secrets from you."

"Okay. I'll brave it. What, exactly, is it you *see* in Teddy?"

She was very quiet.

"I've offended you," he said.

She still did not speak. She would never be able to explain it even if she chose to.

"I'll never ask that again," he said. He looked utterly ashamed. She did not disabuse him of the notion that what she felt for Teddy was deep and abiding love. There was simply no point. She chose Teddy. They are anchored together. She made a vow and she sees no choice but to keep it. And there were years when she did enjoy the best things about Teddy—their love of animals, his happy-go-lucky nature, the way he could tell a story and charm their friends. But it is difficult to recall them now, even when she tells herself to.

In recent years, Walter Berry has become an international lawyer. It's an impressive and important role in the world, and Edith is proud of him. As much as she has grown to love him, she is still glad she didn't marry him. Walter would have had no patience with her, would not have allowed her to spurn her marital duties as Teddy has. Yet his presence in her life as intellectual sparring partner and loyal friend is infinitely more precious. She is grateful Teddy doesn't mind. The way Teddy sees it, he won the contest, and Walter is simply first runner-up. Allowing him to come around just confirms Teddy's superiority. That the "prize" is somewhat shabby and disappointing seems to have no bearing on Teddy's sense of triumph.

Edith lies in bed now, and when she closes her eyes, she sees again the resplendent and daunting Anna de Noailles shaking her hand good-bye: such a warm, ironic smile, the dusky stain of her cheeks, the tumble of her dark, infinite hair, the green feathers at her shoulders shuddering with every breath. Mythic.

Tonight, the salon was not as Edith had expected and yet it was more thrilling than all the other evenings at Rosa's. Can she learn from de Noailles? What if Edith's own smile could be so seductive? What if she had the power to make Mr. Fullerton's cheeks color, to make his hands shake?

And Fullerton, with a face she might find in a John Singer Sargent painting. Those icy eyes. Those sweeping black lashes. Why did he watch her all through dinner? When she thinks of it, she experiences a sweet drawing beneath her ribs. What was he thinking as he stared? And what was he about to tell her when Comtesse de Noailles interrupted by entering the party?

In the next room, Teddy finally comes to bed. She hears the familiar groan as he removes his slippers, the scuff of the sheets, the sigh as he settles onto his soft mattress. She soon detects that distinctive snore that rises only from a heavy blanket of brandy. She doesn't know why tonight—a night so full of new people and ideas and pleasures—the widening distance between them should bathe her in such despair.

Anna Bahlmann slowly climbs the stairs to her room at the top of the *hôtel*. It lies along a hallway she shares not just with Catherine Gross and Cook and Marthe, the Whartons' servants, but with all the servants in the building. The narrow gaslit passage is made to feel wider with walls the color of clotted cream and pretty prints of odd-shaped houses from Japan. Her room is spacious for a servant's room, and in the late mornings, when she comes back for a respite after typing up Edith's pages, sunlight spills from an east-facing window and she likes to lie in its warm embrace. The bed is especially comfortable, with a cherry satin eiderdown and a fat bolster. More than at The Mount, and almost as much as in her beloved rooms at 882 Park Avenue in New York, Anna feels at home here. Now, at the end of her very long day, she finds comfort under the eaves.

Once, many years ago, after years of boarding, she bravely took a flat of her own on the top floor of a house on Ninety-fifth Street. It was airy and clean, and she furnished it with family things her brother sent her from Missouri and a beautiful chest her cousin shipped her from Virginia. She adopted two kittens, and after a long day they would greet her with a symphony of demands. How rich she felt in that little flat! Free. But how lonely! After years graced with the music of other people brushing teeth in the hall bath, arguing, sneezing and singing to themselves, the long silences of her evenings were too accusatory, and ultimately painful, even with feline company.

And then one day Edith came to her and said, "I know you love your little space uptown, Tonni, but won't you come down and live in Number 882? You'll have two rooms of your own, a sitting room and a bedroom. You can bring all your pretty things. The kitties can come, of course. It would be absolutely free, and Gross would love your company. Besides, I need you closer to me. The streetcar has disappointed us one too many times." A month later the narrow house right next to Edith's became her primary home.

But the top floor of this building in Paris houses a special treat: the common room where an ever-changing cast of servants gathers in the evenings. Sometimes Anna sits by the fire with a book. But more often than not, after a page or two, she turns the book upside down in her lap and chats with the servants from other households. She is keen to know what other families are like, where and how they travel, and how they treat their staffs. Tonight she takes her darning egg and a pair of worn stockings and walks down the hall to see who is in the common room. Though it is very late, she finds Louise, one of the friendliest ladies' maids, seated in the most comfortable chair by the fire. By her is one of the footmen, and across the room, a seamstress who has come for just a week to sew a new wardrobe for the very wealthy but very fat lady who lives one floor above the Whartons.

Anna has never forgotten what Louise told her when she first arrived: "My mistress only wears her dresses once or twice and often gives them to me. She gives me her jewelry too. She gets tired of everything."

"But whenever do you wear such grand things?" Anna asked.

"The best ones I have remade for me. The rest I just enjoy having. This was hers." Anna recalls how Louise plucked a golden chain from her bodice. Dangling from it was a heavy gold seal. Edith has drawers of jewelry similar to this, but Anna can't imagine Edith giving away a single piece. Could someone be so rich that things of such value hold no meaning? And at that moment, Anna thought of her own great prize, the secret locket she wears against her heart always. *His* locket. Nothing could make her part with it.

"My mistress smokes opium," Josette, a little French maid with a strawberry mark on her cheek, whispered last week. "Her skin is turning a terrible shade of yellow. Soon her husband will leave her. I see how he looks at her with disgust. I keep dreaming she's died. I fear I'll come to wake her one morning and she'll be cold as ice."

Anna carries these stories with wonder and sadness, thinking about them for days afterward. If one were lucky enough to have such a life of privilege, how could it be tossed aside so casually? She considers telling Edith about the lady who smokes opium, but stops herself. The story was told in confidence. Doctors do not share information outside the sanctity of their offices. As a governess, as a secretary, Anna has spent a lifetime straddling a life of service and Edith's world. And despite her middle-class roots, she is more comfortable as a servant after all these years. In the servants' hall, she's admired. Edith, lately, sees her faults and points them out too often. Sometimes, Anna feels like a mother whose child has grown beyond her, a child who no longer remembers the tenderness they once shared.

Tonight, unsettled by Teddy Wharton's growing melancholy, an issue Edith doesn't seem to acknowledge, Anna chooses the settee near the footman where a glowing oil lamp brightens the corner enough that she can do her darning. She slides the china egg into the toe of one of the stockings and threads up the needle. She is surprised when the young footman launches into conversation.

"I hear your employer is famous," he says.

She looks up, puzzled.

"Mr. Wharton? He's not famous."

"No. It's the missus who's famous. That's what I hear. She's a famous writer?"

This amazes Anna—that even a footman would have heard of Edith. Is her fame now so widespread? True, Anna has helped Edith with nearly everything she has ever written from the time she was in braids. She answers her mail. Reads notes from the publisher out loud when Edith's eyes are burning with allergy. She corrects her spelling. She picks up the pile of pages outside her bedroom door every morning to type and tells her when characters don't seem believable or things don't make sense to her. She offhandedly mentioned to Edith when she first read *The House of Mirth* that it struck her as ironic that Selden seemed to spend a great deal of his time with just the sort of people he disdained, and the next time Anna typed the pages, Lily Bart was telling Selden exactly that. But Edith famous?

"I wish my mistress was famous," Louise says. "Anyone can have money. Talent is something few have."

"That's so," the seamstress says.

"You're Mrs. Wharton's secretary, are you not?" Louise says, sitting forward in her chair, her eyes suddenly bright.

"Yes."

"Well, you must read everything, then. You must know every word of her famous books, maybe even put a word or two of your own in there?"

Anna nods.

"Well, *ma petite*! I'd say that makes you famous too!"

Anna feels herself blush. She's never wanted the spotlight herself. Unlike Edith, who has always expected great things for herself, as though a fairy whispered in her ear at birth, "You are somebody." Anna finds herself smiling as she darns, thinking about the stories she has typed from Edith's scribbled and often indecipherable notes being read by kings and commoners everywhere. And those words that Anna suggested right there with Edith's own. The scope of it, the impact of it makes her dizzy. I am nearly famous, she tells herself with a silvery dart of satisfaction.

Anna is very pleased to be in Paris this year. The cobbled streets remind her of her childhood visits to her grandmother in Germany. Orphaned at the age of two, she was raised by her eldest brother, William, who was only fifteen, and by her Aunt Charlotte, who had a family of her own and little time for her. But with her grandmother, Anna experienced the warmth and sweetness of primary love. Now, in Paris, the smells of pastry, the blue-wet cold of European winter bring visions of those three important visits to Frankfurt. Oh, when her grandmother hugged her, how special she felt! How beloved. Her grandmother would braid her hair and tell her all about her mother's childhood. She taught Anna German songs that they would sing together. On her last visit, it was as though Anna's grandmother knew they'd never see each other again.

"Memories will keep you warm, *mein Hase*," she whispered in her ear. My little rabbit. She sent Anna back to America with a satchel stitched from her mother's favorite childhood plaid blanket. Inside were photos of her mother as a little girl, the mother she never really knew, four pairs of hand-knit socks and, in a velvet case, a silver bracelet engraved with a tiny perfect rabbit. Her grandmother died the following year.

Sometimes on the streets of Paris, when Anna hears tourists speaking German, she can't help but feel a soaring in her chest. Perhaps she will turn and spot her cousins Liesel and Lotte, who used to come to dinner at her grandmother's house every Sunday. But of course, the streets are merely filled with strangers. And though her French is almost fluent, she can't yet express herself as well as she can in English or German.

Many things weigh on her lately. Her bad knee protests when she climbs the three flights to her room; her heels are so tight in the morning, she can do no more than tiptoe. She must start taking walks when Edith is out to tea, to keep her legs strong. She will turn fifty-eight in a month, and the last thing she wants is to feel like an old, crumbling woman, growing more useless by the day. Edith needs her.

And then there is Teddy Wharton. Edith, blooming in Paris like a struggling flower finally planted into richer soil, is willfully closing her eyes to how much Mr. Wharton has faded this winter. In some ways, Anna understands. Happiness can be a blinder. And this is the first time in years that Edith seems deeply happy. For so many years after her marriage, Edith was sickly. She told Anna from the start that things were not right in the marriage bed, and Anna advised her that she'd heard that marriage was often that way. The intrusive desires of a husband were something a woman simply had to tolerate. You did it so you could have children. How Anna wished that Edith might have had a child! She could have become a governess again. She would have loved that child, could have been the honey to Edith's occasional vinegar.

It's hard for Anna to understand why Edith isn't thrilled to have a husband like dear Mr. Wharton. Teddy Wharton clearly worships his wife. It's as if every time Mr. Wharton lays eyes on her, he's located his true north. Edith brings him certainty and calm. If merely *once* in her experience, Anna had a man look at her that way, she would feel as if her entire life had been justified.

It can never happen now. She is too old for men's eyes. When she was young, men didn't regard her with love but there was at least approval. She recognized that gleam when their eyes met hers. Once on a streetcar in New York, a man commented that her deep golden hair, pinned to the top of her head in a braid, was the very color of late afternoon sunshine and made his heart stand still. Years ago, one of the footmen had knocked at the door of her room one night.

"What's wrong?" she'd asked, pulling her wrapper tighter. She imagined that Edith was ill, or had asked for her. The man smelled of bootblack. He must have just finished the polishing. And she could see black crescents beneath his nails.

"Robert. What is it?" Without asking, he stepped into her room and she shrunk back, afraid.

"Anna, beautiful Anna." She felt heat flood her face. The room suddenly was too small. He was a coarse man, a big man. Not young. Not at all educated. Alfred White had told him it was better if he didn't speak too much when guests came because he sounded like a longshoreman.

"Will you take your hair down for me, Miss Anna?" he asked. "Please."

She stared at him. His big florid face. Not a handsome face, but manly, with a strong, masculine chin.

"Please?" he asked. In his kind brown eyes, there was something she couldn't deny: embarrassment, pain, longing? She felt her hair for pins, and began to remove them one by one as he watched—too hungrily. His breathing was odd and noisy. It scared her. But once she started, it was as if she couldn't stop. She was mesmerized by his wheezing and the sound of the pins falling into the china dish. Her heart beat fast and light . . . like a small animal's.

"Shake it out," he whispered hoarsely. He could hardly speak for his leaden breaths. She knew suddenly that taking her hair down in front of him was far more sinful than she'd imagined. She felt exposed, but also thrilled. The way his eyes glowed. The clarity of his desire lit a flame inside her. If he had put his hands out to grab her arms, she would have welcomed it. If he had kissed her, she would have let him.

Instead, he made an odd, wounded-animal sound, squeezing his eyes shut and folding his large body suddenly forward. He shivered in a frightful way.

"Thank you," he gasped. "Thank you." And then he ran from the room. She didn't understand it. She couldn't imagine what had happened. But that night, she wasn't able to sleep. Her whole body felt on fire and she had no idea how to quench it.

For two years—before Robert was asked to leave by Alfred White, the butler, because he had stepped on one too many guests' toes, spilled too many things, dropped too many butter knives as he put away the silver—he'd knock on her door every Saturday night and she would open it for him. In time, he didn't have to tell her to let her hair down. She came to look forward to it, though he never touched her, never choked out more than an "Anna" or "Thank you." It always ended with that sound he made. Like pain. Like misery. And with him running from the room. This is all Anna Bahlmann knows of love.

Catherine Gross, the housekeeper, once spoke to her about it.

"I know he comes to your room," she said.

"Who?"

"Robert. I know he comes. I hear him. I know what you do."

"I don't do anything."

"I wouldn't tell the Whartons. You're like a sister to me, Anna. But for pity's sake, choose better than that oaf Robert."

"Nothing's ever happened with him, Catherine. I swear it."

"Anna. I have ears. I know how a child is made. I *know*."

"You don't know about this," Anna said. She is grateful Catherine cares more for Anna's welfare than for propriety. Still, when Robert was sent away, she felt a gasping emptiness she couldn't share with anyone.

In her lifetime, there has been just one other man that's mattered. And one other memory that soothes her, that slakes her thirst on the loneliest of nights. Edith, who was very young at the time, had received urgent word that her mother was ill in Newport and had gone off to Rhode Island ahead of Mr. Wharton. It was June and Anna had stayed behind to close up the New York house for the season.

Teddy Wharton rarely spent an evening at home when he was in Manhattan. He spent most afternoons and even whole nights at his club or would meet people for dinner or the theatre. Sometimes he brought his friends home and they would drink in his study. Anna would walk by the door and hear the clink of glasses, the laughter. She could always pick out Teddy's voice, deeper and more velvety than the others'. He was a wonderful storyteller. But tonight he was alone. Anna knew he grew melancholy when Edith went off without him. She stood nervously by his study door for quite a while until she finally found the courage to knock.

"Well, Miss Anna," he said, smiling when he found her at the door. "She's left us both alone, hasn't she? Two orphaned children. Come in and sit down. Have a drink with me."

"Oh, no, Mr. Wharton. I couldn't. I don't drink. . . . I just came to see if there was anything I could do for you."

"Cagey girl! I've seen you drink wine at dinner. I've a nice cabernet here." He got up from his chair and, before she could protest, drew a glass down from the shelf and poured it nearly full.

"Sit. Right. Down. There." His eyes were sparkling. She felt a little foolish, but she sat in the chair offered and took the too-full glass of black-red wine by its delicate, glistening stem.

"Go on, then. Drink your medicine, young lady," he said. She thought it amusing that he called her young lady since he was a few months younger than she. The first taste of the wine did remind her of the licorice-flavored tincture her aunt used to give her for constipation. The second swallow blossomed with ripe fruit.

"Well, this is much better than being alone," Teddy said. "Two lost children huddling together in the woods." He smiled, his walrus mustache spreading like a golden fan. "And how is little Anna?" he asked. "Is the missus working you to the bone?"

"Oh no. Mrs. Wharton is always very considerate of me."

"As she should be. You run this household. You do everything and ask for nothing."

"Catherine Gross runs the household," Anna said soberly.

"In theory. But if we asked Edith to choose just one of you to throw out on the street . . . I highly doubt you'd find yourself staring at pavement."

Anna felt herself blushing and could not meet his eyes. "That's a terrible thing to say, Mr. Wharton. Mrs. Wharton would never throw either of us out on the street. Besides, not a thing would happen in this house without Catherine Gross."

He laughed. She watched him take a deep draught of his brandy. He held the glass up to the light as though trying to see through it. "Did you never want to marry?" he asked.

"There was . . . no opportunity."

"But you're a beautiful woman."

"Oh . . ." She bit her lip, shook her head vehemently. "I'm not."

"I've always thought so. I don't understand why you hide your light." She looked over at him. His blue eyes seemed a little queer. He'd been drinking too much. From where she sat she could smell the syrupy aroma of his brandy.

"My light?" She barely got the words out.

"You wear your hair like that, so tight, and your clothing is so . . . forgive me . . . drab."

"Mr. Wharton." She felt ashamed to hear him say this. Anna didn't want to stand out. When her aunt died, it was a relief to know she could blend into any household. She was sensible. She was smart. And she didn't need attention. She was an orphan who rarely got much attention at home, and she didn't mind, really . . . but to hear Teddy Wharton tell her that it was so obvious she was hiding herself, it mortified her.

"Maybe I should go."

"Oh don't, Anna. Don't go. I didn't mean to hurt your feelings. Please."

"I just came to see if I could do anything for you."

"You want to do something for me? You can keep me company. I find you very restful," he said.

She stayed dutifully in her chair. She was afraid to drink more wine. He thought her beautiful. She could hardly contain this thrilling, foreign news.

"Do you think me a fool?" he asked suddenly.

She looked up, startled. "Oh certainly not, sir."

"Edith does. She thinks I'm a buffoon. I don't know why she married me. She thinks I'm a dunce. I see it in her eyes ten times a day. But I married her precisely because she is smarter than me. I'm not afraid of a woman being smarter. I think that makes me quite wise, don't you?"

Anna felt breathless.

"I don't think Mrs. Wharton thinks of you as . . ."

"Yes, you do."

"Any woman would be happy to have you as her husband," Anna said suddenly. She felt her chin quivering.

"Would you have been happy to have me as your husband, Anna?"

Anna wanted to speak. But what were the right words? He was staring right at her.

"You won't answer?"

"I would have been *so* proud to call you my husband," Anna blurted out. The words burned like coals on her tongue. They were a betrayal of Edith. She felt trapped and mortified. She rose suddenly.

"I'm sorry," she said. "I'm so sorry, Mr. Wharton," She darted for the door. Her heart was thrumming up against her throat. She expected him to stop her. She waited for the feel of his hand on her wrist. Words of appeasement or praise or command. But nothing happened. The soles of her shoes slapped the floor as she ran down the hall. She took the steps two at a time to her room. She could never take back her words. Now he knew how she felt about him. Now he would always know.

The next morning, he called for her to come to his study. She'd barely slept all night. She would have to leave, she knew. She would have to find a new post after all these years. Would she have to be a governess again? Would she find someone to whom she could be a secretary? Would Edith even write a letter to recommend her? How could she explain to Edith why she needed to leave?

Teddy sat at his desk, penning a letter.

"Sit down," he said.

"Yes, sir." She was quaking. She wondered if he could see it.

"Last night I said some things I wish I hadn't said. Would you be kind enough to pretend I didn't say them, dear Anna? Would you erase last night's conversation, so we can be good friends again?"

She was silent. He smiled at her. It was the kindest smile she'd ever seen.

"I'm sure I offended you, and I'm sorry, Anna. You're a proud woman. I recognize how you must have felt. Please forgive me."

"Of course," she said.

"I have something for you," he said.

"Some work?" she asked.

He laughed. "No. Not work." He opened up his desk drawer and drew out a velvet box and set it before her on the desk.

"What is it?"

"Open it," he said impatiently.

Even the luminous blue velvet of the box was magnificent. She picked it up gingerly and unlatched the tiny case. Nestled against white satin was a beautiful gold locket on a thick chain adorned with a white enameled dove holding a letter in its beak. The letter was sealed with a tiny perfect ruby. Anna gasped.

"Mr. Wharton, I couldn't take this."

"Why not?"

"Surely it was meant for Mrs. Wharton."

"I think it suits you. Please understand, this is a gift to say I'm sorry. That's all."

A bribe. The gift was a bribe. It couldn't be a love token. . . .

"I don't think I could . . . take it."

"Of course you can. If you don't, my feelings will be hurt. Plain and simple. You type Puss's letters every day and make our lives so pleasant with your quiet and constant companionship. It's just a gift of friendship."

He got up and came around the desk. Taking the box from her, he opened it, released the pendant, worked its clasp and hung it around Anna's neck. She felt the weight of the heavy, twisted chain, the cool solidity of the pendant even through her dress. She touched it with her hand. She had never owned anything so valuable.

"That's a good girl," he said. He handed her the box. "Now, not another word about it. All right? Go see to closing up this house." He turned back to his desk with a grin. "There's so much to do and hardly any time."

"Thank you," she whispered.

Since that morning in his study, when his kind fingers brushed her neck as they fastened the heavy clasp, not a day has passed that Anna Bahlmann hasn't worn that beautiful pendant beneath her clothes. She hasn't slept a single night without its comforting weight nestled between her breasts. It's grown as smooth as a river stone, stays as warm as her heart that beats against it. So many years have passed, the pendant no longer makes her feel miserable or embarrassed or ashamed. It makes her feel beloved. And sometimes when she sees Teddy Wharton smile at her at dinner or in the hallway, she knows that all these years later, he remembers that they share a secret.

m

the
fields
lacqu(

THREE

EARLY SPRING 1907

Delighted by an invitation from Anna de Noailles for tea, Edith rings the bell and a gypsy-eyed *bonne* ushers her into an entrance hall draped in striped silk like a Bedouin tent and redolent of cinnamon. Edith feels as though she's visiting another country. The neighborhood is nothing like the Faubourg. No musty eighteenth-century courtyards or high, forbidding walls (which she, in truth, has cherished). Just a sunny front stoop and window boxes adorned for the winter with fir boughs.

She follows the *bonne* into a drawing room where a roaring fire licks the walls of a seven-foot fireplace. Anna de Noailles leans over her desk, pen in hand. Wrapped in a turquoise silk shawl, displaying bare feet, she seems completely unaware that anyone has joined her.

"Madame," the *bonne* says after a moment.

The Comtesse looks up with a start.

"I've interrupted your writing. I'm sorry," Edith offers.

"Don't be silly." She stretches like a cat. "I invited you to interrupt ·. Come sit down, Madame Wharton."

The rumpled sofa is dressed in the same Caribbean turquoise as Comtesse's shawl, and is strewn with pillows of brilliant yellow. Like of Maine sunflowers opening to summer skies, Edith thinks. The ·ed coffee-bean-colored walls reflect the flicker from the hearth.

It's a dazzling room. Edith could live here, she thinks—though it is nothing like any place she's ever inhabited. The Comtesse slinks over to the sofa. Her feet are brown and sinewy, as glossy as polished bronze. Edith doesn't think she's ever been greeted by bare feet before. As a matter of fact, she's seen few unshod feet in her entire life. She never once saw her own mother's. There is something louche about bare feet—and thrilling.

"Since last we met, I finished reading *Les Éblouissements* and was enchanted," Edith announces. She feels passionate about de Noailles's poetry. She is galvanized by her ability to marry nature with sensuality. The simple, organic poems remind her again and again of Walt Whitman, whom she desperately admires. "Were you writing poetry just now?" Edith asks.

"I couldn't write a thing today," de Noailles says. "Do you have days where no words will come when you beckon them?" She stares directly into Edith's eyes. "One's heart is a shepherd. If only the words would follow like a docile flock. Too often they wander off on their own and we spend days looking for them."

Edith laughs, and can't help feeling that though Anna de Noailles is much younger, she is the wiser.

"Are you living in Paris now?" de Noailles asks.

"Just until the end of spring."

"And then, New York?"

"And then we go to our country place in Massachusetts, not far from New York."

"And what do you think of Paris?"

"I feel at home here. I spent a lot of time in Paris as a child."

"I could live nowhere else," de Noailles says. "But the French are a locked house. I was born in France, yet my father was a Romanian, my mother Greek. They think me a foreigner so I'll never be invited inside."

"And if they don't accept *you*, Comtesse, it's certain *I* won't be allowed beyond the front gate," Edith says.

"And yet Paris is the center of the world, *non?*"

The *bonne* reenters the room balancing a heavy silver tray. Plates of sweets accompany the service: petits fours and biscuits with jammy centers. De Noailles poses high her birdlike wrists to pour the tea. Falling from so far above, it sings a melody into the cups.

"Since Rosa's, I've spoken often of your book," de Noailles says. "I was surprised how many people have already read it. You should hear what they say! I'm angry at myself for not knowing English better."

"It won't be long until the French translation is done."

"And where will it appear?"

"Perhaps the *Revue de Paris*, if they are willing to publish it."

"They published my first poems. I was just a girl. But it seems they publish little by women these days."

Edith takes a sip of tea, which seems particularly strong and fortifying. "Does anyone publish much by women?"

De Noailles shrugs and nibbles at the edge of a petit four. "There are so few of us who write, Madame Wharton. Or perhaps many women write—but only a few put their work up for public inspection. Are you mostly read by men or women?"

"I don't know."

"I'd wager women. Women read with their hearts. They're more eager to journey on words, because their lives are narrower."

"I never thought it mattered," Edith says. "As long as people were reading my books." But as Edith ponders it, in fact she has been most pleased when men think her worth reading. She feels herself redden with guilt.

Anna de Noailles glances up.

"Men validate us, don't they?" she says, as though Edith had spoken her thoughts aloud.

Edith nods.

"Ah," de Noailles says. "We are traitors." And then she laughs. Her laugh is free and young and full of hope.

De Noailles gets up suddenly and walks to the cabinet by the fireplace. She exudes the darkest mysteries of sensuality in every move she makes. In some odd, subtle way, she even stirs Edith. From a shelf she draws a hammered-silver flask. It sparkles in the firelight. Without asking, she pours some of its contents into Edith's tea and then into her own. "We were missing something, weren't we?" she says with a wicked smile, and when she offhandedly touches Edith's hand, Edith feels electricity pass through her fingertips.

"Anna de Noailles is like no one I've ever met," Edith tells Anna Bahl-mann the next afternoon when her secretary carries in her newly typed pages. "Perhaps I will invite her for dinner. You can meet her."

"She would pay no attention to me," Anna says.

"Nonsense. You must see her face-to-face to truly understand her poetry. It's as if she's neither a woman nor a man, but another sex entirely. She's got the mind and the desires of a man and the drive to be heard like a man. And yet all the beauty and allure of a woman. The extraordinary thing is it's all unstudied. She's a force of nature."

"She sounds frightening," Anna says.

"I'll invite her to meet Henry when he's here."

"Well, then, you surely wouldn't want me at the table."

"Of course I would, Tonni. Henry finds you very calming."

"Herz, if you wouldn't mind, may I talk to you about this scene?" Anna asks, selecting a few pages from the batch she's typed. Edith has nearly worn herself out trying to prepare her new novel, *The Fruit of the Tree*, for serialization in *Scribner's Magazine*. The new book is bolder and more important, she deems, than any book she's written before. *The Fruit of the Tree* is about industrial reform, and even addresses a nurse choosing death over life for a patient and friend who suffers after a crippling accident.

But Edith's editor isn't satisfied with the ending. He wants Edith to make the main character's feelings clearer. As a nurse, Justine has opted to give her friend a deathblow of morphine she feels her friend is begging for, rather than force her to live in excruciating pain. After Justine ends up marrying the woman's widower, she never finds the right time to tell him what she's done. When he discovers the truth, she must make a series of confounding choices. Edith has always resisted overexplaining her characters' intentions. Let the psychology speak for itself, she thinks. In life, no one explains themselves, and rarely are people insightful enough to question their own motives. But she has decided this one time to give Mr. Burlingame what he's asked for. He has been annoyingly insistent. Like a fly in her ear. And now she isn't feeling very good about the changes. How disconcerting to have Tonni call it out.

"Have I failed at it?" she asks Anna. "It was a fool's mission."

"Failed. No, but . . ."

Edith feels herself biting her lip, just as she did as a child when Tonni corrected her German grammar or urged her to better support her main theory in an essay on Goethe.

"I wish Burlingame hadn't asked it of me. . . . I think he's wrong."

"So why change it?" Anna says.

"Burlingame thought . . . you agree with me then?"

"It was clear enough before."

"And now it feels like a diatribe."

"He isn't reading carefully enough. It's all there," Anna says.

Edith reaches out and gives Anna a hug, clutches her for a moment as someone might grab a life preserver.

"I shouldn't need a backup on these things. . . . I don't know why I let him talk me into it."

"We all need a backup sometimes." Anna's eyes are as clear as water. Her lashes almost transparent. She stands there, blinking in the sun. "Shall I retype it as it was, then?" Anna asks in a whisper.

"Yes," Edith says. "Please, please do."

Henry James arrives at the Whartons' door with two trunks, four hatboxes and a stained and rather nasty-smelling half-eaten train lunch which he insists be placed immediately on ice. One cannot entirely prepare for a visit from Henry James. He is a jumble of strength, intensity, neediness and vulnerability so tangled, so exquisitely bright, so sharp, so insistent that no matter how well one plans, there is simply no way to know what to expect. Edith sees him as brilliant and flawed. Kind and selfish. Both master and child. Approaching the age of sixty-four, he has grown stout and unwell. During the cold spring trip they took with him the previous year, he was often dyspeptic, and had moments of what Edith thought of as thermostatic issues: he would suddenly and dramatically become hot. Itchy. This would usually occur after dinner. If he was in familiar company, he would apologize profusely, remove his jacket, then his waistcoat and then, with nothing else to remove, he'd go to bed.

Edith remembers her mother going through a similar phase as part of "the change." She didn't think men experienced this too.

But if any man could, it's fitting that it be Henry, for, despite his rich masculine voice and dominant presence, there is a femininity about him that Edith can't help noting. She sees it in his sensuous lips and his perfectly manicured hands. And in his eyes. Henry has the clear, gentle eyes of a child.

Henry once confided in Edith that as a child he was mortified by a stammer so profound it took a Herculean effort for him to share even the simplest thoughts, so even now each spoken word bears the weight of a dictionary falling off a shelf. It often takes him so long to get to the point, a simple story can grow to four, six, eight times its natural size. While Edith knows she's in for an exquisite ride, others are often not as indulgent.

At the dinner party she throws on the night of his arrival, Henry is in grand form, spinning a single story that dominates the entire dinner from soup to dessert. It is a long-winded narrative, even for Henry, and though to Edith it seems wonderful, she sees it strains the patience of even the most tolerant of her guests.

After Henry has retired, Teddy, still pale from a week's bout of influenza, struts into Edith's boudoir and perches heavily on the edge of her bed, sighing.

"Must everything Henry says be a literary reference?" he says. "I never had a class at Harvard so wearisome."

Edith takes a deep breath. "Some things are worth waiting for."

"But every time he speaks, I fear the train will *never* reach the station."

She rises and comes over to him, pressing her hand against his forehead. "You're still feverish, dear," she says. "Go to bed. We want you well for our motor trip."

"Promise me you will not let Mr. James go on while we are trapped in the motorcar with him, Puss."

"I can't control Henry," she says.

"Well, give it a try." He sniffs, shuffles into his own room and closes the door sharply behind him.

Edith is amazed that she has so far avoided Teddy's influenza. Instead, it's Henry who falls ill. Two days after his arrival, he asks Alfred White to inform Edith that he is seriously, possibly fatally indisposed.

"I'm sorry, Ma'am. That is what he told me to convey," Alfred says, looking at his shoes.

Edith hurries to Henry's room and taps on the door.

"May I come in?" she asks.

"If you dare," he says. Henry looks like a great beached whale, lying in the middle of the *lit bateau* with the covers neatly tucked under his armpits.

"I think I shall die," he says. "You'll have to have a piano mover remove me from this lovely bedroom," he announces. He moans and lies back on his pillow. Edith notes that he has put on a beautiful silk dressing gown and wears an ascot. Quite an effort for just lying in bed.

"We'll take very good care of you," she assures him.

She arranges for much tea with honey, all sorts of croissants and toast and stewed chicken to be brought to his room.

Later in the afternoon, Henry asks for Anna. Soft, serious Anna enters his room, shuts the door and doesn't come out for an hour.

Edith, feeling a tad jealous, monitors the door. When Anna emerges, Edith ushers her away from Henry's room. "What on earth did he speak to you about?" she asks.

"He told me what he wanted us to do if he *died*."

Edith can't help but laugh. "He's not going to die. He simply has a head cold."

"I took notes," Anna says, and with only the faintest smile holds up a pad of paper filled from top to bottom.

"We'll have to have these framed for future reference," Edith says. "Good heavens. He wants only *black* horses in his funeral procession. No cars. Very old-fashioned of him."

A week later, when Henry is himself again, guests begin to arrive once more, including Henry's particular request: the journalist Mr. Morton Fullerton.

Fullerton arrives on a Tuesday afternoon bearing an elegant top hat, a walking stick and a nosegay of roses, violets and daisies for Edith.

"For me? Or Henry?"

"You, of course," he says.

"Oh lovely! I appreciate flowers so much this time of year!" She strokes the slick lavender silk gracing the stems. "Thank you."

"The magic of hothouses," he says. "I hear *you* are quite the gardener."

"And who told you that?"

"Charles Eliot Norton."

"You know Mr. Norton?"

The well-known Harvard scholar is the father of Sally Norton, one of Edith's dearest friends. Edith feels flattered that Fullerton bothered to mention her to them.

"He influenced me more than anyone at Harvard. I know all the Nortons, and they seem to know you. I don't wish to be brazen, Mrs. Wharton. But the Nortons say I must visit you when I'm in Massachusetts. That your house is the 'embodiment of you.'"

"The embodiment of me. Hmmm. Largish and white?"

He looks her up and down with a grin. "Well put together. Elegant."

Fullerton's good looks make Edith uncomfortable. She's heard that the glaciers in the Alaska territory hold such an extraordinary azure color they seem to have trapped the sky beneath the ice. And that's how Morton Fullerton's eyes strike her. Caught in the black fringe of his long lashes, they are glistening, chilling, reflective. "Oh, and Sally says I *must* smell the pine trees at night from your terrace."

Wise Sally. To step out on The Mount's terrace in the moonlight, after a pulsingly hot day, and feel the cool breath of pine is one of Edith's greatest pleasures. "I'll count on you visiting me, then?" she asks.

"We'll shake on it." he offers his hand. With her hand enfolded in his, an odd sense of peace comes over her. She reluctantly lets go, but her very skin seems to vibrate.

"Please excuse me while I get Mr. James." She hears a girlish lilt to her own voice.

Henry is thrilled to see Fullerton. His face lights up like a starving man being presented a chocolate cream pie. He pulls up one of the Louis XIV tapestry chairs to sit closer.

"My boy," he says, "you're looking well. The world of journalism hasn't ruined you, I see."

"I am quite good at hiding the damage," Fullerton says. "And you, Mr. James, are looking fine, despite your brush with death."

Henry apparently doesn't hear the irony in his voice, for he goes on in flinching detail describing the misery of his week in bed. Fullerton furrows his brows with appropriate concern.

"I am sure Mrs. Wharton was relieved that you didn't die chez Wharton. It would have been a blot on her reputation as the consummate hostess."

"I am too thoughtful to die in someone else's home," Henry says with a harrumph.

The *bonne* arrives with a spread for tea: tea cakes, pastries and small sandwiches. Henry isn't too shy to fill his plate with little pleasures. Fullerton merely sips his brew. He must be in his early forties, but his body appears fit and disciplined. His face unlined. There's no mark of indulgence in drink or gluttony.

"I hear that Charles Du Bos is translating *The House of Mirth* for you," Fullerton says, turning to Edith.

"Yes, I'm hoping to have it serialized here. To place it in *Le Temps* or *Revue de Paris*. Do you think that's a good idea? That's how it was done in New York."

"A very good idea. But the *Revue de Paris* is the better choice. It's a natural fit for your work. I could speak to the chief editor there, Rivoire. I know him well."

"Could you?" She races on lest she lose her nerve. "And let me ask you, Mr. Fullerton: when Charlie is done with the translation, would you look at it? I am a disastrous proofreader even in English. My brain supplies all the missing words and I don't see the gap. But in French . . ." She makes a moue and a poofing sound, as the French do to express complete hopelessness. "I imagine you are much better at it."

He smiles very slowly, and his eyes meet hers. "Nothing would give me more pleasure," he says.

"I'll write as soon as the manuscript arrives," she tells him.

When Fullerton is gone, Henry grips Edith's hand with childish passion. "He's an extraordinary fellow, isn't he? A beautiful, extraordinary fellow." Edith cannot help but agree.

Edith hasn't been sleeping well. Her nights are filled with dreams that wind around her so tightly she wakes in the dark, aching and imprinted by the sheets. What was the dream she just had? That she and the Comtesse de Noailles were going bathing together in the sea. Edith can't remember the last time she really stepped into the ocean. Sometime in her twenties in Newport. The unpredictability of the waves frightened her. Walter once said, "You'd control the Atlantic if you could, wouldn't you, Edith? That's why you're afraid of it, you know. Because it pays you no heed." But in this dream, she and de Noailles were going to swim. And de Noailles started removing her own clothes right at the shoreline, encouraging Edith to do the same.

"There's no one here. Don't be shy."

She helped Edith untie her corset.

"Evil thing," she called it, tossing it down onto the sand.

De Noailles wanted them to swim naked. Completely naked. The sea wasn't cold like it is in Newport. It was warm like bathwater, bright turquoise like the Mediterranean. Undressed, Anna's skin was dusky and glowing, her nipples as richly colored as autumn apples.

"Come in! Come in," she called out to Edith, stepping in deeper and deeper, until the water reached her neck and she was swept into the bright waves. Laughing and luxuriating in the broth-warm ocean, she waved and smiled. Her hair tumbled around her shoulders. She was a water nymph, a siren, calling Edith forth. But Edith stood shivering on the edge of the surf. If only she could make herself go into the water, it would be warmer. Far warmer. Gooseflesh sprouted on her arms, her exposed thighs. Why couldn't she make herself go in? It should have been so easy. So enticing. But she couldn't step in beyond her knees. What did it matter that the warm waves were so inviting when she couldn't sally forth?

She shivers now in her bed. Alone and awake, she wishes she could close her eyes and swim.

The motorcar is packed. With Charles Cook, the chauffeur, at the wheel, Teddy, Henry and Edith set off to explore France. Nicette climbs right into Henry's lap and he declares by lunch that he has fallen in love with her. If she were a woman, he says, he would throw all caution to the wind and give up his bachelorhood immediately. The weather is lovely and a breeze whooshes in through the open windows. The car flies on its big India rubber tires. They all exclaim that they can barely feel the road.

It's late April when they return to Paris, a jolly crew. Henry says he's practically had the time of his life. Edith is tickled by the disclaimer of the word "practically," but she feels closer to him than she imagined possible. As persnickety and full of irony as he can be—and often is—he experiences everything with a childlike pleasure that she deems the essential element of a good traveler, and in this case, a charming companion. By the time they return to Paris, even Teddy is calling him "good old HJ."

Henry stays on at the Rue de Varenne through much of May, and the Bourgets—Paul and Minnie—visit with him often. Paul has grown fond of Henry, has all the patience in the world for his stories and declares him a genius.

One afternoon, Anna de Noailles comes for tea and to meet the great Monsieur James. She arrives in her silken dress, dewy and flushed as though she has walked all the way from the Right Bank. After Edith's dream of de Noailles naked in the ocean, she feels shy to be alone with her. And since Henry is still out with the Bourgets, Edith is relieved to recall her promise to invite Anna Bahlmann to meet La Comtesse. Coaxed from her room, Anna sits very still on a distant settee in her dull gray dress and gazes at de Noailles with wide eyes. She speaks only when Anna de Noailles asks, "Aren't you going to have a taste of these uncanny little cakes, Miss Bahlmann? Honestly, you will be a changed woman." Anna shrinks back into the pillows and demurs, "Non, merci."

"Miss Bahlmann clearly doesn't wish to be a changed woman," Edith says, laughing. Just then she catches Anna's pained eyes and feels a moment's remorse. But then Tonni leans forward.

"Comtesse, when I read your poem "Imprint," I cried. It made me realize how little *I* leave behind." And then, in flawless French, Anna Bahlmann recites the beginning of the poem.

> "So vigorously will I lean on life,
>   So strongly will I hold and embrace it,
>   That before I lose the sweetness of day
>   It will be heated from my touch."

Anna de Noailles's soft lips part with surprise.

"It spoke to me," Anna Bahlmann goes on to say. "It urged me to make a mark."

"Truly, Miss Bahlmann?" The Comtesse raises her extraordinary dark eyebrows. "I too often hope in vain that my poems will do more than amuse people. You are proof that I have made *my* mark on someone," she says humbly. "I am inexpressibly touched."

When the tea is over, she embraces Anna. "Imprint the world," she whispers into her ear loud enough for Edith to hear. The door closes behind her.

Edith and Anna Bahlmann are left standing in the hall with the Comtesse's lingering scent. Edith takes in the figure of the woman who hovers by her every single day: so transparent in her gray gown, like a wisp of smoke threatening to disperse. She wonders if she has ever really *seen* her before.

Anna Bahlmann lies neck-deep in the servants' tub, caressing the cool nickel faucet with her toes, whispering aloud the same poem she quoted to the Comtesse. She is pleased that the cool tile plumps her whisper with watery sibilance.

> "That before I lose the sweetness of day
>   It will be heated from my touch."

Anna has spent a lifetime allowing poetry to tie neat bows around her life. How gratifying that this time her habit of finding herself in poetry has managed to please the poet herself.

How little the world around Anna has ever been heated by her touch! And yet is there anyone she knows who experiences more from the universe than she? Who else sees beauty in the branchings on the underside of a leaf, thrills at the perfect middle C of a streetcar bell, is electrified by the perfume of rain on cobbles? Edith. Edith is the only other person she knows who finds splendor in the mundane. And that is why she loves her, why she has devoted herself to her. From the moment she laid eyes on the earnest ten-year-old with ripples of straw-berry hair, she knew she'd met her match. A walk in the woods with Edith was a revelation for both of them. A letter from Miss E. Jones burst with description, with news that no one else would have relished.

Yes, Edith was intractable sometimes. She wanted the world to be as she expected. Once, as a twelve-year-old, she tore every page out of a Dickens book because it disappointed her. Another time, she wouldn't write to Anna for a whole month when they were apart, because Anna, called away in an emergency, left the Jones's household unexpectedly.

"You could at least have warned us," Edith said as Anna packed and her young charge watched, her mouth in a jealous twist. Just as Anna was closing the case, Edith grabbed Anna's already packed shawl and yanked it from the bag. "In fact, I won't let you go. You've just come."

"Edith, no one could have guessed Ilsa Barnard would come down with scarlet fever. They need me to take care of her."

"But you are *not* a nurse, Tonni! Let them hire a nurse."

Anna took the furious little girl and held her to her breast. "I'd choose you over Ilsa, you know, if I had the choice. We'll see each other soon. Would you like to keep my shawl in the meanwhile?"

Edith gazed at the nimbus of blue yarn crushed in her fist, sheer and glistening as spider silk.

"No." she said, throwing it back on the bed. "I don't want to be re-minded of someone so . . . so . . . *inconstant*!" After a month of silence with not a single reply to Anna's faithful letters, she wrote, "I have enjoyed all your letters, Tonni. Do come back soon. I have had some very important thoughts about Goethe and no one to share them with. And mother is at a loss without you." How relieved Anna felt, knowing Edith couldn't stay angry at her for long.

For the last thirty-five years, the very center of Anna's life, the touchstone, has been Edith. How can Anna help feeling unspeakably pained when she knows Edith is laughing at her, as she surely was this afternoon in de Noailles's presence? Would Edith have become the writer she is if Anna had not walked in the woods with her and discussed the leaves, the people they met, the reasons things happened? If Anna had not read poems aloud to her, had not made Edith parse the poet's intentions in every line, had not opened her eyes to new ideas, new ways of thinking? Has Edith come to believe she taught it all to herself? Anna kicks the faucet with her toe. The radiating sting fills her eyes with tears. How lucky she is that she's in the bath, where no one can see.

For Edith, the best part about Henry James's visit is that Morton Fullerton drops by often now: sometimes in the morning, when Edith is writing, sometimes for afternoon tea. She is sorry to miss him when he arrives too early. And she discovers that she is a bit jealous of the abundant attention he pays Henry. On his third visit, he brings the proofread manuscript of *The House of Mirth* with him. Even at a quick glance, Edith can see he's done a fine, exacting job.

"I owe you a great deal for this, Mr. Fullerton," she says, eager to see all the marks he's made.

"Since Henry is nowhere to be found," Fullerton says, "perhaps you'll honor me with a walk, Mrs. Wharton. It's the nicest day of the year so far. And you can consider it a payment of sorts, especially since you have been so cruelly ignoring me of late."

"Ignoring you?"

"Well, the last few times I've come to visit, you haven't even appeared. I find that very wounding."

"Mr. Fullerton! I didn't 'appear' because I was writing."

"And you find literature more important than me?" His blue eyes twinkle. He holds out his elbow. "Let's go out before the sun decides it has better things to do."

The air is soft and persuasive and the sun, rather than deserting them, splashes itself all along the high-walled *hôtels particuliers* of the Rue de Varenne. Except for a few walkers, the squeal of passing prams and an occasional distant horse clop, there is no sound but their shoes on the pavement. They are nearly the same height, and their feet find a lilting rhythm.

"So tell me," Fullerton says, "have you ever known anyone like Lily Bart? Someone who's his own worst enemy?"

She glances over at him. "Isn't everyone?"

"No. You don't strike me as someone who risks enough to do damage to herself."

She is startled by his statement. Does she seem so very dull to him?

"I think I should be insulted."

"You shouldn't. I don't find risk takers particularly appealing," he says. "I find them less appealing every year."

"I would like to be a risk taker." Edith envisions Anna de Noailles.

"What good would risk do you?" Fullerton says jauntily. "You know what you like. And you seem to have everything you could want."

Edith smiles to herself. "You don't know me at all, Mr. Fullerton."

The lawns of Les Invalides roll out green and fragrant before them. After the narrow streets, the open space exhales verdant airiness.

"I know why *I* find Lily Bart so compelling." A shadow clouds his eyes for just a moment. "What can be more tragic than someone destroying his own chance at happiness? It's the classic theme. The seductive glow of the wrong option. Wrong options always seem to have ribbons on them for me."

"For you, Mr. Fullerton?"

"I think I'm doing everything right and most of the time I'm just flat-out wrong. And I live with the consequences. I am a very bad sport. I don't like consequences. They're so untidy."

She is charmed by his forthrightness. She thinks him a very rare man, indeed, who can view his own failings with such a cool eye.

In the garden, they locate a bench and sit side by side. She can sense his body heat, and takes in his odor of driftwood and lavender. Edith feels something she hasn't felt in a long time and cannot name. She's been happy of late, but this feeling of expansion dizzies her.

"Look there." He points. "See that honeybee?" On the hedge behind them, a honeybee as fat as a blackberry is trying to wedge himself greedily into the narrow trumpet of a pink flower. Fullerton turns his gaze to her and says, "That's how drawn I am to you."

Edith, speechless, feels her cheeks redden.

Seeing her discomfort, he seems to shift gears. "You are far more disciplined than I, for one thing. Were you always like that? Is it something I can learn?"

Her mouth is very dry. "I had tutors who insisted on discipline. I suspect you could learn it too."

"My school reports all declared that's what I lack most. You, on the other hand, were, no doubt, a stellar student."

"I've always had to motivate myself. No one's ever expected anything from me," she says.

He smiles softly. "I do."

She observes his perfect Greek head, his smoothly shaven chin and combed mustache, his gloved hands. She has never seen neater gloves. Entirely buttoned. Teddy has never buttoned a glove in his life. What does Fullerton want from her? Why should he waste his ammunition on such untasty game—a long-married woman whose beauty has never been her greatest asset?

"We should go back," she says. It's Lucretia whispering in her ear: *Why hope for much? You can only fail.* How strong this need of hers to close off options, to make things safe. Only on the page can she take risks. She abhors this about herself.

They walk back in near silence. Still, their bodies seem to cleave to one another.

"I'm leaving soon, you know," she says. "I'm off to America. Do you have any plans to make a crossing this summer?"

"My family *has* been asking me to come."

"You could visit me at The Mount."

"And view your gardens; take in the much ballyhooed scent of those pines."

They stop by the gate and look at each other. Their mutual gaze extends beyond the fleeting nod of parting friends. Edith relishes the moment to dwell on the extraordinary perfection of his face. Has she ever thought a face so lyrical?

"I don't think I'll come up and see Henry today after all, if you don't mind," Fullerton says at last.

"No?"

"He doesn't even need to know I've come to call. I really came to see you."

Edith is bewildered. Is he really trying to woo her? Or is it wishful thinking on her part?

"Thank you for the lovely walk," she says. "And the proofreading. I'm eager to see what you've marked."

"My pleasure." He bows his head formally. She hopes he might grasp her hand and kiss it as he has done before; she longs for him to do so, but instead he draws away suddenly and walks toward the Rue du Bac. His gait says he knows he's being watched, and also, somehow—Edith is certain—that leaving her has cost him a great deal of energy.

Henry oversees the packing of his many trunks and heads off for a few weeks in Italy before returning to England (*"For Life!"* he says). Edith and Teddy have their own trunks packed. George Vanderbilt wants his apartment back and they must move to Edith's brother's much smaller residence in the Sixteenth Arrondissement. The little house feels cramped and puts Teddy too near at hand so that Edith is surrounded by his bumping about and sighing. In Harry Jones's house, Edith finds it impossible to write or to entertain comfortably. Anna Bahlmann has to share a mean little room in the attic with Catherine Gross and both are unhappy. When the staff isn't happy, everyone feels it.

"We'll be back at The Mount before you know it, Tonni," she consoles Anna, patting her hand. "Before you can so much as blink." Anna gives her a doleful look.

Edith thinks of those last weeks as a fine transition. They make her actually glad to be heading off to Le Havre and the ship home. How happy she has been in Paris this winter. The salons! The people! The talk! The week before departing, she scribbles a note to Fullerton. She tells him that she is "findable" at The Mount in Lenox any time up until Christmas and hopes he will visit.

He writes back:

Dearest Mrs. Wharton,
*   As discussed, I have indeed decided to visit the States this*
summer. There is much on my agenda. A lecture at Bryn Mawr.
A day or two with the Nortons. And a great deal of time eating
mother's cooking and reminding her that despite my so-called
worldly knowledge, she is indeed my favorite cook. Amidst all
that, I hope to see you.

*   Morton Fullerton*

During that last week in Paris, Anna too receives a letter. She slides it
into her pocket and opens it three, five, eight times over the course of
the day. It's from her niece, Anna Louise, in Missouri, imploring Anna
to come.

*   Maybe not just for a visit, Aunt Anna. Would you consider*
coming for good? Is there any way we could entice you? Father
does miss you. Your good company would perk him up consider-
ably. You've worked hard for so many years. Wouldn't you like to
make a home with us in Missouri, as you always said you would?
We would be so happy to have you in our daily lives.

At first, Anna feels a heaviness as she reads the note. Her brother
William is the eldest in their family; Anna is the youngest. William has
recently retired from a career as a teacher, a school principal, a college
professor. He taught German, loves poetry, books, ideas. But William's
life has been marred by tragedy. His son, Lewis, the very soul of his life,
a golden boy, shattered William's world by holding a rifle to his head
and taking his own life after an ill-fated romance. The following year,
William's beloved wife died of a broken heart.

William's heart is equally damaged, but he has not been lucky enough
to die, he tells Anna sometimes. Alone, he's moved reluctantly from

Warrensburg, where he taught, to Kansas City to live with his daughter. Anna's niece has written that there are entire days when he barely speaks. He goes to bed at dusk. He pushes his plate back not having touched a thing. And then, for months at a time, he'll be more like himself, until the dark times return. Anna is no fool. She's seen Teddy Wharton's dark days. Surely her brother's taken a turn for the worse. Otherwise, why would Anna Louise ask her to come now?

So she shudders on receiving this letter. And frets about it. Then she begins to envision what life in Missouri might be like, how calm and enveloping, and she starts to feel giddy at the thought.

She remembers one Fourth of July during a family visit years ago. How glorious the parade was up and down the main street of Warrensburg, Missouri, stars and stripes adorning farm wagons, children waving triumphantly from the seats, dogs prancing in ruffled red, white and blue collars. And the fireworks, the ice cream! It held a wholesomeness and hopefulness she can still savor. On that trip, she visited Kansas City. It hardly seemed more crowded, and offered the same innocence. Entirely different from the world she inhabits now—Edith's world of formal dinner parties, ironic banter. And Anna always feeling as though she's standing backstage.

In Missouri, the stage would be her own. She'd be surrounded by her great-nephews and great-niece! Billy, whose letters make her laugh. Charlie, the two-year-old. And the baby, a girl named Abbott—a baby she could hold in her arms! Well, that sounds fine indeed. To truly be "Aunt Anna." To have a place in the world!

Anna fantasizes telling Edith, "When we return to the States, I believe I will retire. I'd like to go to Kansas City, to be with my family."

She pictures Edith's shock, her hands clasped in distress, pleading, "But Tonni, I need you. How am I to *write* without you to lighten the load? Without your counsel?"

The thought of Edith so openly appreciating her would be worth the terror of breaking the tie. And Teddy. He would grasp her hands in his. His fingers would be warm and dry. He'd realize what Anna meant to all of them. To him in particular.

"Are you sure of this, Miss Anna?" he'd say. "I don't want you to leave." Her heart aches to think of it. She takes his locket into her hand, presses its eggshell smoothness into the nest of her palm and feels a sense of peace she hasn't felt for years.

The morning before they are to go to Le Havre to board the ship—the first morning it hasn't rained in a week—she asks Edith if she might take a walk with her.

"A walk?" Edith asks. "When there is so much to do?" She looks annoyed, but nods and asks the *bonne* to bring their wraps. "All right, then. Let's not take too long." They have been walking companions for many years. As they skirt the park, they say nothing. The sound of motorcars and horses, laughing children and some nearby construction seems to press between them. Anna's heart leaps against her throat. She feels light-headed.

And then she stops. "I've been thinking," she says at last.

"Thinking what?" Edith's voice is stern.

Anna cannot get the words out. She is sure she's going to faint.

"Can we sit down?" she asks.

Edith looks at her with concern. "What is it? Are you ill, Tonni?"

Anna shakes her head. They settle themselves on the nearest bench.

"I was thinking, when we go back, perhaps I won't come to The Mount with you. . . ." Her tongue feels thick in her mouth.

"You'd rather stay in New York?"

She can't swallow. She can barely breathe. "I want to go to Kansas City and be with my family, Edith. They want me to come." For an orphan, could there be anything more seductive than to be wanted? "They want me to *stay*."

Edith pales. She looks into Anna's eyes and Anna realizes Edith's face is dearer to her than any face she's ever known, more familiar than her brother's or her niece's. It's the face she's understood for too many years to count. Tears fill her eyes, then spill hot and plentiful.

"Well, then you shall go home, Tonni." Edith says softly. It's the voice she uses for Nicette and Mitou, the souls she loves most in the world. She strokes Anna's back, just as she does the Pekinese. "We'll arrange a reservation on a train out West the minute we land. You can join us at The Mount later in the summer. I can manage."

Anna hadn't anticipated an interim solution. She could go out for the summer. She could cheer her brother up, help with the children, spend time with her family and then return.

"Of course, you are homesick! I would never keep you from your home or family. I would be happy to pay for your trip."

But is this what Anna wants? No laying down of her burden? No breathing easily at last?

Anna puts her face into her hands.

"There, dearest," Edith says, patting her hand. "No call for crying. We must hurry back. We have many things to accomplish! Especially if you are about to leave me."

It is as cold as a winter morning and still dark as the blue Panhard-Levassor roars away from the city toward Le Havre. Edith turns and watches the rows of electric lamps disappear to a single point on the horizon. She doesn't want to leave Paris. She has been awakened by the daily sting of its beauty, a venom, she knows, that will bedevil her forever. The promise of The Mount doesn't fill her with the pleasure it should. And in the port office in Le Havre, they are informed that the ship has boiler problems and will be delayed by at least two days.

"Boiler problems?" Cook scoffs. "Not likely. That gentleman over there says it's a strike."

"Why is it never simple?" Edith says petulantly, tossing her pale kid gloves down onto the stone floor. "First Anna wants to desert us. Now, this. I take it as an omen that we should turn right around and stay in Paris for the whole summer." Everyone knows that Edith doesn't like surprises. And two in a row! Cook gingerly squats for her gloves and hands them back to her.

"Bite your tongue, Puss." Teddy says. "You would stay at your brother's miserable little place rather than our Mount? Do you know what Paris is like in the summer? A cesspool." When Teddy gets upset, his lips turn as gray as liverwurst.

"And are your needs the only ones to be considered, Mr. Wharton?" Edith says.

Cook steps nervously between them. "Excuse me for interrupting.

But perhaps I can offer you and Mrs. Wharton a short motor trip. In two days you could see a good deal of Normandy."

In the silence that follows, Edith's aspect lightens from surly to serene.

"That's exactly what we should do. Teddy?"

The color returns to Teddy's lips. "You'll get no argument from me."

The servants' trunks are separated from the rest. A hotel is found for Anna and Alfred White and Catherine Gross so they can stay on in the port with the trunks and the dogs.

In short order, the purr of the motor, the Normandy air and beautiful sights smooth all tempers. As they swoop past green fields and apple orchards, long velvet beaches and timbered houses, Teddy reaches over and squeezes Edith's hand. Edith can't help reflecting that despite this potentially sour ending, she has spent a wonderful season in France, one of the best of her life. She senses it the way animals sometimes anticipate an earthquake—pawing the ground, restless—that something is about to shift. It gives her spirits wings.

"Isn't this grand?" she exclaims.

"Brilliant!" Teddy leans over and kisses her brow.

After a full day of touring, they come to a beautiful stone inn in Bayeux. Because no plans have been made in advance, there is only one servant's room for Cook and one last guest room vacant, and no other inns for miles. Exhausted, Teddy turns to Edith.

"Only one room." He looks at her anxiously. "What do you make of it, Puss?" Edith smiles. How could she not be grateful to Teddy for allowing her so full a time in this magical country? Nearly six months.

"Well, Mr. Wharton," she says. "I think we can manage well enough."

It is the first time they have shared a room in years, let alone a bed, and on those rare occasions it has always been a misery. But with the windows open and the scent of the distant ocean wafting in, when Teddy puts his arm around her, Edith wonders if tonight they might have relations for the first time in a very long time. Maybe now, more sure of herself, experiencing a new sense of longing, she might actually enjoy it.

"Ah, dear Puss," he whispers. She's always liked his voice, rich and warm. And then . . . nothing. His arm grows heavy, his breathing even, and she knows he is asleep. She doesn't mind his heavy arm on her. She even feels surprisingly close to him. He is a good man, really. He loves her. But even as she falls asleep, she feels the beat of her unsatisfied heart.

Anna had imagined that her trip to Missouri would constitute a nice, clean break. But instead, it feels like a painful tearing away. The moment they reach New York, Edith busies herself directing everyone and their trunks into various hansoms and taxis and barely takes a moment to hand Anna a book and wish her farewell.

"Something for your journey," she says, then a peck on the cheek and nothing more. Teddy merely nods and in his jolliest voice says, "Have yourself a fine time, Miss Anna." Oh, how Anna wishes she could linger, watch them, watch over them.

At the sparkling new Pennsylvania Station she finds a café where she can sit and sip tea. Pigeons have already gotten in and beat wildly beneath the glistening glass roof. One settles right at her feet, pecking at a crust of bread. She's surprised at the clanging loneliness that surrounds her in the vast station. How long until she sees the Whartons again? She draws out of her carpetbag the neat red leather book of Meredith poems Edith handed her on parting. On the flyleaf, Edith has written, "Dearest Anna, May all your journeys be memorable and bring you safely home. For you will always have a home with us. And for me there would be no home without you. Edith."

If you were on that platform, that afternoon in May, you would have observed a woman no larger than a child, sitting alone in a shaft of light, weeping and smiling and drinking every last drop of good old American tea.

FOUR

When Edith was just five, Lucretia taught her that unhappiness is a moral failing.

She recalls the scene of her indelible lesson: they were living in an ornate hotel suite on the Right Bank of the Seine. Her mother had filled the social season with dinners and balls, and endless rounds of dressmaking and shopping. Edith was given a sealskin coat and hat, a china doll with pink cheeks and a silk velvet pillow the color of raspberries that she took to bed at night. On this winter day, as snow fell outside their window, her father stepped into the drawing room with tears in his eyes and announced that the family's money had run out. Lucretia had bought too many dresses and pearl rings and hand-sewn kid gloves. Instead of being angry at his spendthrift bride, George was devastated. He had married a woman who didn't appreciate art or literature or music. She loved *things*. The family was penniless, about to be homeless, with not even enough money for the fare back to the States. George fell into the big carved armchair by the fireplace, his head in his hands. Choking sounds leaked from his throat. Edith didn't know that fathers were able to cry. She came to him, sat at his feet and began petting his ribbed socks, whispering, "Hush, little Papa."

Her mother rose sharply with a rustle of silken skirts. "Get up, Pussy. Young ladies do not sit on the floor." Her voice was stony and threatening, but Edith didn't want to leave her father.

"Get up!" Lucretia bellowed. "With enough fortitude one can find reason to be happy even in the direst circumstances. And I do not want you to witness this ugly example of self-pity." Her father raised his head, and Edith looked into his eyes. Even at the age of five she could identify hopelessness. Was her father at fault for not being able to mend his own broken heart?

As it turned out, some relative eventually sent money before the family was evicted from the hotel, and the Joneses were able to stay in France for another year, until things began to "look up."

But Edith never forgot her mother's disdain for her father's tears. And her message: *If one is unhappy, it's one's own fault.* Edith therefore can't help but define her own state this summer as an unprecedented bout of weakness.

Summer in the Berkshires has always given Edith pleasure. But this July, she often stands on The Mount's terrace awash in sadness. So much about the house of which she was once so giddily proud now seems a mere impersonation of the beauties that line George Vanderbilt's apartment in the Rue de Varenne. The boiseries in The Mount's library, the regimented allée of lime trees—the very backbone of The Mount's garden—have been transformed by her newly Europeanized eyes into the faux and the failed.

It is a perfect day, glorious without an ounce of disagreeable humidity. Her eyes take in the geometry of her once-beloved gardens; her ears are soothed by the music of the stone fountains. Laurel Lake dazzles like a diamond tiara. But none of the beauty reaches her soul. Her heart is blocked and she feels ashamed.

She's begun writing a new book about a headstrong, social-climbing, money-burning woman. She is taking a risk: this self-absorbed woman is her heroine.

When she's writing, she finds her only pleasure these days. She loses herself in the music of her words, her characters' thoughts, their faces. She sees them all so clearly. Undine Spragg's strong, almost manly hands, her petulant mouth. And dear, weak Ralph Marvell. She can hear his voice as if he is in the room, broken by his disappointment that Undine will never be the woman he wishes she were. Sometimes, when the writing truly flows, it's as if Edith enters a place out of time. She has no sense that hours have passed. Bodiless, she floats above the world of her characters. This is the greatest ecstasy she knows, the reason she returns again and again to the page. But even these ecstatic journeys feel empty without Anna to comment on her writing at the end of the day.

She recalls that when she was a child, she and Anna would be parted while the Joneses summered in Newport. They would reunite in the autumn, but oh, how she missed her Tonni on those long, hot summer days. She would compile notes to share about what books she was reading, the thoughts she had. She remembers writing, "We can read German together and collect autumn leaves and do a thousand things which are nothing to me now, but so much with you."

What a lonely little girl she was! And how utterly Tonni filled that loneliness with her patience and abiding interest. Edith would dream as a child that she could cast a spell on Tonni so she'd never want to leave Edith's family. If she could speak that incantation now, she'd chant it until she could at last see Tonni alighting from the wagon, a soft and expectant smile on her face.

Arriving in Kansas City dirty and exhausted from her train journey, Anna is greeted by her niece's husband, Charles, whom she has only seen in photographs.

"We're so glad you've come," he tells her on the ride home. "You see, William has simply stopped speaking. Anna Louise thinks you're the one person who can make a difference."

Indeed, when Anna is face-to-face with her brother, the first thing she notes is the milkiness of misery in his eyes. Mourning his son, his wife, years past the fact. How grief can still the tongue, limit the soul!

Anna presses herself to him and feels him relax into her arms. Her closest kin, crushed and brokenhearted.

"Here I am, William," she says. "I'm so looking forward to spending time together. It's been too long."

He doesn't say a word. But she feels his acceptance in her presence. She knows that somehow, in time, she will reach him.

Later, in her room, unpacking her clothes into the oak armoire, she can hear, threaded through the Victrola's wheezing Mozart, a counter-melody of family conversation. Her niece, her great-nephews, her niece's husband, chatting about ordinary things. A suffusion of hot pleasure runs from her throat to her belly, as though she has been drinking boiling tea. For the voices that sift up through the floorboards belong to her family! It makes no matter if raising her brother's broken spirits seems herculean. Or that she has not seen any of them for years and years. They are her blood. What most people take for granted every day knocks the wind out of her. How ironic that the only person Anna wants to tell is Edith. "There I was," she imagines confiding, "like a girl in love, because my family was just feet away. Edith, oh Edith! My heart rose like a hot-air balloon!"

Just two weeks into the summer, Edith finds that she no longer just misses Anna but is irritated by her absence. When she writes now, she must work off her own handwritten pages instead of crisp typewritten copies. She wastes precious time copying pages when they get too garbled. And there is no one to question her, no one to say, "Surely you didn't mean *that*, did you?" Or "I don't understand why she would do such a thing. Perhaps a little explanation would help?"

There is no one to keep her social calendar. No one to neatly copy letters. Alfred White brings her mail now, but he doesn't want to disturb her until she's dressed, so she receives no letters until nearly noon. When she'd told a weeping Anna that *of course* she could go to Missouri, Edith didn't realize how much hardship she herself would incur. One night, she mentions her annoyance to Teddy.

He takes a sip of brandy and laughs. "Imagine that! Our little Anna having the nerve to live a life of her own. Serves us all right for taking her for granted."

"Since when is she *our* little Anna?" Edith says with a huff. "She's *my* little Anna and I want her back."

"Funny. I thought slavery was abolished." Teddy must be on his fourth glass.

Edith glares at him. "I have a book to write. You have no idea how hard it makes things for me."

Teddy's voice deflates and Edith can barely make out his response. "No, dearest, only you know that. Is there no one you can hire from town? Surely there's someone who can type."

❀

Two days later, an officious little woman with a birdlike face and a smashed hat arrives at the door—the results of Albert White's inquiries in town. Edith tries to explain to her what she must do.

Pushing a pair of pince-nez onto her nose, she scans a sample page of Edith's work. "If you presume I can read this handwriting, you'd be wrong," the woman says. "Perhaps if you printed it out for me."

"But there are pages and pages. My scribble isn't so terrible, is it?"

The woman harrumphs and shakes her head. "You may be a famous writer, Mrs. Wharton, but you certainly could learn a little penmanship."

Edith gasps.

"Never you mind, though. I'll work through it. You may have to re-read it to make sure I got the gist."

"I need more than the gist, Miss McCrae. I need every word *as written.*"

Miss McCrae looks at her with an arched brow.

"I can do only what I can do. Do you take me for a psychic? Please show me the typewriting machine."

By the end of the day, Miss McCrae's pages are neatly typed without a smudge. But three or four times a page, there are words that have been misread, altered, transposed. There are no comments about the material. No suggestions. But only Anna could have softly, respectfully, provided that.

❀

Anna discovers that living with her brother is like living with a photographic negative, a shadowy ghost of the man she once knew. So she brings him books from the library. She sits for hours talking in a pure, happy voice—as one might converse with a small child who cannot yet speak—recalling his trips to Germany, the poems and philosophers they've always both loved. And she sees that she's making progress. He begins to speak. Just an assent here or there. An occasional dark smile.

And then one evening, a full sentence is born. "Dear Anna," he says, interrupting her reading aloud. "You remind me . . . you remind me of our mother."

"Do I?" she says, smiling. "Can you tell me about her?"

And with that one query, the dike is breached. A flood of memories pour out of William. How their mother had the tiniest teeth, like a child's, and showed her pink gums when she laughed. How everyone remarked that her English was so perfect, so unaccented that she could easily have been born in America. She was proud of that. Their father spoke with an unmistakably German accent, as did all their friends.

William's face animates for the first time in months as he tells her stories of his childhood, of her brothers whom Anna barely knew, of the rainy night baby Anna was born, and how their mother wept, for at last she had given birth to a girl. Anna has never heard any of this before. She cannot even recall her own mother's face. All her life, when people spoke of her mother's death, they sighed. They said she died of rheumatism. But Anna knows it wasn't so. Once, when she was fifteen, Aunt Charlotte told her that just months after Anna was born, when she was still being nursed, the flesh of one of her mother's breasts developed a lump like the stone in a peach. By the time Anna was two years and two months old, her mother was gone. No one's spoken the word. Cancer. Yet, what hurts her is that when they speak of Elise Rasche, it's always about her untimely death, never about her life. No one seems to recall what she loved, how she laughed. Until now. "She read poems aloud to all of us. Even as a baby, you calmed down when she recited poetry."

"You do not know what you have done for me," she tells him as they both climb the stairs to bed, hours later. "You've brought Mama to life." William laughs aloud.

"If only I could bring her back," he says. "Mother and Lydia. And especially Lewis." He closes his eyes when he says his son's name. "If only I could bring them all back."

"Tonight, Mother was in the room with us. Tomorrow, we'll speak of Lewis."

"I don't know if I can bear to," William says.

"It will help. I know it will," she tells him. "It's swallowing down the memories that turns the world so black."

Before he heads for his room, he takes her hand. He looks as if he might speak. Instead, he squeezes her fingers and smiles faintly. It's all she needs to know she's made a difference.

"Papa's so much better when you're around, Aunt Anna." Anna Louise tells her before she goes up to bed that night.

"Oh my dear Aennchen. Do not let your hopes rise too high. There's a very long way to go yet."

"But at least you've begun the journey. You will stay, Aunt Anna, won't you? You will!"

The summer wears on for Edith as slowly as one of Henry James's more recent tomes. So she's overjoyed when Walter Berry arrives from Washington, D.C., for a visit.

Though she's had guests throughout the season, all this summer they've felt like an intrusion. But with Walter, she feels nothing but relief. When his long arms enfold her, she is at peace. When he wanders the gardens each morning at dawn in his snowy linen suit, Edith glances down from her bedroom window, wondering what her life would be like if she could make a clean swap and trade Walter for Teddy. How beautifully he stands out against the kelly green grass and brilliant flowers! How regal his gait! But because she has a far-too-developed rational side, she recognizes the negative aspect of this fantasy: unlike with Teddy, she never could have hidden a thing from Walter. Could she ever have felt free? Even now she feels him watching her with concern.

"What is playing at you, Edith? Are you quite all right?" he asks one evening, wandering into the library after a dinner at which Edith wasn't as talkative as usual. "Am I not the company you hoped for?" He pushes her feet aside and sits right down on the end of her chaise longue, where she has escaped to bury her agitation in a book. How well they know each other!

"I'm fine. And you're always the company I hope for, Walter. Always." She looks at his long, sensitive face, his graying hair. She in fact wishes he could stay forever, take up residence in the guest room, filling it with his law books and ledger-shaped diaries.

"I'm worried about you," he says. "At first I thought I'd caused some offense. Or you weren't glad to see me."

She shakes her head. "It's not you."

He waits for her to continue, raises his eyebrows to coax her to go on.

"I'm restless," she says finally.

He smiles. "Chérie, you've always been restless." It's true. Edith has always had a restless mind and body. She learned long ago that in order to listen well, she needs to distract part of her too-active brain. So she's learned to knit or smoke or tat, just to focus. Her desire for travel is another sort of restlessness. Her interest in new books, new authors, new thoughts: all a manifestation of her restlessness. But restlessness without bravery means dissatisfaction. She wants something, but is she willing to take the risk to find it? All summer, longing has haunted her. She is surprised at its ferocity.

"Cigarette?" She lifts the crystal and silver box from the table beside the chaise and offers it to him. Walter selects one, finds a match in his jacket pocket and lights her cigarette, then his own.

"Would you mind, dear, if I turned off the electric light?" he asks. "It's so harsh and my eyes are tired."

"Of course not." She switches off the lamp for him. For a while they smoke in silence. How intimate it is to be so close to him in the dark. As her eyes adjust, she enjoys the platinum shadows lit only by the intake of their breaths reawakening the ash. She remembers how once Walter seemed so challenging, so intimidating. Now there is no one whose company soothes her more. He takes her free hand suddenly and enfolds it in his. How small her hand becomes in his large one. Through the open French doors the moon is huge, the color of a white-fleshed peach. A breeze blows the voile undercurtains, spilling ivory light onto the patterned rug.

"Come," he says and draws her to her feet.

She has been sitting with outstretched legs too long, and her body aches as she rises, a reminder that she is no longer young. He leads her to the window, from where they can see over the terrace to the allée of lime trees, crisp and neat in the moonlight, and far away, the wispy glimmer of Laurel Lake.

"It's a perfect late-summer moon," he says. "The moon is never so pristine in Washington. It always looks like it's got a scratched lens over it. Here in the mountains, it's clean as a dinner plate."

"You should stay longer."

"No. I'm needed in Washington. I shouldn't have left at all, but I didn't want to disappoint you."

She shakes her head at the word. "Needed. I think I don't know what it's like to be needed," she says.

"You? There are many people who find you indispensable, my love," he says. "Henry James would fall into a heap if you should disappear. As would Teddy. And I most certainly would."

"Walter," she begins. "Do you think there will be any more . . . surprises in my life?"

"Surprises?"

"I've come to believe I've used up my store of surprises."

"Ha." He chuckles softly. "As though we're all allotted a certain precious set. But, Edith, you hate surprises."

"I used to."

"Dearest," he scolds, "you're like your gardens." He gestures out toward the perfectly trimmed moonlit hedges. "You like things just so. Surprise-free. It's what drives us mad about you. And mad for you. It's the Edith we love. And the devil incarnate."

"Maybe so. But now, I feel like I would like my life to grab hold of me and give me a good yank." She thinks of the weeds in her garden. Is she like one of those weeds, in a place she doesn't belong?

Walter laughs. "Really? A good yank? If life did that to you, you'd spank its backside and send it home."

"No," she says. Her fists rise to her waist, her feet planted wide. "You don't understand. It's insulting that you should laugh at me." Her cheeks burn.

He places his large hands on her shoulders, shaking his head with kind, narrowed eyes.

"Dearest. I am not the enemy."

"I didn't say . . . I didn't think . . ."

He leans forward and kisses her brow. His lips are cool and tender. She hears his breath catch. What is he feeling? How sweet his touch! Her heart pounds and she is ashamed to realize she desperately wishes he'd take her chin and kiss her lips too. She would part her lips. She would draw in the sweetness of his mouth. She would be unafraid. Instead, he steps away with a sigh, finds the ashtray on her desk and stubs out his cigarette.

"Well," he says, "it's late, dear. And I have to travel in the morning."

"I wish you didn't." She tries to control the quaver in her voice.

As he leaves the darkened library, desire for him cuts through to her marrow. Later, bound with craving, she finds herself wandering down the hall to his room. She is wearing only her nightgown, barefoot. Her hair is loosened. It is a warm night, and she can hear the crickets rasping outside. Urging her on. Perhaps it is better to risk and make a mistake than to do nothing. She has spent a lifetime doing nothing. Living in a ghostly marriage. Watching other women bloom amidst the spoils of a life she will never know. If she just knocks on his door. If she just whispers, "Before you leave in the morning, do let us be closer. . . ." What is the worst that can happen? She wants to be fearless like Anna de Noailles. At his door, she stands for a long while before she raps. Two knocks. The crickets scream. The clock downstairs chimes. She can taste his lips, feels his arms. . . . But there is no answer. She raps again. And nothing. Is he so soundly asleep already? Is he somehow not in his room? Or is he simply disinterested? She is middle aged, has never been beautiful like so many of the women Walter has escorted. Her heart sinks. How foolish she feels wandering back down the hall to her maiden bed to spend a forlorn night tangled in longing.

When William naps in the afternoons, Anna takes advantage of her stay. She spends time out of the house, exploring the neighborhood. Could she live here? she asks herself. Would she fit in? She walks the boys to the park, and starts to teach them German. She befriends the librarian, Jessie Toibin, who shares books with her that she thinks might reinvigorate William. Though not a single new book has arrived in years—it's a quaint old library—Anna finds many things that please her. On a cushioned window seat in the back of the library, overlooking a wooded knoll, Anna sometimes sits to read and finds solace.

One day, she and Jessie Toibin strike up a conversation.

"What is it you were doing in Paris all winter? I've seen pictures of Paris. And imagine! You've actually been there."

"I'm a secretary," Anna tells her. "For a writer."

Jessie, who is in her early forties, biscuit plump, with steel-rimmed glasses and a sweetheart candy of a mouth, leans forward with interest.

"A writer? Someone I may have heard of?"

"I don't know if you've heard of her. Edith Wharton."

"Oh my!" Jessie sits right down on the window seat next to Anna and puts her hand over her mouth. "Edith Wharton!"

Anna raises her brows. "You know of her? But you don't have her books. I've looked."

"We don't have any books that didn't arrive before you and I were born. But I read every word of *The House of Mirth* in *Scribner's Magazine*. I read it twice! I saved it!" She grabs Anna's arm. "You know her? You worked with her on this book?"

Anna nods, a bit uncomfortable at Jessie's enthusiasm.

"What's it like being part of something so . . . so important?"

Anna beams. "I hardly know what to tell you."

"Is she a nice lady, Mrs. Wharton?"

"Oh yes. She is my closest friend." Anna feels herself blush with pride.

"And to think I know you . . . and you know her. When nothing ever happens around here but new paint on the walls once a decade. And you come along just like that to *my* library!"

From that day on, every time Anna enters the library, Jessie gets up from her desk and gives Anna a hug. And if others are in the library, she is sure to tell them what Anna does "in her real life": "Why, she works hand in hand with the greatest lady writer that ever was!"

As time passes, each time Anna receives a letter from Edith, she feels a pang. Edith describes her days at The Mount, Teddy's childlike joy at the planning out of a new pig house and a visit from Walter Berry. She tells Anna of the conversations she's had, or what she's reading. Presently, she is reading Immanuel Kant in German. "You would find him very exciting, Tonni. I wonder when you are coming back?"

Her life with Edith seems a lifetime away. Is it possible that two such worlds could exist simultaneously? On the days when she receives Edith's letters, she sees her new life in Kansas City through a more critical lens. Is this the life she was meant for? Is she willing to be just one more mouth to feed, one more person to crowd the house? She offers Charles money for her board, but he squarely refuses.

She considers renting a small house of her own, thinking that William might share it, the two of them, aging brother and sister, making a second life together. Perhaps, he would feel less of a burden to his daughter that way. Independent again. But even with his company, which is becoming more loquacious, what would *Anna* do to fill her days? How empty she has always felt without a purpose. Once William is better, will there be any use for her at all? Who will hire a nearly sixty-year-old teacher?

And then she pictures herself handing Edith's freshly typed pages to her, and asking, "Is this character consistent, Herz?" "Is this the right word? Or did you mean 'absolving?'" In her own small way, affecting *literature*! And Edith grateful and loving, smiling in that soft, distant way that is hers alone.

Edith alternates between feeling murderous toward Anna and feeling her absence as an intentional wound. Miss McCrae is more of a burden than a help. If Anna had planned out her trip in advance like sensible people do, she might have had the kindness to find a substitute for herself. From time to time, Anna sends Edith a postcard adorned with a tinted photo of a museum, a library, a grand house. "Found a book about Dutch still lifes at the library," she writes in her perfect, elegant hand. "Did you know that one of the most important Dutch still-life painters was a woman who had ten children?" And, "This house is considered the fanciest house in town. I've visited and it's decorated in the Louis style. It's quite garish and you would not like it at all. The carpets are the color of grass. I thought flowers might sprout from them." The notes are tailored to Edith's interests. Collecting in her handkerchief drawer, they give Edith pause when she reaches for a fresh linen hankie each morning and invoke in her a surprising fondness. Is she angry, or does she simply miss her?

Often, as Edith prepares for bed, she imagines that when she wakes, Anna will be back, moving about the house in her mouse-footed way.

FIVE

LATE SUMMER 1907

Two months pass. William tells the children stories at night now. He stands out on the porch and remarks about the weather, the flowers, the sunset. In the evenings, he walks the neighborhood with Anna.

"I've been thinking of writing a book about the value of literature in the schools. Real literature. Not just *McGuffey Reader* tripe." Anna rejoices to hear the melody of strong opinion in his voice.

"It's not a popular concept, using real literature," he says, rubbing his chin in thought. "Too many teachers are ill-schooled themselves. But imagine how it could lift a classroom to read Herman Melville or Joseph Conrad or Henry James, or even Jack London."

"How indeed! And you're just the person to bring those books to life for them, William."

"Yes, maybe I am."

"Write the book!" She squeezes his arm with encouragement. That very night, he begins to gather volumes from his library, writing himself notes.

A week later, hearing the children shriek with glee at a particularly absurd tale their grandfather is sharing with them, Anna begins to pack her trunk.

"Must you go?" William asks that night, joining her in her room, eying the trunk which is now nearly full.

She nods, smiles, feels tears filling his eyes. "I have a job to do. I'm expected back East."

He sits on her bed and thoughtfully, slowly rubs the tops of his thighs. "I will never forget what you have done for me. You have a place here," he tells her. "You don't need a job. Not anymore."

She looks up at him, at his graying hair, his soft pale eyes.

"I think, William, we both need jobs. It's just how we're made."

"A man needs a job," he says. "But you . . ." He looks at her quizzically.

"You'll write that book. I'll help Mrs. Wharton. Even a woman—at least a woman like me—lives better when she feels useful. You are well. And now I am needed elsewhere." William nods, his eyes lighting with understanding.

Two days later, Anna takes the train back to Lenox, where she feels useful indeed.

On August 31, when Edith awakes, Anna is there with a smile, wearing a soft green dress, her face suffused with light in a way that Edith hasn't seen in years.

"You've come back," Edith says.

"Here I am."

"I can see Missouri agreed with you."

"Oh yes," Anna says. "But I'm happy to be home."

"I'm so glad you think of it as home." For a moment the two women are silent, finding tranquility in each other's presence. Edith takes Anna's small hand and squeezes it.

"You have months of typing to tackle, I'm afraid," she says.

"I'm up to the task."

"Oh, dear, dear Anna. You are always up to the task. Bless you. What on earth have you done with that awful Miss McCrae?"

"White gave her a cheque and we sent her packing."

"Amen! Well, then, you'd better get started. There's plenty to do."

She missed me, Anna thinks. She missed me!

Autumn blows in, bringing fiery hues to the tops of the mountain trees and cool nights for sleeping. Anna works all hours to catch up with the typing. Edith can hear the clucking of her typewriter even after dinner. It's too much work, Edith reflects, but how gratified Anna seems doing it! And Edith finds herself putting in extra hours of writing each morning. She is starting a different sort of novel. The house feels like a newly tuned engine.

"I am intrigued with this woman," Anna says, handing freshly typed pages to Edith one afternoon. "This Undine."

"What intrigues you?"

"Whether I should like her or not. And I *know* I don't like her mother. I suspect I'm not meant to like anyone in this first scene. This masseuse!"

"I didn't mean for you to like them. I meant for you to enjoy reading about them."

"Oh, I did. Right from the start. They are so obtuse for protagonists. Is Undine the protagonist?"

Edith sighs and nods, expecting that Anna just doesn't understand what she's attempting to do. And then Anna sits down across from Edith, a gesture very unlike her. The next thing she says surprises Edith even more.

"I think it very bold of you, Edith. To create main characters who are less than sympathetic. I like it. It feels extraordinarily . . . audacious."

"You like it, then . . . as far as it goes."

"Very much. It's a treat. I don't know how else to put it. It made me laugh. Should I be laughing?"

"Yes. I want you to laugh."

"You haven't done that before. Invited me to laugh at your characters. Sometimes Dickens does that. But rarely the main characters, just the peripheral ones. I think it very daring."

"Thank you, Tonni."

"It's dangerous, of course," Anna says, standing again.

"Dangerous?"

"Because it's almost essential you make them unlikeable . . . well, to a degree."

"Why? Why do you say that?"

"If you have us laugh at them and they are likeable, then you as the writer will be the one who's unlikeable. You will be the one who's cruel."

Edith sits back in her chair and looks at Anna.

"I think I intuited that. I never really looked at it quite like that. It's a good thought. A great thought."

"Thank you." Anna bows her head.

"I didn't know you had a sense of humor, Tonni. And I don't mean this cruelly. Some people have a sweet tooth. Others don't. Some people have an ear for music. Others have ears of tin. A sense of humor is not dissimilar."

"I also have a sweet tooth and an ear for music," Anna says, smiling, before she gets up and closes the door. "I look forward to seeing how Undine makes her way in the world."

One morning, when Anna brings in the tray of letters, a pale blue envelope penned with a confident, educated hand captures Edith's attention. Morton Fullerton writes that he has been invited to give a lecture on Henry James at Bryn Mawr, and if Mrs. Wharton's kind invitation is still good, he would be most pleased to stop and spend a few days at The Mount before journeying up to his family home in Brockton. He wants most of all to see Edith's famous gardens, and could she be enticed to share with him the fragrance of the pine trees from her terrace at last?

That afternoon, Edith writes him back.

The Mount
Lenox, Mass.

October 15, 1907

Dear Mr. Fullerton,

We are so pleased that you have not forgotten your promise to look us up—especially as dear HJ, in a letter received last week, skeptically prophesied: "You won't see Fullerton. . . ."

We shall hope for you, then, either on Friday evening or on Saturday morning, & your "few hours" will, I trust, be elastic enough to extend over Sunday, as I want to show you some of our mountain landscapes, & have time for some good talks too?

I am so glad you are going to talk about dear James at Bryn Mawr.

Yours sincerely,
Edith Wharton

Edith is fortified with new energy as she chooses which guest room will be right for Fullerton. She sees that extra effort is put into refreshing the house after the long summer. The French doors to the terrace are washed. Books in the library are dusted down. An old acquaintance, portrait painter and essayist Eliot Gregory, is scheduled to arrive a day before Fullerton. Eliot considers himself a great observer, but in fact he is a fussy, self-important tittle-tattle with his own popular newspaper column. Sometimes, in the middle of a too-quiet season, he brings just the right pinch of caustic merriment to her mix of guests. But Teddy can't stomach him. And Edith has doubts about Teddy meeting Fullerton as well. Or, if she's really being honest with herself, it's Fullerton meeting Teddy that unnerves her. Somehow the two have never come face-to-face, even when Fullerton came calling last winter to see Henry James. What will Fullerton think when he discovers that Edith is married to a buffoon? It sends ice up her spine. So when word arrives that Teddy's mother is ill in Boston, Edith can't help but feel a moment's guilty satisfaction that he will need to go to her at once. Teddy's bags are hastily packed and Cook drives him to the station.

Eliot, who divides his time between New York and Paris, has a great deal to say about the very people Edith is trying to capture in her new book— the nouveaux riches and their desire to impress, their impact and intrusion on a world that once pretended they didn't exist. In fact, Eliot has something tart to say about just about everyone. (Edith wonders what he says about her when she's not around.)

In Paris, he's found a particularly unconventional garret in a not-quite-chic neighborhood, where his clients, American society wives and daughters, are forced to climb his rickety wooden stairs, threatening to run splinters through the hems of their Worth dresses. "It's an adventure for them," he tells Edith. "They giggle, 'It's so charmingly rustic!' though just months ago they were entertaining people with manure on their boots in Omaha."

While Edith gathers flowers from the garden for Fullerton's arrival, Eliot follows behind her, stooping to observe more closely a particularly beautiful flower, pulling a stem to his nose now and then.

"Did you invite Fullerton," he asks drily, "or did he invite himself?"

"I invited him, of course," she says.

He arches his eyebrows. "Uh huh," he says.

"Why so skeptical?" she asks.

"I live in Paris, my dear," he says. "I hear things."

"What sorts of things?"

"Things better left unsaid," Eliot declares.

Following her into the house, he sits down with his sketchbook on a stool in the scullery and begins to sketch Edith in the light of the large *demi-lune* window while she arranges the flowers one by one in a tall crystal vase. "I want to know what you're keeping from me," Edith says after a while. "Everyone knows something about Fullerton they just won't say."

Eliot shakes his head. "Hearsay should not be repeated," he says.

"Eliot, you write a gossip column in the paper! You tell me something evil about almost everyone we know in common. And you won't say a thing?"

"It is not a gossip column," he says haughtily. "It's a column of observations. And I have not observed Mr. Fullerton doing anything. In fact, the less I observe Mr. Fullerton, the better. He has his share of *admirers*. Let's just say that. Quite a motley crew, in fact." Edith raises her brow, wondering what he could mean. Innuendo is one of Eliot's favorite weapons. For a while he says nothing until at last he turns the drawing toward her.

"How have I done?"

The woman Eliot has drawn, her mouth set just so, her figure straight and determined, exudes efficiency and self-possession.

"Is this how I look?" Edith asks.

"I think you look rather handsome."

"This woman looks as though she needs nobody whatsoever to help her."

"Then I've captured you."

Edith has worked her whole life to be self-sufficient, to make herself as intellectual as her brothers, who had the benefit of university educations, to write as well or better than any of the two dozen male authors she admires. And to do it all on her own. But the woman in the drawing appears unassailable. Edith learned long ago that men are drawn to women who are either undeniably beautiful or alluringly vulnerable. She's never been either.

She sighs loudly. Eliot is famous for making the accepted and the longing-to-be-accepted look more beautiful than they really are. He laughs about it. It is the trick which makes him so wildly popular. But in her case, he seems not to have changed a thing about her. Her chin is as lanternlike as ever.

"Oh dear. Lady Edith isn't happy," he says. He minces his mouth with counterfeit upset.

"No. I think it's quite true to what I see in the glass. But what happened to your uncanny way of making your subjects more attractive?"

"Since you've pointed out to me exactly how I swindle the masses into thinking themselves all beautiful enough for fairy tales, I knew you'd be insulted if I attempted to deceive you as well."

She laughs.

"Watch out for Fullerton," he says as he gathers his pencil and sketch pad.

"Whatever for?" she asks.

"Just be circumspect," he says. "He's a very charming man. Too many people find him irresistible. And," he adds, "if you fall under his charms, I will not protect you. I am the sort of man who likes to watch such a spectacle. The bottom line, dear Edie, is you're on your own." His smile is reminiscent of the Cheshire cat.

It is late and they are already dressed for dinner when Edith looks out the main floor gallery window to discover it has begun to snow. Snow in October! Fat flakes already sparkle on the brick walls of the forecourt and the drive. And then she sees the lights of the Panhard breaking the darkness, coming closer. Her throat and chest tingle.

Downstairs in the entrance hall, Alfred White opens the door and Edith hears him ask for Fullerton's coat and hat. As Fullerton stamps the snow from his shoes and hands off his gray felt hat, Edith comes down to greet him. Nicette and Mitou follow and jump at his ankles.

"I hope you don't mind the dogs," she says.

"Not at all. They're my old friends. Aren't you, fellas?" He squats down to let them lick his hand. He is natural with the dogs and easy in himself.

"I'm so glad you could come. I did so want to show you The Mount!"

"Did you order this weather to create the Currier and Ives feel, to show off your manse at its best?" he says, standing again. "Your reputation as a thoughtful hostess hasn't been stressed enough."

She laughs. "How was your train ride?"

"I slept nearly the whole way here. I'm afraid I look it." He draws his hand over his hair. His slightly rumpled look serves only to make him more pleasing.

"Alfred will take you to your room to wash up. We'll hold dinner for you. You must tell him if you need anything at all." Fullerton has only two leather suitcases and a hatbox. Alfred lifts both suitcases. "We'll just put these on the trunk lift, sir," he says.

"A trunk lift?" Fullerton takes back one of the cases. "Henry tells me that you supply your guests with things they don't even know they need but will need forever after. So I am girding myself to keep from being spoiled. I don't want the rest of my life to be a disappointment!" She watches as he climbs the stairs with the one suitcase, his compact figure disappearing around the landing. In the passage beyond the hall, Alfred starts the trunk lift's motor whirring and clanking just to send a single suitcase up to the third floor.

Fullerton arrives in the drawing room a few minutes later, freshly washed and neatly turned out in a crisp shirt and dinner jacket. His hair is combed in a perfect part, his mustache is smoothed and his eyes are as bright as though he's just awakened after a full night's sleep. His dark eyelashes are starry, still wet from being splashed.

"What a beautiful house," he says. "As charming and restrained and elegant as advertised."

"Thank you, Mr. Fullerton."

"And Eliot Gregory, well! I had no idea you'd be here. Good to see you." The men shake hands. Edith watches Eliot appraise Fullerton with impatient eyes. Fullerton does not look entirely comfortable in Gregory's presence either.

"How was Bryn Mawr and your lecture?" Edith asks.

"It seems the young ladies of Bryn Mawr are quite passionate about our friend Mr. James." Fullerton says. "But they all want to ask questions about the early works. *Daisy Miller*. That's all I heard all night."

"That's because they see themselves in Daisy Miller," Edith says. "Fresh, brash. The new American woman."

"Or because it's his shortest book and the only one they could chop their way through," Eliot says.

"Bryn Mawr was surprisingly stimulating," Fullerton offers. "Women allowed to exercise their intellects. To fill their minds with all the right things. Did you know my sister, Katherine, is a lecturer there?"

"Is she? She must be quite accomplished."

"She's a Radcliffe graduate. I don't think I've ever known a brighter woman. Except for you, Mrs. Wharton."

His face colors as he speaks about Katherine, but Edith hears nothing but the words he says about her. "You flatter me," she says.

"You'll discover something," Fullerton tells her. "I flatter only those who deserve it."

"Then it isn't flattery, is it?" Eliot asks drily.

"What's that?"

"If one truly means the compliment, it's no longer flattery."

"Ah," Fullerton challenges him. "Must the word always be pejorative?"

"What do you think, Mistress of Letters?" Eliot says to Edith. "I'd say so."

"We'll get the dictionary." Edith rings Alfred and asks him to bring the gargantuan red book from the library. While they wait, she pours each of them a glass of dry sherry. Fullerton takes his glass and stands by the fire. He is not a tall man, but there is a certain athletic beauty about him, a lean magnetic energy.

Alfred carries in the dictionary. It must weigh ten pounds. He lays it on the table by the window and Edith opens it to look up the word.

"Fruitery . . . flummox . . . flattery. . . . Well, Eliot may win here," she says after a moment, and begins to read: " 'To compliment insincerely. To play upon the vanity or susceptibilities of . . .' Hmmm. Well, then, if that's what you've done, Mr. Fullerton, I would opt to never be flattered again," she teases. But when she looks up, she sees that Eliot is beaming quite triumphantly and Fullerton is looking sour. What is it with men that one must always defeat the other?

"You get three writers in a room and disaster ensues," she says. "By the end of the evening we will be parsing our words so finely, we will be completely unable to speak to each other."

"Then we will have to speak in gestures," Eliot says. "The servants will have no idea whatsoever what secrets we're sharing. It will ruin their night."

"Will you deign to pantomime with us, Mr. Fullerton?" Edith asks softly. She didn't expect she would have to jolly him out of a mood so early in the evening. But in short order, the warmth of the sherry and the novelty of new snow outside the window reinstate the camaraderie just in time for dinner. Over a leg of lamb, they speak of Paris and Fullerton's friendship with Clemenceau, France's new prime minister, about whom he has written a much-discussed article.

"He's the most brilliant politician I've ever known," Fullerton declares. "He isn't there for self-aggrandizement but for the public good."

"Like our TR," Edith says, referring to her friend Teddy Roosevelt. "Perhaps, years from now, they will declare this a time of wise politicians. I suspect as time goes by, politicians will be made more and more of pasteboard. Now that they can make appearances by motorcar—and be seen even where trains don't go—I'm afraid the handsome and blustery ones will be the winners. That will be a sad state of affairs." They all agree.

By the time dinner is over, the snow has stopped. Eliot says the wine and all the good talk have made him tired, and besides, he wants to pen some thoughts before bed. He shakes Fullerton's hand and kisses Edith's cheek and they can hear his heavy footfall on the stairs.

"Would you like more wine, Mr. Fullerton?" Edith asks.

"No. I'd like a different draught. I'd like to breathe in those famous pines from your terrace. Sally Norton would cut me from her life if I didn't."

They ring for the maid to bring their wraps and hats from downstairs. And Edith asks her to bring Teddy's galoshes as well, which fit perfectly over Fullerton's polished French shoes. Buttoning on her own winter boots, she shivers with excitement like a child. The first snow!

The scent of the pines reaches their noses the moment the French doors are opened. The shock of cold is vitalizing. With the heavy clouds mostly gone, the stars gleam like ice chips in the sky. Ghostly outlines trace the hedges in the gardens and the lindens in the lime walk below. Edith relishes the sound of her feet crunching on the inch and a half of snowfall.

"What a perfect night," he tells her. "It makes me think of my child-hood. The air here is an elixir. I can see why you chose this place."

"Yes. It's very special."

He gestures to the garden. "In this light, it looks black and white, like a steel engraving."

How accurate and clever, she thinks, noting that the scene does indeed seem devoid of color.

His voice grows intimate. "I almost didn't come here, you know."

"Why?"

"The train schedule was impossible. I had to change trains three times. It would have been easier to go directly to my parents'."

"What changed your mind?"

"You." He turns to her. "I wanted more of your company."

She feels an exquisite expansion of her lungs. It is not unlike the one and only time she was allowed to take a roller-coaster ride as a child. Her mother had a headache, so her father took her for the afternoon to the Frascati Gardens in Paris. She can still recall the big sign with its gold and red letters: LE CHEMIN DE CENTRIFUGE.

"We'll keep this a secret from your mother," her father had said. Oh, how special Edith felt that day! They'd had to wait in line in the sun for ages. She remembers her trembling childish anticipation as they were ushered into their little carriage and strapped in with leather straps. Her father put his arm around her and the tiny train began a slow frightening ascent up the steel mountain.

"Are you afraid?" her father whispered in her ear.

"No, Papa. Because I'm with you." And then, at the top of the hill, they were looking out over all eternity. When the coaster descended, she had the sensation that her stomach dropped away, allowing her lungs to expand to ten times their size. And this is exactly how she feels right now. The rush of air into her lungs leaves her speechless for a moment.

"I'm so pleased you decided to come," she finally manages to tell Fullerton, though her voice meters out breathy and soft.

"After being here, Edith, I shall never think of you the same."

She shivers at the sound of her Christian name from his lips.

"No?"

"Houses say so much about people, don't they?"

"I've always thought so."

"Yes, I know you do. The way you describe houses speaks volumes about your characters. You even use "house" in your title of *The House of Mirth*. It's from Ecclesiastes, isn't it?"

"So few people realize that."

"My father is a minister. I grew up with a Bible always at hand. 'The heart of the wise is in the house of mourning. But the heart of fools is in the house of mirth.' Did I get it right?"

"Well done!" she says.

He steps back on the terrace so he can see the house more fully. "If I were a reader and you were a character, I'd say this house belongs to an extraordinarily haunting woman at the peak of her life. Would you like me to tell you more?"

"Yes," she says hesitantly.

"She has seen the world and delights in its bounty, but doesn't need to prove it to anyone. She brings together the classicism of New England with the sophistication of Europe. But there are secrets here. Illusion. Doors that look double on one side but are in fact single on the other. I believe your life is rather like those doors."

"My life?" she asks. She knows that she has grown crimson. "Whatever do you mean?"

"Edith," he says, then nothing more. She revels in the tingling feeling his words have generated. Does he know that she and Teddy are nothing to one another? That she is a free and single soul? The air is icy, the breeze picking up. But the warmth between them is palpable. "And what does your home in Paris say about you?" she asks.

"It says I rent a few rooms from a landlady because I am a poor, lowly journalist." He gently takes her elbow and turns her back, so her eyes meet his. "It says I would rather be at Edith Wharton's house." She hears her breath catch.

"Mr. Fullerton," she says too loudly, "it's late."

For a moment he doesn't let go of her arm. They stand face-to-face in the snow, alone, the fog of their breath blending and swirling together in the cold.

He finally releases her and, leaving her on the terrace, removes Teddy's galoshes at the French doors. Albert, hearing them return, takes the dripping overshoes with a look of distaste. Edith, after stamping her feet at the door, sits on the sofa to remove her boots. She feels self-conscious because she knows Fullerton is watching her.

"Yes? Is there anything I can get you?" she asks. She shudders at how dismissive she sounds. Her tone reminds her of how her mother used to speak to her father.

"No, thank you. I have everything. I'll be going up to bed." There is a touch of hurt in his voice.

"Good night, Mr. Fullerton. Sleep well."

"Call me Will," he says. "My family does."

She smiles weakly. She can't quite imagine calling him "Will." It is too simple, too American.

"Might I call you Morton? Henry sometimes does."

"Call me any name but Mr. Fullerton," he says.

"Good night, Morton," she says and listens to each and every one of his footsteps on the stairs.

The next day, after an excited night tossing, often waking, Edith props herself up in bed and writes, but stops early, feeling the tug of wanting to see Fullerton again.

Eliot and Fullerton are chatting by the drawing-room fire when she comes downstairs. "Would anyone like a tour of the gardens?" she asks. Eliot shakes his head, announcing he is happy to stay inside with old Jules warming his feet. Jules barely lifts his head to acknowledge Edith's presence, and sighs loudly as he settles his chin back down on Eliot's velvet slipper. But Fullerton stands, and with an impish smile, raises his hand like a little boy at school. Wraps and boots are supplied, and the pups intuitively head for the French doors.

As Edith and Fullerton work their way down the icy staircase from the terrace, he holds out his arm for her. She grabs onto the warm tweed of his coat, relishing the solidity of his muscles. Fullerton turns his head to her, his eyes gleaming.

"So, this is how Admiral Peary felt as he ventured out into the frozen wild. Imagine Nicette and Mitou pulling our dogsled."

The thin panes of ice at the edges of the steps shatter beneath their feet. The dogs run ahead onto the pristine garden paths, kicking up flurries of white, letting out shrill foxlike yelps.

Frosted like ice cream bombes, the lime trees, whose beauty arises from how they flutter, now stand encased in ice, paralyzed, like the trees in murals she's seen in old New England houses. Epic. Childlike. Beneath them, Fullerton gathers sticks brought down by the storm and tosses them toward the dogs for a game of fetch. As Edith watches his youthful antics, she feels as though Fullerton is the only object in her world that's moving at normal speed. All else feels slowed. The late morning sun breaks at an angle through the pines, spreading the hedges and frozen beds with buttery light. She can hear her own heartbeat in her ears. How measured it sounds! The snow silences all else. Has she ever felt so extraordinarily sated or content?

The game moves farther and farther along the path toward the edge of the woodlands, until Fullerton has gone so far, he stands and waves and begins to run back to her. He exudes such joy, as though he could not possibly wish to be anywhere else or with anyone else.

Later, as they walk through the beds of frozen flowers, their footsteps match, and Edith can feel the heat and pressure of his arm through her wraps. It makes her too breathless, too giddy.

So she stoops to tap snow off the once-glorious chrysanthemums.

"I do hate seeing the season end like this," she says.

What was just yesterday an efflorescence of russet and spice has grown limp and blistered, black and slimy. "It's a shame you weren't here even one day sooner. The garden was still beautiful."

"I wouldn't have given up this snow for all the flowers you had," Fullerton says. "We'll remember the snow. I might not have remembered the flowers." She is warmed by how he speaks of them as "we."

As they chat and stroll beyond the gardens and through the shady paths, Edith finds it difficult to concentrate on his words—she is so distracted by the insistence of his presence. She feels dented by him. He marks her soul more than anyone she's ever known. She thinks briefly of Eliot's warning. Fullerton is indeed a very charming man.

She can hardly bear to end the garden walk, but the sun is now directly above them and there isn't much more time: they need to eat lunch. The plan is for all of them to enjoy a motor trip through the Berkshires, then drop Fullerton at the Westfield station where he can board a train for his parents' house in Brockton. Afterward, Edith and Eliot will head south to the home of William Sheffield Cowles and Anna Roosevelt in Connecticut. When she tells him they must go back in, he presses his lips together with disappointment.

"Must we? I could stay out here forever," he says.

She nods. "I'd stay with you," she says, "but you have a train to catch. Unless you can extend your visit another day. Might you?" she entreats. She would happily give up her own journey for him.

He shakes his head. "Mother would be wounded to her toes."

Edith shrugs. "Well then . . . come, *mes petits*," she calls out to the dogs. Mitou obeys cheerfully and dances toward the house, but Fullerton has to chase Nicette as she darts away from them down the garden paths.

"Nicette is a nature lover," she calls after him.

Morton slips and slides, running after the puff of fur.

"You devil," he yells. Eventually, he corners her in the Italian walled garden. Picking her up, he displays her like a prize through the opened arch in the wall. "Voila!" he shouts out. How enchanting he looks as he comes into view, warming tiny Nicette against his chest.

Anna Bahlmann peers down from her window at Edith and Fullerton in the snow. She didn't have a chance to greet him last night—he arrived late from the station, long after she had joined the staff for dinner. But she knows his compact shape, his neatly arched back. She met him once or twice in the Rue de Varenne apartment. And even then she thought him a popinjay. Seeing them together now makes her apprehensive. For, even from up here where their voices reach her panes only by riding the wind, she can tell that Edith fancies him. She watches her lean into him like a girl being courted. Anna can hear her laughter, see how animated Fullerton makes her; she gestures openly, touches Fullerton as she speaks. She is never like this with Teddy. She is often icy, or bored. Anna closes the sheer curtains and sits down on her bed with a sinking heart.

It's not my business, she tells herself. But how at odds she feels, for it's most natural for her to love what Edith loves. When it comes to plays, music, books, they have always been of such intellectual sympathy that there is rarely, if ever, discordance in their tastes. And with people, it's the same. Anna is a bit afraid of Henry James but worships his brilliance, as Edith does. And Sally Norton is the dearest human being alive. Eliot Gregory is always entertaining, if treacherous. The Bourgets are a treat. Anna de Noailles is fascinating. So why does she feel this way about Fullerton? Nervous. Distrusting. It makes her cross with herself.

She forces herself to think of her family in Missouri, where her life was indeed her own. She goes to the desk and begins a letter to her niece.

> "*Dearest Aennchen,*
> *How I miss all of you! How is your dear Papa?*"

At lunch, Fullerton suddenly looks up from his soup. "Good God, Edith! There's something I must tell you."

"What's that?"

"The *Revue de Paris* will be publishing *The House of Mirth*."

Edith sets down her spoon and puts her hands on either side of her plate. "That's wonderful. Thank you so much for making that happen, Morton," she says. "What perfect news. You were saving it to surprise me?"

"I was saving it because . . ." He looks delightfully sheepish. "Because I forgot to tell you."

"Well, I'm glad you remembered." When their eyes meet, Edith sees something in his that is indefinable: pride, joy, pleasure at having pleased her? Eliot seems to notice it too, for he flashes Edith a raised eyebrow and a warning smile.

After lunch, Fullerton sends down his bags, and Edith and Eliot each have their cases packed for their overnight trip. Cook brings around the Panhard. Fullerton is amused by it. "I could barely see it in the dark last night, though Cook showed me the electric lights inside," he said.

"Henry says it's a moving divan."

"Oh no, it's much bigger than a divan! It's a moving parlor!"

Eliot sits in front with Cook. Edith, dressed in her heavy serge driving duster and veiled travel hat, shares the back with Fullerton. She is so delighted to be near him, to feel the pressure of his knee against hers. It's a glorious afternoon as the Panhard takes to the road. The snow has mostly melted where the sun has licked it. As they climb the first real peak, panoramic views stretch open and they all sigh with appreciation, even Cook.

"Can you see a single thing?" Fullerton asks her, tugging at her veils. He pulls them back, then—in a sweet, unexpected way—smooths her hair, enchanting her with his touch. "Much better," he says. "You've improved your view, and mine."

The farthest mountains are a dazzling dragonfly blue; the fields glow amber with the syrup of late-afternoon light.

"There couldn't be a more perfect day, could there?" Fullerton says.

"Not in all the world," she says. But halfway up the mountain, they can feel the car shimmy precariously near the edge of the embankment, making Edith gasp.

"I'm sorry, Mrs. Wharton. We'll have to turn off," Cook announces. "It's slippery up here still. We need to put chains on the tires." He turns onto a packed-earth dogleg, meant as an overlook. As he heads back to the boot to find the chains and Eliot joins him, Edith gets out of the car and stretches in the chilly mountain air. Fullerton stands beside her and presents an open silver cigarette case. "Care to?" he asks. She takes a cigarette and waits for him to find a match.

"What do you say," she asks after he's lit her cigarette, "shall we go down and sit on that bank? There's no snow right there."

He nods, and she lifts the heavy plaid rug from the motorcar. The view from the bank is breathtaking. Indigo mountains braid the horizon; fallen and falling red and yellow leaves embroider the landscape. Snow sits in every crevice but the one they've intended as their perch. But before she sits down, she spots it.

"Look. What a sight!" she says, pointing as Fullerton lays the blanket on the ground. A beautiful little witch hazel shrub is shouting with fresh red blooms against the blue-white snow. Instead of the customary yellow flowers, tiny crimson rags undulate on its twigs, like banners of happiness. She crosses the sugary white to snap off a sprig. When she brings it back to Fullerton, he takes the stem between his fingers.

"The proverbial late bloomer, Mrs. Wharton," he says. He glances at her and smiles.

Does he have any idea how empty her marriage is? Does he sense that she is beginning to wonder whether he is the one to fill that emptiness with belated beauty, so that her life might finally flower, like the beguiling and brazen witch hazel?

"I imagine the color of that witch hazel is not so different from the color of your hair as a child," he says tenderly. "Am I right?"

"Yes," she says. "It was red. It gave me no end of grief."

"Well now, it gives *me* no end of pleasure. It's the color of maple syrup," he says. "I wish I could take it down and see it in the sun. Does it ripple?"

Edith feels herself blush. "Yes. It's wavy when I take it down." She's forty-five years old. But in Morton Fullerton's presence, she feels as sensitive and untried as an eighteen-year-old. Deliciously uncertain. She has spent her adult years working to be impressive, imposing, so that people might take her seriously. How has he torn it all down with a few impertinent words?

There is much noise up the hill as Cook and Eliot haul a second set of chains from the boot of the car and drop them in coils on the ground.

When Morton hands back the witch hazel sprig, his hand caresses hers. A silvery dart of pleasure pierces Edith just beneath the ribs, then runs like cold water to her very center. The air is punctuated by the sounds of winter birds and the stirring of fallen leaves.

She self-consciously tucks the sprig into the pocket of her duster, her hands shaking visibly. She's relieved to see that Cook and Eliot are caught up in the job of running the chains beneath the car's wheels and haven't been watching.

While Fullerton glances away, she furtively takes in his strong profile and sky-tinged eyes. When those eyes turn to her once more, she doesn't think she's ever felt another's gaze so keenly.

"If HJ were here," he says, "I suppose he'd compose a fifty-nine-word, twelve-part sentence about this moment," Fullerton says. "He'd say," and he drops his voice, adding the slow exactitude that makes Henry's voice a caricature, "'Despite the late snow, and the air which was too chill to enjoy—though Fullerton chose to enjoy it nonetheless—and because of the company of the lady, a company which he would later recount to his friends with much pleasure, and think about in the quiet of his room, he felt an unfamiliar wave of gratification, which overtook him and made him suddenly note the slightest, most extraordinary detail of the assignation.'"

Edith smiles. "Fifty-nine or so beautiful words, Mr. Fullerton," she says.

"Henry. Call me Henry."

"Ah, but what would Morton Fullerton write about this moment?" she asks.

"I'd write . . ." His voice changes from playful to sincere. The shift is seismic. And his mouth, which a moment ago was pursed with irony, softens. "Mr. Fullerton was perfectly content in her company." Then he glances away again, as though he recognizes he's revealed too much. She imagines having a photograph of this very moment. A caption written in ink below would read, "Edith and Morton on a snowy bank in the Berkshires." She envisions sliding it into the embrace of an etched silver frame, reaching for it on lonely nights.

"Contentment is underrated, isn't it?" she says.

"Yes. It's a very fine thing. One doesn't know until one no longer has it." She wonders: is he so malcontent with his life? Henry recently said Fullerton has much on his mind. How she would like to ease it.

She glances up the hill to see that Cook and Eliot have secured the chains around two of the tires. They seem to be having a fine time with the task. She rises, brushing the damp from her duster, then peers out over the shimmering valley. It seems to hold, like a cup, all the colors of the universe.

After Fullerton's visit, and Edith's trip to Connecticut, Anna notes a change in Edith's routine. Usually she doesn't wake until Agnes, her maid, arrives to rouse her, but now Agnes reports she finds her each morning sitting up in bed, already littering her bed with pages. Ethel, the cook, mentions that Edith seems to have stopped eating. Her plates return to the kitchen seemingly untouched.

"She didn't eat any breakfast at all today, and I made her pancakes . . . which she never fails to eat. Is she ill again?"

"Are you coming down with something?" Anna asks. "Are you feverish?" She places her own cool hand on Edith's forehead.

"No. I'm quite well. Why on earth do you ask?"

"I just thought perhaps you're feeling queer," Anna ventures.

"Not in the least," Edith snaps.

"It's not your allergies?" Anna asks. "Sometimes this time of year . . ."

"It's nothing, Tonni. Stop fussing over me." Her words are stern, but she finishes them with a smile. She is certainly smiling more often lately.

A few days later, intent on a scene in her book, forming her lips around the dialogue, Edith looks up and Anna is standing there with the mail. Scribner's writes that early sales of *The Fruit of the Tree*, her first novel since *The House of Mirth*, are not as promising as Edith had hoped. Another letter is covered with Sally's spidery penmanship, and then there is a thick cream envelope postmarked "Brockton, Massachusetts." Edith waits for Anna to leave before she slices it open. A sprig of witch hazel slips from the envelope. A rare scarlet, just like the bush on the hillside. The note from Fullerton is simple and gracious— about how much he enjoyed his stay at The Mount, the aroma of the pines and the game of fetch in the snow. And how deeply honored he feels to have had the chance to become truly acquainted with a woman as brilliant and special as Edith Wharton.

Later, Edith pulls down a bound book of blank pages that was given to her many years earlier. She tears out the five leaves of a diary she began long ago, and then, sitting at her desk, takes up her pen and writes:

The Life Apart (L'ame close.)
The Mount. October 29th, 1907

> *If you had not enclosed that sprig of wych-hazel in your note I should not have opened this long-abandoned book; for the note in itself might have meant nothing—would have meant nothing to me—beyond the inference that you had a more "personal" accent than week-end visitors usually put into their leave-takings. But you sent the wych-hazel—& sent it without a word—thus telling me (as I chose to think!) that you knew what was in my mind when I found it blooming on that wet bank in the woods, where we sat together & smoked while the chains were put on the wheels of the motor.*
>
> *And so it happens that, finding myself –after so long!— with someone to talk to, I take up this empty volume, in which long ago, I made two spasmodic attempts to keep a diary. For I had no one but myself to talk to, & it is absurd to write down what one says to one's self; but now I shall have the illusion that I am talking to you, & that—as when I picked the wych-hazel— something of what I say will somehow reach you.*

Then she picks up the still-crimson sprig between her fingers, twirls it in wonder and settles it into her newly begun journal.

SIX

LATE AUTUMN 1907

Against Teddy's wishes, Edith arranges for the household to return to Paris far earlier than planned. They aren't even going to enjoy Christmas at The Mount—a tradition only recently established, but that she and Teddy have enjoyed so much. Still, the thought of Christmas in the City of Lights thrills her.

"I wonder if it will feel quite like Christmas," Anna says hesitantly. "All it does is rain in December in Paris."

But Edith's eyes glitter. "The shops will be filled with holiday specialties. *Bûche de Noël.* Christmas patés. We'll bring with us a whole apronful of pinecones to throw on the fire at the Vanderbilts'! It will be the best Christmas we've ever had." Anna admits to herself that she's looking forward to reuniting with her friends in the common room, and settling back into her own sunny garret beneath the eaves with its comfy bed, cherry eiderdown and rooftop views.

Edith dreams of Tuesday-night salons at Rosa's, café lunches graced by Paul and Minnie Bourget's comic banter, a return to the grandeur of George Vanderbilt's apartment.

Most of all, she envisions Morton Fullerton arriving for tea. She can see him at the door of 58, rue de Varenne, in his full Paris dress, radiant with joie de vivre, his fingers casually caressing hers as he bestows on her the perfect nosegay—a fragrant bunch of early violets. Their eyes will meet with knowing communion. This is her chief fantasy, and nothing strikes her as a more blissful tableau.

Teddy, on the other hand, is furious she's moved up the date of their departure.

"Without even consulting me, Puss? Have I no say in your plans? You at least used to pretend I did."

"Well, we *did* discuss it. You just choose to forget."

"I remember perfectly. And when you brought it up, I said no. I didn't want to go early. You're the one who's chosen to forget."

"A few more winters in Paris, and you'll feel just as at home there as you do in New York."

"Oh really?" he says. "Will they all have learned to speak English by then?"

He slams his book closed, sets it down and leaves the room. She lifts the tome from his ottoman. *Basic Pig Husbandry.*

There's one more reason Edith wants to leave. *The Fruit of the Tree* has been such a disappointment. Its initial printing of 50,000 copies sold out at once, but the next edition of 30,000 seems to be gathering dust. Since it's a drama about a mill, about working people, it's apparently not what her newly minted fans expected after *The House of Mirth*. They want "another glimpse into upper-crust society," her publisher tells her—a society, Edith notes, that excludes most of them.

"I've already written *The House of Mirth*, she laments to Sally when Miss Norton comes for a short visit. "Why must I write it again? Why must one be hung on the same peg forever?"

"It's reassuring for people to hang their coats on the same peg every time," Sally offers.

"Be that as it may, I am *not* an old coat."

Despite Teddy's grumbling, the Whartons set sail on December 5 replete with servants, dogs and trunks. As soon as they are settled at 58, rue de Varenne, Edith is swept up in her old routines. Tuesdays at Rosa's, café lunches with the Bourgets, just as she imagined. A walk in the Faubourg with Paul Hervieu. Tea with the Abbé de Mugnier. She feels as though she is coming alive after months in mothballs. Even though *The*

House of Mirth is just beginning its run in the *Revue de Paris*, it is instantly an extraordinary success—perhaps the most unexpected triumph the *Revue de Paris* has ever had. It helps Edith forget about the poor reception for *The Fruit of the Tree*.

Anna de Noailles writes that she is in the midst of reading Edith's "tour de force" in the *Revue*.

> *Dear Mrs. Wharton, you have robbed me of two nights of sleep already, for which I may never forgive you. As a rule, I only allow lovers to compromise me in such a cruel way.*

And then there is Fullerton.

Two weeks in a row, he does not appear at Rosa's salon. So Edith writes and invites him for tea.

"Mightn't we see you? You must catch us up on your adventures." Though she had been certain after the witch hazel sprig that a vigorous correspondence would have arisen between them, all through the autumn he has written only one more vague letter, the sort one might write a very distant acquaintance.

He doesn't answer for two painful days, but at last she receives a petit bleu—a note sent through the magically fast pneumatic tubes of Paris— that he has been quite busy at the bureau, but can spend an hour with her on Monday. The weekend seems four days long, but at one P.M. on Monday, Morton Fullerton arrives at the Whartons' door as dapper as she had imagined. A breath of lavender emanates from his person as he shrugs off his coat. If he has been overworked, he is nevertheless looking more than well: his cheeks are cheerily stained from the cold. Instead of flowers, he proffers a pale green box of gleaming pastel macarons from Ladurée, the pastry shop on the Rue Royale. "I don't know why, but I was passing by and the macarons called out to me," he said. "Maybe I was thinking of HJ. He would have stopped in his tracks for these. Coming here made me think of him. I hope you like macarons."

"Like a rainbow!" she says, pressing back the flap and glancing with a smile at the tenderly tinted treats. She calls the *bonne* and hands over the box so the delicacies can be arrayed on a plate to serve with their tea.

Edith has dressed as carefully as a bride for Fullerton's visit. Choosing pearls because she thinks they reflect kindly on her face, and a shirtwaist the color of crushed roses because it makes her feel young, and a soft, and a flattering gray flannel skirt. She often deems herself harsh looking, and she wants to look anything but.

In the drawing room, they sit in a wash of afternoon light. She expects somehow that he will reach out to her, touch her, or speak to her with the familiarity that had marked their last conversation on that bank in the Berkshires. Instead, it's the more formal Fullerton who graces her sitting room. He doesn't even meet her eyes. And he speaks mostly of himself. Perhaps he is nervous, she thinks. She offers him one of his macarons, and after some deliberation he chooses a framboise as rosy as his cheeks. But he holds it in his hand without eating, and begins to tell her how disappointed he is with the way things are going at the *Times*. He thinks he should be next in line as bureau chief, and yet no promises have been made. Some days he feels he should just gather his things and leave. She tells him he should write a book.

"A man with your clarity and discrimination could write anything he put his mind to," she says. He smiles and visibly relaxes in the warmth of her encouragement. He finally bites into the macaron and sighs.

"My favorite taste in all of Paris, to be honest," he said dreamily. "It wasn't really because HJ likes these that I stopped and bought them," he says. "Or for you, dear Edith. In truth I bought them for me." He looks up at her, and for the first time their eyes reflect each other's mirth. "I'm a very selfish man," he says.

"Are you?" she asks. "I can imagine you might be."

"Women tell me so."

For a moment, she can see the little boy in him. She's glimpsed this before: a too-vulnerable, injured child tucked neatly behind the sophisticate. She knows that he might soon conceal this weakness. Yet, while it's in sight, this side of him elicits feelings in her that she finds strangely stirring.

In short order the look, the openness, is tucked away, and he's back to complaining about his job. Still, his willingness to let her into his personal worries says he trusts her, wants to be close. Yet when Fullerton consults his pocket watch, stands and says he needs to leave—less than the hour he'd promised her—Edith wonders: has she been wrong about him? Was that sprig of witch hazel nothing more than a kind gesture of remembrance? Did he see her just as a friend, or even worse, a motherly figure? She needs to know.

So, two days later, she invites him to the theatre.

> Dear Mr. Fullerton,
>   Do you care for the Italian theatre—& if yes, will you go with me on the 13th to see La Figlia di Iorio? I am going to as many performances as possible, & as my husband objects to the language, I am obliged to throw myself on the charity of my friends.
>   We should be very glad if you would dine with us first at 7:30.
>
>   Sincerely Yrs.
>   E. Wharton

It's true. She's gone to play after play since she arrived, sometimes with Matilda Gay, who gushes about each and every production she sees no matter how dreadful, or Minnie and Paul, who make fun of the actors afterward, imitating their voices, their walks, their most memorable lines. Once Edith even went with Rosa, whom she had to persuade to leave her house—how rarely Rosa goes out! Rosa told her it was the highlight of her month and Edith made a note to draw her out more often. But to go with Fullerton! And to this particular play! A play about a man who falls in love with his son's lover—a play that mingles anger and passion, loyalty and betrayal. She senses that although Fullerton says he doesn't like D'Annunzio, he'll appreciate the simple drama of this scenario. She desperately wants to share it with him even if it means finally exposing Teddy to him at dinner. It must happen sooner or later.

But that afternoon, Teddy isn't feeling well. He's having trouble with his teeth—a throbbing in his back right molars that no dentist can fix, that creates a terrible ache behind his right eye.

"I'm having a deuce of a time determining a specific problem, Monsieur Wharton," the dentist told him. "But we will pull all the teeth back there, to be safe." Teddy refused. He doesn't trust French dentists (or doctors, for that matter). Even the few who speak English. And Edith doubts it will make a difference anyway. She thinks the phantom pain is just a part of Teddy's melancholia. She's seen it before: the slow misery that overtakes him. Winnowing into his teeth, his joints. More each day. Until he ends up in bed, writhing. Too miserable to get up. She fears it.

"If you took a walk, got a little fresh air, wouldn't that help?" she asks.

"What would you know about it?" he barks. The melancholia is always accompanied by a desire to inflict misery on her as well. So she stays away from him as much as she can. She worries how he might act toward Fullerton. But by the time their guest arrives, Teddy is already anesthetized by three glasses of brandy, and is jollier than usual.

Fullerton is ingratiating to Teddy, sitting by the fire with him and giving him almost seductive attention, paying very little consideration to Edith. At dinner he asks question after question about the stables at The Mount, about hunting, about Teddy's early summers in Bar Harbor and Newport and the people they might know in common. Teddy seems to drink up every moment of his presence. By the time they are to leave for the theatre, Edith is glad to steal Fullerton away for herself. Only in the motorcar does she begin to feel the full beam of Fullerton's interest.

"You are looking elegant tonight," he proclaims. "The Paris Mrs. Wharton is very different from the country gentlewoman I spent time with in Lenox."

"Just my wardrobe," she says.

"No. Far more than that. I like both women especially well. But they are completely different. This Parisian woman is a more exciting, younger version of the woman who owns the big white house in the Berkshires."

His interest drips over her like honey.

In the private red-velvet-curtained theatre *baignoire*, she feels the pressure of his knee against hers. It's hard to ignore. The heat of his pulsing blood! However will she focus on the play?

"If you'll allow me to say," he says suddenly, intimately turning to her, "you and Teddy are a surprising match." His voice is soft and quizzical.

It's such an intimate comment. She blanches at its directness.

"Yes. We haven't much to share. Except the dogs. And travel. He doesn't read literature. He only tolerates light theatre. I guess we're known as an odd pair."

"That's what others think. What do *you* think?"

"I think . . ." She looks up at his blue eyes. "I think I was very young when I chose him."

He observes her for a long moment. "Henry said there never was . . . a strong bond between you. Never much of"—he clears his throat— "*anything* between you."

It's obvious what he's implying. She's certainly told Henry too much. Henry's avuncular style makes one think he's the perfect receptacle for confession. But a receptacle that leaks.

"Henry should learn to keep his confidences," she says. Her voice must be too cool, for Fullerton shifts in his chair, stops questioning her and begins to read the program.

"You were very kind to him," she offers after a while.

"Henry?"

"Teddy."

"He doesn't seem a bad fellow," Fullerton said. "But tell me this: why is it our class is prone to naming men children's names?" he asked.

"You don't have a child's name."

"No. I put the kibosh on Willie long ago." He smiles to himself.

"I think I shall call you Willie," she says.

"If you do, I'll call you Puss, the way Teddy does. And make sure everyone else does too. I see how it rankles you."

She laughs. "Just try it."

The lights dim. The play is wonderful, and Fullerton's absorption in it thrills her. When he enjoys a line, or a part, he glances at her and they share the moment. Or sometimes he asks her interpretation of the Italian, especially when he can't decipher the heavy Sicilian accent. His presence, his enthusiasm, his generosity in sharing it more than doubles her pleasure.

At one point in the play, Esmeralda, the young woman, finds herself so overcome with passion that she discovers she can't send her lover away.

"That's something," Fullerton whispers to her, so close she feels his lips against her ear, "I'd wager you wouldn't know anything about."

She shivers and, not knowing how to answer him, glances into his eyes. He doesn't flinch or turn away as most men would. He absorbs her gaze, invites it. And at that moment, with their eyes locked, Edith feels positively pierced.

That night when she gets home, nearly breathless with joy, she writes in her Line-a-Day diary, "Unforgettable hours," and sleeps only fitfully, recalling the pressure of his leg, his scent, his smile and the sensation of those lips on her ear. Later, she thinks that it was the most intimate night of her life.

In the next few weeks, she invites him to lectures, luncheons, but he is busy, and only occasionally says yes.

One Thursday late in February, he attends Rosa's salon. It's an odd springlike day, and he arrives looking flushed. Edith hasn't expected him and finds herself undone by his presence. She even loses the thread of a conversation she's having with Rosa.

"Hello," she says when he finally makes his way to her. "I had no idea you were coming tonight."

"Nor did I," he says. "I seemed to have been drawn by unseen forces." He sparkles at her like a cut stone in the sun. He's come to Rosa's to see her! she thinks. But he doesn't spend much time talking to her in the drawing room. Instead, he joins a discussion of the German policy toward immigrants. And when they're called into dinner, he's ushered to a chair on the other side of Rosa and too far away for eye contact. Worse, he's seated next to Paul Hervieu's attractive young cousin, a Frenchwoman, delicate and soignée, with large dark eyes, a slender neck and tiny, perfect white teeth. Though the dinner conversation includes, as usual, the whole table, Edith watches, her face growing hot as Fullerton bends to whisper things to Paul's cousin. It's the way he looks at the girl as he shares his asides that catches Edith in a grip of possessiveness. She knows she has no claim on him. Yet he's gracing Hervieu's young cousin with the radiant attention he had emitted that night on the terrace at The Mount. And in the baignoire during the Italian play. She tries to take her eyes off them. She attempts to join the conversation, to little avail.

That night, in bed, she feels grief-stricken. What had made her think that dazzling, handsome Morton Fullerton, younger, and unmarried, could ever see Edith Wharton in any other way than as a friend?

In the morning, she wakes with the same sense of mourning. And matters are made worse by Teddy, who is lately sinking deeper and deeper into a dolorous funk. This morning, he won't get out of bed at all. Catherine Gross comes to her door literally wringing her hands: Alfred White is worried. Mr. Wharton is not himself.

When Edith steps into Teddy's room, he's slumped in bed, awake but with his eyes at half-mast. He's hardly eaten for days, though Edith has hired a new cook and asked her to try some of his favorite American dishes. His skin has taken on a gray cast, which makes his reddish mustache look enormous and pinned on. His eyes, through their lowered lids, glisten like those of a cornered animal. Gripping the covers tightly, his hands look mottled and dry. He says he can't get up. It's his gout. But she knows it's the same neurasthenia, which overtook him four years earlier: nervous depression, exhaustion and general hopelessness.

"Then you needn't get out of bed at all," she tells him soothingly. "We'll have the maid deliver lunch on a tray. And you simply stay here and rest." Not struggling against his moods is what finally pulled him out of his neurasthenia last time.

She finds herself wishing to go back to bed herself. Concern over Teddy looms between her and her fiction this morning. So she writes Henry and Sally, each of whom would be sympathetic to her tale of woe, and then grabs an umbrella to go out in the rain for a walk. Every fiber of her is restless and pained. This is her life: Teddy's misery and the rain, the failure of *The Fruit of the Tree*, a sense of homelessness: she no longer can live in New York, The Mount has lost its shimmer and Paris seems tainted now by her misinterpretation of Fullerton's interest. What a fool she's been to believe that for once she could have a real life!

The following day, she suggests that Teddy travel to Cannes on the train: the Curtises, longtime acquaintances, have invited them both for a week at their villa near the sea. She is relieved that he has some enthusiasm for the plan. In the past, Edith would have left Paris with him, even fussed over him, though it would have meant giving up her own plans. But this time she tells herself he'll be happier without her impatient presence. The Curtises think he's an entertaining fellow, a good sport. Even though it's too cold for the beach, they'll get him out for a walk on the promenade and ply him with good wine. They'll make him forget his complaints. She imagines him returning with color in his cheeks.

"Do you really not want to come, Puss? I don't know why you want me to go off without you."

"I've made promises to people here. And I want to see you get better. A nice visit will do you good. You don't need me along. I've got my book to write. And Anna's here. If you want, I'll ride with you to the train station."

He nods grimly. "As if that's a reasonable substitute."

Teddy knows he's being sent away. When she loads him onto the train, she feels she is shipping her recalcitrant child off to boarding school. He leans shyly out the train window to wave good-bye as the train glides away, until they can no longer see each other and she is alone. She takes a deep breath and stands quietly until she is the last person on the platform.

Alone in the motorcar, she feels weightless, gutted. What will she do with herself? At least she can work on her book. She thinks of Undine Spragg; what would *she* have done having unloaded a husband? Found herself another.

Back on the Rue de Varenne, Edith pursues her own answer: a petit bleu is waiting. She opens it without taking the time to find her silver letter opener, tearing it, much to her dismay.

> *Dear,* [Oh, his neat, tight, perfect handwriting!]
> *You left the Comtesse's the other night without saying good-bye. I trust you are all right?*
>
> WMF

It took two days for him to write. But he has addressed her as "Dear"! She charges down the hallway to her desk, then pulls out a blue slip and writes him back,

Cher,

 Thank you for your concern. I needed to get back to Teddy, who is still doing poorly. I'm sorry I didn't take the time to part more gracefully. I have just this morning sent him off to Cannes where he can get some rest with friends.

 Do you know the village of Herblay? Where our dear friend Hortense Allart raised her mighty pen? Since I am on my own for the next few days, I wonder if you would like to explore it with me. Saturday, perhaps? Shall we hunt for the house where she served up her womanly wiles? Cook will drive us and we can make a fine day of it—HJ will be wildly jealous.

 Yrs. EW

Henry and Morton and Edith and nearly everyone in Paris have been simultaneously reading a newly published biography of Hortense Allart. Like George Sand, and also from the first half of the nineteenth century, Allart lived a life of free love and still managed to pen histories of Florence and Athens, essays on religion, openly sexual novels and sizzling erotic letters. She did as she pleased, refused to marry, slept with French literary lights such as Chateaubriand and Sainte-Beuve and gave birth to two children by two different men. Later in life, she finally married—an architect who tried to control her in every way and made her weep daily. "A lesson to us all," Henry wrote. "Of course, Fullerton and I have already heeded this by avoiding the altar altogether."

It's a blustery February day when Edith and Morton set out for Herblay. Paris is festooned with ice, and even with travel rugs tucked in around each of them, the motorcar is so chilly they sit close in the back-seat to preserve body heat. At one point, their gloved hands, pressed down onto the seat, accidently touch and he wraps his pinky finger around hers. It feels innocent and kind, something a child might do to express affection. And yet his merest touch infuses Edith with heat and hope.

They pause for lunch in a small town along the way at an inn called Au Bon Coin. It is indeed a good corner. Edith thinks she has never tasted anything better than the hearty chicken in red wine, tarragon and tomato sauce, though she is so sated by Morton's presence she can't eat more than a few bites or drink more than a few sips of wine. His appetite seems unaffected. Digging into his boeuf, he talks at length about their "dear friend Hortense," and how it would be wonderful if only she would break through the walls of time and greet them at Herblay, "a baby at each breast." Edith laughs. She feels again like a girl in her teens, self-conscious and glowing with feeling, full of stinging desire.

Bundling back into the motorcar, they drive on to Herblay, and, at a distance from the town, overlooking the Seine Valley, they at last come upon the miniature twelfth-century church. The exterior of St. Martin d'Herblay is so simple it might as well be a child's drawing of a house of worship. Before entering, they stop to take in the leaden Seine slipping through its bend far below. For just a moment a dart of sun turns it a molten bronze, and the whole scene alters, as though someone has pressed the lever on an old stereopticon.

Morton says, "One could do with a view like this. Perhaps you and I should move in." He gestures to the church behind them. It does seem almost small enough to be a house. "A few lace curtains and we'd be all set." Edith wonders if he says intimate things like this to other women.

Inside the chapel, the silence has a velvety quality, and though the structure is made of stone, it radiates warmth—which strikes her as no less of a miracle than loaves transforming into fishes. Beneath the Romanesque arches, Edith takes a seat. It's the rare church that makes her regret she's never felt drawn to religion. If she prays for Morton's continuing presence in her life, will God heed her or strike her down?

When the curé, a willowy, faded man in a worn cassock, steps out of the vestry to tend to the candles, Morton approaches to ask him what he knows of Hortense Allart. How sturdy Morton looks beside the rusty old priest. For one fragrant second, Edith feels entirely happy just watching him, thrilled to be near him. She feels as though electricity has run to her fingers, her toes, the roots of her hair. She can hear the curé's hoarse voice proclaim, "Allart? Non, monsieur, je ne connais personne de ce nom. Elle habite la région?"

"Elle y a résidé, il y a une cinquantaine d'années," Morton says. "Elle était écrivaine."

"Désolé." The curé shrugs. "Je n'en ai jamais entendu parler."

"How's it possible?" Morton asks Edith, settling into the chair beside her. "He has no idea who she is. Never heard of her."

"Well, God has spared him. If he had known, he would have been offended by all that she stood for." Edith looks up to see a particularly comic gargoyle peeking out from the groin of a vault. He seems to be winking.

Pulling their wraps up to their faces, they step once more out into the cold. Across the street from the church, with its own view of the valley, a blowsy stucco house with brown shutters leans into the wind, its roof curtseying one way, its windows the other. Splintered flower boxes dangle beneath the windows, still clutching clumps of dirt, dried stalks and seed heads. Once, the house must have been beautiful. Edith can imagine children running in and out of the hobnailed door, can see Allart standing in her yard looking wistfully out toward the river, her hair pulling from its pins in the breeze.

"I feel a ghostly presence pointing the way," Edith whispers and gestures to the house across the way with her chin.

Morton laughs. "The book did say she could view the church through one set of her windows, the river through the other."

Battling the gusts, they cross the road side by side.

"Shall we knock on the door?" he asks. "Maybe the owner knows of her."

"If there *is* an owner," she says.

Continuous rapping brings no response. So they edge around the cottage where summer's weeds have shattered and matted in the cold, creating a carpet as soft as the Turkey rugs at George Vanderbilt's apartment. Morton has no compunction peeking into the grimy windows.

Dusty furniture sits forlornly inside. A heavy carved bed with torn curtains around it. A table. But no effects. A damp emptiness rises from the rotting wooden window frames.

"The era where a woman could do as she pleases seems long gone," he says.

"Did that era ever exist?" Edith asks.

Morton turns to her. "If not, I hope it's about to."

She smiles. He takes her elbow and goes on.

"I've never understood why there should be a difference between our expectations of men and women. Especially a woman like you."

"Thank you," she whispers. She loves the pressure of his fingers, his optimistic tone.

"I didn't say it to flatter you."

"No, after your trip to The Mount, I imagine you won't misuse that word again."

He looks at her askance, then breaks into a laugh.

"Promise you will never flatter me," she says. Her voice is coy and joking, but she's not.

"I do solemnly swear I shall never flatter you, Edith. Ever. Besides, you're far too clever to be flattered."

"Morton . . . I'm hesitant to ask, but are you flattering me?" Their combined hilarity echoes back on the wind. How harmonious it feels to be with him! In some ways, she has never met a man who displays less pretense, less guardedness. In other ways, she instinctively knows that he hides a great deal. Is it this dichotomy that makes her so dizzy?

When they come around the other side of the house, battered by the most monumental gust yet, he pulls her close to shield her and she senses he's about to put his lips to hers. The whole world becomes drugged and dreamlike as his beautiful, masculine face draws close. Yet suddenly, confoundedly, what she feels isn't the fluttering of her heart, or the warm flow of passion. Instead, she is watching herself in third person, thinking, "Who is that dreary woman? She is *destined* to disappoint him. Where the well of that woman's passion should be shivers an inch of gelid water skimmed over by a pane of ice . . ."

As if he is reading her mind merely by searching her face, he lets her go suddenly, the kiss not taken, and says, "We ought to be getting back, oughtn't we?"

Two nights later, after a meal that makes Edith glad she hired the new cook—filet of sole braised in butter, squab perfumed with juniper berries, haricots verts in a bath of tomato and thyme—Morton sits in the dark red fauteuil near the parlor lamp at 58, rue de Varenne, reading out loud to her from *Le Revue de Paris*. Tête a tête in the heated embrace of the Rue de Varennne, she feels utterly happy—has she ever been so happy? It's after dinner, and, with Teddy out of town, Morton's removed his jacket and looks rumpled and husbandly in his shirtsleeves in the pool of lamplight.

Edith feels effervescent. This is what it would be like to be married to a man she truly loves: the hiss of a fire, the crisp sound of his voice enlightening her about an article she's already read but didn't quite grasp, her needle dancing through linen stretched between the circles of her embroidery hoop. He questions the article, a mostly unfavorable revue of Meredith's poetry. She selected it—for she didn't know quite what to make of it when she first read it. How is it that he is able to draw so much more from the words than she, discern weaknesses in its argument that eluded her? She is impressed with his acuity, his sensitivity, his sheer brainpower. Has she ever known a man so undeniably bright? She is giddy with happiness.

How can she not indulge herself with the dream of what life would be like if nights such as this were habit. Habit! Never has this dull tweed word ever meant anything so rich with possibility. Utterly different from her present existence, in which every surprise has been wrung from each day. If merely sharing a weekday meal, reading together, being domestic side by side could bring such joy, how infinite the possibilities! She'd wish to live to a hundred. She would age like fine wine. His wisdom would seep into her work, into every single breath she took!

He closes the magazine and sets it in his lap, then picks up a tiny, phenomenally valuable crystal clock on the side table and observes it silently for a few moments.

"George Vanderbilt has an eye," he says. He glances around with satisfaction.

"Yes. It's extraordinary here."

"Is this where you sit every night after dinner?"

She nods.

"Good. Now I can imagine you here when I am not."

He feels what I feel! Edith thinks. He wishes our nights were intertwined! And she sees it: a glimmering glass of crystalline bliss balancing between them. She will never forget this moment, this night!

And so she ventures further. Oh, to have him confirm it, so she can lie in bed later and savor his affirmation!

"Having you here is so gratifying. I wish it were so every night," she says. She hears the girlishness in her voice. But a worried look crosses his brow. He presses his lips together and catches her with a sideways glance. "I'm just wondering what you want from me, Edith," he says softly.

"Pardon?" Maybe she's misheard him.

"What I'm wondering is, do you wish us just to be intellectual companions?"

"Well, it is nice that we are, isn't it? Not so easy to find someone so utterly compatible."

"And not so hard."

Edith's mouth goes dry. "I don't think I understand. . . ."

Is there someone else? Is this what he's telling her? She's been brave, and now will he send her back to her dark hiding place? Why?

"Maybe you overestimate my ability to interpret you," she says. She hears the imperiousness in her voice.

"Do you have feelings for me?" he asks.

"I . . . I . . . do. . . ." Should she have said no? Will he now say he doesn't have feelings for her?

"Well, you must know how I feel about you."

Oh, why doesn't he say it? Why must he torture her?

"I'm not sure I know," she says.

He shakes his head. Not annoyed. Amused, it appears.

"I didn't take you for coy. It's very simple, really. I want you, Edith. Desperately. What I'm trying to parse out is whether you want me."

She has never heard words so bald, so unornamented. He is a Harvard man. Couldn't he have stated it more gently, more romantically? Even Teddy was more romantic. What does he want? To *have* her? She feels herself blanch.

"You see, I can't tell if you're toying with me or are serious," he says.

"Morton."

"Because you're married, be that as it may, and I am a single man. And you might be just flirting."

She feels indignation straighten her back, puff out her chest, send fire to her eyes.

"I don't flirt," she states coldly.

He laughs at her. "How little you know yourself," he says.

"I know myself quite well."

"So why do you put yourself out at every turn? And a moment later demur? You're a tease."

Edith gasps, hears her perfect goblet of happiness shatter, spilling every drop.

He has spoiled it. Spoiled everything. She feels sick with disappointment.

She stands. "Perhaps you should go, Mr. Fullerton."

"Now, dear." He stands too, and puts his hands on her shoulders. She doesn't want him to touch her, not feeling the way she's feeling. Men are so clumsy. So heavy-footed.

"Listen. Look at me." He tilts her chin upward. "I merely want what every man desires from a woman he cares deeply about. I find you impossibly alluring. Don't you see? Being intellectually sympathetic is only one part of the equation."

How can she tell him? How will she explain it? She is a freak of nature. *Mismade* . . .

"Some women are made for that sort of thing," she starts carefully. How can she tell him this? "It seems perhaps . . . I am not." Her voice is very quiet. Pained. She feels utterly chastened.

"So it's true," he says. "What Henry says about you and Teddy? There's . . . *nothing* between you?"

Edith closes her eyes for a moment. She can't hedge now. She shakes her head. "It didn't feel right from the start. For either of us."

Morton shakes his head. "It's incomprehensible . . ."

"That nothing would happen?"

"That you would stay married. That you wouldn't seek out something that *did* feel right. You *are* human, after all."

"You mean . . ."

"One would imagine you'd seek out desire . . . for anyone."

"But women are different from men."

"Are they? It's not been my experience. It was Eve that proffered the apple, wasn't it?"

"What are you saying about me?"

"That you are curiously devoid of passion."

Her indignation propels her toward him. "That's unfair and unkind. I have a great passion for life."

"For life. Perhaps. But have you gone through life with no bodily desire whatsoever? I suppose the point of men choosing snow-white women is that they can be the ones to awaken desire in these women. But I've always believed a woman has the capacity for desire. Or she doesn't. I wonder if you do."

"Are you being purposely vicious?"

"I'm being honest. Straightforward. Which I believe is far more respectful than flirtation and innuendo. You're a grown woman. I can speak candidly, can't I?"

"But you're accusing me of being bloodless."

"It's been said of you."

"And do you speak of me with others? What right do you and Henry . . . Henry, of all people . . . ?"

He shakes his head. "What do you want from me, Edith?" He stands to face her. They are the same height. Eye to eye.

Edith finds herself completely speechless. Until she finally stammers, "I'd like . . . I'd like you to leave."

"Are you certain that's what you want from me?" he says. He looks so cool, so amused by her anger. Even in shirtsleeves, he is polished and self-possessed. Perhaps it is better to spend an evening with Teddy. He would never rile her so. "I'll ring Alfred for your coat." Her voice is quavering. Absurd.

Edith has a horrible sense that he might go home and laugh at her. She wouldn't mind any other reaction. But to be laughed at! To be derided!

"My dear," he says in a suddenly soothing voice, "you are a very proud woman. And you have good reason to be. You may be the brightest woman I've ever encountered. I am painfully drawn to you. But passion and pride rarely occupy the same space. And that makes me hesitate."

"You don't know anything about me."

"I'd like to," he says. He strokes the tender insides of her elbows for a moment, and looks into her eyes, flashing her a soft, thoughtful smile. "Am I wise to go against my better judgment? I wonder if you are courageous enough to find out what's hiding inside you."

When he releases her, she feels as though she is falling down a well. The door closes behind him and she is safe again. Safe. Is that really what she wants?

She writes in her diary, "You hurt me. You disillusioned me. And when you left, I was more deeply yours. . . ."

"Perhaps we can spend the day together Saturday," she writes him. "I have always wanted to see Montfort-l'Amaury. Have you ever been?" She wonders whether, after their last conversation, he will be willing to spend a minute more with her. But he sends her an immediate petit bleu saying he would be very happy to have a chance to spend a whole day together. *Nothing would suit me better.*

Her immediate sense of elation alarms her. She checks herself. What if he expects that his desires will be instantly met? But an entire day together in the country with the only human being in the world who has the ability to make her happy! How can she not revel in the possibility of it! I will speak to him with a *coeur ouvert*, she tells herself. I will tell him how afraid I am. I will put myself in his hands. . . .

Possible scenes etch themselves on her mind. A tender walk in a field, holding hands. A country churchyard with a thousand clues among the gravestones. Morton picking wildflowers that he tucks in her hair. He touches her cheek. He runs his fingers along her collarbone. These scenes carry her forward toward Saturday, fill every waking moment.

And then Friday night, she receives a wire: ON MY WAY HOME FROM CURTISES' EARLY. STOP. STILL VERY BAD. STOP. TRAIN TO ARRIVE SATURDAY LATE MORNING. STOP. TEDDY.

SEVEN

WINTER 1908

Anna comes into the room to see Edith with her face in her hands. It's been years since she's seen Edith cry. Early in her marriage there was a great flood of tears. Many of them soaked Anna's breast.

"Nothing good will happen for me," Edith used to moan. "I am doomed." Anna knows not to openly soothe Edith when she's miserable. One must merely be present and silent. Edith is nothing if not dramatic. And when wrapped in her own misery, she doesn't wish to be jollied out of it. As a child, Edith's tears rose from frustration or anger. But now, somehow, Anna can read that these tears rise from sheer despair. What could be making her feel so?

"Edith?" she asks softly.

Edith raises her pale face. She looks as though she's been caught doing something unspeakable.

"Oh. Tonni," she says wearily. "You have my pages?" Her eyes are swollen. Her lips thin and pained. Anna hands her the typescript and steps closer.

"Do you wish to talk?" she whispers. How long since Edith really confided anything in Anna? Though once, she confided everything.

Edith shakes her head. And then, sheepishly, she lifts the yellow sheet from her desk which contains the wire.

Anna takes it and knits her brows. "Does it make you so sad just to have Mr. Wharton return?"

Edith closes her eyes and shakes her head. "He's no better," she says.

"You know it takes time for him to get better. Especially when he's so melancholy. Last time it took months. He needs your patience."

Edith's nostrils flare. "Nothing I do seems to have any effect."

"He was patient with you, all those years you were ill. He was kind to you. Remember how he brought you flowers every day and books, and cheered you up? Again and again . . . unfailingly. He's a good man, Edith."

"Don't lecture me."

"I don't mean to lecture. I meant to remind you."

Edith nods. "Sometimes I think nothing good will ever happen for me."

"I know, Herz. But nothing good is happening for Teddy right now either, and he needs your patience. Your loyalty." Anna places her hand on Edith's shoulder but Edith turns her face away, a signal that Anna should leave. Still, she stands there for a moment, waiting to see if Edith will say more, will reach out to her again. Instead, there is only silence.

Perhaps I was too harsh with her, Anna worries all through the evening. But she feels angry too. How could Edith be so selfish to find distaste in her own husband's return? That night, Anna's lovely soft bed beneath the eaves feels as though it's made of nails, her pillow of hardwood. When she gets up, her bones aching, and goes to the window to look out over the roofs of Paris, she sees a bat circling and circling over the hammered silver moon. She closes her eyes, allowing the cool moonlight to paint her eyelids, feeling far too small to make her dent upon the world.

Edith, unable to sleep, sits close to the fire. Having finished a terse pneu to Morton—"Cannot join you as planned"—she now sits with the new diary open on the desk and composes a poem on a separate piece of paper.

L'Âme Close

My soul is like a house that
Dwellers nigh can see no light in.
"Ah, poor house," they say,

"Long since its owners died or
Went their way." Thick ivy
Loops the rusted door-latch tie.
The chimney rises cold against the sky
And flowers turned to weed down the
Bare path's decay . . .
Yet one stray passer, at the shut of day,
Sees a light trembling in a casement high.
Even so, my soul would set a light for you,
A light invisible to all beside,
As though a lover's ghost should yearn and glide
From pane to pane, to let the flame shine through.
Yet enter not, lest as it flits ahead
You see the hand that carries it is dead.

When rereading the poem brings tears to her eyes, she carefully transcribes it into the diary she has begun for Morton, then turns off the light and searches blindly for sleep.

With Teddy home and confined to his bed, bellowing and complaining and clearly furious at his wife for not having joined him on his journey, Edith gives up any hope of comforting him, grabs her wraps and, without the slightest notion of where she might go, leaves the house. Paris is perfumed with a surprising spring breeze. There are men strolling down the street, cloaks in hand, though it is far too cold not to wear them. And a parade of babies slides by, aired in their carriages by nannies and mothers while the weather is cooperating. It would have been the perfect day to explore Montfort and Edith's disappointment is bitter. What has Morton chosen to do today instead? she wonders. She hadn't the heart last night to explain to him why she must cancel their plans. It was too wounding to even think of what she'd miss. And describing Teddy's illness makes her feel weak and compromised. He already questions her for staying with Teddy all these years. His pneu back sounds bewildered and a touch angry. "As I recall," it says, "you were the one who asked me to come. Perhaps you were not able to locate your courage after all."

With nowhere to go, Edith decides to see if the Bourgets are home. It's entirely unlike her not to phone or write first. But the Bourgets never mind surprises, and if they are out, Edith will take a long walk—stride across the length of Paris and back if she must—to dispel the feeling of corrosion that courses through her veins.

At their neat sunny apartment on the Rue Barbet de Jouy, Minnie welcomes her, book in hand, wearing a light blue tea gown and the softest expression.

"I'm so sorry to come unannounced," Edith says. "But one more minute in the presence of Teddy's misery and I thought I would do damage to myself. He's grouchy and toxic and not fit for anything."

"Paul is out," Minnie says. "But you couldn't have come at a better time."

Edith notes as she comes closer that the softness in Minnie's face is the aftermath of tears.

"Whatever's wrong, Minnie?" she asks. She lays her hand on her friend's arm, and Minnie motions for Edith to sit.

"I'm not sure I can speak about it," she says. "It's too early for tea. Have you had luncheon?"

"You don't need to serve me anything. I merely came for company. Tell me what's troubling you."

"I wonder if I can trust you to keep a confidence," Minnie says nervously. Minnie is the most even person that Edith knows. She sails through life with grace and good humor. Tears are the last thing Edith expects from her.

"You can trust me with anything," Edith says.

Minnie nods and worries her bracelets for a moment—a pair of old Etruscan-work snakes, wrapped tight about her left wrist. "I believe Paul is *seeing* a woman," she says.

"No . . . are you quite sure?"

"Ever since *Un Divorce* opened, he has been a different man. He struts around like a peacock. He is everyone's darling. 'The play of the year,' they call it. But it started even before then. His absence in this past year, well, I assumed it was the play . . . the stress of the play, not who's . . . *in* the play." Minnie grows crimson about the ears, but her lips pale. "I found a petit bleu in his pocket last week that said, 'Saturday at noon?' and nothing more. And at a quarter to noon, he darted out the door with a very guilty, happy look on his face and his most flattering suit."

"But it could have been from anyone."

"I know who it's from," Minnie says huskily.

Edith shakes her head. "Someone in the play? An actress in the play?"

Minnie closes her eyes very tightly as if trying to block out an image.

"You don't mean Mrs. Davreau?" Amélie Davreau is the most beautiful woman in Paris. Her hair is the color of butter, and her figure like that of a china figurine.

"I don't wish to say. . . ." Minnie's voice cracks at the end and Edith knows she's spoken the unspeakable name. Amélie Davreau is so beautiful, she is the only actress on the Paris stage who wears no heavy stage makeup. Her dark-lashed lavender eyes can be read across the entire theatre. Even Edith fell in love with her during the play. Her grace and her modesty were so unique for an actress, so appealing.

"But how do you know it's from this . . . woman?"

"When he speaks of her, his voice changes. I've wondered for a long time what might be going on between them. Men have no idea how sensitive a woman can be to the smallest clues. When we are all three in the same room together, it's as though I'm not there, even when I am. She is slender and fine. The very opposite of me. He hangs on her every word. He quotes her when she's not around just to hear himself say her name. She's married. Why should she want my husband as well?"

"Some women get no pleasure from their own husbands . . . ," Edith says. Minnie glances over at her with a clouded eye. Can she read what Edith is thinking? She blinks at her for a moment, and Edith feels the heat of her own wayward desire.

"I know you are unhappy with Teddy. But it isn't as though you would simply stomp off and have a love affair with another man."

Edith can't swallow. She wishes now that Minnie had called for tea.

"I try not to be old-fashioned," Minnie goes on. "But I guess I'm not as modern as I profess to be. Or as Parisian. I do believe one should honor one's vows. And if that's old-fashioned, then I'm happy to be."

Edith puts her hand to her face to cover up what must be a painful flush. But Minnie is looking out the window, paying no attention to Edith's distress.

"You're not a bit old-fashioned," Edith says, just to keep Minnie talking until her blush has subsided. "But perhaps they are merely friends? Perhaps nothing's . . . happened at all? Sometimes men just set their hearts on other women and do nothing but pay them attention."

"You see, that's the point. Does it matter? I don't think it does. It's that he has feelings for another woman that hurts the most. I know men think that if they are physically faithful they are in the clear. But it's not so for me. It's that he desires her. That he thinks of her when he's not with her. I watch him. I see him. He's a man who loves women. Who desires women. I fell in love with him for that, really. I have no patience with men like Paul Hervieu, who would rather read poetry and pick flowers. So if he has been faithful or not, he's wounded me. I thought I would always be the one he desires the most." Minnie pulls a crumpled handkerchief from her sleeve and dabs her tears, which are falling too quickly to catch.

"You don't know it's not so."

"I know his world has shifted. A woman knows when she's no longer the center of someone's sphere. It's just cruel, Edith. If you loved someone, how could you hurt them like that?"

"Maybe if you spoke to him. Maybe if he knew that you knew . . ."

"When a person has a different sense of right and wrong, what does it matter? When the man I love no longer thinks I am enough, what does it matter? When we live in a time where sin is more delicious than loyalty, what does it matter?"

"Perhaps," Edith says, as evenly as she can, "sin has always been more delicious than loyalty. . . ."

"Not by people who are guided by what they believe in, rather than by a fleeting urge. . . ."

Edith feels as though Minnie is speaking directly to her. She closes her eyes. But the bright sunlight of the day she was meant to spend with a man she longs to love, a man who is not her husband, burns her.

For two days, there are no notes between Edith and Fullerton. She wishes to explain to him what caused her to cancel their day together, but after her talk with Minnie, she feels chastened and unable to pick up a pen.

When Minnie writes that she'd like Edith to accompany the Bour-gets to the Renaissance Theatre that night, Edith is more than happy to say yes. She is relieved to leave the house. Teddy has not improved. But, happily, Anna says she will stay with him. Teddy is more himself with Anna anyway. What is it about Anna that everyone finds so consoling? Small children, miserable old men find her a balm.

Knowing that Teddy's in good hands and off her own, she's curious to see how the Bourgets will relate to each other. And she wonders if Minnie is inviting her to see for herself the change in Paul.

It's grown cold again and rain is threatening to turn to snow, so Edith offers to take the three of them in her motorcar. Snuggled into the back-seat with their theatre coats and muffs, she feels happy for the first time since her lost Saturday. But she does notice that Paul has seated himself on one side of her, Minnie on the other. And Edith is required to carry the bulk of the conversation. When they speak, they mostly speak to her or through her, not to each other.

The theatre is as unreal as a carnival, thumping with sound and color and energy. Settled in the Bourgets' baignoire, she enjoys the parade of women in their gowns and gloves, the men in their stiff suits, the jumble of perfume, conspicuous jewels, and half-heard conversations. Women peer out over fans or gossip behind them. Held up to this circus of humanity, Edith's long days at the Rue de Varenne with gloomy Teddy seem utterly moribund.

Seated next to poor Minnie, Edith perceives that while her friend is present at the play, she is not truly watching it. The same clouding of her eyes, the same pressing of her lips as Edith observed the other day convey her pain. While the actors prance and argue and weep on stage, twice Edith reaches out and touches Minnie's shoulder, her elbow. Once, Paul notes the gesture and looks at her askance, but she merely smiles sweetly at him.

And then, before the first act is over, Edith hears the muffled squeak of someone opening the velvet door to their baignoire and the thump of it closing on its own. And with the scent of lavender, she realizes that Fullerton has seated himself directly behind her. She turns to take in his gaze, clear as a child's, and his gentle, beautiful face lit by the lights of the stage. He mouths the word "Hello," and she finds herself visibly shivering. But his eyes warm her: they are kind and beseeching and flash a sweet shyness in their blue glance. He must wonder what she feels toward him, since it was she who put him off in that scribbled pneu. Edith gets the sense that Morton isn't used to being put off. If he only knew how much she suffered by losing their day together. If he only knew how much she's since longed for him. He must see it in her face, for the meeting of their eyes is electrifying. A communication of such kindness, sympathy and desire, no words could impart it, no touch has ever affected her so. What flows between them feels as though it might ignite the baignoire. Or the whole auditorium. How is it that Minnie hasn't turned to see it, or that the play itself hasn't stopped in deference?

How can anything stand in the way of what is already happening between Edith and Morton? She has never been one to believe in predestination. But as clear as Minnie's sad figure next to her, fate stands in front of her with outstretched hand, and no shaming from Minnie's situation, no moral qualms can keep her from taking hold of those warm fingers.

When the curtain drops on the first act, Morton stands and greets Paul and Minnie as though it is the Bourgets he has come to see. He kisses Minnie's fingers. He charms her with kind remarks about her dress, which he says is the color of an angry sea. And he tells Minnie that she is the one who surely must appreciate this daring play since she's the only one among them with a developed sense of right and wrong. The struggle of the main character surely must speak to her. Edith wonders how on earth he knew this about Minnie? Minnie blushes under his ministrations and color flows back into her cheeks. Edith is happy to see it—Minnie is the one who needs his attention. He makes Paul laugh as well, comparing the play they have come to see unfavorably to *Un Divorce*, which he says makes all other plays this year seem shabby. Not nearly as brilliant or insightful. Not nearly as polished. But the entire time he is speaking to the Bourgets, Edith knows he is doing it for her benefit. She has never felt so secure in her sense of connection with anyone. And when he glances her way, she feels the buzz, the heat of their bond. This must be what happy women feel, she thinks. I have waited a lifetime to know it.

Fullerton stays in their baignoire for the length of the play and walks them out to their motorcar, refusing a lift home, saying he'd prefer to walk in the rain.

"But sharing the play with all of you has made this evening one to remember," he says, once again kissing Minnie's hand and looking into her eyes, shaking Paul's hand mightily, then giving Edith the ultimate warm glance as she is last to climb into the motorcar.

"Soon? Please?" he whispers.

"Perhaps I have misjudged Fullerton," Minnie says on the ride home. "It *was* kind of him to come by and see us."

"I believe he was flirting with you, Minnie," Paul says. "Was he?" He reaches over Edith and squeezes Minnie's hand.

Minnie laughs like a young girl and looks down. "I believe he was," she says, with burning cheeks and a voice brimming with pleasure.

"He certainly was," Edith says. "What impudence to flirt with a woman right in front of her husband!"

"Well, a roué like Fullerton is all about overconfidence," Paul says with a harrumph, clearly playing up his displeasure. When Edith drops off the Bourgets, they say it was a fine evening, and Minnie takes Paul's elbow as they open the gate to their building. But Edith knows: no one enjoyed the theatre that night as much as she.

Anna sits with Teddy Wharton, reading out loud to him from the *Journal of North American Agriculture* about ileitis in pigs. Teddy says the pain in his head precludes him from reading to himself. And Anna's voice is as soft as silk, he tells her.

She doesn't mind reading aloud. It reminds her of her teaching days, when the best way to calm a rowdy student was by reading a story aloud. Even the most restless child could be settled by a good tale. Well, this is no story, but she finds the article enlightening too, for she knows nothing about pigs. How interesting that stressed pigs are most at risk of ileitis. Anna did not know that pigs could become stressed.

"Pigs are sensitive," Teddy tells her. "They have feelings. And faces that show those feelings, like our little Nicette and Mitou do."

"Indeed?" Anna says. "I don't think I shall ever eat ham with the same feeling again."

Teddy laughs, for a moment forgetting his pain. His guffaw is deep and rich. Her life has been adorned by his laughter for years; when he is away, she pines for it.

"Next time we are at The Mount, Miss Anna, perhaps you'll come down to the new piggery with me and meet some of my favorite sons."

"I'd be honored," she tells him.

"Lawton. You'll particularly like Lawton. He will steal your heart!"

"I've never had my heart stolen by a swine," she says jollily.

"Well, since most women do at some point or other in their lives, it's about time you did," he tells her. "It's what makes it hard for nice fellas like me. But honest, Lawton is a gentleman . . . er, a gentlepig."

"I'll look forward to our meeting," she says soberly.

Teddy sits up in bed and leans toward Anna.

"Listen, Miss Anna. We ain't young, you and I, but we're both open to experience. People don't know that about you, I'll wager. I'm not even sure Pussy does. But you're an explorer, I think. You like learning new things. I've always admired that about you."

"Thank you," she says, honored, though the teacher in her cringes at his ungrammatical speech that seems suddenly in vogue with the upper class. She imagines that Edith must hate it.

"And the other thing we have in common is that people don't appreciate us. That's what I think. They think we're simple because we're not clever with quips and such. But it don't mean we're not smart and have our own important thoughts, you know?"

She nods. It is fine to see him smile.

"It ain't good for me to be here in Paree, and that's the truth. Paris is no place for a man like me. I'll go to theatre. And I don't mind a good restaurant meal. But if you get right down to it, I find happiness outside. Where there are trees. Paris is too cramped. Too mean-spirited. What do you say we both go back on the first steamer out of Le Havre? Spring is a fine time to be there. Still snowy, but beautiful. I'd be better if I were there. You could sign on as my nursemaid."

"There, Mr. Wharton," Anna says. "No sudden moves." She's flattered by Teddy's suggestion, but what would Edith think? "You need your rest and a doctor's care. Dr. Kinnicut isn't there this time of year. Besides, Mrs. Wharton needs me here to help her with her writing."

"So you choose Pussy over me. I should have known." His face collapses like a child told he can't have a toy.

"Now, that's not fair. I work for Mrs. Wharton. You know that."

"I know that you and I get on like a house afire. And that I don't feel that way about just anybody. You are good company, Miss Anna. Good company, which is what I need right now."

"Which is why I'm here with you this very minute." She puts her hand on his arm and squeezes it. He closes his eyes.

"You do soothe me, I'll tell you that. You're the best medicine I know."

"Well, let me go on, so we can find out more about pig ileitis. We've got research to do."

Teddy lies back on his pillow. "Go on, then. Go on," he says. And then right in the middle of a sentence, she hears him say very softly, "You are a gift to me, Anna."

Edith has lost all sense of ordinary days. For wherever she goes—and there is much on her calendar in the early spring—thoughts of Morton follow her. She has tea with countesses. She takes walks with Minnie, who happily feels that Paul is paying more attention to her. She dines with dukes. But at every table, she speaks to Fullerton, whether he is there or not. She describes every scene to him in her mind, every ironic observation of Paris. On Tuesday, she dresses carefully, certain he will appear at Rosa's: her rose-colored shirtwaist again, with an amethyst brooch at her throat and golden earrings (ah, she *must* be fitted for more attractive, younger looking clothes!), but he doesn't come. She leaves early, telling everyone she's tired from a bad night's sleep. And then she manages to have one, her sleep pitted with a longing that wakes her every few hours like a fever.

The next Saturday, she and Teddy drive out to St. Cloud for a luncheon with her brother Harry, Eliot Gregory and essayist André Chevrillon. She is worried about bringing Teddy out into public, for he has become stranger and stranger. Interrupting in the middle of others' sentences. Moaning sometimes about the buzzing and pain in his head.

Starting arguments. Wandering off without warning. Anna says he just needs more of Edith's attention, and so Edith nervously agrees on this lovely March day to "air him out." Once in the motorcar with him, she rues the decision. He has a pinched look on his face like a man with smelling salts under his nose. She begins discussing a book she's reading, a long essay about Darwin which she thinks will interest him since he is so fond of animals and breeding, but quite soon his openly rude sighing tells her he's bored. So she starts to talk about who will be at the luncheon, but he doesn't even acknowledge her chatter. Still, she's hoping that once he gets there, he'll be glad he's come. He doesn't like Eliot, but at least he'll speak to him in English. And Teddy is always comfortable with her brother, who loves horse racing and can make small talk about breeds and skeletal structure and jockey fitness.

It is the sort of day when kites might have flown in Central Park. The air is still chilly but the breeze is surprisingly warm, and, with some imagination and forced good cheer, she can conjure up the Parisian spring to come. What is Morton doing on this beautiful half-cloudy day? Strolling down the Boulevard St. Germain, keeping his eye out for her?

The restaurant in St. Cloud is the sort of place with glassed-in rooms that make you feel as though you are eating outside even when the weather is too chilly. Tables are set with pink napkins and buckets of chilled champagne. Eliot greets Edith with a "Halloo," so she seats herself next to him and across from André Chevrillon. She directs Teddy to sit on the other side of Eliot, across from her brother.

"Good to see you, Ted," Harry says. "What do you hear about the horses these days?"

"I don't hear a thing. I'm in Paris and they're over there," Teddy says ruefully.

"You and I will have to motor out to Villemer then," Harry says in his easy way. "A fellow's raising some beauties out that way. I'm thinking of snatching a few up for my farm."

Champagne is poured, and, feeling certain that Harry's got Teddy distracted, Edith relaxes into a conversation with André about French politics. Then her heart lurches. Across the restaurant she sees a golden sight: Morton in his crisp suit, a garnet waistcoat, his top hat in hand, crossing the glassed room toward their table. When he spots her, his smile flows like light into a room after a cloud uncovers the sun.

Eliot leans toward her and, making sure his voice is too low for Teddy to hear, whispers, "Put your tongue back in your mouth, my dear." She glances at him sharply. But even his tart comment can't take away the pleasure she feels in Morton's sweet presence.

"Monsieur Chevrillon, Mr. Wharton. Eliot . . . Mrs. Wharton." He takes each of their hands with a gallantry that would be comic if it were not so graceful. "And sir, I don't think we've met."

"This is my brother," Edith says.

"Well, what an unexpected honor!" Morton declares, then chooses the empty seat beside Edith.

"Dearest," he whispers to her. She looks to make sure neither Eliot nor Harry is watching before she lifts her face and throws beams of kindness on him.

"I had no idea you were going to be here," she says.

"Eliot invited me."

"Eliot?" Edith feels a moment's panic. Is this some sort of trap that Eliot's concocted? Eliot was the one who told her to "be circumspect," who said Fullerton was not to be trusted. He also said if she was drawn in by him, he would be only too happy to watch the spectacle. She shivers.

"Pigs?" she overhears Eliot saying to Teddy. "Eating them is the only thing I ever plan to do with pigs. Hideous, filthy creatures." Edith sees that Teddy's face is growing red.

He booms. "Not hideous. A great deal more sensitive than a jackass like you. And likely more intelligent."

"Teddy!" Edith cautions. Why, oh, why did she bring him? She is furious at Anna for suggesting it.

"Now don't get all het up, Ted," Harry says. "Most people don't realize that pigs . . . are not what they seem."

Morton leans past Edith so he can be heard by Teddy and Eliot. "It's ironic you should be speaking about swine. We ran an article in the *Times* just last week about how researchers have discovered that pigs are some of the most intelligent creatures on the planet." Edith notices how Morton's blue eyes sparkle like aquamarines. "They say they have the aptitude of dogs. They may even be smarter."

"That's right, Mr. Fullerton. That's just right," Teddy says. Edith flashes Morton a grateful smile. And when she does, she feels his smooth warm fingers interlocking with hers under the tablecloth. The sensation overtakes her, almost stings in its intensity. But at the same time, Eliot is leaning toward her with an aside.

"Your Mr. Fullerton could charm the peel off a banana," he hisses to Edith with a snort. "And has, I've heard."

"Hush," Edith says, elbowing him. She's aware of how ironic it is to be elbowing Eliot, the man who warned her away from Morton, while at the same time holding hands with the man in question.

She looks over at Harry, who is observing her wryly. He smiles. "This is a lovely place for a meal!" he says. Ah, the classic Jones attempt at distracting from a set-to. Surely he learned it from their father, who was often called on to defuse uncomfortable situations created by their mother but rarely did it gracefully.

"Well, why don't we order our luncheon," Eliot proclaims, opening his menu. "I hear the sole meunière is divine."

"When will we have another day together?" Morton whispers to Edith.

"I might just have the boeuf," she says. Then, shaking her head sadly, she gestures toward Teddy with her eyes." I wish I knew," she says so softly she can hardly hear her own voice.

The longing, the passion in his eyes jabs her. Perhaps their time apart since his visit to the Rue de Varenne has quickened his interest.

"Senlis," Morton says to her.

"Pardon?"

"We could go to Senlis. It's everything they say it is. And not so very far by motor."

"Yes, Senlis is a lovely place," Eliot says too loudly, proving it hasn't taken much to hear their conversation. "If you're fond of the medieval, that is. And you are, aren't you, Edith?" Edith lets go of Morton's hand. "You're our own little Eleanor of Aquitaine. . . ."

"Perhaps you could come with us," Morton says, taking the bait.

"Oh no. I'm sure you two wouldn't appreciate extra company."

"Your company, Eliot, is always appreciated," Morton says with too flowery a spin. Eliot glares at him. Edith gets up.

"I'm going to go have a cigarette before the sky opens up. It's getting dark out there." She can't get away from the table fast enough, desperate for the outside air, however cold it may be.

Out in the courtyard, she draws a cigarette from her purse and lights it. Her hands are shaking. It has indeed grown chillier, and that dark cloud lumbering toward them looks like snow. She leans against the pergola and closes her eyes. Come summer, this courtyard will be aflutter with flowering vines. The outdoor tables will be adorned with candles and pink napkins and zinnias, and the chairs which are now tilted forward on their front legs and resting against the tables will cradle colorful cushions to comfort lovers who've come for a meal away from town and a breath of cool air. How nice if she and Morton could steal away in her motor and spend a few hours in the dazzling summer sun together. But the thought evokes pain rather than joy, because come summer, they will be an ocean apart: Edith, imprisoned with Teddy at The Mount, Morton slaving for the *Times*. They have a mere three months together until they must part. How she aches thinking of it!

She finishes the cigarette and is wondering if she should smoke another when she sees Harry crossing the courtyard with a concerned expression.

"I think you'd better come back, Edith. Teddy's making a bit of a ruckus."

Following quickly on Harry's heels, Edith discovers Teddy standing over Eliot Gregory, bellowing. He's raising a butter knife in his hand as though it is dangerous. The entire restaurant is watching. His face is as red as a side of beef. His other hand is gripped into a fist. Morton is standing beside him, attempting to settle him down. But Teddy is focused on Eliot.

"How dare you say that about my wife! I tell you, a man can only take so much. You rotter! God, my head is bursting. And you bait me. You taunt me."

"Now, Ted. I hardly said a thing. . . ." Eliot looks like a scared child. "I can't imagine what I did to set you off."

"Teddy!" Edith comes up to him and gently wrests the knife from his hand. "Come on, dear. I'm sure Cook would be all too happy to take us home." Her voice is as smooth and even as she can make it. "After all, you're not feeling well. It was selfish of me to take you out, feeling as you do. . . ."

Edith sees that Morton is watching Teddy with raised eyebrows, and then his gaze moves to Edith's face with distress.

"Look, Edith, don't trouble yourself," Harry says with unexpected cheerfulness. "I'll motor Ted back. You stay here and have luncheon with your friends."

"Harry, I . . ."

"No, do as I say." And then he leans toward her. "You could use a rest. Besides, Ted and I can have a nice chat. And my dyspepsia knocks out my appetite these days anyway. What do you say, Ted? You wouldn't mind returning to Paris with an old friend, would you?"

Teddy shakes his head.

"Oh, Harry, that's kind," Edith says. "Really kind."

"Nonsense. I want to talk to my brother-in-law. What better opportunity! Catch up on horse talk. Come on, old boy. I want to show you my new motor. It's a stunner."

Edith is relieved to see Teddy following her brother meekly. When they have left the restaurant, everyone settles back in their seats with a heaviness, and relief. For a moment, there is total silence, a group of four people gazing at their plates. And then, suddenly, like children after a playground skirmish, they simultaneously begin to giggle.

"Is he often like this?" Eliot asks. "Good God, Edith. It's rather frightening. I'd have him committed if I were you."

"Easy," Morton says sternly.

"What did you do to set him off, Eliot?" Edith asks.

"Don't blame me. Absolutely nothing. A little teasing about how successful you are. And how's he going to have to be quite the man to hold on to a famous lady like yourself. He's always been up for a bit of ribbing before."

Edith gnashes her teeth. "To say that that was unwise in his present condition is an understatement."

"Well, how was I to know he had a *condition?*"

Edith shakes her head, narrows her eyes. "I knew you liked your mischief, but I didn't think you could be so cruel."

"Let us set aside our differences and get down to the business of eating," André says. "All this drama gives me an appetite. Like being at the theatre. Garçon!"

By the time they've completed their lunch, fat flakes of snow have covered the glass roof and coated the drive.

"How did you get here?" Edith asks Morton as they stand on the threshold of the restaurant, Edith ruing that she didn't wear her boots.

"The omnibus."

"The omnibus? Not even a cab?"

"I am not a rich man," he says plainly.

"Well then, drive back with me. We'll have a nice chat." She says this right in front of Eliot, turning defiantly to catch his eye. She kisses André good-bye but nods coolly at Eliot. He squints at her sheepishly.

"I had no idea he'd go off like that, Edith. Honest. . . ." He holds up both hands like a bystander at a bank robbery.

"Well, perhaps you ought to have," she says sharply, knowing full well that making Eliot Gregory an enemy is a surefire way to find oneself caricatured in his column.

Cook pulls up with the Panhard, and Edith and Morton climb in. Once the doors have closed, the snow-coated light inside is soft and gray and comforting, as though a quilt has been thrown over the entire motorcar. Through the shrouded window, she can see only the faintest outline of Eliot skulking off to his motor. She stamps the skin of snow off her shoes and it sparkles as it melts on the floor of the Panhard.

"Well then, this is much better than you waiting for an omnibus in this weather."

Morton smiles with relief. "Far better," he says. "Thank you, patroness." He takes her hand, examining it for a moment then sliding his thumb over each of her fingers, twisting her rings straight. "I'm awfully worried about you," he says, when the road noise has created enough of a buzz that Cook is unlikely to hear them. "I had no idea Teddy's condition was so precarious. Is he always like this?"

"This is as bad as I've ever seen him."

"You must feel cursed, trapped. I can't even imagine. . . . My poor dear."

"I'm glad you know now. That you've seen it firsthand and don't just assume I'm simply carping about my husband. I feel guilty complaining about him. He's the one who's suffering."

"It's frightening to see someone change, isn't it?" Morton gets a faraway look in his eye, as though he is drawing on a memory of his own.

"Last time he was ill like this, he was melancholy. It's more than that now. Now he's obstreperous, unpredictable."

He takes her hand and kisses it. Then he leans over and kisses her nose and, with a finger, tenderly smoothes the lock on her forehead. She knows she should be worried that Cook might be watching, but this kindness is so necessary to her right now, so exquisitely what she wants. To get just what one wants when one wants it: has it ever happened to her before? How rare, how deeply satisfying it feels. And the richest part of his ministrations is that she feels so utterly understood.

"It's heaven to be with you," he whispers.

"When I saw you in the restaurant today, I felt as though I were dreaming. I was so happy. And to think it was Eliot who invited you. . . ."

"I had no idea he had designs in asking me to come."

"It was as though he were trying to spin a drama. . . ."

"I wish we could steal away from everyone," Morton says. "And just go where no one cares who we are. . . ."

"I've never felt so in need of escape. But Teddy . . . I hardly feel I can leave him. Anna helps. Anna always helps."

"She doesn't like me."

"Oh, nonsense. Anna doesn't have an opinion about people."

"I'm quite sure you're wrong about that." The solemnity of his voice carries a warning.

Edith shrugs. "It's always seemed to me if I like someone, she does as well."

"She's protective of you. She doesn't trust me yet. But if she's willing, maybe we can employ Anna to babysit Mr. Wharton, and we'll go off for a nice drive somewhere. Next Saturday perhaps, when I'm free for a full day. I need to be alone with you. I need to *be* with you."

"A full day. Just those words! Could a day ever feel so full as to spend it with you? An entire day without the whole world needing our attention. Oh, Morton. Can we really make it happen?" She hears herself, and knows she sounds young, overexcited. Foolish, even. And yet the idea of having so much time with the one person who pleases her most is irresistible.

"But do you understand what I'm saying, Edith?"

She looks up at his face. "I think I do." Does she? Is he saying he wants the sort of intimacy she is uncertain to be able to give him?

But Morton hasn't dropped the thread of Teddy's distressing behavior. "You don't think Teddy would ever become . . . truly violent. . . ."

Edith is quiet for a moment. "He's always been a kind man. He's blustery more than dangerous."

"The way he held that knife to Gregory . . ."

"It was a butter knife."

"But if he ever found out you and I . . . had feelings for each other . . . what would he do?"

Edith can't help but smile at hearing that Morton has feelings for her, however obliquely. "He won't find out," she says.

Morton shakes his head. He doesn't appear soothed by her words.

"Teddy wouldn't do anything that might hurt me. He loves me."

"It's because he loves you that I worry."

"You know he and I have been nothing to each other for years but two yoked oxen. I'm sure there have been other women. . . . I've accepted that."

"That's different."

"Is it? Why?"

"Women are more forgiving about such things."

"Are they indeed?"

"He thinks you couldn't have feelings for another man. You never have, have you?" Morton looks up at her with worried eyes.

"No," she says softly. "I never have. Never before you."

"Edith . . ."

"Look, we're in Paris already," she says, pointing through the clear space in the front window where Cook has continually reached around from the side window to clear the snow. Through the peephole, the Champs Élysées is coated with sugar. The shop windows are steamy. There are almost no cars on the normally crowded thoroughfare. And even the horse-drawn vehicles seem to be moving at an exceptionally slow pace.

"I'm sorry to be here so quickly," Morton says.

Edith weighs asking Cook to drive around for a while. To give them time. But she knows in this weather it's too much to demand. And their progress will be slow enough in the snow.

"Next Saturday?" he says.

"Yes. Next Saturday."

They look at each and settle back in sweet, smiling silence.

That night she writes in her new diary, "I should like to be to you, friend of my heart, like a touch of wings brushing by you in the darkness, or like the scent of an invisible garden, that no one passes on an unknown road at night."

EIGHT

SPRING 1908

Morton writes her often now. Mostly scribbled petits bleus that whisper to her thoughts that occur to him: about books or conversations that remind him of her. About how he is haunted by his memory of their being together "like a ghostly breeze that blows on my thoughts, shuffling them all like cards, sweeping them right off the table."

On Saturday, with Teddy growing worse and worse (throwing a crystal paperweight, weeping, shoving aside his food), Edith and Morton still manage to steal away, but rather than for a full day at Senlis, only long enough to walk the streets of Montmartre together. Oh, what an exquisite Saturday it is! Not quite spring, but so much warmer than the Saturday before. Shoulder to shoulder, they talk about what they once hoped to accomplish in their lives.

"The first time I was able to read a book, I thought, This is what I want to do every day for the rest of my life," Morton says. "I lose myself in reading."

"I find myself in reading!" Edith says.

"I find myself in reading your books. I've gotten hold of *The Fruit of the Tree*. When I am reading it, it is as though you are reading aloud to me. And I've ordered your short stories as well."

When they share good-byes, he whispers, "We didn't have our day together. We need to. I need to be alone with you." He caresses her cheek tenderly.

She peers into his eyes and says nothing.

"I fear you don't understand what I'm saying." His frustration is visible.

She opens her mouth, but words don't come.

"What are you thinking?" he asks.

"When can I see you again?" she says.

The next day, she writes him a letter:

> *Do you know what I was thinking last night, when you asked me and I couldn't tell you? Only that the way you've spent your emotional life, while I've—bien malgré moi—hoarded mine, is what puts the great gulf between us, sets us not only on opposite shores, but at hopeless distant points of our respective shores. . . . Do you know what I mean?*
>
> *And I'm so afraid that the treasures I long to unpack for you, that have come to me in magic ships from enchanted islands, are only, to you, the old familiar red calico and beads of the clever trader, who has had dealings in every latitude, and knows just what to carry in the hold to please the simple native— I'm so afraid of this, that often and often I stuff my shining treasures back into their box, lest I should see you smiling at them!*
>
> *Well! And if you do? It's your loss, after all! And if you can't come into the room without my feeling all over me a ripple of flame, and if wherever you touch me, a heart beats under your touch, and if when you hold me, and I don't speak, it's because all the words in me seem to have become throbbing pulses, and all my thoughts are a great golden blur—why should I be afraid of you smiling at me, when I can turn the beads and calico back into such beauty—?*

On that Tuesday and Thursday and the following Tuesday as well, they
lunch together at faded restaurants far from the Faubourg where none
of their acquaintances would deign to dine. Places with worn doors
and broken shutters, and soft smiles shared across butcher-paper-
covered tables. Sometimes there are kisses in the vestibules of the
restaurants before they charge into the street to say good-bye with a
handshake. Edith has never known kisses like this. Deep and slak-
ing. Heart-shattering. She and Teddy never once kissed like this! She
relives these kisses late at night, drinking from them again and again as
if they were endlessly refilling carafes of intoxicating wine. A single sip
can make her drunk. Oh, the silken siren's call of the inside of Morton's
lips!

The restaurant on the second Tuesday is a sweet surprise: a tiny bistro
that smells of baking bread, with a view of the river and bunches of riot-
ously colorful silken flowers in flimsy vases on each table. They hold
hands beneath the table. Forget to eat. Quote poetry.

And then Morton says, "Today is the day."

"For what?" she asks, game and excited.

"To be alone together."

"Here in Paris?"

"That seems to be where we are."

"You're . . . you're serious?"

"Of course."

"But I . . . how would we do that?" Her voice is light but careful.

"I've hired a room."

"A room?"

"There is a small inn not far from here. It's why I chose this restaurant. We can eat quickly, go out the back door, walk from here, then
return, and Cook will merely think we've had an extended lunch."

"Morton, that's madness. We couldn't possibly."

"I need to be with you, Edith. I long to be with you. To touch you.
Don't you want to be alone for a few minutes . . . ?"

"I don't want this to be about sneaking through back alleys," Edith
says. "And a few minutes? Is that what we want? A few stolen *minutes*?

There's too much that's fine between us to sully it with that sort of behavior."

"That sort of behavior is what people do when they love each other," he says, his voice churlish.

"And speaking to me like that. Is that what people do when they love each other?"

"If you loved me, being alone together would be exactly what you'd want."

"But I'm a woman. I express my love in a different way."

"I told you: there are women who express their love exactly as I do. And if you are not that sort of woman . . . perhaps you are not the right woman for me."

Edith feels her lips begin to quiver. "Maybe I am *not* that sort of woman at all. I'm a woman who loves poetry and tender touches."

"And what makes you think there wouldn't be that as well?"

The waiter brings their food but neither of them takes more than a bite or two. The silence between them is painful and weighty. The windows of the restaurant are open and the newly warm air blows in with the scent of flowers; sunshine shot with gold spills onto their table. If only Morton were suggesting instead that they walk down the avenues with the horse chestnuts just beginning to flower! If only he wanted to celebrate the spring together, like lovers do, instead of suggesting something so crass, something so beneath her. When the waiter has cleared the dishes, and Edith has paid—for Morton does not even reach for his purse in the face of the bill—he refuses to go back with her in the car.

"I'll go out this way," he says. "I have somewhere I need to be."

"But Cook will drop you wherever you wish to go."

"Not today. I have to go pay for that room. Just because we're not using it doesn't mean I don't have to pay for it." How petty he sounds! He heads for the restaurant's back door. She follows him to the doorstep.

"Wait," she says.

"I don't like to be played," he says. "It's brutal."

"It's not my intention to play you. I'm nothing if not honest. We just need to find a way to make it work for both of us. I didn't ask you to hire a room."

"It's never going to work if you'll continue to be impossible," he says.

The word stings her like a slap. How much of her life has she spent trying to be reasonable? To think and act as rationally as a man? But for him to call her *impossible* . . . the way he would a cotton-brained woman . . .

He is a few steps down the street when he turns back to see her standing in the doorway, letting the alley's unsavory air into the restaurant. She hears a stir behind her.

"Fermez la porte, Madame!"

Closing the door behind her, she steps outside into the fetid alley, shivering without her wraps. He comes back to her and takes her shoulders in his hands.

"It's not too late to say yes."

She shakes her head, slowly and with certainty all the while, breathing in the damp scent of the restaurant's garbage.

He squints his eyes as though he's trying to understand her, but they're speaking different languages. He walks away.

"Morton," she whispers. Her voice drifts out into the street, full of questioning and mourning.

✦

She cannot eat. She cannot sleep. And worse, she finds no pleasure in writing. It is as though her pain and shame washes away her thoughts, her once phenomenal ability to lose herself in a story, in words. Every time she conjures up the word "impossible," she shivers, she freezes. In the middle of the night, she gets out of bed and goes to her letter-writing desk. Her hands shake as she writes:

> *Cher ami,*
>
> *Of the extent to which I have been tiresome and "impossible" and not worth giving another thought to, I am perfectly and oh so penitently aware—ne doutez pas! I "walk dreadfully illumined," believe me.*
>
> *On the practical side, as to your particular suggestion, it would be "the least risk," but possibly the greatest, to follow your plan, even if I could—as assuredly I should—finally overcome my reluctance.*

At least believe that I am unhappy, more than I can say, about it all.

And now when you "make a sign" I'll answer—whenever you make it. Only arrange somehow beforehand.

I'm not worthy to write to or think about. My only merit is that I'm unsparingly honest. But that's not a charm, alas!

I'll let you know the moment I am free. It might be Monday or Wed. Next Friday, Sat., Sunday are absolutely mine, en tout cas. I beg instant cremation for this.

E

Anna notices that Edith is not herself.

"Are you ill?" she asks as she drops new pages off for Edith to work from.

"Not at all," Edith says, hoping that a breezy tone will make it so.

"Well, you seem unhappy."

"I can't imagine why you think so."

Her dismissive tone still doesn't make Anna leave.

"You've been quite busy this spring," Anna goes on.

"No more than usual."

"I think quite certainly more than usual. . . ."

Edith looks up sharply.

"Do you have something to say to me?" she asks. Lucretia is long gone, but Anna's frown is as condemning as her former mistress's. "Do you?"

Anna goes white but shakes her head. Yet she's not ready to back down.

"It's Mr. Wharton I'm concerned about."

"We're all concerned about Mr. Wharton. You're *always* concerned about Mr. Wharton."

"He's worse this time, Edith. Last night I came to see him for a few minutes and he was saying terrible things. About how he no longer wished to live with his pain."

"I haven't heard him say that sort of thing."

"No, he might not say them to you. . . ."

"But he does to you?"

"He said if he were at The Mount and had his rifles near at hand . . ." Anna can barely set the words one before the other. Her voice, normally sweet and lilting, is heavy and slow.

Edith sets down her pen. "Tonni, he does it to get your attention. Like a child."

"Are you so certain? I've never heard him speak this way before."

"What should I do? What could I possibly do to help?" Edith snaps.

"He might see the doctor again. And you might spend less time with"—she clears her throat—"Mr. Fullerton."

Edith hears her breath catch. She takes in Anna's small, pinched face. Her once-soft lips are narrow now. Her reproachful gaze makes her look years older than Edith. Has Anna ever loved any man? Could she ever understand what Edith feels for Morton? How longing can alter a soul, change a woman forever? How a single kiss as passionate as his could change all expectations?

"What makes you think I spend time with Mr. Fullerton?" she asks in a measured tone.

"Cook told me," Anna says.

"Am I being spied on then?"

"Spies are emissaries of an enemy. Could you ever think of me as your enemy?"

Edith is surprised how boldly Anna stands before her.

"If you are asking me not to see Mr. Fullerton, who has become my dear friend, then yes, you are my enemy," she says.

"Edith . . . I have no right to ask anything of you. But Mr. Wharton is suffering. I believe he knows something. . . ."

"There is nothing to know."

Anna closes her eyes, clearly not believing what Edith is telling her.

"That will be all," Edith says. Has she ever spoken to Anna so curtly?

"All?" Anna asks with a gasp. She leaves the room, but her reprimand echoes for a long while after she's gone.

Anna is shaking when she leaves Edith. It is nearly four P.M. She can't imagine what to do with herself. She cannot go back to her room or even up to the servants' common room feeling the way she does. She thinks about visiting Teddy, but in his sensitized state, he might well notice her upset and she wouldn't know how to explain it. She stands against the wall in the main hall of the apartment and tries to breathe. She's not the sort of person who confronts others, having learned long ago it could be a dangerous way of life for a person as peripheral as she.

Instead, when she is upset she finds comfort in putting things in order, cleaning everything that isn't perfectly pristine. When she lived with Aunt Charlotte, she'd alphabetize all the old volumes by author, line up the spices from the most to least used, slap the lamp shades with a damp rag, forcing them to release their soft fur of dust. And most satisfying: she could kneel right down onto the hearth to scrub the tiles with soap and water and make them shine again.

"Anna's got cleaning fever," her cousins used to say. "Come to *my* room, Anna." She soon got smart enough to demand a penny or two for her services. Aunt Charlotte was mightily pleased that all the children had suddenly become so neat.

Now Anna goes down to the kitchen where the cook and a scullery maid are peeling vegetables, chattering in rapid-fire French.

"Where's Gross?" she asks. One by one, they shake their heads, make a moue, shrug their shoulders. So she opens up the butler's shelves where a forest of Vanderbilt silver shimmers: candlesticks, jam jars, ashtrays, serving pieces. On the bottom shelf is a fat glass tub of silver salve and a stack of rags. Anna chooses a particularly tarnished divided dish engraved with a flourished V, and, retrieving a handful of newspaper from the trash bin, she lays it out on the scrubbed kitchen table and begins her task. The cook and the maid stare at her as if she is mad. Rubbing the dish's voluptuous shoulders as hard as she can, the tarnish begins to melt. As the piece comes alive again, Anna finds it easier to breathe and not care that the Whartons' entire world has been turned upside down.

And what if Teddy *were* to die? Edith suddenly wonders as Anna leaves her room. What if he were to take his own life, suddenly, cleverly, even here in Paris? There are a thousand seemingly innocent poisons all around them. Or, she thinks excitedly, what if melancholia isn't the cause of Teddy's excruciating head pain, but a tumor the size of an orange! No one could possibly guess it's growing there. What if one moment from now he whispers her name and keels over and is released from his suffering! Edith is mortified to come upon these thoughts in her brain. Like fat toadstools growing on a manicured lawn. A spider slipping across a lacy pillow. What are these iniquities doing here? She doesn't really want her husband to die, does she? And yet she cannot shake the idea of how it would feel to be free of his misery. She would make a fine widow, the sort everyone would gladly invite out. How proud they'd feel for effecting a charitable act. "Poor Mrs. Wharton. She's been through so much. It wouldn't hurt to have her to dinner." They would call her brave. Applaud her unexpected good cheer. And she'd have endless time with Morton. Days and days to grow closer, to entwine like wisteria, and become one strong branch. For, after all, isn't that all they need? Time. Alone. Together.

Oh, these cloven thoughts. Not worthy of her. And yet they linger. They wind and wind, all around her heart. If she had gone with Morton to the inn that day, would that have been more depraved than what she is doing now: longing and pining and dreaming of the death of the person to whom she's pledged herself? Now she knows why she has closeted herself with books and secret dreams, caught in a cement of fear. How safe it was in that prison!

When Anna is feeling more like herself, lifted by the table of polished silver she's left behind, she slips quietly into Teddy's room to sit by his side for a while, allowing the nurse who's been hired to have a moment's respite.

"Miss Anna," he whispers when she settles down beside him. He reaches out for her hand, and she gives it. He has unusually delicate hands for a man. Elegant, but freezing cold. She folds both her hands around his and rubs softly.

"Help me to die," he whispers.

"I know you are suffering, Mr. Wharton. But you don't want to die. You have a great deal of life ahead of you."

"Edith doesn't love me anymore."

"Nonsense."

"You don't know," he whispers.

Anna shivers. "You mustn't speak like this."

"You don't know what I know," is all he says.

"Tell me all about the pain in your head. Maybe together we can make it go away."

"It feels like a horse is stepping on my brain. Right here." He points to the place between his brows, just above his fine nose.

Anna reaches out and touches the offending spot. She rubs it in a soft circle.

"Imagine my touch is erasing that pain," she says. "Just as you might erase a pencil error." Anna imagines absorbing his pain through her fingers—how she wishes she could. She knows she could deal with it better than he. She is so much stronger.

"You can't help me," he says. "No one can help me."

"I can. You have to let me. You have to give up your pain. Imagine just letting it go . . . up and out through my fingers."

He groans, and she almost wishes she could kiss his brow as a mother might. Or hold him in her arms, the way she would hold her young students when they wept.

"Let it go," she whispers. "Shhh, let it go, my friend. That's it. I can see the pain is lifting. Can you feel it?"

"Yes," he says, his voice rising. "It's better. Don't stop."

"I'm right here."

"Don't stop doing that."

"I'm not going to stop. We'll make you better. And then you can go to The Mount. Can you imagine that good mountain air? You're in the barn, in the room with all the saddles. The light burns golden through the window."

"Yes."

"The sunlight makes all the saddles glow. Choose one. Your favorite. The horses are waiting. Have you chosen one?"

"Yes."

"Take it down off the peg. And after your ride, you'll take the time to stop at the new pig house. Imagine it's built now. We'll visit all our lovely squealy fellows. They're so happy to see you. They've missed you. Lawton misses you."

"Anna, dearest Anna!"

"Shhh," she whispers, her heart beating sweetly. "Imagine being there. Let's make you better. Then we'll all go to the mountains together. It will be a wonderful summer. Cool and beautiful and fresh."

"We'll go together," he whispers.

In the morning, there is a petit bleu scrawled in Morton's familiar, clear hand.

> *Dearest,*
>
> *I accept your apology. Perhaps I should learn to be more tender with you, or more patient. But passion makes me a bounder. Still, I cannot blot out my desire for you. Perhaps if we weren't in Paris . . . would that make a difference for you? An inn far away in a wood somewhere, where we could lie abed and hear the cuckoos . . .*
>
> *I don't know when I can get away next to travel so far, or stay away for long. My sister is coming to Paris soon, and the bureau is hell-bent on paralyzing me with endless, unmanageable assignments. But the day will come.*
>
> *Yours with love,*
> *Morton*

"I've rarely seen anyone so deeply depressed, so wretched," Dr. Bastien tells Edith, drawing her aside into the library where the fire is crackling. "But I believe there's a reason for Mr. Wharton's misery. It's gout. In his head."

"Gout?"

"The pain. The noises. The moods. It's gout."

"I didn't know that was . . . possible. I thought because his father had a history of melancholy . . . He killed himself, you know. . . ."

"Perhaps his father had gout as well."

"Sit down, doctor, please." She points to Teddy's favorite leather arm-chair by the fire. How she hated finding Teddy there day after day. "Well, that's good news, then," she says. "It's something that will pass like the gout in his knee? He'll get better? I've never heard of it, gout in the head."

"It's rare and troublesome. It causes startling shifts in mood. Anger even. Sadness, like Mr. Wharton's. But it can be treated."

"How?"

"Rest, mostly. No alcohol. No heavy foods."

"The only thing that's helped him in the past has been taking the waters," Edith says. "When his knee was disastrous, it did the trick when nothing else made a whit of difference."

"It might be worth a try," the doctor says. "It certainly is known to help gout in the joints. Of course, it makes the condition worse for a short while, forces a flare-up, but by doing so, it may clear the system. . . ."

"He went to Hot Springs in the United States last time. He could go now." Edith tries to modulate the joy in her voice.

The doctor looks at her with a cocked head. Why is he staring at her that way?

"And you?" he says drily. "Of course you'll go along with him? He's far too ill to travel alone."

"If I don't go, a nurse will. Or Albert White, our butler. Or both."

The doctor nods. He clears his throat. "He said something to me I found a bit disturbing."

"Yes?"

The doctor blinks his pale spiky lashes closed, wets his lips, then opens his eyes with intention. "It could be the gout, of course. It might be making him delusional. But he said you . . . well, it's not my busi-ness . . . but he suggested you might no longer care for him as you once did. That you've been . . . distracted . . ."

"It's the gout. I can't imagine what he's thinking." Edith hears the snap of her voice. She stands. She feels herself burn. Her chest, her face. "Thank you so much for stopping by," she manages to say.

"Whether or not it's true," the doctor says, not even attempting to hide the disdain in his voice, "perhaps you should take care to prove otherwise. Mr. Wharton needs to feel secure. He needs to feel beloved. It's essential to his recovery. Do you understand what I'm saying?"

Edith tries to swallow, but hasn't a bit of saliva. She decides then and there they need to find a new doctor in Paris.

※

"Perhaps I should go with him," Anna says upon learning that Teddy is to be shipped out immediately.

"It's not necessary," Edith tells her. "You're not strong enough to help him with his needs. Albert will go. He trusts Albert. And we'll hire a nurse. Some young English-speaking girl will be quite happy to take a trip to Hot Springs."

"Of course," Anna says. She turns to the window so that Edith might not see her disappointment.

"I need you, Tonni. I'm deep into my book. I couldn't possibly manage without you at this stage."

"No, I understand. Will he be all right?" Anna asks, turning back to Edith. She knows she has tears in her eyes. "Will they really be able to help him? He's in so much pain. He's suffering so. . . ."

"The doctor says there's a chance. I know he's not getting better here in Paris. He despises Paris, as you know. What choice do we have?"

"No other choice."

"Well, then, stop looking like that," Edith snaps. Anna presses her handkerchief to her mouth and hurries out of the room.

"And please finish your typing. I need my pages," Edith calls out after her.

※

But even though Edith can't help feeling happy that Teddy is leaving, she is also not of one mind. The morning Teddy's trunks are hauled down to the motor and Teddy follows, wrapped in a heavy coat, his face white and swollen, his eyes distant and liquid, Edith feels a surprising sadness.

"I know you'll be happy in Hot Springs, dear," she tells him, taking his elbow, kissing his cheek. "Remember how it helped you last time?" She waits for his answer. "Dear, remember?"

Teddy barely looks at her, and doesn't say a word. She knows he doesn't want to go. Not without her. A good wife would wrap up her affairs and board the ship with her ailing husband. She would sit on a deck chair embroidering, making sure he ate his supper and felt beloved. She might be unhappy, but she would go. While Teddy has hardly been a good match for Edith, and has often been a trial, she is fully aware that there are far more malicious, difficult, selfish and unkind men in the world.

Maybe she is *not* a good wife. Maybe she has *never* been a good wife. Maybe she is no better than her mother, whom Edith has often thought of as a *terrible* wife. The notion haunts her. And Tonni's mute resentment doesn't help. Every time she steps into the room to return typed pages, to ask a question, to comment on the manuscript, Edith feels pierced by the arrow of her contempt.

But Edith knows what she must do. She cannot help Teddy. She is impatient with him. Unloving. Easily irritated. Just what Teddy doesn't need right now. What he does need is a cure. In the geo-heated waters, he once found what he sought: relief from pain. Perhaps he will find it again.

The disturbing sadness parts with him, though, and once he is gone, Edith cannot dismiss the giddy sense of freedom she feels. He is gone, and did not need to die to be out of her life. Now, she can spend more time writing, more time reading, thinking. She will no longer have to feel she is holding up the world with her very tired arms. And she can make plans without the sense that she is sneaking away. That's all she's wanted, isn't it, to not feel underhanded in spending time with Morton?

But, free at last to spend time with Morton, it's as though there's a conspiracy against them. As Morton predicted, his superior loads assignment after assignment on him, assignments that even swallow his weekends whole. Still, Edith is baffled that somehow, suddenly, Morton seems reluctant to see her. One day after a number of notes, begging him for his time, he writes that he has just an hour for a walk in the Tuileries. "Meet me at the Louvre," he writes, "just beneath the Diana of Goujon."

It's a damp day, though everyone is trying to pretend that spring is moving forward. Children run between the statues, nannies push prams, shivering in the breeze. She shivers too, wondering if he's coming at all.

When he finally arrives, rushing across the courtyard, she discovers a pale Morton, his face pinched, his eyes distant.

"Are you all right, dear?" she asks, gently touching his arm.

"It's not a good day," he says. She can see the energy crackle from him as from a Tesla coil.

"I'm sorry." She modulates her voice, the way she might with Teddy when he's out of sorts. "What's happened?"

"You couldn't possibly understand," he says. "We should go if we want any time in the Tuileries at all."

"Yes."

She listens to their footsteps echoing together on the gravel.

"Is my worldview so narrow?" she asks after a while.

"I don't know what you mean."

"You said I couldn't possibly understand what's bothering you. You might try me."

"This has nothing to do with you," he snaps.

"I'm sorry."

He shakes his head. "You wanted to see me?" he asks.

"I don't understand," she tells him. "You longed for nothing but time alone together and now that it's easier, you eschew it. And we're seeing each other less."

"Well, we're together now."

"Yes, but you're not talking to me."

"I'm talking to you. You hear my voice."

She shudders. "I know I've been tiresome. Who'd want to be with a tedious woman like me? And I'm aware how busy you are, how the bureau has tormented you for days. Is that it? Is that why you've been reluctant to commit more time?"

"I have my reasons," he says.

"I'm sure you do. Just share them, please."

"There are things you don't know about me. Pressures you can't possibly imagine."

"I can imagine them if you share them. It's not much to ask. I can support you better if you tell me."

"I wish I could." He doesn't look at her. His eyes have a glazed, far-off stare.

"I don't like it when you're being mysterious. I suppose some women might find it exciting. It merely makes me distrust you."

"Distrust me, then. . . ."

How could things have become so awfully derailed between them? If only she'd gone with him that day to the inn. Why is it so hard for her? Other women in love would have followed, would have lain down with him in those sheets, enjoyed his whispers and caresses.

"Is it your work?" she asks.

"I told you I don't want to discuss it."

A warm tear escapes and runs down her cheek. Perhaps it's over. Perhaps there's someone else already more willing than she. A younger woman, no doubt more beautiful. What woman wouldn't respond to his attractiveness, his magnetic charms? She barely suppresses a sob, and feels him glance her way.

"So," he says, suddenly falsely bright. "Tell me what you hear from Henry. He writes he's coming to visit!" Seeing her cry, he must pity her, and is trying to make small talk.

"Yes," Edith says, ruing the quaver in her voice. "He's coming. In May."

"Splendid. I wrote him about us, you know."

"You did? About *us*?"

"He was pleased. He said you should be treated with the sweetest care. He's right, of course."

She can hardly believe it. She looks at him and cannot read his face. If Morton has told Henry their secret, then he *must* have lasting feelings for her. She should be angry—having been exposed as a philanderer to the one person she most admires—but Morton says Henry's glad for them. In which case she's thrilled to include him in the conspiracy.

"He says he loves us both, and can absolutely see why we might love one another."

"Is that what you told him? That we love one another?" she asks, her voice brightening.

"More or less . . ."

"Which is it, more . . . or less?"

Morton just shakes his head and laughs, but she can see it's with aggravation.

"What did you tell him?"

"Well, I don't have a copy of the letter in my jacket, Edith. I suppose I told him we have feelings for each other."

"What sort of feelings? Like good friends, I suppose."

"Do you know you really can be vexing?"

"I'm not trying to be vexing. . . ."

"We're not even lovers. And yet you'd like to manage every word that's spoken about us. Everything we say to one another. As though we're characters in one of your books and you can rewrite the scene to suit yourself."

"That's unfair. I have a right to know what you're saying about us to Henry. . . ."

"I'm under a great deal of pressure. Don't you understand? I try to please you. Really I do. And yet there's nothing I can do to make you happy."

"You *do* make me happy."

"And that's why you're crying, I suppose."

Edith searches for a handkerchief in her purse and dabs her eyes. By now they have reached the carousel, and the colors and sounds of small children full of delight wound her more than soothe.

"I'm sorry. I don't mean to irritate you or wheedle or make things difficult. That's the last thing I want. I want to be valuable, to be supportive. I thought with Teddy gone now you would be happy. . . ."

"My upset has nothing to do with you," he says.

"Really?"

He looks down and his eyelashes glisten in the light. Then he raises his eyes with unexpected tenderness. His mouth softens. "I've been harsh. I'm sorry. There are things you couldn't possibly understand. Once they're settled, we'll be like we were. But better . . . because Teddy's gone."

She nods. "That's all I want."

"Have patience with me, my love," he says. "As I've had patience with you."

"Yes. Fair enough," she says before her voice trails off and the sadness feels once again like sacks of rocks weighing on each of her shoulders.

She doesn't hear from him at all for four days. And then Morton's sister, Katherine, arrives.

"Will you join us for dinner?" Morton bleus her one morning. "My sister wishes to meet you."

Edith is stunned and thrilled. If Morton is choosing to introduce her to his sister, the clouds of their previous meeting must have passed. They agree to dine at Gerald's, a restaurant with dark velvet booths and quiet carpets that reminds Edith of the theatre. Edith picks up the Fullertons in her motor. Morton gets into the car first, settling next to Edith. Oh, the feel of him, the warmth of him beside her! Quietly, she slips him a note.

He takes it, but, worrying over Katherine's entrance into the car, he holds it in his hand, between his index finger and middle finger like a cigarette, rather than sliding it into his pocket for later inspection.

Earlier in the day, after receiving his petit bleu, Edith had thought it important that she bridge the gap between their miserable meeting and this dinner. Now she wishes she hadn't bothered. For whatever reason, she hadn't imagined that slipping it to him would have been so awkward.

> *Dearest* [she wrote on this, her third attempt],
>
> *Are things better now? I have been worried far too much about you since our last meeting. I was reluctant to write. But when you told me you wanted to meet for dinner tonight, it stirred my courage like embers in a fire. I do hope you've forgiven me for whatever trespasses I've committed.*
>
> *Your E*

When Katherine has fully gathered her skirts into the motor and Cook has closed her door, Edith leans over to see her. Tiny and beautiful with dark wavy hair, which she wears pinned up in front but loose around her shoulders, she seems more like a child than a woman. Her face strikes Edith as an Italian cameo. Perfect and unlined with a sweet, mysterious smile.

"My sister Katherine," Morton proclaims. He is more than a little proud of his sister, presenting her to Edith like a decorated cake. "Two great women meet."

Edith reaches over and shakes Katherine Fullerton's tiny hand.

"I hope you are enjoying Paris?"

"I love Paris," Katherine says. "I'd be happy to make it my home." She glances over at Morton with a knowing smile. Has he offered to have her come to Paris for good?

As they are getting out at Gerald's, exiting on Edith's side, Morton, perhaps having forgotten he was holding her note, drops it on the motorcar floor, and Katherine says, "Oh!" right before she steps on it and picks it up. Thank God Edith didn't write "Morton" on the outside of the envelope.

"Is this yours, Mrs. Wharton?" she asks, holding it out as she slides from the car, her blue eyes wide and innocent. "I'm awfully sorry I stepped on it."

"Oh dear. It certainly is." Edith feels the vein in her neck pulse with warning. She should be angry at Morton for carelessness, yet she finds even this pleases her. Perhaps he *wants* Katherine to know that they are more than friends. She tucks the note into her purse, wondering if she should give it to him at all.

Later, Katherine announces over soup in a voice as soft and melodious as a girl in her teens, "My brother says wonderful things about you, Mrs. Wharton. In practically every letter. He sent me *The House of Mirth* last year and I was quite taken with it."

Edith looks fondly over at Morton, but he is too rapt with Katherine to share her smile.

"I've even passed the book on to other women at Bryn Mawr. There was a great deal of excitement about it. It's rare to find a book by a woman. But to find one so accomplished! It's presently everyone's favorite book at the college. And to think you're friends with Will! It's so clever of him to acquire such illustrious friends."

Edith is amused how formally she speaks. Though her voice is soft, she carries more authority than most young girls. Morton said she is a lecturer at Bryn Mawr! Edith tries to imagine how her life would have been if *she* had had the opportunity of such a notable job and so much freedom. Edith can't help being impressed.

She is surprised how physically protective Morton seems of Katherine, touching her blue silk sleeve often during the meal, especially when she says something he deems clever. Katherine clearly adores him, glancing over often for approval. "Don't you think, Will?" she asks. And yet she is brilliant. Sharper than almost any woman Edith has known. She meets Edith measure for measure in discussions of Dante and Meredith. She writes poetry. She teaches at a university. She has decided to write a novel, which she has already outlined. She has hands as delicate and white as porcelain. Edith wonders why just sharing a meal with Katherine should give her a jealous ache. Maybe it is simply Katherine's shining youth, and the aura of possibility she wears like a halo.

"Mother says that Will is not living up to his potential at the *Times*," Katherine says in a semi-teasing voice over dessert. "She thinks if he came back to Boston, he could be a professor at Harvard. And then she could see him more often."

"Harvard!" Edith says, surprised.

"I could never leave Paris," Morton says flatly.

"Charles Elliot Norton would vouch for him. He'd be employed immediately. He told mother so. Especially now with all of Will's worldly experience. He's always been fond of Will."

"Is it something you've considered?" Edith asks, bewildered.

"It's something that Mother and Katherine have cooked up to control me," Morton says. "And nothing more. Now don't go spreading unfounded rumors," he tells Katherine. She sighs and pushes her mouth out into a pretty pout.

"Katherine thinks if she keeps saying it aloud in front of others, it will come true," Morton says. "I'm afraid that would be a *different* Morton Fullerton."

"A happier one, perhaps," Katherine says.

"A miserable one with a very large belly stuffed by motherly love and sisterly intrusion. No thank you."

"Mother says Will is the most stubborn Fullerton in the history of all Fullertons. And you should meet Father!" Katherine says.

"Please stop quoting Mother, or I shall have to leave the table and go to the bar and chat up the barkeeper," Morton counters.

"Because he's the eldest, he's very spoiled," Katherine confides in Edith.

She laughs. "I can see that," she says, but Morton doesn't look like he's in on the joke.

✿

The next morning on Edith's breakfast tray is a petit bleu.

> *Dearest,*
>
> *Thank you for being so thoughtful as to meet my sister. She can speak of nothing but you. Was there something in that note I should see?*
>
> *Yrs. MF*

✿

"I met Fullerton's sister," Edith tells Anna. Maybe if she begins to speak of him, Anna will see him less as a threat. "As lovely a girl as you can imagine. And do you know she teaches at Bryn Mawr? She can't be more than in her early twenties, and yet she has a job teaching at a college."

"Is she terribly brainy?" Anna asks.

"Oh yes, but not at all worldly. Rather naïve, I think. But Morton is so proud of her. His whole face lights up when he speaks of her accomplishments. Can you imagine, Tonni, if I'd been able to teach college? Or you? If such a thing had been possible when we were young? I wonder what our lives would have been like."

Anna nods. "It's hard to imagine."

"Ah, if I were younger," Edith says. "I'd do it all over again. Every part of my life, except for the writing, of course."

NINE

SPRING 1908

The following weekend, with Katherine on her way to a convent in Tours to work on her novel "without distraction," Edith finally has her full day with Morton: a motor trip to Montfort l'Amaury. It starts out like many April days, the Paris streets veiled in rain, but by the time they reach Montfort, the sun is brilliant. Leaving Cook far below in the motorcar, Edith and Morton take the stone path up the hill to explore the ruin of an old castle built in 996. They laugh at how winded they soon are, trudging up the rocky lane.

"Two old folks on holiday," Morton says.

"Must . . . see. . . . the . . . sights!" she pants. At the top, they find themselves deliciously alone. The castle towers catch the April wind with a harmonic whistle. Early flowers, violets and woodcock orchids ruffle the bases of the rustic old structures. He picks a fat fragrant violet and slides it through the buttonhole of her shirtwaist. She touches it with delight.

"I've never been here," he says.

"It's wonderful," she declares, knowing that anything would seem wonderful to her today. All the clouds between them seem to have parted. And the sweetness has blessedly returned. They walk the perimeter of the ruin. Morton holds Edith's hand as she balances along a line of mortared stones that once were part of a wall. Ducking under an old doorway, they find themselves within a reverberating silo-like expanse.

"Hallooo there," he calls.

"Hallooo there," she repeats.

"Ah, see," he laughs. "The perfect echo." He laughs aloud and indeed his laughter is multiplied. They peer up into the furnacelike structure, and as their eyes adjust, they see that windows from upper stories send down faint beams of light, but not enough to warm them. Edith shivers. He takes her into his arms.

"Mine," he whispers and holds her against his chest. She can feel his heart beating against her own through his clothing. His hands slip beneath her wraps and study the line of her waist, then ride back up to her bosom, cupping each breast. A sensation so exquisite it makes her gasp.

"Ah, so there *is* someone alive in there," he whispers. He pushes her stole from her shoulders and it drops carelessly to the stones, but she is hardly aware, focused on his hands, which radiate a special power. He tweaks her nipples through the fabric of her bodice. Blood rushes to them, and she knows they are changing form, blooming like flowers, pressing forward into his teasing fingers. Not once in her life has she ever felt this quickening, this ripening, this surge of feeling. That night in the library with Walter, she felt something. A longing. But this is so much more. This is what women know that she has never known! This is what Anna de Noailles celebrates! No one has touched her like this. No one.

"Don't think," he whispers. "Just feel."

"Morton . . ."

He brings his lips to hers, parting them with his tongue. Feeling. Just feeling. Not thinking! She is drawn to search the soft insides of his lips with her own tongue. She can hardly bear the satiny sweetness she finds within. They have kissed deeply before, but she has never given back. How extraordinary it feels to give! At last, to *want*! He sprinkles light kisses along her neck, brushes her ear with his lips, sending fire all through her.

"This is what we've been waiting for," he says, having trouble finding his breath. "What we've needed." He unbuttons her shirtwaist. As he does, the violet falls. She thinks to stop him and rescue it. But no. He is worrying the layers of her clothing. Like peeling leaves from a cabbage! The lace-encrusted corset cover. The tiny-buttoned chemise.

"But here, Morton?" she asks. "What if someone else arrives?"

"Just this," he says. "Let me. I must . . ."

He pushes her farther into the darkness. The walls give off a smell of old smoke and damp earth. Finally freeing one breast into his hands, he holds it like a precious treasure. How round and fruitlike it looks in the dusky light, cupped by the elegant beringed fingers of both his hands, her nipple a perfect coral rosebud. He leans down and kisses it and accepts the hard nub into his mouth, his tongue caressing round and round. A sound leaks from her throat, so sudden and unexpected she wonders if it's coming from someone else.

He lifts out her other breast, still caressing the first. If he hadn't, she would have done it for him. How hungry she is to have him kiss it too, to feel his tongue anoint and tease her nipple. More than twenty years of privation, of dull despair melt from her, leaving her throbbing and damp and aching.

And then she hears voices. Coming up the hill, it seems.

"No!" she utters.

"No?" he asks.

"Someone's coming!"

Laughter, voices. Quite a few voices. She turns from the doorway and struggles to hide her breasts beneath her chemise, to resettle her corset, to button her lacy *cache-corset*, to fasten her shirtwaist. She wants to cry.

When she turns back, Morton looks mussed and annoyed. He pulls a cigarette from his silver case and sets it between his lips, watching her. His face is blotched with color. She feels as though her own lips are burning. She pats at her hair, uncertain how she must look.

"Maybe they won't come in."

Morton shrugs. "What if they do? You look fine. You're not a marked woman yet."

Edith shivers and retrieves her stole from the ground, shakes it off. And she lifts the violet. Somehow in their moment of passion, it's been stepped on. The purple petals have been crushed to grapey juice. She drops it and watches it fall limply to the stones. She is struck by how distant Morton seems. Having felt like one single being for a glorious moment, she can hardly bear the distance! If only he would touch her. Or take her hand. Or smile. Instead, he offers her a cigarette, and she accepts it, finding comfort in the distraction. The shivering inside doesn't want to stop, even with the hot, calming draw of the smoke.

He must note it because he gestures for her to follow him outside. "Come on," he says. "Let's sit in the sun."

They step out of the same door they entered what seems like hours ago. Sunlight is flooding the grassy space beyond the castle, warming the castle walls. Morton settles onto a white stone doorstep polished by a thousand years of footfall and holds out a hand for Edith to join him. In the distance they see their intruders, a band of local boys, laughing and slapping each other's shoulders, tossing stones down the hill and at each other. Perhaps they never would have entered the castle structure after all. Edith's heart is still beating as though she were in the path of a train. She feels she will never be the same.

Knee to knee, hand in hand—oh, how happy she is that he's taken her hand—they bask in the piping sun.

"Tell me," he says finally. "Are you happy?" He does want to be close. He *does* have feelings for her! How could she have doubted?

"I didn't know I could feel this way," she whispers. Morton brings her fingers to his lips and kisses them.

"It's just the beginning," he says. "Maybe those fellows are right. Maybe one *can* awaken desire in a woman. I thought it a myth, like unicorns."

"I am your unicorn," she says.

Glancing at his watch, he frowns. "Time seems to have gone mad," he says. "It's nearly one. Aren't you hungry?" She nods. "We'll eat somewhere in town, then walk in the forest before we go back."

"What's it called? La Forêt de Rambouillet? We could get lost in the forest like Hansel and Gretel. I wish we never had to go back."

"I wish that every night in my dreams," he says. "Come on. Even unicorns must eat."

If Edith has known joy, it has never felt like this. For this sensation is a mixture of ecstasy and misery she could never have foreseen. She tries to shake off the latter, but it simply won't retreat. Having tasted just a sip of the nectar, Edith is ever more aware that soon it will be gone. It is early April. By the end of May, she will be on an ocean liner heading to the United States. But she *must* enjoy the journey. It is all she has, all she may ever have.

A note comes almost every day now. It is brought in on my breakfast tray with other letters, and there is the delicious moment of postponement, when one leaves it unopened while one pours the tea, just in order to savourer longer the joy that is coming! Ah, how I see in all this the instinctive longing to pack every moment of my present with all the wasted, driven-in feeling of the past. How I hoard and tremble over each incident and sigh! I am like a hungry beggar who crumbles up the crust he has found in order to make it last longer! . . . And then comes the opening of the letter, the slipping of the little silver knife under the flap (which one would never tear!), the first glance to see how many pages there are, the second to see how it ends, and then the return to the beginning, the breathless first reading, the slow lingering again over each phrase and each word, the taking possession, the absorbing of them one by one, and finally the choosing of the one that will be carried in one's thoughts all day, making an exquisite accompaniment to the dull prose of life. . . . Sometimes I think the moment of reading the letter is the best of all—I think that till I see you again, and then, when you are there, and my hands are in yours and my soul is in my hands, then what gray ghosts the letters all become! . . .

Edith knows that happiness is as rare and slight and fragile a thing as a Bernardaud teacup. One unfortunate tap can shatter it to useless shards, never to be drunk from again. For years, she's sipped life from an ugly earthenware bowl. There was no pleasure in drinking from it. But no matter how often she dropped it, it did not break. In some ways, that was easier, for there was nothing at risk. Now that she's held such blinding bliss in her hand, can she ever go back to supping from that heavy, ugly vessel?

After her honeyed Saturday with Morton, Edith wakes from the dream of such rare happiness giddy and oddly nervous, lost in all but the simplest conversations, unable to read a word on a page (except for his gorgeous, wonderful letters—he writes full letters now, not just petits bleus), or work on her own writing with any momentum. Her writing time is consumed by lingering moments of blind staring, trying to recapture the rapture of their prismatic day together. And as the days of the week pass, she finds her joy exacts a toll.

> I am a little humbled, a little ashamed, to find how poor a thing I am, how the personality I had molded into such strong firm lines has crumbled to a pinch of ashes in this flame! For the first time in my life I can't read. . . . I hold the book in my hand and I see your name all over the page! I always thought I would know how to bear suffering better than happiness, and so it is. . . . I am stupefied, anéantie. . . . There lies the profound difference between a man and woman. What enlarges and enriches life for one eliminates everything but itself for the other. Now and then I say to myself, "Je vais me ressaisir"—mais saisir quoi? This pinch of ashes that slips through my fingers? Oh, my free, proud, secure soul, where are you? What were you to desert me like this. . . .

Anna, also, feels unmoored. Without Teddy to care for, worry about, she too has lost her focus. She can envision his face as she types Edith's business letters, as she walks the streets of Paris. She carries this emptiness wherever she goes. It becomes a bubble through which she sees a faded world. The gay cafés of Boulevard St. Germain and the beautiful quiet parks near Les Invalides are softened and altered by this sad gray lens. She waits anxiously each day to hear if he has landed in the United States, whether he has arrived at Hot Springs and if the warm, flowing waters have given him relief at last. She even thinks of writing him herself. To remind him why he must get better: so that he can be there for the unveiling of the swine house at The Mount. So he can introduce her to dear fat Lawton.

Once long ago when Edith wasn't well and she was in Europe, Teddy wrote Anna a letter. He addressed her as Miss Anna. His handwriting was simple and blocky like a child's. His spelling was execrable. She remembers he told her that he was concerned because Edith "don't seem like herself these days," utilizing for one of the first times that glib, ungrammatical way of speaking that irks her. That letter sits in a box on the top shelf of a cupboard in the house on Park Avenue, where Anna has stowed a cache of Edith's letters too. She wishes she had Teddy's short missive now, so she could trace her finger along the curls of his words to her.

These days, when she asks Edith if she has heard anything about Teddy, she finds her in a softer and more amiable mood. Edith smiles at Anna more and her voice is light and generous, as it used to be, long ago when she was a wonderful, odd little girl. In those sweet years, Edith thought Anna the greatest authority on life and literature, the only one who truly understood her. Anna wishes she could understand Edith now. But how can she when nothing Edith does makes sense? When she chooses a bounder like Fullerton over a good-hearted, loyal, upstanding man like Teddy Wharton? And Edith's feelings for Fullerton can't be ignored. A woman in love is an ostentatious thing. If Anna is in Edith's room when her breakfast tray arrives, Edith's hazel eyes alight on the note that always seems to accompany her breakfast like a hawk landing on a mouse. She never opens his letters in front of Anna, but Anna knows it's her cue to excuse herself, for from the moment the letter arrives, Edith seems to go deaf.

"Do you think she's gotten herself *entangled* with him?" Gross asks Anna with a look of dread when Cook tells them Edith is having lunch with Fullerton again. "I mean *in the worst sort of way*. She seems utterly changed."

"I wish it wasn't so," Anna tells her, biting her lip.

"Can't you talk to her, warn her?" Though she is the more outgoing of the two, Gross is never one to confront her mistress.

"What could I possibly say more than I have said? What?"

They both know through Cook that Edith and Fullerton have gone on an outing to some far-flung locale and disappeared for hours by themselves. And there are those lunches a few times a week. If Edith weren't acting so fluttery, Anna might not pay attention to it. She's always had male friends—from the great Henry James to much younger fellows with keen eyes and nervous laughs. But this one is different. Anna's known Edith too long not to be sure of it.

One day, after luncheon, a letter arrives for Anna from Kate Thorogood, Sally Norton's housekeeper. Anna looks forward to Kate's monthly missives. They are always newsy, wise, full of quotes from poetry and thoughtful sentences. When Anna and Edith visit Sally Norton at Shady Hill, Anna spends as much time with Kate as possible.

Kate's letter tells of worry over Sally's bronchitis and the miserable wet weather they've had to bear this spring in Cambridge. She writes of people that Anna's been introduced to in the past, and then, surprisingly, her letter mentions Morton Fullerton.

> Since Miss Norton has said that Mrs. Wharton is now great friends with Will Fullerton, I suppose you know about his odd engagement. It's rather the talk around here. At first, I heard through my friends that there was quite an uproar in his family over it. He went down to Bryn Mawr last summer and just up and asked the girl to marry him. But now his family is telling everyone that a marriage will soon take place, and his mother is planning his wedding breakfast.
>
> The facts of it are rather more than I can fathom. I mean, to be engaged to one's own sister! Perhaps I'm just not modern enough, but it makes me gasp. Of course, she is not really his sister but his cousin. Still, they were raised together as siblings (as you and I were with our cousins) and I can't help but find it an outrage. Can you imagine marrying one of your cousins? Do you know if Mrs. Wharton is invited to the wedding?

The letter begins to shake in Anna's hand and Anna feels as though she's holding a lit explosive. Her heart is racing, her mouth is so dry she can't swallow. Could it possibly be true? Fullerton engaged . . . and to his sister! Why, just a few weeks ago Edith dined with Fullerton's sister, didn't she? Edith and she talked about how remarkable it was that the girl taught college . . . at Bryn Mawr. But she didn't say a word about an engagement. Could she possibly know?

Anna heads straight for the kitchen, which, happily, is empty. Too late for luncheon, too early for dinner preparation. Rather than seek out Catherine, who will only laugh at her when she tells her what she has in mind, she heads straight toward the silver cupboard and pulls out the largest, most tarnished tray she can find. Anna thinks it must be ten pounds. Its repoussé rim boasts oranges and apples, artichokes and corn cobs. And in between them are crevices as deep as a woman's little finger is long: all nearly black. The V in the center is elaborately carved. Anna scoops the tarnish cream in a great greedy blob onto her cloth, spackles it onto the V and begins to polish. She rubs so hard her wrist soon burns.

If she tells Edith that Fullerton is engaged to his sister, Edith will think it just a clumsy plot to discredit Fullerton. Because who could ever believe such madness?

Eliot Gregory would probably love to be the bearer of such shocking gossip. Let someone else break the information to Edith.

Anna stands in front of Edith at her writing desk, her hands clasped, feeling all energy and intent drain from her. When she came into the study, Edith was writing a letter, and Anna's intrusion made her turn it upside down on her desk with childlike furtiveness.

"What on earth is the matter with you, Anna?" Edith asks. "Just say what you've come to say." Her voice is not harsh, her eyes not truly angry. But her brusque words send Anna even deeper into the morass of silence that provoked them.

"There's something I need to tell you," she says to Edith. "But maybe it would be best to come back later." She steps backward toward the door.

"Is this about Teddy?" Edith asks. "Because I've heard from him, just this morning. He's arrived in Hot Springs."

"Is he there at last? I'm so glad." She feels a breathtaking weight lifted from her, imagining Teddy bathed in warm, soothing waters.

"Of course, there's no word yet, but I have great hopes they can help him."

"Oh, I dearly hope so. He's so despondent, in so much pain."

"Yes, so he tells me again and again," Edith says. It hurts Anna to hear how dismissively she speaks of her husband. "What did you come to say, Tonni?"

Again, this morning, Edith didn't leave Anna a single page to type. Not one. And Gross said she didn't touch a bite of her luncheon. She looks high in color too. Keyed up.

"I've heard something," Anna finds the courage to say. "About Mr. Fullerton. I didn't want to tell you, but I decided you shouldn't . . . wouldn't want to hear it from others."

Edith's eyes fly to Anna's face. "What about him?"

"I got a letter from Kate Thorogood. Do you remember her?"

"Kate . . . Thorogood?"

"Miss Norton's housekeeper."

"Oh, your friend Kate. She wrote about Mr. Fullerton?"

"She said that he's . . ." Anna looks at her shoes, which need polishing. When she is done with this misery, she can polish her shoes. Then scrub the shoe polish from her fingernails. She would like to scrub the very skin from her hand. Edith will hate her when she reveals what she knows. Why did she embark on this terrible path?

"He's what?"

"He's engaged to be married."

"What?" Edith bursts out laughing. "Mr. Fullerton? That's absurd. To whom? To whom does Miss Thorogood think he's engaged?"

"To his sister."

Every ounce of color drains from Edith's cheeks.

"That is *not* a funny joke."

"I didn't think so either. His sister was adopted by his family. She's a cousin, in fact. And last summer when he was at Bryn Mawr, he asked her to marry him."

"That's . . . why, that's impossible! He came to The Mount right after Bryn Mawr. He didn't breathe a word." Edith's nostrils flare.

"His parents objected at first. But now they are telling everyone there will be a wedding. Kate asked if—seeing as you're such good friends with Mr. Fullerton—you're invited to the wedding."

"There's a misunderstanding."

"I hope so. It did seem odd to me. . . ."

"Odd? It's grotesque!"

"I was just going to write her back and say there had been some mistake. But I thought I should speak to you first, in case you knew something."

"If he were engaged, I'd know," Edith says. Her voice is cold with confidence, but her eyes betray her. They dart about the room, full of question.

"I'll go now," Anna says.

"You don't like Mr. Fullerton, do you? Why?"

"I hardly know him."

"But you've already told me that you don't approve of our relationship."

"I merely said that it would be good if you spent less time with him—when Mr. Wharton was here, it upset him."

"The simple truth is," Edith's hazel eyes narrow and, when they catch the light, flash yellow. "The simple truth is you don't want me to be happy because *you're* not."

Edith could not have hurt Anna more if she'd slapped her across the face. The words hang in the air like gunpowder, sulfurous, volatile. Anna tries to find her composure, but the pain addles her. And when she does speak, each word comes out on its own, slowly, devastatingly. "All I've ever wanted is happiness for you," Anna says.

When Edith was little, Anna called her Herz. Heart, in German. Edith used to sign her letters to Anna "Herz." All these years, Edith has held Anna's heart. But where is Edith's heart?

"And you think my happiness will ever come from an imbecile like Teddy Wharton?"

"Please! Please don't call him that. You can't see who he is anymore. You've forgotten how good he is."

"I can't bear being with a man as flat as a piece of paper. . . ."

"If you just gave him some sign you still loved him . . ."

"I never loved him."

Anna gasps. "Edith . . . you don't mean that."

"I mean it," she says, her voice so icy it wraps crystals around Anna's heart. Anna can taste tears on her tongue. Her throat burns. It is the kind of silenced inward weeping only a woman who lives a tangential life could know. Poor, dear Teddy!

Anna takes a deep breath and tries to find the even tone she used to use when her students provoked her. "He loves you. He counts on you. You made a vow. You have a responsibility. If we all pursued nothing but happiness, the world would crumble. The ill, the old would be alone with no one to care for them. We'd be adrift in a sea."

"Look at me," Edith says. "Do you see me before you? Well, it's a miracle, because I've been dead for years," Edith says. "Like a ghost. I've been snuffed out by my sense of duty toward Teddy Wharton. I am finally tasting life. How can you ask me to spit it out?"

Anna sits down in the chair by the desk, singed by Edith's incendiary gaze. What can she say? What can she do? She is not equal to the task. "Is Fullerton the sort of man you can trust?" she asks softly after a while.

"He wouldn't lie to me. That's why I know he's not engaged to anyone. I've never met a man more gentle, kind or giving. You don't know what I know about him."

"No," Anna says. "I don't know anything about him." She stands shakily, starts toward the door, then stops. "You should ask him," she says, turning. "Ask him about the engagement. He should know what people are saying about him, even if it's not true."

"Please go," Edith says. "I want to be alone for a while."

Suddenly Anna can't wait to be out of the room. The air in the hall is cool, inviting.

"Tonni?"

"Yes?" She turns back one more time, hoping for an apology, a softening word. Instead she sees that Edith's chin is tilted upward, her face as defiant as ever.

"I deserve to be happy," Edith says. "Even you can't tell me I don't."

Anna stares at her for an icy moment before she pivots and escapes.

Dearest, can I see you in the morning around 9:30? I don't wish to be a bother, but perhaps I can be of use in carrying you to your ministère and we can talk en route. Do say honestly if this is inconvenient.

E

Edith is disappointed to see that Morton is not in one of his better moods. She knows immediately, even before he speaks. His mouth looks pleasant enough beneath the dark arc of his mustache, but the appearance of two parallel grooves between his brows spell annoyance. She's sorry to catch sight of them now.

"It was good of you to let me see you," she begins in her most cheerful voice.

"What was the hurry?" he asks.

"I didn't think you'd mind a ride to the *Times*."

"It throws me off. I'm used to the walk. It's my time to sort myself out, to think."

"I'm sorry then . . . I never want to be a bother. . . ."

"I doubt you wanted to see me just to provide a conveyance."

He told me he's never good in the morning, she thinks. I should have waited. Why didn't I wait?

"No. It's just that I've . . . well, I've heard something . . . ," she says. "Something very odd about you . . . And I wanted . . . I needed to ask you about it."

"Go on. . . ." There's malice in his voice. He is not so beautiful when his expression is pinched with annoyance.

"I heard that you're engaged to be married." Edith watches his face carefully, and what she sees unnerves her: his mouth twitches, he swallows before he speaks and he doesn't even break into a smile, as she expected.

"And who am I supposed to be engaged to?" he asks carefully.

"Katherine."

He closes his eyes for a brief moment. As one might when confronted with one's worst fears. And then his face completely transforms, and the change is even more unnerving because it is so patently false, so nonchalant.

"To Katherine? That's absurd."

"Is it?"

"Where did you hear this?"

"It hardly matters. It came from someone who knows your family in Massachusetts."

"You know how news gets perverted as it travels. . . . Didn't you play that whisper game as a child?"

"I heard that Katherine's not really your sister."

He licks his lips. "Well, that's true. At least the gossips got that right."

"But she is your cousin?"

"Yes."

"Your first cousin?"

"Yes. Am I on trial?"

"I'm sorry. I don't mean to harangue you."

"Then stop."

He crumples his leather gloves in his hands. And she sees how a pulse twitches in his forehead. She knows he can't wait to get out of her motor. What will happen now? Edith wonders. Why did she even ask him about Katherine? Just the thought of her young, breezy beauty gives Edith a twinge. But what if he does have feelings for Katherine? It's not as though Edith's ever expected him to marry *her*, even if she were to free herself from Teddy. She's never imagined she'd be lucky enough to have Morton as her lover for more than a blink of an eye. As long as he wants her, pursues her, isn't that enough? And how delicious it's been. Will their beautiful connection now be snapped like an electric wire in a storm, sparks flying? The truth is overrated, she thinks.

They've reached the building where the *Times* keeps its offices. In the light rain, people on the street have popped open their umbrellas. Through the motorcar window, she watches a parade of them bob along the sidewalk like mourners on their way to a funeral.

Morton touches her hand before he gets out of the car. It should be a comforting touch, but his palm is cold and damp.

"Don't spoil what we have," he says.

When he is gone, she feels grief stricken, foolish, doubtful.

"I'd like to go back home," she tells Cook.

"No errands this morning?" he asks. "I thought you wanted to stop at the bank."

"No errands."

Anna thinks a great deal about happiness after her talk with Edith. And it strikes her as a foreign topic, for it's something she hasn't expected for years. When she was young and just a guest in Aunt Charlotte's house, she deemed happiness something for other people. Her cousins were clearly beloved even though Aunt Charlotte and Uncle Heinrich were stiff and strict. And other children at school with bows in their hair and pet dogs and summer plans all seemed to have a little golden key that opened a door to happiness along their way. When she became a governess, she noted the blooming cheeks of her little charges, how oblivious they were to the dangerous world in which we all reside. They knew they would always be protected with trust funds and family jewels, and significant plans for their futures.

Sometimes in those days, Anna tried to imagine that her life would turn out like Jane Eyre's. Back then, she could see herself as the little orphaned governess who finds love and a new life in her job. But Anna's employers were never handsome, mysterious gentlemen with mad wives in the attic. Just bored married men with tired eyes. Her own happiness came from the offspring of these men, their unspoiled delight at discovering new books, new ideas. And no child ever made her as happy as Edith did.

She doesn't believe she's ever been as close to the precipice as she now feels. Teddy gone. Edith angry at her. She wonders, just as she did the night she was mortified after telling Teddy she would have been proud to have him as a husband, whether she will be orphaned again and have to begin anew at the age of sixty. She imagines ringing a doorbell at a strange house and saying, "I'm here to apply for the position of governess."

Once more, the house is in an uproar, because the lease at 58, rue de Varenne, is nearly up. Edith will soon be moving to Harry's cramped townhouse on the Place des États-Unis. At first, Harry said he had business in Germany and wouldn't be there at all, but at the last minute, his trip was canceled. So because Harry and his staff will be present, Edith is sending Gross and White home.

"It was crowded enough last year. And it would only be worse this year," she announces to Gross. "We needn't make the same mistake twice." Gross is happy to be returning to Park Avenue. She hasn't been feeling well, and a few weeks of rest are just what she might wish for.

But Anna has no doubt *her* services will be required. After all, Edith will be in the Sixteenth Arrondissement for more than six weeks. She will want to keep writing, although there has been little to show for her efforts lately. Edith is still asking not to be disturbed in the mornings, but only a few half-written pages are left on the floor outside her door these days, when before there were almost more than Anna could type. If this were the only effect of Morton Fullerton on Edith's life, it would be enough for Anna to resent him.

So Anna is stunned when Edith calls her in one afternoon to tell her, "Tonni, perhaps it's best if you go back to Park Avenue with the rest of the staff. There's no need to put you through the cramped accommodations at Harry's. I'm even asking Harry to put up Henry James, which I wish I didn't have to do, but what other choice do I have? Harry's happy to have him, but there will be no room at all."

"Edith . . ." She is momentarily speechless, then composes herself. "I'd be willing to stay in the smallest room in the house, a broom cupboard, if you could find use for me. Surely, there's correspondence to attend to?"

"I can write my own letters for a while," Edith's voice is breezy but oddly strained. She shuffles the letters on her desk, not once raising her face to Anna.

Edith has never sent Anna away before. In fact, if anything, she likes to complain when Anna—as was the case last summer—is gone for reasons of her own. And though her explanation of why the change in plans appears thoughtful, Anna can smell fraudulence.

"Has a reservation been booked for me?" she asks.

"I've told White to book your passage."

"I see."

Edith glances up at last. "I think it's best," she says, catching Anna finally with frank eyes. "Don't you?"

TEN

SPRING 1908

On Edith's first full day at Harry's, Anna de Noailles is scheduled to visit at 3:30 for tea. All spring, Edith's been inviting
her to come to the Rue de Varenne, but despite their best
plans, she never did make it. Now Edith will have to
entertain La Comtesse at her brother's, which is less than ideal. Overdecorated, over-Americanized, the house embarrasses Edith. Especially in
light of the sleek Bohemian sumptuousness of de Noailles's own manse.

And Edith feels both overexcited and miserable. Time has been a
loudly ticking clock. Amidst the move to Harry's, Anna's apparent sadness at being sent away and Henry's upcoming arrival, Edith has had no
room to reflect, no time to breathe. She is giddy with the passion Morton
has unearthed in her, yet once again he has been withdrawn: his notes
are short, his *Times* assignments longer. Edith blames Anna for sharing
the news about Katherine. And she blames herself. Why did she ask him
about it at all? Even if Morton were—and how could he be?—engaged
to Katherine, would Edith feel differently about him? Would she love
him any less?

As expected, de Noailles is late, and Edith hopes once again a note
will arrive saying she's been forced to change her plans. But just at five,
when Harry's oversized American grandfather clock starts to chime, the
Comtesse sweeps into the parlor, laughing and bright eyed, sporting

a beautiful crushed-satin hat the color of Arizona turquoise and a translucent aqua dress with an aqua slip boldly displayed beneath. Edith has never seen clothes like this before, and she can't take her eyes off them. To be so original! To be so fearless! Oh, to be so inimitable as de Noailles!

"Well, look at you, chère Edith," Anna says the moment she and Edith are side by side on Harry's stuffy chesterfield. "You've found yourself a lover!"

"What . . . ," Edith stammers. "What have you heard?" Edith feels the blood rush to her ears.

"Relax. Not a thing. You just look changed. A blind man could see it. Marvelous! Rosa says Mr. Wharton is away. Be an industrious little mouse and have yourself some fun for now is what I say."

"Perhaps we should keep our voices down. My brother isn't here, but his servants might well tell him. . . ."

"Hah!" Anna says. "Who cares what anyone thinks when you look so well? Like you've been sipping a magic tonic! Are you happy?"

"Yes. . . ."

"But a bit miserable too, no? You have to be a bit miserable in love or it doesn't amount to much."

"Really?" Edith is taken aback. This is the last thing she expects to hear from de Noailles, who she assumes is all about pleasure. The *bonne* arrives with the tea, taking far too long to set it out on the tea tables in front of the sofa.

"Why does one have to be miserable in love?" Edith asks when the *bonne* has at last curtsied in her insipid little way and disappeared.

"Well, think about it. Love must come with a soupçon of torment or even a great deal of torment, or how can it leave a lasting mark? What would Romeo and Juliet be without their troubles? The most ordinary fairy tale must have something to keep its lovers apart: someone evil, or a spell, or a nasty little gnome. Well, you're a writer. You know this all too well. If Lily Bart married Lawrence Selden in the first scene of *Chez les Heureux du Monde*, why would we have bothered to keep on reading?"

"But in real life . . ."

"You don't want a boring lover who worships you to your toes. A good lover should distress you a bit. 'Does he really love me? Maybe not.

Maybe there is someone else. Someone who gives him more pleasure than I do! Is giving him pleasure this . . . very . . . minute!' Well, you know. It makes you want him more."

"Oh!" Edith says, knocked flat at the thought. She tries to pretend her gasp is a chuckle, but of course, Katherine Fullerton's rose-petal face appears instantly before her.

"A good lover lets you hang on the edge of agony before he takes you to ecstasy. The very act of love, the pleasure of love is enhanced by sheer misery, no?"

Edith parts her lips, understanding what de Noailles is saying. She thinks of the ecstasy she felt in Montfort. If it had been delayed even a moment . . .

"I see your lover *does* know the power of anguish. He must be French."

"Well, no."

"No? An American?"

"I don't wish to say," Edith says.

"Oh, don't bother. If he's an American I know who it is."

"You do?"

"Of course! It's that boulevardier: Fullerton. Again, a blind man could see it."

"How? How do you know?" Edith is stricken. She and Morton have been too open, too foolish! If de Noailles knows, everyone most know.

"My dear. Enjoy the moment. I would never interfere. I have my secrets too."

"But I must hear. How do you know?" While she's waiting for the Comtesse's answer—for Anna is nibbling at a biscuit and watching Edith with amusement, purposely torturing her as her proposed ideal lover might—Edith asks herself if maybe she's a little pleased that her secret is out, that the whole world knows that someone as worldly and handsome and desirable as Fullerton has chosen *her*.

"Well, how shall I put this?" de Noailles says. "You're rather his type."

Edith is crestfallen. "His type?"

"Of the moment. Once it was older men . . . but now, it's older women. Not that you're old, mind you. Not that you're old."

"Men?" Edith feels her mouth open, and has a sense of losing balance, dropping, falling.

"Oh, stop asking me," de Noailles says. "You can be such a bore. Enjoy the moment."

Edith says nothing. She knows she is as red as can be. And her hands have lost their steadiness.

"Oh, don't tell me you didn't know Mr. Fullerton has a reputation. Surely you knew *that*, *ma chère*?"

"I assumed . . . but I didn't know what you're telling me. . . ."

"Well, so let's discuss your writing, and I'll tell you all about mine!" De Noailles taps her on the knee. "But first, is there no liquor in this house?"

"Wait, I want to know more about Mr. Fullerton."

"Absolutely not," de Noailles says, straightening her long neck. "Ask him yourself. I am here for the liquor and the company. Not to give you a biography of Mr. Fullerton. Go on. Tell me about what you're writing. Have you created any characters based on me?"

❀

Edith won't do it: won't ask Fullerton about what Anna de Noailles told her. Asking about Katherine did damage enough. And what if Morton *was* involved—in his youth—with some older man. What if he was? She can't obsess over what happened long ago. Years ago, in her stupid youth, *she* chose Teddy Wharton over Walter Berry, and what did *that* say about her?

Still, now that desire is her new play toy, constantly rekindled by the smallest reminder, she cannot help picturing a graying, elegant man propping himself on his elbow on some Oriental daybed, gazing down over Morton's beautiful body, testing the smooth surface of Morton's young chest with his beringed fingers, exploring Morton's masculine lips with the tip of his buffed thumbnail. It makes her shiver with a sort of agonized delight. De Noailles is right. The very inappropriateness of it, the shocking thought of it makes her heart pound. She will not, cannot ask him. The image is too delicious to spoil.

❀

Tucked into an overly ornate chair in Harry's library, falling asleep over a book about xenophobia in French culture, she is jerked awake when the *bonne* raps on the door and says there is someone waiting to see her in the parlor. She isn't expecting anyone; her hair is pinned up artlessly. A week at Harry's with little contact from Morton has taken its toll. She's wearing her old shirtwaist and a gray flannel skirt that's more comfortable than comely. She can't imagine who would visit without calling or writing first.

"A gentleman? Did you get his name?" Edith asks.

"Yes, but I can't remember." A *bonne* so careless wouldn't survive a day in *her* household.

Still holding her book to her chest, Edith peeks in through a crack in the parlor doors. In the velvet bergère by the fire sprawls Morton Fullerton. He looks so young, so carefree. Leaning his elbow on the armrest, his head cocked sideways onto his hand, he appears so at home he could easily be the lord of the manor. With his slender legs outstretched, he seems taller than he is, perhaps merely because his confidence is so oversized. She envies him this, and is also wary of it.

"Hello," she says, gliding into the room. "Did you tell me you were coming?"

"No, I'm a terribly rude, bad boy. I had to pursue a story just across Thomas Jefferson Square. I wanted to see where you've been hiding."

"Well, you found me."

Just seeing him sends a shock of new energy through her. Since their trip to Montfort, desire sits on the very surface of her skin these days. Anything the least sensuous seems to set a spark. And Morton has allowed this flame to smolder in her alone. Oh, how she wishes to touch him! At the same time, she is certain she will be reduced to ashes if he places his fingers on her.

"This seems quite the house. Take me on a tour," he says. "I've never been to Place des États-Unis."

"It's just like my brother to choose to live in Paris but reside on a street called American Place," she says.

"Ah yes. Sophisticated Mrs. Wharton wouldn't be caught dead here . . . and yet here you are!"

She shakes her head. "Why is it I feel the way about you that I do?" Oh, the effort to sound dry when he washes over her the way he does!

He flashes a clownish smile, then kisses her lightly on the cheek by her ear, sending waves of delight through her.

"Will you give me a tour?"

"It's not a very big house," she says.

She leads him on a short exploration of Harry's rooms, from the overdecorated parlor with its heavy silk damask drapes, the dining room with its ten paintings of ships all lined up as a grid on the wall and the library with its gilded chairs.

"Harry and I don't share the same taste," she tells him. "This is my room for the moment, though pink is far from my favorite color."

"Like cherry ice cream," he says, looking about. "Makes me want to lick it." He shuts the door with his back and pulls her toward him.

"The servants," she says weakly.

"Hush. They're not even your servants. And I've missed you."

"But you've barely written and made no attempt to . . ."

"I've had concerns. It had nothing to do with you." He turns her around and presses her up against the door, raising her hands above her head and insinuating his body against hers. The feeling is unbearably delicious. To be so totally owned. How easily she melts under his touch, dissolves to nothing. But not here!

"Morton. You disappear for days . . ."

"Stop talking," he says sharply, then kisses her as urgently as he used to in the dark doorways of restaurants, and at Montfort. Oh, how she wishes to reject him. Instead, she is shamed to hear herself panting.

"I'm being watched here. The woman who brings my breakfast tray . . ."

"Hush. . . . Wouldn't you like to feel again what I made you feel at Montfort?"

"I can't."

"You can."

He walks her backward to the bed, pressing her down onto the cream *matelassé* coverlet.

"No," she pushes at him lightly.

"My dear." He runs his hand up her leg.

She continues to push back at him. "No," she says. When his fingers insinuate themselves beneath her underclothes, her reaction is sudden and violent; her whole lower body shoves him back with enough force that he stumbles against the chest of drawers and almost falls.

For a moment there is a hideous silence. Morton straightens himself proudly, yanking down his waistcoat, smoothing his hair, not looking at her.

"Well," he says.

Edith is mortified. She stands, her knees quaking. "Not here. That's all I'm saying. . . ."

"Sometimes you are an awful lot of effort."

"I'm sorry." She closes her eyes, remorseful. "I didn't mean to hurt you. Did I hurt you?"

He glares at her, not answering. "HJ is coming soon. You understand?" he says.

Her lips quiver.

"Then we'll have no time alone together . . . even if he does approve of our *enchevêtrement romantique*."

"Just not here. Not here at Harry's."

"And then you sail. 'Not here.' It's an excuse, you know. It's an excuse because you have no heart."

"I do have a heart. . . ." In fact, she feels it sinking, clanking away from her like a rock down a well. She must know him better, feel closer to him before she can feel close in that other way. "What sorts of concerns have you had?" she asks.

"What?"

"You said you've had other concerns which kept you from me. What sorts of concerns?"

"I told you it has nothing to do with you. Why would it help to share my worries?"

"It might make me feel nearer to you. . . ."

"Women always think it's a good idea to know more about a man. But what they discover rarely does anything but upset them."

Edith opens the door and heads for the parlor. All her remorse, all her longing freezes in her veins. He wants her to give up everything, and intends to give nothing in return. He follows her down the hall straight to the front door. The scent of his lavender cologne precedes him.

"Thank you for visiting," she says, opening it.

"Listen to the ice in Madame's voice. You push me away, and don't even offer me tea to ask for forgiveness?"

"There's a tea shop just at the corner."

"I have a mind to start shouting until all the servants come running." And then his voice rises to an ear-shattering volume. "Mrs. Wharton's breaking my heart!"

"Hush," she says, exasperated. "All the servants here speak English." The *bonne* is already running into the room with a concerned look on her face.

"Is everything all right, Madam?"

"We're fine, Celeste. Mr. Fullerton is just leaving."

"Yes, Ma'am."

When the *bonne*'s footsteps retreat, Edith turns to him. "If you want tea with me, or anything, things will have to change. I can't keep up with you. One minute you have no time for me. The next you're on my doorstep."

"Ah, we'll have tea soon and far more," Morton says, snatching his hat from the stand in the hall and flashing a broad, assured smile. "Because fortunately, dear, you love me."

❁

Henry and Edith have a plan. Instead of his coming directly to Paris as usual, he'll sail to Le Havre and take the train to Amiens, where they can enjoy the cathedral together. He writes her:

> *To see the cathedral in the late afternoon will be of the last refinement. And it will be adorable to have WMF—kindly tell him, with my love, how immensely I feel this.*

Knowing that Henry is far too fastidious to ever act on his adulation for Morton, could *never* have been the older man with whom Morton dallied, Edith sees that she has been appointed his surrogate. She smiles at his note. He wants Edith and Morton to be together.

When she tells Morton about it on the telephone—all the rage she felt the last time she saw him had astonishingly melted away—he agrees to join her in picking up Henry at the train station in Amiens. "After

Henry goes to bed, the rest of the night will be ours," he says. "If you promise not to hurt me in the process."

The morning of Henry's arrival, however, Edith wakes, her heart pounding to the sound of a terrible deluge. Thunder. Rain rushing down the streets in torrents. Wind rattling windows. No day for a motor-flight of any kind. She immediately wires Henry to come straight to Paris instead of Amiens, and dashes off a note to Morton as well. As she sips her morning tea, she is astonished at how relieved she feels.

Arriving in Paris larger, more winded and red-faced than ever, Henry is happy to be welcomed into Harry's dry and fussy little house.

"In retrospect, I see that a side trip to Amiens might have killed me. I must be grateful to the gods for concocting this wretched rain."

He is pleased that Harry has agreed to let him have the yellow bedroom overlooking the just-budding rose garden. Before he takes a nap to fortify himself for the rest of the day, he hugs Edith warmly.

"You are so exceedingly important to me, dearest Edith," he says with stentorian grandeur, as the servants mill about with fresh towels and fire stoking. "Or I should *never* have dragged my weighty, miserable soul across the channel. I want you to drink in my stay, because I may never come again." Edith begins to close the door when she hears Henry calling through it.

"When I wake, will I get a glimpse of Miss Bahlmann?"

"No, I'm sorry. She's gone back to the States."

"Why on earth would she desert you? That doesn't sound like her."

Edith bites her lip and demurs. "I sent her back."

Henry frowns. "What did she do to deserve that?"

"She disapproves of Morton," Edith says.

"Ahhh. Well, in the future, you can always send her to me. I know she doesn't disapprove of me. And I find her very useful."

Park Avenue could not look more foreign to Anna if it were Tverskaya Street in Moscow. After such a long season in Paris, the houses (especially 882 and poor 884 with no window boxes and tired curtains) look small and plain and rather oddly unpeopled. Though Anna has always appreciated New York more than Edith, perhaps she has finally caught Edith's Americaphobia as one might catch a cold. Everything looks smaller, more provincial and more foreboding than it has ever seemed to her before.

It takes a good two weeks of unpacking her trunks and reacquainting herself with her treasured things: her books, her favorite mulberry-colored teapot, her Aunt Charlotte's mohair armchair, to feel comfortable once more. But she has to admit, she is remarkably happy to be away from Edith. How painful it was to have to hear from Cook two, three times a week about her lunches with Morton Fullerton. And Anna wouldn't have even minded that so much if Edith hadn't appeared so unconcerned about Teddy, so defiant of all the things she's been taught, of the vows she once took so solemnly. In some odd, angry way, Anna wishes she would never have to lay eyes on Edith again.

After some days, Anna is surprised to find herself revitalized by familiar smells and sounds of New York. Even the steam train rattling through the open tunnels on Park Avenue warms her heart. Everyone is talking about how, come June, the law is forcing the railroads to switch to electric trains only. It feels like an era passing. New York is growing up. And she has missed so much of it. If she stays with Edith, she will miss more.

One day, Anna walks to the Metropolitan Museum of Art and wanders among her favorite Greek and Roman galleries, and then spends time among the American paintings, something she has hardly ever done. She stops at a George Inness painting titled *Autumn Oaks*, with its light just breaking through the clouds and spilling onto the golden-green grass. There is a sort of innocent optimism about American paintings that feels spirited and true.

And then, as Anna stands there, tears well up in her eyes. A rush of them. She fumbles in her handbag for a handkerchief, sits on a bench near *Autumn Oaks* and tries to hide her face from others in the room. What's come over her? She feels suddenly, excruciatingly brokenhearted.

How happy Edith is with Morton and Henry, gathered at luncheon in the courtyard of the Hôtel d'Angleterre, the three of them relaxing under a mauve umbrella, sipping cold white Bordeaux. The breeze in Beauvais is as sweet and warm as July. Two little girls sit cross-legged on the stone pavement under a fringe of fragrant wisteria, playing clapping games in high, cheerful French. The waiter is whistling. Sweet-faced *pensées* bloom around a stone fountain plashing with water. Canaries sing in unison in a fat silvered cage by the restaurant door. Was there ever so sweet a symphony?

"Oh happy day," Henry declares, clasping each of their hands. "We are together at last! And in such a lovely place!"

Edith smiles at him, and then at Morton, who initially didn't want to come to Beauvais at all but now looks as happy as she's seen him in a while. How startlingly handsome he is when relaxed. She watches Henry gaze over at him fondly. He, too, revels in Morton's beauty.

"It will be uncomfortable with the three of us," Morton had fretted when she invited him. "I'll want your attention. He'll want mine."

"Please come. The thought of you not being there makes me sad. You *must* come."

Having them both here now, how could she feel more magnificent? Free and happy to be out of Paris and Harry's house of servants and strictures. Today in the sunshine and country air, she feels ten years younger.

"If only one could put a day into a potion and drink it whenever one likes," Henry says. "I would choose today and Beauvais."

"I would choose today," Edith agrees.

"I would choose the day I graduated from Harvard," Morton says.

Henry shakes his head and laughs. "You're a scamp, dear man."

Morton looks up through his lashes at Edith. "It *was* wonderful being young," he says sheepishly. "But this is lovely too."

After the lunch is cleared, they linger over coffee and cigarettes.

"My two dearest friends are friends!" Henry declares. "This is a gift of the most generous sort. In my experience, one's friends never like one another." He sighs with contentment, and Edith feels awash in Henry's benevolent approval and distracted by the sweet pressure of Morton's leg against hers.

She realizes that with Henry along she is more talkative than when she's alone with Morton. Henry's open attachment to her makes her more self-assured, more amusing. She's always so worried when she's alone with Morton that she won't please him. That he'll judge her wanting.

Now after luncheon, strolling the streets of the village, pausing briefly at the twelfth-century church of St.-Etienne to admire the stained glass, and then walking on through the marketplace in the square, she feels carefree. Stopping at a booth selling thickly embroidered gypsy scarves, she wraps one around her hair and poses for them. Together they insist on buying it for her. "The real Edith," they declare. "A mad gypsy at heart."

"We should buy you these too," Morton says, lifting some painted gourds from the table and shaking them at her. "No? Too much. Ah then, Gypsy. We'll leave you as you are." All around the square, fruit trees are in bloom, snowflakes of cherry and apple blossoms swirl on the breeze. Edith feels perfectly giddy.

Together, with Edith in the middle, they climb arm in arm in arm up the narrow lane toward the cathedral. And then suddenly, there it is: the choir of the great church, a dizzying circle of ivory vaults rising like a dream against the azure sky.

"One can almost see it turn," Morton says. "Wheeling cosmically through space."

"Its own planet," Edith says, breathlessly.

He takes her arm and presses it to him, enfolds her hand in his warm one. If her life could end this moment, she'd be happy. She reaches out her free hand and takes Henry's plump one.

"I'll never forget this day," she says. "Never."

Later, while Henry makes a tour of the ambulatory, Edith and Morton wait for him, basking in the sun—as in Montfort on the warmed stone steps—leaning against one another. She has never felt closer to him, even in that old ruin. For here she feels their hearts entwined in view of the whole world.

"Dear, are you happy?" he asks her, just as he had at Montfort.

"I don't think," she tells him, "I ever imagined being so happy."

I must pack this day away in a great flurry of excelsior and cotton, she thinks. Soon, it will be just a memory.

ELEVEN

Only after such days, the blankness, the intolerableness of the morrow—the day when one does not see you! What a pity that one cannot live longer in the memory of such hours— that the eager heart must always reach out for more and more! I used to think: "If I could be happy for a week—an hour!" And now I am asking to be happy all the rest of my life. . . .

Poor hearts, in this shifting stream of life, so hungry for permanence and security! As I wrote these lines, I suddenly said to myself, "I will go with him once before we separate."

It would hurt no one—it would give me my first, last draught of life . . . why not? I have always laughed at the "mala prohibita"—"bugbears to frighten children." The antisocial is the only one that is harmful "per se." And, as you told me the other day—and I need no telling!—what I have given already is far, far more. . . .

After they have put Henry on the train at the Gare du Nord, with kisses and a basket of food, trying not to notice the tears shimmering in his pale eyes, they wave the train down the track and are alone at last together. Their bodies cleave toward one another, their hearts racing.

"Shall we?" Morton says in a voice so rich and secretive, Edith can feel the vibration of it in her own throat.

The train to Montmorency is on Track 5 and they hurry, not touching but leaning toward one another. Leaning and longing. She can feel his presence to her marrow. The train glistens in the shafts of white light from above as though lit by angels. Others are sliding open the doors and entering. They walk far down the platform to find an empty car. Alone in the sunny maple compartment, their hands reach out beneath Edith's spread skirts and grab onto each other. When the train jerks forward, Edith knows she has not felt more thrilled, expectant and fearful since that day at the Frascati Gardens preparing for her one and only ride on the Chemin de Centrifuge.

Soon the countryside rolls out beside them. The sweetest green of the new leaves. The blossoms of every kind of fruit tree. The just-born beds of lettuces and beans. And the *châtaigniers*, the chestnut trees, lacy margins between the fields, their white-blossomed cones thrusting toward the sky. Not a word passes between them. Sometimes, on other journeys, Morton has grown quiet, lost in thought, far from her. But this silence is shared, carried between them like a child, one hand in each of her parents' hands, being swung joyously over a curb.

During Henry's visit, they were able to steal just moments of time alone. An occasional dinner when Henry was off honoring other invitations. A walk now and then in the Luxembourg Gardens squeezed from the lackluster substance of their busy days. But sometimes there was a sparkling, thrilling kiss in the shadows. A dangerous press of bodies in a doorway. Too many days their plans fell through, though. Morton was too busy. At the last minute, plans were canceled. Never before has Edith suffered such swings from euphoria to despair. The thrill of hearing Morton call her "mon amour." The desolation when no note arrives. These swerves of spirit are new and frightening. Elation collapses like a soufflé snatched clumsily from an oven. And then her heart soars again when her breakfast tray provides a note saying Morton could hardly work all day for thinking of her.

But now, at last, there is nothing standing between Edith and Morton. And as the train chugs toward Montmorency, she wishes to leave all her sadness behind, to be open to this man in a way she has never allowed herself to be—with anyone. All her life she has been "good." But how has it served her to be true to a man who has never given her pleasure? To do what is expected of her, but do nothing to increase her own joy?

Morton, she suspects, has never been good or cared for the appellation. What did Anna de Noailles say about him? That he had a reputation. Why were men allowed to pursue their desires while the world turned a blind eye . . . but women became "fallen women," "ruined souls" if they did the very same? The dishonesty of it, the unfairness of it swells her with determination.

The day is hot, and the train grows warmer as it flies beneath the sunshine. Morton leans over and slides open a window. The breeze wafts in and Edith unbuttons the top button of her dress to catch it. Morton smiles at her when she does and she beams back.

The train leaves them off at a shady station, Morton helping her down, his hands about her waist. A walk through the streets of Montmorency shows them pretty vanilla-colored houses and flowers everywhere.

"So this is where Rousseau walked and had deep thoughts. Shall we go up to the church first?" Morton asks.

"To pray for our souls?" Edith teases.

"Yes. Seems only right," he says. "Then we'll see Rousseau's house."

Edith has read only a bit of Jean-Jacques Rousseau's writing. But she knows he focused on how children are born "natural" and how society ruins us, perverts us, sends us away from all that matters. For the first time in her life, she is delving deep for what is in her soul—the childlike soul that all these years has been strangled by strictures. Morton takes her hand. Ah, the joy of being so open, so free.

They walk quietly through the St. Martin and she takes in the stained glass windows, the smell of long-ago smoke, the cool damp that seems a relief on such a hot day. And then they walk just a few streets away to the white house with the many-paned windows where Rousseau lived. Just before they enter, in the front garden of the house, amidst the blossoms and the flutter of new leaves, he kisses her.

"Dearest," he whispers.

She feels as though happiness might immolate her. But she enters the house, feigning deep interest, inspecting the rooms where Rousseau wrote, dreamed, thought new thoughts that stirred a nation. The tiny desk where he penned *The Social Contract* strikes Edith as humble. She is grateful that Morton is thoughtful enough to let them be tourists for a while. Maybe he is only feigning interest too. He never lets go of her hand. Oh! She is smitten. Lost. She did not know that her ability to love could be so expansive, so generous. He could break her heart and she would not stop loving him. There is almost no disappointment he could conjure that would break the spell of her love for him. This alone seems a gift.

The church bells are chiming noon when they leave Rousseau's house, and the sun is high.

"Are you hungry?" he asks.

"Yes."

"Come. I know just the place." The inn is called La Châtaigneraie, and the courtyard where they are led to a quiet table is indeed surrounded by chestnut trees festooned with towering snowy coneflowers. A sweet young girl takes their order. Her father, presumedly, pours the wine. A mother with a sleeping baby sits at a far table with her husband, laughing at his banter. A butterfly alights on the vase of flowers set in the middle of their table.

If I die soon, I will have at least had this, she thinks. I will have known happiness. If I had died just a few weeks ago, I would never have believed what I was missing. The thought wounds her in a strange, delicious way. She wants to keep poking at it, reminding herself to take it all in.

She drinks more wine than she should. The giddiness she already feels marries with the alcohol to take away her last ounce of reluctance.

"Have you planned where we're going?" she asks Morton.

"Just upstairs," he says when he's paid the bill and smoked a cigarette. "Are you ready?"

She nods.

Their room is large and full of light and peeks through the lacy chestnut blossoms out over the courtyard. It's just a simple space beneath the eaves, with wallpaper of blue morning glories climbing from baseboards to ceiling, and a cotton rug. Morton cranks open the windows and Edith sits on the bed.

"This is lovely, isn't it?" he asks her.

"Yes." She wonders if he has ever brought a woman here before. They were kind to him in the courtyard. Did they recognize him? She swats the thought from her mind.

She is afraid she will fail him. And if so, this could be the last time they are together. This new worry flits around her wine-dazzled brain.

He sits beside her and reaches for her chin, gently tilting her face toward his. His eyes are as kind as she's ever seen them.

"You're afraid," he says.

"Yes."

"We needn't make this fearful at all. Not at all."

"I'm not good at this," she says. "At so many things in my life, I've worked hard to excel, to learn. At this, I am an abject failure."

"Perhaps you've never given yourself a chance. We needn't scare you today. There's nothing to fear. I promise."

"I fear it all," she says. "It's as though I'm broken. It hurts me. It always hurts me."

"You weren't broken at Montfort. You were alive. I know I'm right about that, yes?"

She nods and feels tears quivering in the inside corners of her eyes. "I never cry. I detest women who cry. Why do I always cry with you?"

"I don't know," he says, and puts his arm about her. "But we won't make you cry, no matter what. Or do anything that will make you sad. We'll just be here together. Alone together! No one watching. No one interrupting us."

She turns to take in his face. He is the most beautiful sight she's ever seen. She reaches out and touches his glossy black mustache. Never once has it hurt her lips when he's kissed her, as Teddy's always has. And his cheekbones, so noble and high in color, as sweetly tinted as Duchesse de Brabant roses. His lower lip so strong, so masculine. Other women have come before her in his heart. Others will follow. She's no fool. Morton will never love her as she loves him. But how beautiful, how freeing, to know she doesn't care.

He cradles her face in his hands and kisses her lips so gently she barely feels it. And then he kisses her eyes, her nose.

"My love," he says. "My darling." His voice is lulling.

She feels so young before him. So untested. How absurd it is to be a forty-six-year-old woman with no experience. Why isn't he laughing at her?

His lips trifle with the curl of her ear. "Do you know, you have the most beautiful ears. Like seashells." She touches her ear with pleasure and feels herself blush.

"There's some color in your cheeks again!" he says. "Now you're here with me!"

Don't miss this! Feel everything, she tells herself. And remember.

He removes his own jacket with a ceremonial seriousness, carefully places his shoes side by side under the chair by the desk, unfastens his pocket watch and sets it gently on the bedside table along with the crisp square of his white linen handkerchief. Then he goes about the business of unpeeling her layers. Madness that women should dress with such complexity! Like Valentine candy hiding beneath layers of ruffled papers.

"Can we draw the curtains?" she asks.

"And rob me of one of my greatest pleasures? Seeing you? No one can see us."

"I'm afraid to be seen by you."

"But you're beautiful!" he says. When he's managed with her help to remove her corset, he tenderly traces the red lines and welts of its cruel embrace with his fingers, "Poor love," he says, then leans down and kisses her puckered flesh. "It's cruel what we put women through. Men would never tolerate it. And for what? As though you're not beautiful without it."

Nearly naked now, she struggles to cover her breasts, so exposed in the dappled light. He has stripped her down to just her drawers. They are voile, refined and elegant, edged in Burano lace and fastened with mother-of-pearl buttons as tiny as a baby's first fingernails. All these years of exquisite underwear and not one man has ever seen any of it.

She reaches up and slips the studs from his sleeves and shirt, aids in the removal of his collar and cuffs. He laughs. "Well, aren't you helpful," he says, hanging his shirt on the chair. When he strips off his thin jersey undervest, she discovers his chest is surprisingly broad and muscular, covered in dark curling hair. His nipples are as brown as walnuts. He lies down on the bed beside her, propping himself on his elbow to see her better.

"I've dreamed of this," he says. "Of you. From the day we met."

His words fall on her like water on a parched and dying plant. She feels herself leaning toward them, drinking every sweet drop.

"All I want," he says, "is to make you feel marvelous. Do you understand?"

She nods.

"I hope you'll feel things you've never felt. Wonderful things."

"I just don't know if I can . . ."

"Shhh . . ." He puts his fingers to her lips. "Anything that doesn't feel wonderful, we won't do, we won't continue. If you don't like anything, you'll tell me."

She laughs, for she feels like he is stating the rules before a game, the way they do before lawn tennis.

This is happening, she tells herself. This is really happening. No dream. No story conjured late at night alone in her bed. But a real moment, with his ticking watch on the bedside table, the sound of his breath, the dark perfect hairs on his wrist, the tiny scar on his cheek, the dot of black in his blue eye, the scent of lavender mixed with another more dusky sweetness. Her senses are heightened, thrilled by every detail. Will I remember? Will I remember? she wonders. When he leans down and kisses her, she feels it in layers. First, the sweetness of his lips, then the soft searching of his tongue, the weight of him, and at last, the extraordinary heat of his chest against her breasts.

Drawing away from the kiss, he runs his lips down her throat, makes circles around each breast as he did in Montfort, lingering and teasing her with his tongue; then his kisses move down the meridian of her belly, which makes her gasp. How has her body become such a crucible of sensations? Ordinary places feel sensitized. When his fingers find the tiny buttons of her bloomers, she worries that they're too small for a man to unfasten. But he conquers them one by one, slipping them gently through the fine-stitched buttonholes. She realizes as he slides them from her hips that she has never been thoroughly naked before a man. With Teddy, she wore her nightgown. And there was no touching, no sweetness.

"My God, you're beautiful," he says, modeling the lines of her waist and breasts and hips. "As slender as a young girl." So many touches, so many caresses, it's as though he has a thousand hands. His face is lit with pleasure. He really thinks me beautiful! she tells herself. He parts her legs and with his fingers softly begins to explore. What she feels is so exquisite, so beyond anything she's ever known.

"You're flowing with honey," he says. "You want me, Edith. Do you know it? Do you realize? Not all women respond like this. You want me."

"I do?" she asks. "I do!" she says. The same exact words she spoke twenty years ago at an altar, a shivering numb bride. What a different meaning they hold now. She did not want Teddy Wharton then. She never wanted Teddy Wharton. She must not think. She must feel. . . .

Suddenly Morton's gentle probing locates the very bud of all sensation. By parting the petals with soft touches, he has exposed her long-suppressed desire. Stroking the spot with circular caresses, he makes her arch her back, lose her breath. The sensation is nothing she's ever known or imagined, fiery and tingling and urgent. And when he slides down to press his mouth to this very spot, this vortex of pleasure she never imagined was part of her, and worships it with his lips and tongue, something happens. First, she sees nothing but white light beneath her lids. Then a sensation like quicksilver shoots to every part of her. She gasps, she calls out his name. Ripples of flame roll over her again and again and again. The convulsions stun and thrill her. An effortless ecstasy, close to agony. The shock of a body sliding into cold water, biting on a lemon, standing too close to a flame. But with no pain. No pain; just utter rapture. As intense as pain, but for the first time, pleasure.

"What's happening to me?" she says when she can speak. "What's happened?"

Morton smiles down at her, pleased.

"You don't know?" he asks.

She shakes her head.

"It's never happened before? You never made it happen yourself?"

"No. Is it all right? Am I all right?" She is still softly shuddering.

He laughs aloud. "You climaxed, darling. *La petite mort.*"

"*La petite mort?*"

"Each time we die to be reborn again."

"This has happened to other women?"

"Not often enough," he says, amused.

"It's normal?"

"In a perfect world."

She sits half up, feeling utterly spent and blissful. More relaxed than she's felt in her entire life.

"Can it happen more than once in a lifetime?"

"It can happen every day. Ten times a day . . ."

"No," she says, lying back down. "I wouldn't want that!"

Morton roars, and then kisses her, still laughing. She feels how hard his heart is beating. Her own lips feel swollen and sensitive. He lifts her hand and draws it to his chest.

"Touch me too," he says, his voice dark and longing.

His chest is perfectly modeled. The vestigial breasts, like a statue's, hard as stone but covered in dark fur. He guides her hand lower. She has never felt a man's member before, has never imagined how heavy it might feel, how firm. He lays it into her hand like a gift.

"Are you afraid?" he asks.

"No," she says, and it's true.

He shows her how he wishes to be stroked. She feels awkward, but interested. She wants to do it right. She wants to make him happy he chose her. Is there anything she wouldn't do to please this man who seems like an offering to her from the gods? The answer to a thousand hopeless prayers . . .

Morton seems swept away by her touch. His member, velvety on the outside, so marble hard on the inside, satisfies her hand as much as her hand seems to please him.

"It's perfect," he says. "Perfect." His voice is ragged. The out-of-control sound of his words frightens her. But she remembers the pleasure he bestowed upon her. She wants to give it back. His breathing is torn, worrisome, interlaced with moans that move her inexpressibly.

"Edith," he whispers, his voice husky, lost.

"My love," she says, observing how his back arches, his eyes shut tightly. The arcs of his glistening black lashes flare on his cheekbones. His lips part. He stops her hand very suddenly and sits up, then raises his body over hers.

"Guide me into you," he whispers.

"I . . ."

"Don't be afraid. I promise I'll stop if it hurts. Guide me in." How kind he sounds. But she can tell there's effort in what he's saying. She takes hold of him. There's no going back now. She is stepping over the line. But they are doing this together. Lovers. Partners. His member feels even more swollen. Far too big. She doesn't quite know where it should go. But it knows. In a fluid, honeyed movement, he is entering her. The feeling is as far from pain as she can imagine. No resistance. No friction, just shining light and sensation.

She hears a sound spring from her lips. A sound she has never made before.

"Am I hurting you?" he asks.

"No. Don't stop."

He plunges fully into her and holds for a moment, and then pulls away, enters again and pulls away. Just as he has done a thousand times to her before in other ways. A metaphor for everything he's been to her. Approaching. Retreating. Mustn't think. Can't think. Suddenly, it's easy not to think! His breathing is torn and insistent. Together, the sounds they make could be agony. How close agony is to joy! She never knew. Never knew. Never knew. She is caught in the vortex again. The quickening. She finds herself thrusting upward to draw him in deeper. She wraps her legs around his hips. She wants more. She wants all of him. They are one. Ensnared in the swirling. The sensation is even stronger this time. Every nerve ending sparking. White light! She gasps and cries out like someone falling.

And then he cries out too. She feels his whole body shudder. Even inside her. Shivering. Quaking. Tears flow down her face. They will not stop. When she opens her eyes, all she can see are the frills of white blossoms through the open window kaleidoscoped by her tears, shimmering in the soft blue breeze. It feels like the beginning of the day all over again.

"You're a brave girl. I knew you would be. A wonderful girl." He touches her face. "You're crying!"

"Only with joy," she says. He kisses her nose.

"I've made you happy." He sounds so pleased, she feels effervescent. "You did it beautifully, Edith."

"Did I?" she asks.

"Brilliantly. You are very special. Very, very special, *chère!*" His voice is paternal, and soothing. She is preternaturally proud.

He lifts himself off and lies down beside her. "Lie in my arms for a while," he whispers, accepting her into the crook of his shoulder. "Before we go back to being tourists. But," he says, after a moment, "I think it's safe to say I've taken you somewhere you've never been."

"You have," she whispers. "The most wonderful place. I hope to visit often." Later, as they gather their things, she leans out the window just far enough to snap off a sprig of chestnut flower. Sliding it into the pocket of her skirt, it's the last thing she does before they go out into the world together, lovers at last.

TWELVE

We met the other day at the Louvre, and walked to St. Germain l'Auxerrois. Then we took a motor and went over to Les Arènes de Lutèce and then to St.-Etienne-du-Mont. . . . Then we walked to the Luxembourg, and sat for a long time in a quiet corner under the trees. But what I long for, these last days, is to be with you alone, far off, in quietness—held fast, peacefully, "while close as lips lean, lean the thoughts between" . . . there is no use trying to look at things together. We don't see them any longer. . . .

Edith watches helplessly as each day ticks by and the calendar forfeits its leaves. At eleven-thirty on a perfect May day scented with an aroma not unlike gumdrops, just five days before she is to sail, Cook drops her off at the station and she wanders into the echoing crowds. The electrically broadcast announcements for trains buzz incoherently. The vendors promise buttery pastries and coffee. Feeling lost, and sick at heart, she searches for Morton. What if he doesn't come? It's possible. With Morton, anything is possible. Then, there he is, elegant and crisply turned out, leaning by the entrance to the platforms, waiting. His face completely alters when his eyes find her, his mood turning playful. Her own heart opens and sings out like a bird sprung from that ever-ticking clock. Climbing aboard the train, Morton lifts her to reach the first step, then kisses her right in the doorway.

Openly, deeply. He laughs like a naughty boy. It's part of his pleasure, pushing her to do things she once wouldn't have dared.

But she's energized. Thrilled to be with him.

"A full day together," she says.

He squeezes her hand and leads her to a compartment where an older woman in black sits, tatting with ecru thread. She nods and smiles at them, her hands flying in circles and knots.

"Bonjour, Madame," Morton sings out.

"Bonjour." The woman looks from Morton to Edith, then back to Morton again. Then she lowers her head again to her lace making. Morton takes the moment to grab Edith by her waist and pull her to him, kissing her with tongue and lips, daring the old woman to watch. But the old widow's eyes are fixed on the results of her airborne bobbin, conjuring tiny picots with ease and artistry, choosing not to note their embrace.

The train is soon slicing sweetly through fields of grain and beans. And before long they disembark at Senlis. Edith has seen it before, but knows that with Morton by her side, the great Gothic cathedral perched atop the hill will look more splendid, touch her more. There's been no talk of an inn. Edith wonders if Morton has arranged for one, and realizes she will be disappointed if he hasn't. Night after night since Montmorency she has been lying in bed re-creating the light-filled room they shared overlooking the courtyard of chestnut trees. The faded bed-spread. The sky blue ceiling. The ivory blossoms crushing themselves against the window. Now there will be a new memory!

The medieval granite of Senlis's streets has been smoothed by thou-sands of pilgrims from afar seeking solace at the Notre Dame cathedral. Could a young girl from Nazareth have imagined this carved monument to her purity? And why should we worship purity, Edith wonders? Her own purity, or at least her blindness to the sensual, has happily and finally been removed like a stone from her shoe. An ocean can part her from Morton, and time can sway his heart from hers, but nothing can take away the power of the knowledge he's given her or the exquisiteness of its memory. In time, taken out and remembered, perhaps the memory will grow worn and smooth like these streets. But it will never be torn from her heart.

The cathedral is remarkably cold beneath the beating sun, and she shivers under its humbling vaults. Morton takes off his jacket and drapes it around her quaking shoulders. After the tour, she is happy to escape to the warm streets to view the complex frieze on the side of the church. And then they find a small restaurant just down the hill, where they are fortified by buckwheat crêpes and glasses of velvety red wine.

"Let's walk along the ramparts," he tells her, taking her hand across the table. "The old Roman walls." Again the mischievous smile, the twinkling eyes.

"Yes. That sounds wonderful."

Full of luncheon and softened by the wine, wandering along the cliff-like ramparts holding Morton's steady arm, she is suffused with a sense of peace completely foreign and delicious. She, who has spent a lifetime restless, is wrapped in syrupy calm. She revels in it. No one has cleared the land in years, perhaps ever. It is all natural and sunburned, full of hiding places and castlelike openings. And then they come upon a lilac bower, a shimmering wall of flowers.

"Come," he tells her and draws her in beneath the drooping purple tassels. "I've rented a room here."

The dappled shade is full of color. Blue shards of sky, lavender buds, an emerald bed of moss. The scent of lilacs is so heady Edith is drunk with it. Morton draws her down to the mossy cushion.

"Lie down," he whispers. "Lie down with me." She drops to the cradle of moss, spreading her skirts out around her, then lays her head down, her heart thrumming. He settles in beside her and touches her face, traces her lips, her eyes. They have discovered utter privacy in nature's arms. Yet just over Morton's shoulder and through the flowers Edith can see the glittering belfry of the church. Morton slides his hand up under her skirt, whispering, "Come away with me. Come away."

Oh, the pleasures they find on their journey!

Later, on the train back to Paris, the black velvet night brushing the windows, they hold hands in silence. The communion couldn't be clearer. This is how animals in the fields speak to one another. How birds in their nests share their thoughts. Glances and air moving in and out of lungs and hearts beating side by side. Then, as they watch the fields gliding by, just striped shadows of charcoal and ebony, the sky is torn open at the very bottom and an orange flame appears. It rises, eerie, domed, and in a moment transforms itself into a yellow moon wavering in the earth's last heat, moving upward like an illuminated balloon.

Edith gasps, and Morton squeezes her hand.

And just when the glory of the moonrise feels as if it's enough to burst her heart, a nightingale's aria wafts in through the open train window, its bittersweet melody echoing against the edge of the fields. The song clings to the train for a long, long while, as though, perhaps improbably, the bird has perched on the locomotive's roof, stealing a free ride to Paris. At that moment, Edith perceives she's never been closer to the essence of life. Never again will she know so much about sensation, about possibility, about love. One hour like this ought to irradiate a whole life, she thinks. At last, I have lived.

Spring lingers in New York. Soon, raging heat will cook all the odors of too many people and too much life into a devastating stew. Anna has spent enough summers in New York City to know it. But now, everything feels washed and new. In a very short time, Edith will be home. After these few weeks alone, with no demands on her time, Anna has reclaimed herself. She has taken on work as a tutor for some children down the street. She has spent a good deal of time at the library. She has visited her various friends around the city, climbing up to the elevated trains and, for the first time, down into the IRT subway, despite her rheumatic knees, which don't hurt as much as they did in damp, cold Paris. Sitting on the wicker seats, she thrills at the speed of the underground trains, the subterranean breezes that blow in through the opened windows. She feels strong, and happy. Hopeful.

Word of Mr. Wharton in Hot Springs is very positive. What a good idea it was to send him there! Though she doesn't think Edith cares enough about Teddy, Anna can't help but acknowledge she made a fine decision in sending him where he could at last find help.

The pressure of her longing to see Teddy again is disconcerting. The thought that summer at The Mount will be filled with their closeness makes her feel suddenly ashamed, confused. Her dream of walking down to the new piggery to see him worries her. He is her employer. He is Edith's husband. And no more. He never will be more. . . .

And what will it be like to see Edith again? Will Morton Fullerton show up in Lenox with his perfect, starched French shirts? Cook told Gross in a short note that "Mrs. Wharton is never home. Always off somewhere with MF." Anna fears that Edith will be even more impatient with Mr. Wharton. Unhappy without Fullerton. And maybe more impatient with Anna as well.

When she speaks about her fears with Gross, Catherine shrugs.

"What are we to do? Edith will do as Edith chooses to do. No one ever has had any sway over that woman."

The trunks once again are hoisted from the cellar of Harry's house and set into Edith's room. Just the sight of them sickens her. Food has no meaning. Sleep is insubstantial and often interrupted. By the middle of the week, Edith is already seasick before her journey has begun, terrified to return home: not just to the emptiness of life without Morton, but to the tyranny of boredom at her husband's side, to the narrowness of a world she once deemed exciting. And to Anna. She's thought a great deal of Anna. She's pined to have her helpful hand. All one has to do is tell Anna what the gist of a business letter should be, and Anna presents it in ten minutes, crisply composed, neatly typed and ready to sign with two shivering carbon papers slipped between the copies. Edith has missed her quiet support, her point of view on her daily pages, and sharing books that have thrilled or interested her, because no matter what Edith likes to read, Anna appreciates the contents, provides feedback. But Anna's recent censure of Edith's behavior is painful. And as long as Edith is in love with Morton, that censure will surely stand.

One night, tossing in Harry's awful *lit bateau*, she dreams that Anna is standing by her bed with a dripping candle. She is younger, almost beautiful, the way she was when Edith first met her, with translucent eyes and braided straw-gold hair that Edith liked to twist and pet. Anna is smiling as she gazes down at her beloved charge, but at the same time, tears are flowing from her eyes, as in paintings of suffering Madonnas, whose goodness always shines through distress. When Edith reaches out to take her free hand, the vision disappears only to appear again at the foot of Edith's bed, but this time Anna is weeping blood and it's staining the ivory matelassé coverlet, rolling to a puddle on the floor. The memory of the dream is so real that in the morning, Edith has to check the blanket to reassure herself it was only a dream. What will she do about Anna? Talk to her? Tell her that her love of Morton isn't going to go away? Confess to her? Fire her? Does she have a cold enough heart to do that?

That morning on her breakfast tray a petit bleu from Morton announces that he has procured tickets at the bureau for an afternoon dress rehearsal of Albert Samain's play-poem *Polyphème*. She won't think of Anna—she tells herself—not until she returns home, sees her face-to-face. And then she'll know, if their encounter is awkward, what she must do.

After the play, Edith and Morton, reveling in the dappled daylight on their faces, walk side by side through the Tuileries. They stroll past the carousel and the Grand Bassin, where children are crouching, pitting their wooden boats against one another and stop to admire Marqueste's sensual statue of a centaur abducting a nymph.

"I am your nymph," she tells him. Morton smiles but says nothing.

Finding a stone bench overlooking the river, she wishes she could take his hand but knows it would be foolhardy in the heart of Paris where friends might pass. At the moment, Edith wishes she weren't so conventional.

"Will you miss me?" she asks, ashamed she needs to.

"Of course."

"What will you do when I'm gone?"

"What I always do. Go to the bureau, write stories, eat at the restaurant, go home, sleep in my bed."

"Will you remember Senlis? Will you think of Montmorency?"

He looks at her out of the corner of his eye.

"Do you really think I haven't been touched by what we've shared?" he asks.

"I don't know," she says. "I wish I knew."

A breeze is rising from the Seine, scented with river water and warm mud. She puts her face into her hands. She doesn't want to feel bereft. In just a few days, she will be gone. Why spoil the precious time they have together?

"Stop," Morton says, "you musn't," and tugs on her arm, encouraging her to sit up. He takes out a cigarette and lights it, hands it to her, then lights one for himself. She sees her future, alone in the Tuileries, gazing at the suggestive Marqueste statue with longing, resting on this bench alone, reflecting, Once we were here together. She doesn't want her memory of this moment to be sad. He blows a puff of smoke, his eyes directed at the river. She follows his gaze, to the flat-bottomed boats gliding toward distant locales. And the tourist barges, filled with festive sightseers. She remembers how Teddy wanted to take one of those boats with her. She shivers.

"A week from now, I'll be halfway across the ocean," she says.

"In a beautiful cabin with champagne and silk bedspreads. On your way to your perfect summer house where cool breezes blow. A week from now, not one thing will have changed for me. Paris will be steaming. Everyone will escape. I'll still be here, soaked and sorry with all my worries."

But Edith hardly hears him. All she can imagine is standing on the terrace at The Mount, looking across the gardens at the lake. All alone. And all that's been awakened in her—the passion, the animal frankness she is just coming to know—will be forced back to sleep. She blinks back tears before they can fall. She doesn't want him remembering her weak and miserable. She wants him to remember the cheerful, game woman she's tried so hard to be. So she turns her face and smiles at him. He beams back, and she tries to note every detail of his face. Even the tiny mole on his cheek, the uneven edge of his eyetooth that must have been chipped in childhood. She tucks each detail into the hole in her heart.

When Edith arrives home, a letter is waiting on the front hall table. She lifts it. Seeing Anna's familiar penmanship gives Edith's heart a queer little jerk, and for a moment, she's lost in a flood of affection.

Dearest Edith, [How much it matters that Anna still cares to write "dearest"]

It has been a most beautiful, early spring here in New York. Flowers have appeared in all the parks and in front gardens all around town. I had forgotten that New York can be so beautiful. Like you, I had come to think of it as a trial more than a joy. But my walks have been sweet and satisfying, and it is very nice to renew acquaintances all up and down our block. Mrs. Van Peebles has given birth to a new baby, with a head of fine yellow hair like a fuzzy chick. And Lillah Bennet, the youngest daughter at 892, is engaged to be married to a very handsome young man. I have taken work tutoring the Lawndale children in 942 for a few weeks before school begins. They have read nothing of value, it seems. I do not know what is taught in school these days, but it is shockingly lean.

In the midst of all this, Gross and I escaped for a week to Virginia where we visited Mrs. Schultz, the mother of one of my old pupils. You met her once, and though she is very old, she is just as plucky and funny as she ever was. Gross fell in love with her and said we should adopt her like an old dog—which was a very unkind thing to say but struck a chord with me. She is indeed the sort of person so endearing and unique you wish you could pack her home with you.

I've missed you and thought of you often, and am saddened for how we parted. I do not know if you think of me, dear Edith. If I have not been supportive of your choices of late, I ache for it. I thought it would be good to let you know this before you return: that I wish to be a good friend to you in all ways, even if we are not of one mind.

*I hear from White that Mr. Wharton is improving every day,
and I am so relieved and grateful to you for finding an answer
at last to his terrible misery. Some days I worried so about him,
I imagined you sent him away because you did not wish to have
him near. How could I have thought such a thing? You had his
best interests at heart and the happy results speak for themselves.
I know Mr. Wharton will be traveling from Hot Springs to
Boston any day to see his sister and mother. I don't know if he'll
stop in New York. I will feel so joyous to see him recovered if and
when I do see him.*

*I've always wished to be of service to you, not a trial. I know
I have been a trial of late and I ask forgiveness for your old friend
and servant,*

Anna

Edith tucks the letter into a drawer in her trunk, hopeful that, if
nothing else, seeing Anna will ease her battered heart, not aggravate it.
Dear Anna. Dear good Anna.

On the last day before Edith sails, she stands in the pink room, surrounded by flirtatious dresses, satin-lined cloaks, gauzy tea gowns, ready
to be pinned into tissue and hung in the trunks. Each one enfolds a
memory for Edith. From the black velvet gown with the delicately
stitched bodice that she wore on their first outing together (Will he like
me in it? she'd worried when she put it on, turning this way and that in
the mirror), to the navy serge with the white modesty panel and pleated
skirt she donned the day they found shelter and privacy beneath the lilac
curtain under the ramparts of Senlis, their last moment of ecstasy together. The dresses are a compendium of her "coming out" year. She will
never don one again without breathing in a sweet memory from the
months that have changed her life. She steps to her desk and lifts the
diary, where she has written about Morton, and holds it close to her. It
documents every twist and turn of her heart.

I will give this to him tonight, she tells herself. He can hand it back to me tomorrow. She isn't afraid. Maybe if he sees it from her point of view, if he knows that what she's wanted from him is exactly what he's given her—love without commitment or long-term expectations—his love for her will grow. He'll admire all that she's tried so hard to be: unselfish, grateful, open, giving.

They meet for one last dinner at Antoine's, a restaurant just across the Seine from the Faubourg. He's waiting for her when she arrives.

"You look peaceful," he tells her.

"Maybe that's what a man feels when he stands before a firing squad. There is nothing one can do to delay the inevitable, and so it's best just to stand tall."

Morton laughs. "You *are* a brave soldier," he tells her.

"I want to give you something," she says. "It's a diary I've written for you."

"Isn't a diary meant for the writer's eyes alone?"

"Yes. But this was written to you, from the moment you came to The Mount last summer."

"Really," he says, and looks intrigued. He holds out his hand and takes the leather-bound book, pages through it.

"I want you to read it, and give it back to me at the ship tomorrow. Can you? Will you? I must have it back."

"If you like," he says. "Will it make me blush?"

She laughs. "You don't strike me as the sort to blush."

"Will it describe in graphic detail everything I've done to you? . . ." He raises his eyebrows comically.

"Done *with* me," she corrects him. "No," she says, feeling heat rise to her ears. "It won't do that."

"A pity," he says. "I'd like to see how the great Edith Wharton might describe *that*. . . . We could take a room tonight, you know," he says. "At that little hotel I told you about. We could have one last time. Together. In each other's arms. If you pay for it. I'm afraid I'm rather low on francs."

She looks at him, so guileless, so greedy, like a little boy. She shakes her head. "I'd rather think back on Senlis. Or La Châtaigneraie. I don't want to soil the memories with a mean little tryst. We're more than that."

He shrugs. How long will it be, she wonders, until he finds someone else? Until someone younger, more beautiful or more willing comes along, and he forgets how they once felt about each other? Surely, he will remember her through the summer? Maybe into the fall . . . and then? She picks up the menu and bites her lip, gathering all her stored strength just to say, "So, what shall we order for our last supper?"

At the train to Le Havre, Morton is dutifully waiting with her diary under his arm. She takes the leather book and tucks it into her hand luggage.

"Dearest," she whispers, and longs desperately for just a moment alone, a whispered word, anything that speaks of all they've been to each other. She successfully begged Harry not to come and see her off, just so that she might have that moment with Morton, so that words might be spoken which she can enclose in her hand and clutch all the way to New York. But all around them, like a thrumming conspiracy, are people they know.

"My God, Pussy, what good luck to see you!" Her cousin Le Roy King steps between Morton and her, and throws his arms around her shoulders.

"Don't you look splendid! Are you off today as well? Don't tell me you're on the *Provence*? This is just too lucky, I say! Let's make certain we're at the same table for dinner tonight. We'll pop champagne and I'll catch you up on Bunny and Abel and what's been happening to the whole ugly brood. Where's my good friend Teddy? At Hot Springs? Who'd choose Hot Springs over Paris? He's a madman!"

Morton is looking out into the crowd, his face unreadable, smoking.

"Have you ever met my friend, Mr. Fullerton?" she asks. "He was good enough to see me off. I'm afraid we have a bit of business to discuss before the train leaves."

"How do you do there, Fullerton. Seems we've met somewhere, but I have no idea where. We didn't go to school together, did we? I'm an Eli. You? Harvard. Gosh. *Harvard*, old man, what were you thinking?"

While Le Roy prattles on, Edith watches Morton for a sign of annoyance, or even misery, at their parting. But there is nothing to decipher.

She feels as distant from him as if she were already halfway across the Atlantic. The idea sends a dart of pain through her chest. No wonder the words "broken heart" were created. She does feel as though her heart is a dried-out tea biscuit, left on the floor and stepped on.

"Last time I traveled, two of my trunks were lost or stolen. Never did find them again. . . . Someone out there is wearing my evening clothes!"

"Le Roy, let's plan on dinner tonight," Edith says, finding a spot to break into his monologue at last. "Right now, Mr. Fullerton and I have a few last-minute business items to discuss. He's handling my stories with the *Revue de Paris* and we must chat about the coming few months. You wouldn't mind giving us a moment, would you?"

"Just remember to look me up on the ship then, dear," Le Roy says. He shakes Morton's hand with absurdly good cheer and then, thank God, he is gone.

Morton boards the train with her and helps settle her luggage onto the overhead rack. His eyes already look bored. Or is it just fear that makes her read impatience into his expression. Could he really be happy to see her go? He has read her diary. He knows what he has meant to her. She wonders if it was a mistake to share the words with him. Like snapping open her ribs and presenting her heart. Perhaps she trusted too much. She had thought of it as a gift of her love. But maybe he sees it as an expression of her need for him. He has always balked when she's asked too much.

"Dear Mrs. Wharton, are you on your way for the season?"

Edith looks up to see the Abbé de Mugnier insinuating himself into their compartment, another gray-haired gentleman behind him. The unfairness, the misery of so many people milling about! She feels she is being punished.

"This is my brother!" the good Abbé says. "He's on the *Provence*. Are you as well?"

She nods and shakes the Abbé's brother's plump little hand.

"And you too, Mr. Fullerton?"

"No, I've just come to see Mrs. Wharton off."

Edith loves the Abbé and his wonderful sense of humor. But she longs to make him disappear altogether. She fears she will begin to cry.

"Well, I hope you and my brother get to spend some time together while at sea. I think you'll find you have much in common. Meanwhile, I'll leave you two alone to say your good-byes." He looks from Edith to Morton with a wry smile. My God, Edith wonders, does he know? The train whistle hoots its dire warning.

"I'd better go," Morton says.

"But we finally have a moment alone!"

He closes his eyes with what could be impatience, or sadness. "I've never been very impressive at good-byes. I'm much more comfortable slipping off and writing a note later. . . . Besides, you know I plan to come to the States some time this summer."

"Will you write a note? I feel as though I'm being torn in two."

His eyes are kind. "I know," he says. Perhaps these are the only kind words she'll get from him. Her heart sinks. He kisses her quickly on the mouth, but she grabs his shoulders and takes one last deep draught from his lips.

He straightens up. His cheeks are stained with color.

"Bon voyage. I've written something for you in your diary," he says before he disappears through the compartment door.

"Thank you," she whispers.

She sits alone, chilled in the May heat. She can't feel her feet. Or her nose. Perhaps she is hyperventilating. Or close to death.

She spots Fullerton outside her window. He waves and smiles, and as the train squeals and jerks forward, she holds up her hand and smiles too, though to smile at this moment seems as incongruous as looking joyful while someone is slitting her throat.

Once outside of Paris, she reaches into her handbag for her diary. On the last page he's written a whole page of script.

> *What Mrs. Wharton isn't saying is how she was transformed this winter from a cold, formidable, frigid wife to a warm, open lover. How she discovered the heat of passion and learned to impart it too. How she was willing to lie naked with a man who was not her husband and discovered that the gates of hell did not squeak open. As a pupil, as a lover, as an adulterer, she was insatiable, giving and true. Does she know there is so much more*

to teach her, so much more for her to learn? I hope the day will come when we can begin again.

Not a word about love. Not a word about their souls becoming one. Maybe that's not how men think. Maybe he is being self-protective, knowing she is married. Maybe love is not what he felt at all? But lust. No. She can't believe it. She closes the diary and shivers as the train carries her farther and farther away.

THIRTEEN

EARLY SUMMER 1908

Anna arrives at The Mount a few hours before Edith's scheduled arrival. Just the crunch of gravel on the drive sets her heart pounding. At last she is back to her real life—where she can make a difference to someone, make her small dent upon the world. The Lenox air is a good ten degrees cooler than New York City's. Gross preceded Anna by a full week, so she could spur the local staff into folding and storing the off-season canvas covers, dusting and washing floors, walls and ceilings, expelling unwanted creatures and whipping the place into "Edith" shape. Flowers already grace the big vases in the hall. The house smells scrubbed and fresh, exuding country air and baking, and hope for a beautiful summer.

Anna's small room sits at the end of the hall on The Mount's servant floor with a view of the forecourt and a bed whose linens whisper of lavender. Anna is thrilled to find it empty and ready. Like a book that is yet to be written. She shoves open the windows as far as she can, and lets the breeze pour in, carrying with it the sweet whinny of horses in the barn, cows lowing in the field. With her view of the forecourt, Anna will hear the gravel singing again when Edith and Teddy arrive. And she wants to know first thing. How she longs to see them both!

She changes out of her traveling clothes—the blue serge suit that once was Edith's, the high-collared broadcloth shirt, now damp at the neck from the sweltering train. She pulls her old gray-green dress out of her carry-bag. It has happily been washed so many times its nap feels like velvet, and even having been bunched in her handbag, it breathes out its wrinkles in a moment. It is a quiet dress, the kind that makes Anna disappear into the background. She merely wants to observe: to see Teddy, well and strong and happy once again. To look into Edith's eyes and know whether she has forgiven her for the warning against Fullerton. She wonders what happened with Fullerton all spring. Has he disappointed Edith yet? She splashes her face in the basin and enjoys a cool, wet linen rag on the back of her neck. If Edith hasn't forgiven her, what will she do? Where will she go? The thought slows her down for a moment, and as she buttons up her fresh dress, she gazes at herself in the dressing mirror. She is too old to start over. Too shy. Too tired. But she has never been one to sink. She is a swimmer.

A knock at her door announces Holly and Jeff, the two local brothers that come every summer to open the house. They've hoisted her trunks off the trunk lift in the hall and ask to set them in her room as though they are requesting a favor.

"Good to see you, Miss Anna," Holly says. "I read that book you gave me."

"Did you?" Anna can't remember which book.

"This Mark Twain fella, does he live on the Mississippi?" Ah, it must have been *Huckleberry Finn*.

"Not anymore," Anna says. "He did once. There are more of his books in the library in town if you wish to read on."

"Well, maybe," Holly says. He tips his hat at Anna as they leave.

All of Anna's dresses and hats find their rightful places in her armoire. She's brought too many books, she fears, but she stacks them on her dresser in neat piles. She won't have time to read them all, but she couldn't bear to let them sit lonely and dusty in her empty room on Park Avenue. And then, just as she opens the book she's chosen from the pile, she hears gravel scattering and rushes to the window to see Mr. Wharton climbing out of the wagon. Standing tall, he pauses for a moment, doffing his hat, glancing around at the grounds, up at the house.

"Looking just fine!" he declares. The familiar sound of his dear, rusty voice, so full of hope, eases her in a way she hasn't felt in months. "We're here at last," Teddy says. "Here at last." He turns and helps Edith out.

Edith, taking in the house as Teddy did, appears thinner, and even from up here, Anna can see there is no light in her eye. She looks crushed, uncertain. Not emotions Anna usually sees in the grown-up Edith Wharton.

Anna gives them time to settle. She hears the clatter of the trunk lift, voices weaving through the halls and, after a time, Edith's voice just below in her room. She is telling Gladys, the new maid, where she wants her things. But Anna doesn't go down to see her. Not yet. She tries to read her book, though the words float up from the page without mean-ing. When she hears Edith heading back down to the parlor floor (she would know her footsteps anywhere), Anna follows.

Edith is in her library, seated at the desk, looking out over her room, and her face is ghostlike and lost, like a child parted from her mother.

"Hello," Anna says.

"Tonni." Edith stands and takes Anna into her arms, then straight-ens her arms to look into Anna's eyes. "I'm happy to see you," she says. But she doesn't look happy at all. It's not because of me, Anna tells her-self sternly.

"A good crossing, Herz?" Anna asks.

Edith's chin quivers.

"It was a nice ship," she says. "The Abbé's brother was aboard, and my cousin Le Roy. And you? You had a nice spring in New York, it seems."

Anna nods. "Very nice. Do you have work for me?" Anna asks. "I would so like to know where the book has gone. I've thought often of Undine, and wondered about her fate."

Edith shakes her head. "Later maybe," she says.

"Are you all right, dear?"

Edith shakes her head ever so slightly, closes her eyes. Her lids are the color of violets. She hasn't been sleeping. Anna knows the signs. Edith is a language she's spoken fluently for years and years.

"Well, Miss Anna!" Teddy enters the room with such energy, the books seem to shake on the shelves. His face is full of light, too red. Almost absurdly happy compared to Edith's. "I got me my wife back, and now my good friend Anna. It's a fine day indeed. How's by you, little Anna?" He seems to take up the room today. The last time she saw him, he could hardly walk, speak, and most of all he seemed to be shrinking in his bed. His head hurt, his whole body screamed in pain. She doesn't mind that he is so full of life now, that he has no sensitivity to Edith's gray mood. She just feels blessed to see him renewed.

"You're looking well, Mr. Wharton!" she says.

"Pussy knew just the cure: I needed them Arkansas waters. Did me a world of good. I owe it all to her. Ever had Arkansas fried chicken? They spice it up with some of that cayenne pepper. Could cure anyone. Might even make *you* grow, Anna. Pussy's looking like she could use some too. She's skinny as a little boy. Guess she missed me so much, she couldn't eat." He leans over and squeezes Edith's shoulder. She recoils so obviously, it even surprises Anna. But if Teddy notices, he doesn't show it.

"I've always liked fried chicken," Anna says encouragingly.

"The pig barn is nearly done. The hennery. We're finally getting this place shaped up. Have you gotten around? Taken a look?"

"No sir. I just arrived this morning too."

"Pussycat, you up for a hike in the mud? I can't wait to show you how the piggery is looking."

"Not now, Teddy," Edith says. "Letters." She reaches into her desk drawer and pulls out a handful of writing paper.

"You're in the country at last and you want to write letters to all the intellects in Paris? The girl don't have a clue how to conduct herself in the backwoods. How about you, Miss Anna? You want to come down and see the new barns? I'm itching to show them to someone who might exhibit some appreciation."

"Well, I certainly am looking forward to seeing them. But Mrs. Wharton might need me."

"Go with him," Edith says. "Go. I have a headache anyway. And letters. Letters to write." She looks beseechingly at Anna. Take him off my hands! her eyes beg.

"If it ain't one of us with an aching head, it's the other. Come on,

Miss Anna. You better go find your boots because it's a mud pile out there."

Teddy, kneeling in the muck, hugging his beloved Hampshire porker Lawton, catches Anna's eye. "You did me a good turn back in Paris, Miss Anna. And a man don't forget that sort of kindness." Anna is surprised to hear his voice grow soft and thoughtful. Especially in his new ebullient mood.

"I felt you needed a friend," she says after a moment. "I am always your friend."

"The kindest of friends. Am I right in thinkin' you and Puss had yourselves a falling out?"

Anna steps back with surprise. "No. No," she says. "What makes you think that, Mr. Wharton?"

"Seems like she sent you back early this spring. I was surprised to hear it."

"She didn't think there was room at her brother's when it was time to move there. She sent back Gross and White too."

"Them, sure. No need for them at Harry's house. But you . . . well, she needs your services no matter where she is. And you never took up much room in your life. You want to tell me what's eating her?"

"Eating her?"

"You know perfectly well what I mean. Bothering her. She's not herself. You think I'm just a blunderbuss who don't see these things, but I assure you, I do."

"She's probably tired from the journey. I guess you, more than anyone, know what it's like to feel done in."

"I was sick with gout. Doctors diagnosed me. What's ailing Puss?"

Anna shrugs. She's doing all she can not to color, not to give anything away. The last thing she wants is Teddy mentioning Fullerton. He knows, of course. He always knew that Edith was being beckoned away from him. That's why he grew so ill. Anna never doubted for a moment that Edith's moral lapse was one of the triggers of Teddy's ailments.

"You think I can win her back?" he asks very softly.

"Win her back?" Anna says.

"Don't toy with me, Missy. You know what I mean. We speak the same language, you and I. You understand me better than she does. She's all I got, Anna. All I ever cared about. I can't compete on her intellectual plane. But I'm not ready to give her up." He stands, and reaches out as though to grab Anna's shoulders, then turns his hands upward to show they're full of mud and drops them to his sides.

"Please. Tell me what I can do to win her back."

Anna feels for him. His plea twists her soul.

"Listen to her. Ask her questions. Ask what she's thinking. What she's reading."

"When I do, I hardly know what she's jawing about these days. Her head is filled with ideas I'll never be able to sort out."

Anna nods. "You could still let her talk. Act like you want to understand. Have her explain things."

"And make myself out like a fool?"

"Acting interested doesn't make you a fool."

He shakes his head. "When we have those conversations, she picks up right away that I don't get a word . . . reminds her why she don't need me no more. . . ."

"The main thing is," Anna says, "she's away from Paris now. Here at The Mount you share a different life. You can remind her now how much she loves her gardens; together you can enjoy the dogs—do the things you've always cared about as a . . . as a couple. She's a different person here. Remind her of that."

He smiles, and his eyes clear.

"That makes good sense," he says. "I don't know what I'd do without you. Come on!" His face is animated again. His voice high and full of joy. How quickly his mood has returned to frantic joy. It disturbs her. "You've just gotta see the hennery. It's the best hennery in all the land!" She follows him through the mud, through the straw. All the places Edith no longer wishes to go.

✿

Edith's letters to Morton are too long, too frequent. But, as she composes them, she can see Morton in a chair just on the other side of the room, listening, his head cocked just so, a cigarette teetering between his lips, his eyes squinted to avoid the smoke, his legs outstretched. Listening is one of his greatest skills. And thinking about him, feeling him there, as she writes, her letters begin as one long howl of pain, because, of course, he *isn't* in the chair. He will *never* sit in that chair! Then somehow, she gathers herself, regains her poise, and goes on to report her days, her small bits of news, her hopes, her memories, just to undercut the obvious grief written all over the first page.

This grief affects her fiction too, though she's back to writing as soon as she wakes. Like a trained dog, she tells herself. But there is a new darkness stealing over the novel. A sense that nothing good will ever come to pass in her fictional world either. It's easier to write letters, even if she is unsure how Morton will take their frequency.

"I am ashamed to write so often, because with this life I lead here, there's absolutely nothing to tell," she writes. But she fills the pages, one after the other. Anything to make the "conversation" last longer. Sometimes she tries to be magnanimous, to balance the foolish prattle.

"Write. Don't write," she tells him. "Which means always when you want to, and never—not once!—when you are busy, or in the least feel it as a thing-to-be-done. I don't want to put any more of those into your life."

Then one morning a letter arrives announcing that it's possible that Morton will not make it to the States at all this summer—in fact, come winter, he doesn't even know where he'll end up. Things are not good at the *Times*. He's sure Edith will understand how disoriented he feels.

Edith wants to find sympathy for him. But the disappointment is too bitter. Maybe he is escaping *her*. Maybe it's just Morton's oblique way of ending things. Who imagined her despair could grow so large?

She writes him, her pen stabbing at the paper:

> *Don't write me again. Let me face at once the fact that it is over. Without a date to look to, I can't bear to go on; and it will be easier to make the break now, voluntarily, than to see it slowly, agonizingly made by time and circumstance.*

For a good two hours after the letter has been handed to White, to be stuffed into a mailbag destined for the next steamer, she believes she has done a noble thing, that in order to maintain her dignity she simply had to cut off the one person in her life who made her feel truly alive. But then, the plates of the earth shift. And all she wants is to be in contact with Morton Fullerton.

She sends for White.

"Did that letter go out?" she asks, hearing the wobble of desperation in her voice.

"Of course, Madam," he says. "It went out a few hours ago."

"And there's no way to stop it?"

White doesn't speak for a moment. He licks his lips and looks at her as one might observe a mad person.

"Not that I know of," he says. His voice is forcedly soothing.

"Thank you," she says, but she cannot even look at him. Now she is lost, bloated with despair and self-loathing.

And her day gets worse: White brings her a cable that states that the motorcar which, after some mechanical work, was to follow her on the next ship to the States has burst a tire on the way to Le Havre. The mechanic then lost control and smashed the poor blue Panhard into a tree. He, fortunately, sustained only minor injuries. But the car needs extensive repair, and won't cross the ocean for weeks. In her misery, Edith finds it too easy to envision herself in the backseat of her plush car, lifeless and bloodied against the red leather, her head thrown back on its broken stem, her eyes open and staring. And the vision gives her relief. A cessation of pain. A dramatic ending to all that seems too much to bear. She wallows in the apparition for a long time, like a child splashing in a warm bath.

As Anna types the new pages Edith hands her, she's struck by how selfish and unlikeable Edith's character Undine Spragg has become. Her God is money. Status. Fashion. She doesn't even care for her own child. Edith is heeding Anna's warning to make sure that Undine is unlikeable. But maybe she's gone too far. Such an odious character to be the eyes and ears of a novel! Anna sees something else that surprises her: every time Undine opens her mouth, Anna is sharply reminded of Lucretia. She's never mentioned the likeness to Edith, but it's clearly so.

Lucretia was not ungenerous to Anna. And she had beautiful bearing. But she could be harsh. And selfish. And oh, how she longed for acceptance from the wealthy and mighty. It was her goal in life to be important in society. To be considered among the finest, even if the family couldn't afford her aspirations. She bought too many meaningless things to fill a strange, growing emptiness. She found her husband disappointing, too bookish, lacking in ambition, just as Undine finds Ralph Marvell in Edith's book.

But the thing Anna found most reprehensible about Lucretia was that she was unkind to her own daughter. Lucretia made it no secret she thought Edith a changeling. In Lucretia's eyes, Edith read too much for a little girl. She *thought* too much. She cared too little for fashion and standing. Just like her father, George Jones. They were two of a kind and made Lucretia feel like she was the one who was lacking, the outsider. Of course, they were the outsiders in the real world. They were dreamers, wallflowers. Good thing there was a governess to deal with Edith, because Lucretia didn't have a thing to say to her.

Whether or not Edith has recognized Undine as Lucretia's very double, she's grown angrier and angrier at her protagonist as the pages of the book compile. In the chapters that Edith's written since her return to The Mount, Undine has become a scapegoat for all of Edith's anger and misery.

And miserable Edith is. Short-tongued, snippy, icy, silent. Anna wants to speak to her the way they used to, share books, thoughts, ideas. But now is clearly not the time.

"Undine has certainly become a handful," Anna tells Edith one day when she can hold back no more.

Edith sets her pen down, pushes back her chair and sits in silence for a moment. "And shouldn't she be? You were the one who said . . . ," she asks.

"It's not a criticism. I find her interesting. I find *it* interesting that you've chosen to make her so utterly . . . abhorrent."

"I don't really wish *you* to judge my characters," Edith says, her voice as gelid as Anna has ever heard.

Anna is crushed. She's been judging Edith's characters for years and years.

"I just was commenting. . . ."

Edith looks up with raised brows. "Is there anything else you wish to say?" she asks.

"I'm sorry. I didn't mean anything by it." Anna, close to tears, heads for the door.

"Tonni."

"Yes."

"You'll have to forgive me just now."

Anna nods. But she's shaken. Confused. Just as she does with Teddy, Edith is blocking her out. Blocking them both out. And it hurts.

The Mount is beautiful, the lime trees just leafing, the first of the perennials in the fountain garden tender as babies. But Edith has never felt more blind to what's on offer. Except for one day, out in her garden, when she thinks she hears a nightingale. Its haunting melody dilates her heart like a flower bursting its bud. Do nightingales live in New England? And sing during the day? It can't be. And yet she perches on the stone bench, eyes closed, sucking in the sound. Oh, how it recalls to her the radiant moment on the night train from Senlis, side by side with Morton, his warm hand in hers.

Her eyes fill with tears. They spill and spill with longing. She stays out in the garden for a long time afterward, waiting for the tears to dry, for her eyes to clear, afraid of running into Anna.

If only Anna would go away. Every time she steps into the room, Edith knows she's sniffed out her black mood, and thinks she's getting her due for ever having loved Morton Fullerton. It doubles her misery to feel sorrowful in front of Anna. Anna is too kind-hearted to indulge in schadenfreude, but considering how she protects Teddy, how she warned Edith about Morton, surely she feels that Edith's despair is a natural conclusion to her folly.

Teddy chews at her nerves even more. He strikes Edith as simply too excited. At dinner, he talks and talks about things that don't interest her at all. He laughs at nearly everything, as though the world is a comedy written just for him. He has taken to calling her "Pussycat," which makes her want to knife him. And he can't sit still. He can't read a book. He wanders around the house wraithlike at night. More than once she's felt his presence and has awakened, startled, from dreams to find him standing in her open bedroom door, staring. When she asks, he says he's just checking on her, enjoying her presence.

"Awfully sorry if it disturbed you," he chuckles. His jollity is what disturbs her.

"Don't you ever sleep anymore?" she asks him, wondering whether or not this is an improvement over the man who did nothing but doze in the armchair in Paris, hardly moving all day long.

"I don't need to sleep these days," Teddy says. "I feel perfectly fine with hardly any sleep at all. Aren't you glad, Pussycat?"

She wakes in the morning and things are moved, disturbed, opened, eaten. How easy Teddy makes it to hate him! It's almost too much to bear: comparing this hollow fool to Morton. She *is* grateful for one thing: that Teddy pays no heed to her melancholy, seems entirely unaware of it. He has no ability or interest in knowing his wife in depth. What a blessing!

At least more letters from Morton arrive.

"I passed through the Rue de Varenne yesterday and felt certain that you would come to the window of 58 if I stood there long enough." "I bought myself an entire box of raspberry macarons yesterday and ate every single one like a lovesick girl. Today I feel miserable. I shall have to buy a new waistcoat." She inhales them, rereads them, sleeps with them by her bedside in a neat stack hidden beneath her Line-a-Day diary. Sometimes, half-awake, she reaches out and touches them.

And then suddenly, Morton stops writing. It's like a faucet squeakily shut off after flowing freely. Not a word. At first she thinks he's merely busy. Tangled in an annoying assignment from the *Times*. But then three days pass, five, ten. Despair falls on Edith like a blanket of wet snow. She's terrified that he's seriously ill, or maybe has had an accident. Perhaps *he* is the one in the backseat of a car, dead, twisted, broken. Just the thought of it takes her breath away. Destroys her.

She goes to her library and sits at her desk, where the corner windows ensure a breeze. Even as she picks up her pen, her hands are shaking. She knows how important it is to display an even tone, a detached good humor in every word. Still, how painful it is to sound objective when her heart is crashing at every possibility for his lack of communication! She cannot, as hard as she tries, imagine a positive reason why he hasn't written.

When I sent you, eight days ago, that desperate word: "Don't write me again!" I didn't guess that you were already acting on it! Not a line from you in nine days—since your letter of June 2d. Eleven days at least must have passed without your feeling the impulse to write. . . .

You know I never wanted you to write unless you wanted to. And I always understood it would not go on for long. But this is so sudden that I almost fear you are ill, or that something has happened to trouble you.

Think! You have not even answered my first letter, my letter from the steamer, which must have reached you on the 10th; and five steamers have come in, that might have brought an answer to it.—Don't think I don't mean what I said when I last wrote, or what I reiterated to you so often before we said good-bye: that I don't want from you a sign, a gesture, that is not voluntary, spontaneous—irrepressible!—

No—I am still of that mind. Only, as I said, this is so unbelievably sudden. My reason, even—my reason much more than my feeling—tells me it must be some accident that has kept you silent; and then my anxiety begins its conjectures.

Send a word, dear, to reassure me. And if it's not that, but the other alternative, surely you're not afraid to say so? My last letter will have shown you how I have foreseen, how I have accepted, such a contingency. Do you suppose I ever have, for a moment, ceased to see a thousand reasons why it was inevitable and likely to be not far distant?

Allons donc! You shall see what I am made of—only don't be afraid to trust me to the utmost of my lucidity and my philosophy!

—But no! I don't ask you to say anything that might be painful to you. Simply write: "Chère camarade, I am well—things

*are well with me"; and I shall understand and accept—and think
of you as you would like a friend to think.—Above all, don't see
any hidden reproach in this. There is nothing in it but tenderness
and understanding. I am well, and the week since I wrote last has
managed to get itself lived. And the novel goes on. And people
come and go.—I can't tell you more now, but another time,
perhaps—*

And now and always I am yr so affectionate E.

But still day after day passes with no word. She lies in bed and wonders: how could he have taken her literally when she wrote "Don't write"? Yes, her words have been misleading, contradictory. But Morton understands women better than other men. Surely he knows she breathes for him. Surely he knows.

"Since when have you not been able to decipher my handwriting?" she finds herself storming at Anna. "I've never had pages back from you so mistyped!"

Anna seems to shrink before her eyes. And she is already the smallest adult Edith knows.

"Have I truly misread your pages?" Anna's voice is so tiny it's barely audible.

"Yes. Here. I wrote, 'He found her less restless and rattling than usual.' But you typed 'He found her less restless and railing than usual.' Railing. What on earth were you thinking?"

"I'm sorry."

"And here. 'The other lay cold in his clasp, and through it there gradually stole on him the benumbing influence of his thoughts. . . .' 'on him,' Tonni? I wrote 'to him.'"

"I . . . I don't know how I made the mistake. 'On him' must have seemed right. 'Stole to him' . . . didn't seem right perhaps. . . ."

"Oh, and are you choosing my words now? You wish to redirect my life, comment on my characters and now redirect my writing? Why don't you just write the book yourself. Perhaps you think yourself better qualified."

Anna gasps and steps backward. "I . . ." And then she turns and runs from the room. Later, the pages show up at Edith's bedroom door, retyped. And Anna seems to disappear. For two or three days, Edith doesn't see her at all. Her pages are typed and set at her door each day, but Anna isn't apparent at all.

✿

Anna can scarcely leave her room. Her limbs are heavy. Her heart doesn't seem to work hard enough to sustain her. Sometimes she peers out the window and sees Teddy, so jolly these days as he tramps to the barns and back. Perhaps they have exchanged sturdiness and misery. He is fine, and she has sucked up his wretchedness like a leech used to suck out bad blood.

She attends dinner with the servants but hardly touches the food, rarely speaks. When Gross stops her in the hall to ask if she's all right, she says, "Of course." But her heart is in pieces. Too shattered to mend. If she went back to New York, she could find a room in a boarding house. She has saved some money. Surely she could become a social secretary to someone. Perhaps the Lawndale children will need a full-time tutor? No. Far too close to 882, and memories. She will have to be strong. She will have to begin again. How tired it makes her feel.

✿

At last, Edith resolves to cable Morton. He's left her no choice. She must make a trip to town to do so. She could never give the task to White. She could never expose herself so.

She stands in the cable office shaking, trying to pen the note. Why didn't she compose it earlier, at her desk? Why did she wait until now, with the telegraph man standing at the counter on the other side of the room, watching her?

Am concerned for your safety STOP No word for days STOP Tell me you're alive and well STOP Nothing else matters STOP

Ridiculous. Too dramatic. She tries again.

> Haven't heard from you in weeks STOP Am concerned
> STOP Please tell me you are well STOP That's all I need to
> hear STOP

No. There isn't *enough* urgency. She must let him know that he has made her suffer! That he has withheld from her the one thing that keeps her alive. Otherwise he might not respond! And how would she feel if he didn't respond even to a cable! She dies a little just imagining it.

> No letter for three weeks STOP Am sick with worry
> STOP Have I done something to upset you STOP Please let
> me know if you are all right and ease my mind STOP Always
> yours STOP

No words will ever be right. She'll just have to send it flawed. She hands the paper to the operator and he nods, counts the words, tells her how much she'll owe. She is quivering as she draws the appropriate bills out of her purse, fumbles with the change. She wishes she had the courage to grab back the cable request sheet. Surely it would be better to send nothing. How desperate will she appear to Morton, if indeed he is alive? And yet, she *must* do something. She can't go on not knowing if he's dead in the backseat of a car. Angry or in love with someone else. Could he be with Katherine? She feels her skin growing damp. Her hairline, her neck, her breasts are prickly with perspiration. She is breathing as she used to in those dark Newport days when she could barely draw air in and out of her lungs. She finishes paying and forces herself to go outside and sit on the bench by the Lenox post office. She prays no one will come along and spot her. Sitting perfectly still, she stares at the ground, waiting until the feeling of dread passes.

The problem, she tells herself, is that once she expected nothing out of life. She knew that no good thing could come to her, and accepted her fate. Now that she's tasted the opiate of love and happiness, she craves it, aches for it. And, denied it, she is left with a sense of misery so profound at moments she feels she can't go on. *Is* it better to have loved and lost? To have discovered the one thing most worth knowing? To have shared her heart so selflessly? There are moments—like this one—when she doubts it.

No! She must have more mettle than this! Where is her proud self? The one who lived on books and flowers and observations and words—a million words—that arranged themselves so satisfyingly? Where is the woman she's worked so hard to become?

Edith sends one of the maids to bring Anna to the drawing room for tea. Nervously, Anna seats herself in the needlepoint bergère across from Edith. She can't even bear to look up, so she stares at her hands. But her eyes are unseeing. Her heart is rattling in her chest like a motorcar with a faulty engine.

"Would you like a cake?" Edith asks.

"No. I ate too much at luncheon." In truth, she ate nothing.

"The new cook is very good, isn't she? I think the food is the best we've had here since we've taken up at The Mount."

Anna nods, still can't look up. If she sees Edith's face, will she see a Gorgon before her? Will she turn to stone?

"Tonni, I want to offer you something," Edith says. "A present, really. I hope you'll hear me out, and be open to it."

Anna's nerves keep her from sitting still. Her legs jerk as though they wish to run.

"All winter while we were in Paris, you talked about how you wanted to get over to Germany, about your time there when you were young."

Anna nods but has a hard time remembering ever telling Edith that she wished to go back to Germany. Maybe she mentioned it once when they were talking about German poetry. But surely she didn't speak of it all winter as Edith implies.

"I want to give you a gift of a trip abroad."

"You . . . I don't understand."

"We're quite fixed for money these days. It's rather stunning how well the books have done. Especially *The House of Mirth*. It's such a success in France."

"Yes."

"I want to send you to Europe for the rest of the summer. Germany, Italy, wherever you like. I owe it to you."

Now Anna raises her head and gazes on the woman she has known best in all her life. She is expecting to see an ugliness in her familiar face, but Edith simply looks like Edith. She is pale, and her mouth is sweet and kind, as it was when she was a child offering Anna a flower she'd picked from the field.

"You owe me nothing," Anna says.

"But I do. I owe you everything. In truth, I'm not much fun to be with right now. I'm not myself. I fear I've been unkind to you."

"I seem to irritate you," Anna ventures.

"It's not you. Everything irritates me right now. I am suffering. And only you know why."

"But I don't know why. You haven't told me anything. . . ."

"You know the source of my suffering. I don't want to tell you what's happened. You'll only gloat."

"Gloat!" Anna is shocked. "I could never gloat at your pain."

"I talked to Teddy about it. And we both want to send you to Europe as a thank-you. If you want, you can come back in the autumn for a bit, and until we leave for France in the winter. Or, you could stay the rest of the summer and autumn and meet us in Paris. That's another option. . . ."

"You don't owe me anything."

"I knew you'd be hard to persuade. I knew you'd fight me on this. But I want to do something nice for you. And I thought once you mulled it over, you'd be pleased. You needn't tell me now. Think it over. Talk to Gross. You could of course go back to Missouri. That would be fine as well. I just want to give you something. A trip. A gift. Teddy does too. You were so kind to him when he was ill. Far kinder than I was. He reminds me all the time."

Anna says nothing. The offer lodges in her heart, radiating pain, and she's trying to sort out why. Because Edith can't bear the sight of her. How has it come to this?

"What have I done to make you want me to leave?" Anna asks. There. She's set it out for both of them to see.

"Oh no. You mustn't think of it that way."

"I'm happiest when I'm helping you. You know I am."

"But wouldn't you enjoy some time away? Some time to see your childhood places. You have cousins in Germany. Imagine seeing Weimar again. Goethe's home. And Italy. You've always said you long to see Italy. We'll pay for the nicest sort of travel."

Anna can see how beseeching Edith's eyes are.

"Do you really want me to go?" Anna asks. "I know you haven't been happy with my typing."

"It's not that. Heavens. It's not that. That was me. Being absurd."

"You weren't happy when I was gone last summer."

"Perhaps this time you could help me find a replacement. A temporary replacement that I could trust. If you were doing the choosing . . . well . . . the woman we had last summer was a nightmare. . . ."

"You send me away from Paris for the whole spring, then you send me away again. Perhaps you are through with me. I'd rather you just say so. You're not responsible for me. I could go back to teaching. I could find a place of my own in New York, like the apartment I had on Ninety-fifth Street. I'm not afraid." Nonetheless, Anna can hear her voice quavering.

"No!" Edith jumps up. "I couldn't bear to lose you. You musn't think that's what I want. I just need time."

"It's because I warned you about him. I wish I'd never told you what I knew."

"Oh Tonni."

"Why must *he* come between us? It isn't right. It isn't fair."

"It isn't. But there it is."

Anna feels utterly exhausted. She would not have changed anything. Warning Edith was something she had to do. Sometimes friendships go bad, she tells herself. Relationships soften and rot like old fruit. They have their time, and then they shrivel and grow putrid. She feels her shoulders shaking. She doesn't want to cry in front of Edith. She can't.

Edith comes to Anna, kneels down before her.

"My beloved Tonni," she says.

Tears spill from Anna's eyes, making it hard to take in the woman who once was her dearest friend, her very heart.

Edith reaches up and wipes a tear from Anna's cheek. "You are like a mother to me. But sometimes when we are at our most foolish, we don't want our mothers to see. Don't you understand?"

Anna shakes her head. "I don't judge you," she says. "I worry for you. But I don't judge you."

"I judge myself," Edith says. "I feel like a fool. And when I see you look-ing at me the way you do . . . I . . . Take this trip. Do it for me. You will enjoy it, you'll see. Perhaps one of your cousins can travel with you. Take this trip and make it the gift I intend it to be. Get away from me before I hurt you."

Edith reaches out and puts her arms around Anna's waist, settles her head in her lap, just as she used to when she was a child and Anna was her savior.

"Please," she begs. "Do it for me."

✿

Even with White's help, there's some difficulty getting a reservation on a ship. But it is done. Then there is the task of finding Anna's replace-ment. Someone must take the position! Besides the task of typing and editing Edith's daily pages, boxes of mail are arriving monthly from Edith's publisher, full of letters from loyal readers—people saying that reading Mrs. Wharton's books has stirred them, thrilled them, disturbed them or lifted them up from the drudgery of daily life. Someone must answer them all, and even with a mostly standardized note, the process takes time! Anna calls a secretarial service in New York City. Four women arrive one afternoon on the train. They sit on a bench in the downstairs reception hall waiting for an interview in the servants' din-ing room. They are young and fresh and thrilled to seize the opportunity to work for the famous Mrs. Wharton. But none of them possesses the sensitivity, the learnedness or the patience that Edith requires.

So Anna writes to her friend, Miss Fannie Thayer, and asks if she would consider taking the position for a few months. She has known Miss Thayer for twenty-five years. When they were young girls, they were great companions, enjoying the museums and the theatre together. Even skating in Central Park. They learned to be typewriters at the same school, and lived in the same boarding house, their rooms side by side. Sometimes at night, in bed, they would each knock the rhythm of a song on the wall and tell each other in the morning their best guess at which song the other was tapping.

Fannie is well over sixty now. She is rather large and heavy and wears silver-rimmed glasses. She reads incessantly. She particularly loves "the romantic poets," Wordsworth and Shelley, and quotes their poems mistily whenever the occasion arises. She admires Goethe. Anna thinks Edith will love her.

And knowing this, for a moment, Anna hesitates. Up until now, Edith's had no one with whom to compare Anna. Except for the woman last year who was no competition. If Edith tries out Miss Thayer and discovers what it's like to have someone better qualified . . . well, she already is sending Anna away. Things between them feel very tenuous indeed.

But Anna hires her, coming to the conclusion that serving Edith is more important than protecting herself.

Then she focuses on her trip. Letters must be written to her cousins. Trunks reappear in her room and give her a sinking feeling. She was so happy to unpack them just weeks ago. Now she must fold and hang everything again. She wishes she'd left half her books in New York after all. She'll have to wrap them up for White to ship back to 882. And then she has a chilling thought: perhaps she will never be a part of this household again. Perhaps her trunks, on returning from Europe, will be sent to a room in a rooming house, and all the things she left at 882 shipped off to storage. And she will live in that rooming house for the rest of her life, alone.

One afternoon in the hallway, she runs into Teddy.

"Our intrepid traveler!" he booms, his eyes glittering. "Edith told me how much you've longed to travel abroad. I do hope you'll spend all the money you can. We've got scads of it these days and I can't think of anyone I'd rather give it to." He beams at her and she can't help smiling back.

"Thank you," she says.

"You must send Puss passels of letters she can read to me. Will you do that? I love reading travel letters. Almost as good as taking a trip oneself."

"Of course," Anna says. "Of course."

Then he does something absolutely unlike himself: he bends over and kisses her cheek.

"I shall miss you, dear Anna," he says. "You should be happy. You deserve to be happy."

His lips are cool and kind. She knows she will never forget the feel of them pressed to her skin.

Edith insists on traveling in the wagon with Anna to the train station. She chatters as the roads slip by, about how she wishes *she* were on her way back to Europe, and how Anna must visit Munich and Tuscany. But by the time they are sitting together on a bench on the platform, it is as though they've run out of words. Anna watches as her trunk is hoisted aboard. Saying good-bye, they both wipe tears from their eyes, and hug and say how much they'll miss each other. But as the train heaves itself from the station, Anna can't but note Edith's dear retreating face lighting with relief.

FOURTEEN

SUMMER 1908

Eliot Gregory writes that he would "love a nice weekend in the country" and wonders if his "dear friend, Lady Edith" might accommodate him. Edith can't bear the thought of having to deal with Eliot right now, with his baited questions, his puckish joy at throwing her off balance and his jaundiced view of Fullerton. But she can't imagine how she can say no. If she tells him that her guest rooms are too full, he'll know it's a lie. If she cuts him, as she has mostly done since his dreadful taunting of Teddy at St. Cloud, he'll make her life miserable, reveal God-knows-what to whom. So she writes yes, of course, he is most welcome to join her. She just has to hope that Teddy's ebullient mood will stave off a disastrous encounter between the two of them. At the end of her note to Eliot, she writes, "Teddy's been quite ill so extra indulgence on your part would be most appreciated. I know you understand."

Scheduled to arrive at the same time are Sally Norton, who can only stay for a short while since her father is ill, and Carl Snyder, whom Edith met the previous winter in Paris, a young oceanographer who is now living in Woods Hole studying fishery management and conservation. "We think the seas are so vast that we can't make an impact on them," he writes Edith. "But our hunger and greed as a species are far more vast.

And will lead to devastation, I feel certain, of the creatures that now sustain us."

Carl is a dreamy, thoughtful young man. More romantic than a scientist has a right to be. He and Morton attended a series of lectures together on the future of the seas, and Edith finds pleasure in imagining a late-night chat with Carl about the secrets of the oceans or his new topic of interest, the origins of life. Whatever the topic, it will no doubt be esoteric enough to send Eliot yawning to bed. Edith imagines she and Carl alone in the drawing room, all the French doors open to the terrace to let the cooling breezes in. Their talks would naturally turn towards the lectures Carl and Fullerton so enjoyed in Paris, and then to Morton himself. Just hearing Morton's name from Carl's young lips would make Morton more real to Edith, and how desperately she needs that right now! Living in this letterless limbo, she can hardly believe some days that Morton ever existed, ever loved her. Ruddy young Carl can conjure him up again for her, recalling the best winter of Edith's life. Oh, how she longs for it!

Sally arrives first and Edith is sorry to see she has grown stouter and her hair has silvered. Even her clothes are looking shabby and out of style. Alone in her house with no one but a desperately sick father and an ailing sister to fill her days, poor Sally seems suddenly older than her years. Edith wishes they would have more time alone so she could comfort her. No one was kinder to Edith when she was first married and ill and afraid. No one stood by her more solidly than Sally.

"I'm worried with everyone coming, we won't have enough time alone," Edith tells her.

"No, it's what I need." Sally smiles and squeezes her friend's arm. "It's been so long since I've been social," she says. "Being with a house full of people will do me good."

Eliot arrives next with too many trunks, a manservant whom he's brought from Paris, and his own special tea, which he declares he must have four times a day to remove the poisons from his body and preserve his "youthful appearance."

"I can leave some for you, Edie," he says with a wicked smile.

"Oh, do share some with me," Sally says. "It might provide just what I'm missing." Eliot sits right down beside Sally and they start chatting as if they were the best of friends.

"You wouldn't believe what's been going on in Paris these days, Miss Norton," he tells her and she lights up with interest. Edith is relieved. Perhaps the two least likely people of the house party will fit together like the pieces of a crazy quilt.

When Carl arrives, looking scuffed from the train but displaying his charming, boyish grin, she couldn't be happier.

"I'm so honored you've invited me," he says, taking off his crushed hat and holding it to his chest. "What a ridiculous train schedule. I spent hours in Boston. I don't suppose Mr. Fullerton is here?"

"Oh no, he has his duties in Paris," she tells him. But she thrills at Fullerton's name. And without any coaxing on her part at all! "There are plenty of others upstairs for you to meet, once you've settled in, of course. I do hope we'll have lots of time to chat during your stay. Tomorrow I'll take you through the gardens."

Dinner goes well. Teddy is full of chatter about the pigs and the hens and the new horse he's just purchased. He doesn't even seem to remember the exasperating incident with Eliot last year. He loves Sally and has many kind things to say to her about her father, whom he's known for years. He likes Carl well enough, since Carl loves all animals and shows interest in Teddy's menagerie. The houseful of people helps Edith too. With their chatter and needs, she can momentarily forget her misery over Fullerton, and her worry about how he might respond to her cable—which she now wishes she hadn't sent.

But when Teddy goes up to bed, Eliot begins his mischief.

"Lady Edith was quite the belle of gay Paree this winter, you know, Miss Sally," he says. "See how her cheeks glow? This is what comes from the wild life she's been leading."

"Oh really?" Sally says. She perks up, no doubt not having the least concept of what Eliot's alluding to.

"Eliot, stop!" Edith says. "Or I'll have to take you out to the woodshed."

"You know, Miss Norton," he says, ignoring Edith altogether, "to look at her, you'd think butter wouldn't melt in her mouth. Look at that prim little smile of hers. You'd think all the dear girl does is read all day and write her novels. But she is a changed woman in Paris, let me just say."

"Oh, do tell us, Mr. Gregory," Sally says. Edith tries to flash a warning look Sally's way, but she seems not to notice at all. She is practically flirting with Eliot, which of course, couldn't be more absurd, because Eliot's only interest in women is to make them uncomfortable or to flatter them into handing over large sums of money for his paintings.

"Let us all retire to the drawing room," Edith announces. "It will be much cooler there. The servants will bring the wineglasses. Just leave them. Or some liqueur would be nice, don't you think?"

Sally looks a bit perplexed at Edith's interruption and then it dawns on her that Edith doesn't want to hear what Eliot is about to announce. Edith can see the awakening in her eyes.

"Oh yes. That would be lovely. It will be more comfortable there," Sally says. Edith takes her arm. While Carl and Eliot are arranging themselves in the drawing room, Edith draws Sally through the French doors.

"Come on, let's walk out to the terrace. That will be even more pleasant."

"Whatever was he going to say, Pussy?" Sally asks.

"Oh, he's a troublemaker. The worst sort. You know I'm too proud to be teased."

"What does he have to tease you about?"

Edith looks out over the lake. The sun hasn't quite gone down and the lake glows strawberry pink.

"For some reason, he thinks Mr. Fullerton and I spent too much time together this winter. You know, Morton was a great friend to me, with Teddy so ill. I presumed on his good nature to attend plays with me and go out for dinner. Eliot's just the sort of piranha to think it's a good reason to take a nip out of me."

"Oh. You *did* mention Mr. Fullerton a good deal in your letters. . . ."

"Yes. He's a special person. I felt quite close to him. I needed that, this winter. I really did."

"The Fullerton family is confused about his behavior. I mean, the word was he was going to marry his sister, Katherine. Do you know about that?"

Edith feels herself pale. "Yes, it was mentioned to me. I think it's all a misunderstanding."

"Do you? His mother was already planning the wedding breakfast for this summer. And then suddenly everything was hush-hush about it. I mean initially, she and the Reverend were opposed, and just when they acquiesced, Morton seems to have called things off. Or didn't call things off, as I understand it. Just walked away from the whole thing as though it never happened, breaking his sister's heart. I don't suppose that had anything to do with *you?*"

Edith closes her eyes. She feels as though the earth is shifting beneath her feet. Oh, if only it were so!

Seeing she's not going to receive an answer, Sally continues. "You once called him mysterious. Was that the word you used? Father always said that he both loved him and couldn't understand him at all. That no one really knew what was going on in that agile brain of his. I remember he used the word 'agile.' I thought it was a strange word to use. But maybe appropriate. Father has always been so good with words, you know. It's heartbreaking to see Father fail, Edith. It angers me so much. Such a brilliant man. So alive in some ways. Unable to finish any of his projects. Too weak to sit up much of the time. Oh . . ."

Edith hears the tears in Sally's voice. Relieved that she's dropped her inquiry into Fullerton, she puts her arm around her friend's shoulder. She reflects on how rapidly and urgently Sally's been speaking. As though she's barely spoken to anyone but family in weeks. Months maybe.

"I'm so sorry," she says. "I wish I could do anything to make it easier for you."

"Oh, you do. You do. Inviting me here was the best sort of thing you could do. We shouldn't even speak of dear Father. It's just so good to focus on other things. Even Mr. Gregory's gossip. I'm enjoying it all. I really am."

"I'm glad."

"There wasn't anything . . . *untoward* about your relationship with Mr. Fullerton, was there?" Sally asks.

Edith feels her blood freeze. Even Sally wants to know.

"Sally!" .

"Oh, I'm sorry. I couldn't help but ask. You blush when you speak of him. I've known you too long not to wonder. . . ."

I'm in love with him, Edith longs to blurt out. I have never loved anyone the way I love him. Oh, if only she could tell her friend! If only she didn't have to swallow down her misery at hearing about Katherine, her sense of betrayal. If only!

But Sally is a maiden, never married. A daughter more than a woman. How could she possibly understand that this winter, at the age of forty-six, Edith gloried in taking off her clothes in a rented room surrounded by chestnut blossoms, or that she lay stark naked on a bed of moss under a lilac curtain and in a place where anyone might have discovered them, feeling more ecstasy than she has ever known, an ecstasy that she never imagined possible? Sally loves her. But could not understand. She would try, but she would fail. And it would throw a barrier between them. So Edith merely smiles and says, "Nothing untoward happened. Just good, close friendship. Nothing more."

Sally searches her eyes, her face full of questions, and then, with a small pinched smile, says, "Of course."

Just as she imagined, the rest of the party goes to bed early, leaving Edith with Carl in an empty drawing room with open doors, a soft caressing breeze blowing in. He helps Edith light a cigarette and then he leans back in his chair and watches her.

"Don't you smoke?" she asks him.

"No, I never took to it."

He does look astonishingly young. Maybe he is in his late thirties, but his face is as smooth and sweet as a boy's, his eyes as trusting and clear.

"Would you mind if I ask you a question?" he says. He has an open Midwest accent and a formal politeness that pleases Edith.

"No."

"You seem upset about something. I just wondered if there's anything I can do."

"Upset? Do I? Frankly, I'm a little worried about Mr. Fullerton. He was writing me practically every day. And then . . . You haven't heard anything from Paris, have you?"

"No." Carl looks at her with kind, searching eyes. "But with his job, I don't suppose there's any way we can know what Fullerton's up to. He may be involved in some extraordinary story. I'm awfully sorry if it upsets you, though." Flashing his Midwestern smile, he reaches out and plucks her hand from her lap. She's surprised how her skin sings from his touch. She lets him envelope her smaller hand between his big farm-boy mitts for a moment. He's just a young man. Does he think of her as an old woman who just needs his sympathy? When he lets go, she's almost sorry. She has no romantic feeling toward him. But still, she's shocked at how much she enjoyed the fire of his touch. She wishes Morton were there to see Carl Snyder holding her hand. To have his heart squeezed by jealousy, if just for a moment.

"Let's go out on the terrace," she tells Carl.

"Alrighty."

She discovers that Mitou and Nicette are already lying like two tiny bear rugs on the cool clay tile a hand's width apart in the diminishing heat of the day. The moon is just a sliver, barely sending light down onto Laurel Lake. On a quest for mosquitoes, a family of bats are displaying their acrobatics, sending off ear-challenging shrieks of joy.

"Aren't they beautiful?" Carl says, his voice young and full of wonder. "People fail to appreciate bats. Do you know, in Australia there are bats as big as cats. They call them flying foxes. They have faces as big as . . . as large as Mitou's. They are quite beloved." Mitou lifts his little foxlike face and gazes up at the bats with ennui, then sighs and leans his chin again on his paws.

"I think it's just as well we don't have bats like that here," Edith laughs. While Carl continues to marvel at the bat display, Edith leans over the banister, looking benevolently down at her garden. All the years she nurtured it! All the seasons when it was her only joy. She watches as a slender moonbeam pierces the lime allée, sending the faintest carpet of light down the aisle between the trees. Carl settles against the banister too, nearer to her than she ever might have imagined. She can feel the pressure of his arm. It doesn't seem possible he would flirt with her. And yet she feels herself stirring, longing. She thinks about Morton's visit less than a year ago. And how they stood on this very terrace in the virgin snow. How he grabbed her arm and forced her to turn toward him. She couldn't have imagined that someday that desire would be met, leaving a bigger hole than it filled. Tears spill from her eyes and she turns her head from Mr. Snyder, horrified that he might see.

"Mrs. Wharton," he whispers. "Edith?"

"I'm sorry," she says.

"Have I said something? Have I done something to upset you?"

How endearing of him, Edith thinks, to blame himself. Most men would never have imagined that the cause could be them. In this case, Carl is blameless.

"It's nothing you've done. I don't know what I'm crying about. Women cry sometimes." Lately, too much crying has been done in this house. Yet, how she hates the words that have tumbled from her mouth! What a denigrating thing to say about women.

"Not you," he says, his voice shimmering with admiration. "I rather doubt you cry much at all." She thinks if they stay out on the terrace he might kiss her. He is standing so close. As though a woman who has discovered a taste for lovemaking might give off a scent other men are drawn to. The thought oddly warms her. All these years, no men came within feet of her. Even Walter, who loves her in his own way. But she doesn't trust herself with Carl Snyder. Her body is interested in him, even if her mind isn't.

"We should go in," she says.

"Won't you confide in me?" he whispers. "I'm awfully good at keeping secrets."

She looks up at his broad bland face and clear eyes, his taffy-colored hair and small, perfect nose. Most women would call him good-looking. She views him as a child.

"You are a lovely boy. So kind."

His face falls. She realizes the word "boy" has wounded him.

"It's just . . ." she goes on, "I've never been one to confide. And some secrets are best kept."

He nods but his eyes pale with disappointment.

"I understand," he says. She shoos the dogs in and nervously finds her way to the sofa. The dogs settle on one side of her, scratching to dent places for themselves in the cushion. Carl sits close to her on the other side. Sofas and chairs all around, and still he chooses to nestle close.

How little Edith knows about being the object of interest. She wrote about Lily Bart, who drew men to her like gnats to a fruit bowl. But she has no experience of her own.

Carl's face brightens and he strokes the inside of her upper arm with a disconcerting familiarity. The sensation unbalances her.

"Edith, do you have any idea how famous you've become?" he says. "I wonder if you do. When I was in New York, and mentioned I was heading here, the excitement it generated would have stunned you, I think. They say you have become . . . I think the word I heard was *legendary*!"

"Legendary?" Edith is astounded and flattered. Could the legions of stuffy, impossible people who surrounded her while she grew up in New York really be speaking of her with words like that?

"Have you ever met anyone less legendary?" she says in the most offhanded way possible.

"You are legendary to me," he says. He leans closer to her, making her catch her breath.

"So tell me about your work, dear," she says. "I do want to know all about it."

He looks at her querulously, for of course her question has been too broad and clearly a way to put him off, but, taking the cue, drops his hand from her arm and begins to weave a thread about his research, his interests. She breathes a sigh of relief—how distracting it was to feel his touch—and settling into the sofa, allows herself to imagine the vast ocean floor, the prismatic world of fish, seaweed, nets, bubbles, the ocean as the crucible for all the world's animals, even dinosaurs and birds. Lulled by his even, midcountry drawl, she begins to yawn.

"I'm boring you," he says.

"Oh no, not at all."

"Well, I'm boring myself."

"It is getting late," she says.

"Edith . . ."

"Yes."

"I do have such regard for you."

She smiles softly, self-consciously.

"That's very kind of you to say. Come, let's go up to b— Let's go up to our rooms."

She stands and stretches, gesturing for Carl to go first. As she climbs the steps, she knows that if she asked him to come to her room, he would. Once, such a thought would never have occurred to her. Now these depraved ideas follow her as closely as her dogs. After she nods good night at Carl's door, she picks up Mitou and kisses his knobby little head.

"Ready for bed, my man?" she asks. Nicette yips at her ankles for equal time.

Anna's stateroom on the *Amerika* is the most beautiful she has ever had. It must have been Edith's doing, for it's the sort of stateroom Edith always takes for herself: high in the ship where one can hardly sense the rocking. It feels like a comfortable bedroom in a townhouse, adorned with exquisite painted furniture, hand-decorated cupboards, crystal decanters fitted into silver rails so they won't slide, Bouguereau-style paintings screwed to the wall. The bathroom is bejeweled with nile green tile and a mammoth tub with silvered faucets.

In the grand dining room, Anna is seated with couples dressed in satins and furs, the men in patent shoes who set their cigars on the table in anticipation even before the meal has begun. Anna shivers in her own sleeveless hand-me-down evening gown, feeling out of place, even with Teddy's locket at her neck. Champagne is poured into the flute that sits at the point of her knife and she drinks it to gain courage. Or more accurately, to numb her self-judgment. The champagne persuades her to tell the table that she is an assistant to a writer named Edith Wharton. This seems to elicit little excitement from anyone. Perhaps no one at the table reads. She tells them that she's taking some time off to see more of Europe than she's ever seen before.

After supper each night, she squeezes through the crowded Palm Court where ladies sip velvet-colored cocktails shoulder to shoulder with bored-looking gents tipping back scotch. When she ascends the grand staircase to the door that leads outside, she looks down on the clot of bespangled ocean goers, and wonders what it must be like to have such a social, well-padded life. She feels singled out, utterly different from the rest of the people on board.

During the day, the deck is filled with loungers and laughers and chatterers, but it's quieter come nightfall except for a few women smoking together like naughty children, and several couples leaning close, whispering. Standing at the rail, Anna gazes out over the navy nothingness where just that morning the sea sparkled. In her lonely life, she has never felt so alone. As she leans out over the invisible waves, her heart feels as vast and as dark. All her life she has been an optimist. But now, she feels she is tumbling and doesn't know where she'll fall.

On the third evening, standing on deck, she spots an older German man trying to ask one of the crew members if he has seen a walking stick which was carelessly left behind. But the crew member doesn't speak German, and so she steps in to sort out the confusion. In fact, the crew member knows that an elegant silver-tipped walking stick was found just that afternoon, and he goes inside the ship to retrieve it from the lost and found. The German man is thankful for her intrusion and asks if she would like to stroll with him as they wait for the stick's return. He is a small man, impeccably turned out, wearing a sharply honed Vandyke and golden-rimmed spectacles. His shoes seem more pointed than his beard and very fine. He smells of leather and starch. She doesn't think she has ever seen as white a shirt as the one he sports, or a set of buttons as beautiful: made of iridescent nacre and gold. He appears older than she and very wealthy.

"My name is Thomas Schultze," he announces. "Can you be so kind as to tell me your name?"

She tells him, and he asks how she has come to speak German so well.

"Mein Familie ist Deutsch," she tells him. She tells him she has spoken German all her life.

Thrilled he can speak to her in his native tongue, he tells her that he is from Essen, a widower and the proud owner of four factories that manufacture steel. His family has been making steel since the early 1800s. And they are the ones who invented nickel steel, of which this very ship is made. He has just visited steelmakers in America to discuss new techniques.

"And what else is the steel from your factories used for?" Anna asks.

"For buildings, motorcars. Soon, steel will hold up the entire world in its *unerschütterlich* arms."

Anna is amused by his dreamy poeticism.

"A world of steel!" Anna says.

"In order for buildings to scrape the sky," he continues, his dark eyes exuding certainty, "they must stand on steel. Motorcars will soon be made entirely of steel. In a car factory in Untertürkheim, they are this very moment experimenting with a hundred-percent steel car. I've seen it. No wood at all, even in the frame. Bravo steel!" He raises both arms to the sky in triumph.

"You like what you do," she says, amused.

"It is the greatest gift a man could have: to like what he does. Every day. No one could wish for more. And you, Miss Bahlmann, do you like the way you fill your days?"

Anna smiles and nods. "I do."

"And what is it you do?"

"I work."

"Good works? Charity?"

"Real work. I am a secretary for a writer. Her name is Edith Wharton."

"But . . . you're joking. . . ."

"It's no joke."

"I don't understand. You travel in first class. I have seen you come out of your stateroom. It's just down from mine."

"You have?"

"But now you say you are a secretary. How could a secretary—any secretary—afford a stateroom on the *Amerika*?" Anna is surprised at his question. An American gentleman would never ask a question so baldly referring to one's finances.

Still, she smiles and tells him honestly, "It was a gift from my employer."

Anna expects now that Thomas Schultze will tip his hat and move on. Surely knowing that she is no better than a stowaway in his upper-class world, the king of nickel steel won't want to be seen with her.

Instead, he offers her his arm. "You must be very good at what you do," he says, "to receive such a reward. I admire people who do their job well. I admire unerschütterlich people."

"You don't object to women working?" she asks, tucking her hand into the crook of his elbow.

He shakes his head. "My wife didn't work," he says. "Once the children were gone, she wasn't happy with her life. She simply had nothing to do. Sometimes, I think it's what killed her. She was not unerschütterlich in any way." Unerschütterlich, meaning stalwart, unshakable. It is a German word one rarely hears, and yet he's used it three times.

"I'm sorry," Anna says.

"No. She's been gone a long time. We married very young and hardly knew each other. You're not married?"

"No."

"Never?"

"No."

"But why not?" he asks.

"That is an embarrassing question to ask a woman," she says, again noting that no American gentleman, or Frenchman, for that matter, would have put the question to her.

"It's a respectful question. A bright woman like yourself. And pretty too. Why on earth would you not be married?"

"I'm not pretty." Anna thinks of her eyes, which her cousins used to say were so light colored, they made her look invisible. Who could love a woman with invisible eyes?

"You are modest. Another admirable virtue."

"You are most kind."

"Will you dine with me tomorrow night? The people at whose table they've placed me talk and talk and I . . ." he moves his face close to Anna's and his bushy gray eyebrows rise with amusement, "I don't understand half their English. But I'm too proud to let them know. I took the Hamburg/*Amerika* line thinking I would have the pleasure of German companionship, but you are the first person I've had the chance to speak to in German. Even half the crew doesn't speak German. So, will you join me, Miss Bahlmann?"

"I'd be honored," Anna says.

"No," Mr. Schultze says, tipping his hat, "*I'd* be honored. Eight P.M.? Table for two?"

Anna smiles and nods. Imagine what people will think when she shares a table for two with Mr. Schultze. She can hardly envision the stir!

And so for the rest of the journey, she dines with Mr. Schultze. She walks with Mr. Schultze. She sits on the deck and reads side by side with Mr. Schultze. Every night before she goes to her cabin, he kisses her hand with the graciousness of a bygone courtier.

"How nice that you have made friends with that older gentleman!" one of the ladies who had shared a table with her says when she passes her in the grand salon one morning.

"Yes, he's very kind."

"I do believe I see a blooming romance. Perhaps he will ask you to marry him." The woman, who must be about forty, is the sort of long-nosed, gossipy soul that will pass on all she is told to the rest of the table, to the ladies with whom she plays whist, to the cabin maid and anyone else who is foolish enough to listen.

Anna laughs. "It's nice of you to be interested in me. But it is a friendship, nothing more."

"Well, we're all cheering for you, Miss Bahlmann. He looks like quite a catch, although since no one can understand him, no one is certain who he is."

"He manufactures steel," Anna says. She is happy to pass this on to whomever Mrs. Brewer will grace with the tale.

"Indeed!"

"He owns four factories in Germany."

"Well, that *does* make him sound quite prosperous. And aren't you lucky that you speak German and can converse with him. It appears your journey abroad will not be for naught."

Anna winces.

"My journey abroad will not be for naught, no matter whom I meet. I did not come to meet a man."

"Come, Miss Bahlmann. Every single woman wants to meet a man. It's what we women are made for, no?"

"I am made to aid in the writing of novels, Mrs. Brewer. To make my employer's life simpler. And to teach. That's what I was made for."

Mrs. Brewer purses her lips. She gazes at Anna.

"And do you wish to tell me that even if you had the opportunity to marry a steel magnate, you'd turn it down to be a typewriter for some lady novelist?"

"Yes," Anna says. "That's precisely what I wish to tell you," she says and then rushes away. "I have to meet my friend the steel magnate in the Palm Court." She wonders how long it will be until her conversation is on the lips of everyone on the *Amerika*.

One night as Anna and Mr. Schultze stroll along the deck under a shimmering moon, he asks her, "Do you think while you are in Germany, you might come and visit one of my factories?"

"Do you really want me to?" she asks.

"Well, I don't know whether you'll be in Essen or Stuttgart. But if you are, I'd be so pleased to show you. My factories are dreadfully noisy, and I'm afraid that the smell of steelmaking isn't very pleasant. But the energy there, the very *brawniness*, will excite you. I guarantee it."

"Then I'd be very pleased to come if I'm nearby. I would like to experience the world that excites you so much."

He reaches out and takes her hand in his, swings it subtly as they walk, and glances at her, smiling like a shy young beau. She notes the surprising softness of his skin, the sweetness of his touch. She thinks if she had met him thirty years ago, she might actually have fallen in love with him. She can imagine herself moving to Germany as a young bride, making a home for Mr. Schultze, setting his table with silver and laying out his clothes each day. She can imagine watching as he grew wealthy and important. But now, the thought of romance is a puzzle piece that no longer fits. She wishes to gaze on the house where Goethe was born in Frankfurt am Main and the house where he died in Weimar. To drink Italian wine overlooking a field of sunflowers. She wishes to meet many people from many lands and speak to them in all the languages that she knows. And then, she wishes most of all to return to Edith and Teddy, to Gross and White and Cook. To 882 and her books. To the life that has been kindly allotted her, that she does not wish to trade in, as flawed as it may suddenly be.

After Sally and Eliot have each been delivered to their trains to resume their own lives, Carl Snyder lingers in Edith's. He spends afternoons perusing books that Edith has recommended, sitting cross-legged on a bench in the cutting garden. At night, after Teddy has gone to bed, he perches close to his hostess, telling her the books she's given him are the education he never got, having been so caught up in science classes as a young man. He watches Edith with that sad, longing look he never loses. He's taken to touching her hand often, kissing her good night. Once he embraces her before bed, and she feels his heart beating wildly against her chest. While Carl's infatuation warms and amuses her, her misery over Morton's inexplicable silence squeezes her every breath. She dreams about him. Nightmares every time. He is laughing at her. He is telling her he never loved her. He is dancing with Katherine.

On the thirty-first, a stack of correspondence arrives in the afternoon post. A postcard from Anna from the *Amerika*. How joyous she sounds! She says she has made a wonderful friend on board, and is grateful for the beautiful stateroom that Edith has given her. She describes the women in their jewels and the color of the sky at sea. Edith misses her. She cringes at having sent her away to protect her from her own bad temper.

And then Edith lifts an envelope of heavy woven paper. Even before she sees the handwriting she knows who's sent it. She feels surprisingly angry and thrilled in equal measure. If Morton only *knew* how much he's made her suffer. For a moment, she is afraid to slice it open.

It's better to know, she finally tells herself, remembering with an ache the elation she used to feel slipping her knife into his petits bleus each morning. How connected she felt to him back then, as though a glistening strand of spider silk always shivered between them, stretching when they were apart, turning when they turned. Now there is far more than Carl's vast ocean parting Morton's heart from hers.

> My dear,
>   I have just received your cable. I am sorry to have worried you. Simply put, I thought it best, seeing as you were suffering from the distance between us, not to write. You did, after all, tell

me not to write, and I took you at your word. I felt it better for your new novel if you had no thought of me. And after all the good true moments we've shared, I want you to be as joyous as you were beneath our curtain of lilacs. (Every second of that hour for me was but the promise of dearer moments to come.) I did not want to think of you miserable and pining for someone far away who could give you no peace.

You see, there have been worries with me I can't share with you at present. I count on being able to tell you by autumn that these dreadful problems have sorted themselves, and that I am no longer worried. And then I will be kinder to my dearest friends. It is difficult to be generous when one is under a cloud of anxiety, n'est ce pas? But after your year of concern over Teddy, you know whereof I speak, chère.

Last night I saw La Princesse de Clèves at the Theatre des Artes and thought of you and how you would have enjoyed it. It is too hot here, and the theatre was steaming. Two women fainted. It hasn't rained in three weeks and with this heat, the Seine has never been lower. I fear for the fully filled tourist boats. I imagine they will scrape the bottom and stick there like ugly wads of American chewing gum stick to streets where tourists have dropped them.

You said you couldn't bear the dwindling and the fading of our feelings for one another, and though my feelings have not faded, I thought I was doing your bidding. But if it was only a moment of misery that made you write it, then I am yours,

. Morton

He is *mine*, she thinks, and smiles at the thought, touches the very words. *I am yours.* All this time he says he didn't write her because he thought it best, and yet . . . is he being honest? How can she be sure from thousands of miles away?

Teddy comes trudging into the library in his socks, perspiring, panting.

"No shoes?" she asks.

"I was mucking out the pigpens. My shoes were covered in mud. I left them downstairs for Laurette to clean. Dear little Lawton always looks sad when I leave. Won't you come down and see him? Carl has. He says he's the finest pig he'd ever seen. I do believe I love Lawton as much as our little babies." He lifts Nicette from the floor and cuddles her against his sweat-soaked shirt. "You have competition, Lady Nicette."

"You should take a bath," Edith says. "You smell of the pigpen."

"Nicette likes it. Don't you, girl? You like it that I stink!"

"Put her down and take a bath," Edith says, quietly attempting to push Morton's letter beneath the newspaper that came with the afternoon post.

"What are you up to?" Teddy asks, looking over at her desk. *Up to?* Does he suspect? Or is it just an innocent question? These days, she hardly knows how to read him.

"Just reading through my mail. Go wash yourself. You make the whole room reek." She envisions his belly, which, with all his drinking, has recently become ridiculously globular, poking out of the bathwater.

"What is that? A postcard from Anna?" he says, grabbing Anna's card with his free hand, turning it over, reading it. Edith pushes Morton's letter even farther beneath the newspaper.

"She's having herself a fine time already. Happy to see it. Dear woman. Do you want to read it, Nicette? It's from Miss Anna! No. You just want to eat it. That would be rude. What? Don't look hurt. It just doesn't belong to you. It was addressed to your Mama. Nicette, Nicette, Nicette, I do love you!" He buries his damp face into her fur-muff back.

And then he sets her down and heads for the door.

"All right then, au revoir, Pussycat!"

Edith shivers at how wrongly he pronounces the French. "Oh Rev-oy-er." She hears him pad down the hall. Good God, the man leaves a trail of stench behind him. Edith closes her eyes, wishing she never had to open them to Teddy Wharton again.

That night, she writes back to Morton. At first his letter felt like a great relief. Especially his hopeful mention of the lilac bower. But then the poisonous anxiety of so many days of silence boils up while she sits at dinner with Carl and Teddy chatting about cattle, and she feels more indignant than relieved. Joyous? He wishes her to be joyous? The absurdity of it makes her want to bang her head against the wall.

Having shed Carl's clinging presence by telling Teddy that the two of them should take a walk along the ridge to see the best view of the sunset, she settles at her desk and begins:

> *At last, my dearest, your letter of the 21st . . . Que voulez vous que je vous dise?* [Already she is angry in French. Will she make it through this letter without screaming at him for his cruelty?] *Your silence of nineteen days seems to me a very conclusive, anticipated answer to my miserable cry! You didn't wait to be asked what was "best"!*
>
> *But don't read a hint of reproach in this. I have spent three weeks of horrible sadness, because I feared from your silence that within ten days of our good-bye the very meaning of me had become a weariness. And I suffered—no matter how much—but I said to myself: "I chose the risk, I accept the consequences." And that is what I shall always say.* [She must make him see he hasn't fully destroyed her—although so many days he did, he has. . . .]
>
> *Only, cher, one must be a little blind—or else a little relieved at the "reasonableness" of my attitude—to read in my note of the 11th anything but an appeal for frankness—a desperate desire to know, at once, and have the thing over.* [Could he have truly believed she meant "Don't write"? Was he so insensitive to have believed her? Even poor oblivious Carl Snyder would have known better!] *Don't be afraid! I can only reiterate it. Anything on earth would be better (I've learned that in these last three weeks) than to sit here and wonder: What was I to him, then? I assure you I've practiced my "Non dolet!"*

She scolds him for wanting her to be joyous. She excoriates him for suggesting that not hearing from him or thinking about him would be better for her novel. If he were any other man, she would have dismissed him as a complete fool, a manipulator, a cad. But these words were from Morton. Her beloved.

It would be a great joy if you could send me a line once a week—only never, never under compulsion!—And, when your plans are settled—about coming to America,—if you were to tell me it would be kind. Even if you're not coming, I should be rid of the ache of wondering. . . .

Dearest, I love you so deeply that you owe me just one thing— the truth. Never be afraid to say: "Ma pauvre amie, c'est fini." That is what I meant when I said I couldn't bear to watch the dwindling and fading. When the time comes, just put my notes and letters in a bundle and send them back, and I shall understand. I am like one who went out seeking for friendship, and found a kingdom. Don't you suppose I know that the blessedness is all on my side?

That night, she expects to sleep well, but she's miserable in her lonely bed, her pillow a mountain range, her sheets on fire. And then with no sheets, she shivers. With no pillow, her neck twitches and burns. But her physical wretchedness is the least of it. She struggles helplessly between sadness and fury. Feelings she has tamped down for weeks and weeks, now released like Pandora's terrors, flying around her room, biting at her heart. Sighing and flailing, she finally gets up and sharply parts the drapes to look out over the valley. Clouds circle the moon, ever moving, crossing the nearly full orb, weakening its mighty beam. Down below, bathed in milky light, she sees Carl pacing the terrace in his robe. He must have awakened too. Or never slept. Does he suffer from longing as she does? For her. For *her*! She can hardly believe it. She wishes she could ease him, even imagines going down in her robe to talk to him. To hold him. To kiss him. But she doesn't. Her heart is tied up like a hog headed for market. If only she could send Morton Fullerton to market instead! All summer she has hated her own husband, imagined him dead, for he stood between her and the one soul she's loved more than any other. Now her anger is beaming across the Atlantic to that very soul, to the café where he sits at night with his books, his thick coffee. No, it's already morning in Paris. He is walking to his office, his ebony mustache catching the sunlight, his eyes as blue as the cornflowers on china. His crisp, perfect clothes. His polished shoes. She wants to slap him. She wants to hold him. She wants to be near him. She wants to open her clothes again just once for him. Just once! She wants everything she can't have. The pain is excruciating. Cracked ribs, torn muscles couldn't hurt more. She once heard of a man in so much pain he scratched his very eyes out. She would. She could! Instead she cries, lets out a sound like a banshee into the silence. Teddy is drunk, won't hear a thing. Carl is far downstairs. She cries and cries. Until, damp and weak, she tumbles at last into a dead sleep.

In the morning, she drags herself to breakfast. Carl is there, wan and quiet.

"I saw you last night," she tells him. "Out on the terrace. Are you all right?"

"I'm going back today," he says very quietly.

"Are you? I understood you were staying through the weekend." He catches her eyes and stares at her, smiling weakly.

"Do you want me to stay?" he asks, his voice rising with hope.

She hesitates too long. This is how Morton must feel, she thinks. Trapped into a lie to ease my pain.

"I'm going," he says. "You want me to go. I've been here too long."

"I think you should go if you're ready to go," she tells him.

He nods and closes his eyes.

"If someone could take me to the train."

"Of course."

She sees the sorrow, the defeat in his eyes. He is as angry at himself as he is at her. For loving someone so unavailable to him. She understands that also . . . far more than he knows.

That afternoon after Carl has gone, a letter is delivered telling her that Walter will arrive at The Mount the following Friday on his way up to see his ailing mother before he leaves for Cairo, where he has been appointed a judge at the International Tribunal. Edith feels a sense of relief that could only be compared to letting out a breath after holding it until one's lungs burn. The thought of laying her sadness in his large hands eases her immeasurably.

On the morning of Walter's scheduled arrival, Teddy is preparing to go fishing for a week with a Peter Van Gelder, a New York friend who drives up in his own motorcar. It's starting to rain, and, already in a nervous buzz, Teddy insists on packing too many accessories and jackets and three pairs of waders because he can't decide which he likes best. When Teddy goes back into the house for more, Peter leans toward Edith.

"Edith, do tell me. Is he quite all right? He seems a bit *wild*."

Edith steels herself. If Teddy doesn't leave the house, she thinks she might go mad. She's been looking forward to Teddy's leaving almost as much as she's been counting the days until Walter's arrival.

"Nothing to worry about. He's a bit overexcited lately. But not sad like he was in Paris." She can see in Peter's eyes that he's weighing whether he should take Ted on the trip at all.

"You'll have a wonderful time," she reassures him. "You know how much Teddy loves nature! You're doing the kindest thing by taking him."

Teddy arrives back just in time to keep Peter from speculating further.

When they drive off, Edith stands in the rain waving gaily and feels alive for the first time in days. By afternoon the sun is not just out, but glistening, as Walter arrives in the wagon. His lanky body, which always strikes Edith as taller than she remembered, and his energetic certainty fill The Mount with a fresh sense of hope.

"My darling!" he declares, doffing his straw boater and enfolding her in his arms. "When I am with you, I feel at home."

She loves his dry, exotic scent, no doubt bought years ago in Paris, his elegant clothes always so rich—today a beautiful white linen summer suit, velvety at the edge from too much washing. She wishes he would hold her in his arms for an hour. No one makes her feel more at peace than Walter!

In Hamburg, Thomas Schultze insists on staying for a few days to show Anna around, and he begs her to change her itinerary to accompany him to Essen to see his factories. But even after hours of walking together through the streets and over the canals of Hamburg, enjoying the musical theatre and dining in the cafés, she cannot imagine their ship-board friendship going further than it's gone. She has never seen this turn in her life as an option and it confuses her. Why should Thomas, wealthy and smart, choose Anna of all women? Why should any man choose her? At her age. Her hair more white than golden . . . and still a maiden.

After a vibrant staging of *Die Brautwerbung*, they stop for a glass of wine in a small restaurant near her hotel. The room is dark and a sole violinist bows sad melodies that twist and lose themselves in the walls of dark velvet curtains.

"So will you come to Essen with me tomorrow?" he asks, leaning forward. "We could stay a month in Hamburg, there is so much to do! But I have *so* hoped you'll let me show you Essen."

His eyes are shimmering. He has a young spirit, she thinks. And he is good company. Not too domineering or opinionated, but with firm, clear views of the world. And a desire to know more about everything.

"I'm tempted, Mr. Schultze. But my cousins are waiting. And my time abroad is limited. I must go on with my trip."

"You haven't enjoyed Hamburg?"

"I have. Immensely."

"And my company?"

"Even more." She looks down at her hands.

"And you won't, then, come on to Essen for a few days?"

"I . . ."

"Look at me, Anna." He has never called her by her first name before. His deep, thoughtful voice reaches her very depths.

She looks up to see his face in the candlelight.

"Why won't you change your plans?" he asks. "I was hoping you could meet my daughters, get a taste of my life . . . see my factories."

"My cousins are waiting for me to arrive. . . . I've looked forward to my trip for so long, you see, and I have so little time to take in what I've planned."

Disappointment crumples Thomas's mouth. But he nods.

"Are you sure?" he asks.

"Yes."

There is a long moment of silence. Anna sips her wine, feeling a tumultuousness inside that the wine can't settle. She is afraid he will argue. And she will say yes just to please him. She doesn't want it to come to that.

But Thomas is not the sort of man to argue or cajole.

"Do you think you might send me postcards of your journey?" he asks at last. "It will give me something to look forward to. And I can imagine my dear Miss Bahlmann in beautiful places doing wonderful things."

She smiles at him, thinking him a very special man.

They walk back to her lodgings together and the silence is companiable, though sad. When they reach the doorway of the hotel, she holds out her hand in farewell. Instead, he steps forward to take her face in his hands. He gazes at her for a long while, as though he is a camera imprinting her image. And then he kisses her lips. Just a moth's wing of a kiss. Later, as she travels through Weimar and Frankfurt, Baden and Rothenberg, she will often fall asleep thinking of that modest kiss—the haunting brush of a man's lips against hers—the first she has ever known.

FIFTEEN

EARLY AUTUMN 1908

Sleep will not come to Edith—no matter how she tries to change her habits; her thoughts or even her level of anger at her impossible situation with Fullerton. (Not a letter. Not a card. For weeks and weeks *again*!) She begins to fear her own bed. Because she knows in it she will wrestle with sleep and lose. When morning seeps through the curtains, it always finds her emotionally spent. She writes, but how difficult it is to remember where she left her characters, what they are thinking or how different they are from one another! Guests come and go, filling her guest rooms and parlor. She laughs with them. Eats with them. But feels nothing. *The walking dead.* She has heard these words before, but now she knows precisely what they mean.

She hears that Dr. Kinnicut, the doctor she trusts most for both Teddy and herself, has come to Lenox for the month of September. He writes that he's all too happy to see her at his rented house, a stately white colonial right in town. He views Edith over his reading glasses as she tells him about the torment of her sleeplessness. He nods, the only doctor she's ever known with such sympathetic eyes.

"I'm sorry you're suffering so," he says.

He takes a deep breath and pens a prescription for a sleeping powder.

"Just a few grains before bed and you'll be fast asleep," he says. He smiles, this cheerful reliable man with a bald pate as pink as a rose.

"Works every time," he says. Well, why not believe him? If Dr. Kinnicut thinks it will work, it surely will, she tells herself. By the time she is back at The Mount with the packet from the pharmacy, she is immersed in a glow of expectation she hasn't felt in weeks. At this point, sleep seems almost as desirable as a night with Fullerton. After dinner, she excuses herself from her guests and follows Dr. Kinnicut's instruction, stirring the powder into her evening cocoa. Even the few grains infuse the cocoa with a poisonous tinge, but she drinks it down, determined.

She settles into her bedroom armchair to read *Jenseits von Gut und Böse* while waiting for the drug to take effect. How she's enjoyed Nietzsche lately, even in her wounded state! But suddenly, she might as well be sitting on a high, bright cliff, for her bed appears far away, her dresser, the mirror on her dressing table flickering, dancing, shimmering in lamplight. A wave of nausea overtakes her, but she can't quite understand what she's feeling. She stumbles to the bed, which she thankfully had turned down earlier, but even before she turns off her light, the drug sends her plummeting toward a dreamless ocean. Oh! The feeling of falling is so real. So dangerous. *Falling. Asleep.* As she says the words aloud, they take on new meaning.

She wakes in the morning and is certain the cliff of her last waking thought has collapsed on top of her. The heaviness of her limbs, her brain, startles her. The morning light feels evil, pressing through the window, reaching out to pry apart her sticky eyes. Her head could not be more swollen and useless if she had drunk an entire bottle of brandy by herself. The light by her bedside is still burning. She never turned it off!

Most mornings, she wakes and grabs a handful of paper from the nightstand, dips her ink in the well she keeps there and begins to write immediately—before her trip to the bathroom. Morning is her best time. The time of her greatest clarity. Even after a sleepless night. But today, she can barely lift her head. And her thinking has been reduced to primal thoughts. Sip of water. Bathroom. Sick. Must be sick.

She wakes again and it is late. The sun has flooded the room. Her head is not as groggy as it was. Someone is at the door. Teddy.

"Do you plan to sleep all day?" he asks. His voice hurts her ears. "Are you unwell?"

"What time is it?" she asks.

He pulls his watch from his pocket.

"Seven minutes after eleven."

She sits up, startled, miserable.

"This won't do," she says aloud.

"I'll say it won't," Teddy agrees. He closes the door and if it is not with a definite slam, it certainly sounds like one to her bruised brain.

❀

The fun Anna has with her cousins Liesel and Lotte! Lounging in a green-hued café in Gottingen, sharing feathery potato dumplings, Westphalia ham, and beer—such beer! They chuckle over a mention in Anna's guidebook of Otto-the-One-Eyed's reign over Gottingen—"Imagine. A Cyclops ruled Gottingen," Lotte declares. Anyone watching them could see they have the same happy, drifting laugh, the same soft gray eyes. They could be sisters. Three round-faced, older, single women. In their company, it is easy to put aside thoughts of Thomas. To block thoughts of Edith, except, of course, remembering to send each of them postcards. How Anna labors over the condensed little messages she pens on the back, making sure they are charming and informative. But at night in her room at the Friedrichsbad Spa, she aches, without knowing why.

❀

After two and a half weeks of laughter and getting to know one another far better than they ever have, Liesel and Lotte return to Frankfurt and Anna travels on to Verona and Venice alone. Unafraid. The silence soothes her. The sights are beautiful with or without a companion. "I am a lone animal," she thinks proudly.

Yet sitting in her sparkling room overlooking the Grand Canal, she has a weak moment. How much more fulfilling it would be to share this scene with someone about whom she cares. She pens a real letter to Thomas, describing the sound of the water, the singing, the light off the canal washing her ceiling and glass chandelier in watery ripples. And she says he would enjoy it all. She wishes he were there. Later in the week, as her elevator cage settles in the lobby, Anna, a pink mohair stole wrapped about her arms, ready to make her way to a café for dinner, spots Thomas through the gilded bars. He is leaning on the hotel's front desk, speaking her name.

"Thomas?"

He raises his face, beams at the sight of her.

"My dear," he says. "Don't you look well!"

She feels her heart thudding. He is not a handsome man. His features are weathered, and maybe he was never beautiful. But his eyes are remarkably gentle, and so happy to see her.

"I didn't expect. Why are you . . . ?"

Through the hotel's arched windows, the early evening light on the canal is buttery and glowing, as it was when she wrote him the note.

"Perhaps you will join me for supper," he asks, extending his arm.

"Of course," she says. "I'd be delighted." Isn't it best to let gravity take her than to flail, than to struggle? She tucks her fingers into the crook of his arm and they saunter down the dock to a waiting gondola.

"This is my gondolier, Giuseppe." The man nods at Anna and helps her into the craft.

As the vessel swings its way into the heart of the Grand Canal, Anna hears Thomas sigh with pleasure.

"I am a fortunate man," he declares.

Edith receives a postcard from Anna hand-painted in the most glorious shades of sea and sky.

> I had a sudden opportunity to run off to Greece and enjoy a friend's hired yacht, and after all you told me about this exquisite country, I didn't see my way to turning down such a generous offer. Athens was marvelous but sweltering, and after visiting the Parthenon—which simply snatched the breath from my lungs— we have driven to Cape Sounion by motorcar. The breezes here are delightful, the pines are as green as parrot feathers and the air is perfumed with "rigani"—Greek oregano. Do you remember the scent? It makes me weak in the knees. Have you ever tasted

retsina, the pine-resin wine? It's awful and yet curiously makes
me want to drink more! I do so wish you were here to enjoy this.
I know it would raise your spirits, dear.

Anna in Greece? Joyous! Having made a friend who can hire a yacht?
"We have driven down." Who are *we*? A party of people? Another maiden
friend? And she knows that Edith's spirits need raising. The woman is
clairvoyant! Edith, indeed, feels like she's sinking daily. It's been weeks
since she felt like herself. Her head hurts. Her heart aches. But Anna has
never sounded better! Edith is relieved to find the card lifts her own
heart, that she doesn't begrudge dear Anna her glistening fragment of
happiness, though her own happiness is so miserably fleeting.

"The woman who loves a fool, is a fool," she tells herself sternly.

I will forget him, Edith vows. I will reclaim myself. After weeks of intense writing despite her exhaustion, she slips the first six chapters of
The Custom of the Country into an envelope and hands it to Miss Thayer
to ship out to *Scribner's Magazine*. And thus unburdened, she begins by
spending hours in her garden weeding—something she almost always
expects the gardeners to do. She had forgotten how much pleasure there
is in yanking up weeds, rendering a bed pristine again. At night she
focuses on her guests—this weekend an opera singer, a French poet. She
reads Nietzsche. In the mornings, she writes a new short story about a
woman who misreads a man's intentions. She thinks she is winning
the battle.

And then, a few nights later, suddenly heart-thuddingly awake, she
finds herself so bloated with anger at Fullerton she paces the room rather
than struggle for sleep on her bed of nails. And eventually she descends
to the library, seats herself at her desk and picks up her pen.

Dearest HJ,

I beg of you. I urge you to help me. I don't know what's hap-
pened to Morton. He's broken my heart with his inability, or
perhaps I should say "refusal," to answer any of my posts. What
could be hampering him? Do you know if he is ill? Or has he

*found someone else to love? Has he written to you this summer?
Would he tell you if it were so? I am at wit's end. I am desolée.
I thought we meant something to each other. I thought he felt for
me all that I felt for him. You saw us. Did you see deep true
affection or did I only imagine it? I feel sometimes as though I am
going mad. I don't know where to turn. And so, of course, mon
cher maître, I turn to you. Burn this immediately!*

Edith was born to be a lady. And a lady never pursues, never complains,
never makes a scene and certainly never makes a fool of herself. So if
Fullerton isn't going to be available to her in any way—and surely only
a cad could be so callous as to drag her heart through this ditch of
incomprehension—then she will have to run the other way. Walter
writes from Massachusetts, where he is visiting his mother:

> *I know you've told Teddy you wouldn't leave for Europe until
> after Christmas this year. But in his present state, nothing seems
> to faze him anyway. Do you think you might get away? You know
> I must be in Egypt, and the Provence is the last ship I can sail.*

It's true, Edith reflects. Teddy, these days, with his pig house and
chicken palace, is happy all the time like a five-year-old. And since his
fishing trip, he is giddier than ever. The mysteries of his brain are in-
creasingly hard to fathom.

> *And you, dearest one, are not sleeping. You're quite
> miserable—though you won't tell me what's troubling you. Didn't
> the doctor suggest you go somewhere, anywhere else? So break
> with this scene and join me. You're always happier in Paris. Or
> perhaps you can cross the Sleeve and visit Henry at Lamb House.
> He's begged me to convince you to come. It will be much better
> for you to have a travel companion in the state you're in—why,
> you'd forget your passport, your pearls and heaven knows what
> else—and there's no one's company I'd prefer to yours. Do say
> yes before the ship is sold out and they make you sleep in the hold.*

So Edith announces to Teddy, and anyone else who will listen, that her insomnia and her hay fever have gotten the best of her. She requires a change of scene and quickly. Teddy shrugs and says he will book into the Knickerbocker Club until it's time for him to go on his hunting trip, and then perhaps go off to Hot Springs for another cure. (Oh, if only he were *always* so acquiescent!) The servants begin to roll up The Mount's mattresses and bring the oatmeal-colored drop cloths up from the storage room. Usually, this tucking away of her summer life makes Edith sad. But not this year. Teddy bids a tearful good-bye to his beloved Lawton, and the pig keeper reports to Edith that Lawton was literally whimpering at the farewell. Could a pig possibly be so smart?

Edith loves the thought of England, and time with Henry on his own turf. She feels so full of energy at the thought, she even quickly writes a comic story. When was the last time she felt up to that? And as she and Teddy and Fannie Thayer load themselves into the motorcar for the trip to New York, the dogs between them and at their feet, yipping and crazed by all the commotion, she feels as expectant as a young girl heading toward a ball. Teddy will be dropped off at the Knickerbocker Club, and Edith will check into the Belmont—no point opening up 884 for a single night. Besides, at the last minute, they've found a tenant to fill it. The servants can stay at 882 until winter.

And Anna! Anna's ship is supposed to arrive this evening—such good timing! Edith will send Cook down to the pier to fetch her. How she looks forward to seeing her dear friend! She imagines Anna's pale skin burnished by the Greek sun, roses in her cheeks. Tonni's cheeks! How she loved to press her face against her governess's face when she was a child. Tonni's cheeks were always warm and soft as velvet. She would hold Edith close and sing German songs. Hold her the way her own mother never would. As though she were happy to be in her company. As though she were precious. Edith wants so much to show Anna that she still cares about her—that sending her off this summer was a gift, not a snub.

Tonight, she imagines Anna's clear, shining eyes across a restaurant table, retelling her adventures and explaining the mysterious friends who whisked her off to Greece.

But Cook is soon back at the Belmont. Unfortunately, Anna's ship has been delayed by inclement weather in the Atlantic. The *Bremen* isn't expected to dock until late the next day, two or three hours after Edith's own ship, the *Provence*, is set to sail. Fannie Thayer, who has set herself up in Edith's hotel room to organize her papers, shakes her head with distress.

"She'll be crushed, you know. Anna's been longing to see you. . . ."

Edith debates. Should she not go? Should she wait until the next ship in one week's time? But how can she? Walter needs to get to Cairo now that he's been elected to the tribunal. There is a job to do! Counting the three days he plans to stay in England, he told her, this is the last possible date he can sail. Still, Edith fears that Anna will think she's been snubbed again. It wounds her to think that she allowed anyone—even Morton Fullerton—to come between her and her dear Tonni, who never wished her anything but kindness.

And so she writes. Writing is her best way of communicating. But not with Tonni! She had so longed to see her face-to-face, to make things right.

> Dearest Tonni,
>
> The disappointment of not seeing you before I sail! I know it seems heartless, unsympathetic and unnatural. I know Miss Thayer thinks it is.
>
> Well, I've had insomnia badly for two months, and Dr. Kinnicut, who came to Lenox early in Sept., tried different things, of a mild kind, but said, "If it goes on, you must have a change."
>
> It did go on, and got worse, and I came to town to see him about three weeks ago, and he said more emphatically, "Do go away at once." The trouble is that the least little sleep drug stupefies me the next day, and unfits me for my writing, which is such a joy and interest to me—and that makes me restless and bored. So I felt he was right.
>
> At the same time, he urged Teddy very strongly to go back to the Hot Springs for another cure, before going to his shooting in

Dec. Teddy has had the best summer he has had in years, as the result of his Hot Springs visit, so it seemed as if he ought to do this. [Isn't it better to tell Anna that he is going to Hot Springs because he has had success there? Why worry her by mentioning his overexcited state, which is the real reason she hopes he goes. Tonni would never approve of her leaving him in the shape he's in.] *Therefore I should have had to stay alone in Lenox all of Nov. or go with him, and I disliked the idea of that, as the hotel is very much over-heated, food very indigestible, etc.*

So I decided I would go out to Europe six weeks ahead of him; but I should have waited over another week in NY expressly to see you, if it had not been that Mr. Berry (who has been appointed a judge of the International Tribunal at Cairo) suddenly decided to sail on the Provence—that is, as soon as he was appointed, he settled on that date as the latest. It gave me the opportunity of having a companion instead of crossing utterly alone, and as I knew no one going out in Nov. I was very strongly tempted, and decided I had better go with him.

If I had felt well, I should not have minded being alone, but the insomnia has pulled me down, naturally, and it made all the difference having him with me. Dr. K. thinks my bad hay-fever was one of the causes, and he assures me it will all be over in a short time with complete change, as my general physical condition is good. But I want to break it up before it becomes anything like a habit, because it unsettles my whole mental life, and leaves me so good for nothing.

Miss Thayer will tell you that it hasn't yet affected my spirits, or prevented my writing what she considers a very funny story!!

I write this in great haste, as I was so sure of seeing you today that I didn't allow myself time. But you shall get a real letter from the steamer.

Dear Tonni, I do hope you understand that it is not heartless or inconsiderate of me to go off like this, and that it wrings my heart not to see you, and hear from your own lips the story of your summer.

Teddy will tell you all the details; I only want to assure you that I wouldn't have gone without seeing you for a few days first if I hadn't dreaded the long solitary days at sea and the sleepless nights.

I have a feeling you'll understand, and not be hurt, and above all, not worry. That's the thing I want most. I am well, essentially, only this special thing has to be cured.

Your devoted EW

Anna is thrilled as they steam past the Statue of Liberty. Oh, to be home at last! She breathes in the oil-infused perfume of New York Harbor, and glories in the crush of buildings and motorcars she spots on shore. What a journey it was, bringing her experiences she never imagined she'd encounter in her life! But during her most rousing moment abroad, she wished not any other outcome than this: to return home to Edith. Edith's most recent letters sounded kind, contrite. Perhaps at last they can be what they were to each other once more. How Anna longs for that.

Cook is waiting on the pier, looking nervous, his hands held behind his back as though he is hiding something.

"Miss Anna," he says, doffing his cap. "Welcome home. Have we many trunks to collect?"

"Just one." She smiles at him, and sees that he's aged: his boyish face has begun to tighten around the eyes, and loosen at the chin. How many years has she known him?

"What is the plan? Are we to go straight away to Lenox? Or are we stopping at 882?" she asks. "There are some books I'd like to pick up there first, if it would be no trouble."

Cook bites his lip. Another steamer moving out of the harbor lets out a low and mournful howl.

"We're *only* going to 882," Cook says. "You see, Mrs. Wharton's had to go on. She's awfully sorry. She gave me this note to give to you."

"On? Go on to where?"

"To France. On the *Provence*."

Anna feels as though her feet have been knocked out from under her. The late October wind whips up the river, forcing her to pull her wraps more tightly.

"To . . ." Her mouth is dry. Her heart is slamming too loudly. "To France?"

"Then back to England on the ferry." Cook holds out the letter. "Take it. Please."

She accepts the ecru envelope. It says in large looping letters, "Tonni."

"She knew you'd be upset," Cook says sotto voce. "It worried her." He looks away as he scrabbles to find a cigarette in his pocket, then takes it out and lights it.

"I'm . . ." Anna feels slapped.

"She says the letter explains everything."

"I'm sure it does."

"You don't want to open it now? I can wait."

Anna presses her lips together. Perhaps coming back was a mistake. Perhaps she should have more seriously considered her other options.

"I'll open it when we get to Park Avenue," she says. She folds herself into the motor.

"I'll come back for the trunk," he says. "Could be a long time until they winch it down. "Ready?" he asks.

She closes her eyes. The letter burns in her hand.

SIXTEEN

LATE WINTER 1908

All through the autumn and winter, Edith steeps herself in the social swirl of England to make up for the one wretched afternoon she spent in Paris with Morton Fullerton after the *Provence* landed. She had persuaded Walter, against his better wishes, to accompany her on the train to Paris rather then heading straight across the Channel on the boat-train as planned. It came to her on the *Provence* that she simply couldn't go on to England without knowing why Morton had stopped writing. It isn't that I want his reassurance, she told herself. I expect the worst. I merely deserve an explanation. Then I can cut him out of my life with certainty.

"Just one day. Honestly. I have to sort out hiring a cook for the coming season," she told Walter. "We've never had a good cook at the Vanderbilts' and it's essential I find one this year. Teddy's spirits are at stake. Besides, don't you want a day or two in Paris before you go off to Cairo?" It did indeed turn into two days, as Fullerton couldn't see her on the first, and hardly found time, he told her, to see her on the second.

She and Walter had to hole up at the ridiculous Hotel Dominici because the Crillon was fully booked. And then there were those few miserable moments with Morton. Oh, if only she hadn't insisted! But she shook it off. She had to. And went on with Walter across the Channel to England, which has never been more welcoming. The country suddenly seems to suit her so well. She can stupefy herself with the parties, with the introductions, with the glitter and glamour and joy of the place. England joyous! She had never imagined it could be so.

There are dinners with Lady this and Lord that. Time alone with HJ, and time to meet and befriend his crowd: Gaillard Lapsley and Howard Sturgis (who crochets and has a hulking male nephew named "Babe"); and time to meet new friends, like young John Hugh Smith, who, like Carl, seems surprisingly drawn to her. And the people she meets! Legendary. At one dinner, she is seated between Philip Burne-Jones and John Galsworthy.

"My maiden name is Jones. Do you think we may be related?" she asks Burne-Jones.

"If you are hoping for an inheritance, I can say certainly not," he mutters, sipping his wine.

She and John Galsworthy have much more to share, observing everyone at the table with whispered irony. She thinks she must read his books in case they meet again.

If only she could tell Morton all that she has done and who she's met. But no. The very *thought* of Morton is indigestible these days. The way he sat across from her at Le Fouquet that night, and had nothing to say to her. Nothing. When she begged him for an explanation of his curtailed communication this summer, his nostrils flared. His lips pressed together.

"Don't ask me," he said at last. "I told you I'm having problems. I'm probably harming myself just *being* here with you. You don't understand." She can see him now. How his face looked mottled, how his eyes darted to the door again and again.

"But dear, I *want* to understand."

"Well, you can't," he said, his words breathtaking in their chilliness.

"Is it Katherine?" she finally blurted out. "Are you in love with Katherine?" Edith was mortified for asking. Why, oh why had those words fallen from her lips?

He closed his eyes and shook his head. Disdain. That's what his face read. After all she gave him! All she trusted in him!

"Then just say it's over. Say it."

Again, he just shook his head.

"You won't? You won't put me out of my misery."

"If you just give me time . . ."

"Can't you be honest and say it's through between us? Are you too much of a coward?" She wanted to pummel him. To slap him. Her first instincts were physical and childish.

"Is that what *you* want?" he asked drily.

"Of course not."

"Then I won't say it. Edith, I must get back to the office." He rose and put on his coat. He didn't offer to pay.

The word she came away with from the meeting was *cruel*. He was outright *cruel* to her.

So she swallows England whole, dancing and dining, saying dry, witty things to aristocrats, poets, novelists and hangers-on. In London one night, a week before Christmas, and after two glasses of red wine, in which she almost *never* indulges, she sits down at the lovely little writing desk in her room at Lady St. Helier's house and writes:

> *Dear Mr. Fullerton,*
>
> *You have, if they still survive—a few notes and letters of no value to your archives, but which happen to fill a deplorable lacuna in those of their writer.*
>
> *I shall be in Paris on Monday next—the 21st—for a day only, and I write to ask if you would be kind enough to send them to me that day at my brother's.*
>
> *Perhaps the best way of making sure that they come straight into my own hands would be to register them.*
>
> *Yrs sincerely,*
> *E. Wharton*

But of course, when she arrives in Paris, there are no letters from Morton.

Edith hastily escapes Paris for a tour of Provence with the crocheting

Howard Sturgis, his outsized nephew and Cook, who's arrived early with the motorcar to whisk them all away.

WHILE Edith steeps herself in distraction, Anna is left to wrestle Teddy. Though he is staying at the Knickerbocker Club and she at 882, he visits the very first day after her arrival. Knocking on the door around teatime, he appears stiff and uncomfortable in his city clothes, his slender-cut suit which barely accommodates his expanding belly, his sharp-folded collar and silky tie. She hardly recognizes him.

"I want to welcome you, dear little Anna," he says, lifting Nicette, who has appeared from behind Anna's skirts. "How I've missed your face," he says, holding the little dog and looking right into her delicate foxy countenance, making Anna wonder if he is referring to her or Nicette.

"I want to hear every single detail of your infamous journey." He looks at her now with mischievous eyes.

Anna is warmed by his attentions and finds some Louisiana crunch cake in the kitchen that Gross bought at the Charming Door bakery and lays it out like daisy petals on a china plate. They sip tea together. He eats three pieces. And then asks for brandy, which White provides from his own stash.

Swirling the brandy snifter, Teddy tells Anna how crushed Edith was that she missed seeing Anna.

"I'd say she was crying. She was disappointed, I'll tell you that. I was already at the Knickerbocker, and we were on the telephone, so I didn't see tears myself. But she begged me to explain to you that it was a matter of timing, and to read nothing whatsoever into it. Those were the words she used."

Anna nods and traces the rim of her cup with her finger. She wants to believe him. But she can't know until they are face-to-face, until she can see for herself if Edith will look her in the eye. She shivers.

"Cold?" Teddy asks.

She shakes her head. "Maybe someone is walking on my grave," she says.

"So tell me about the trip. I read some of the postcards. I want to know more."

Looking up, she sees he means it. So she launches in. Avoiding any mention of Thomas, she describes her reunion with her dear cousins, the German castles and Roman ruins she found most memorable. She describes how the taste of the beer in Munich seemed to her bitter and refreshing, the way rain smells on cement when it hasn't rained for a long time.

"Ain't that the grandest description! You should be writing, instead of Pussy. Maybe you've been writing all her books and I'm the only one that didn't know it."

Anna blushes.

"Now, Mr. Wharton, you know that's not true," she says.

She goes on to depict the shimmering light in her ethereal hotel room in Venice. The taste of the retsina in the Peloponnese. He sighs. He lights a cigar. He pours more brandy.

At six o'clock he rises and straightens out his too-tight jacket.

"Miss Anna, seeing you is, without a doubt, the nicest thing that's happened to me all month." Anna can't help but be pleased. How lucky she is to have dear Mr. Wharton as a friend!

But then, Teddy starts showing up nearly every day to see her. To the point that Gross says, "He's here again? Whatever for?"

Anna shrugs. "He must miss Edith. That's the only explanation I have. And the dogs. Maybe he comes to see the dogs."

He does make a fuss about the dogs every time he comes. Holding and kissing them. Getting right down on the floor to play with them sometimes.

One afternoon, rising from a rip-roaring session with Mitou and Nicette, he sits down in the chair across from Anna and looks her in the eye. She notices then that he is looking drawn and cheerless.

"Truth is, I only feel settled these days when I'm around you," he says.

She is taken aback. "That's very nice," she says as neutrally as she can.

The overexcitement of the summer, the alarming way his eyes used to glimmer with manic jolliness, is now fading to a heavy glare, a rounding of his shoulders, an undeniable sadness.

"Edith don't care for me. That's what's weighing on my mind, Miss Anna," he tells her. "I don't think she's written me a single letter in two weeks. I bet she wrote you."

Anna says nothing.

"She has, hasn't she? Tell me."

"She does care for you," Anna says. "You just need to see her again. When we reach France in February, you'll be reassured." But Anna knows it's not true. Edith has written her a number of times. Nice full letters of her whirlwind tour of England. Why should she lie to him? Because he is too fragile to be slapped with the truth. She tries to talk with him about happier times, about things to look forward to. But for all her struggle to uplift him, his spirits seem to be sagging more daily, like a broken roof in the rainy season.

One night in December, just as she is brushing her hair for bed, the bell rings. In a few minutes, Alfred White knocks on her bedroom door.

"Mr. Wharton's here. He insists on seeing you, Miss Bahlmann."

She pulls on her wrapper, shaking. She fears he's bearing bad news from Edith. A car accident in France? A fire at The Mount?

When she comes into the drawing room (Alfred insists on staying as well), she sees he's sallow.

"Mr. Wharton. Are you all right?" she asks.

"Sit, Anna. That will be all, Alfred."

White leaves reluctantly; Anna still sees him peeking in from the hall where Teddy can't detect him. The fire in the drawing room is just sputtering. It's cold enough that the draperies are puffing out with the draft from the poorly sealed windows. She shivers even in the chair she chose, the farthest away from the window. Teddy hasn't taken off his coat, or sat down. He's pacing. He comes toward her.

"I don't feel safe when I'm not with you," he says. "I wonder if I can't move in here."

Anna gasps.

"Mr. Wharton. You can't possibly move in here."

"Why not? I own the place." She stands to see him better, to not feel so small beside him, though even when she stands, she's inches lower. She smells the liquor on his breath.

"I think maybe . . . perhaps you've had too much to drink," she says.

"I haven't. I haven't."

"Sit. Sit down," she says. He shakes his head. "Sit down, *please*."

He does finally, hunching in his chair. His coat still hangs about his shoulders. His lips are gray as they were last winter when she worried about him so.

"You miss Edith," she says in her most soothing voice. "That's it, isn't it? And yet it's only a few weeks until we can go back to the Rue de Varenne. I know just seeing her will set you right. And the hunting trip. What happened to your hunting trip?"

"I don't care about the hunting trip. And I don't want to go back to Paris. Damn Paris to hell. I'd rather *die* than go back to Paris." Any words about dying shake Anna, knowing what she knows about his father. Shot himself in the face with a pistol. She feels her lips quivering.

"But you'll be near Mrs. Wharton. And when you're together again, you'll feel better."

"It's not her I need. It's you. I miss having you near," he says. "I don't feel myself. If I could just move in here . . ."

Anna feels so unbalanced, she sits heavily in her chair, searching desperately for words.

"You canceled your time in Hot Springs. We must make that appointment again. Allow me to do it for you. I know Dr. Kinnicut will be very disappointed you didn't go. So we'll set that right. Edith wrote me that Kinnicut urged you to go. We must make it happen."

"Anna . . ."

Anna looks over at the hallway to see if Alfred White is still standing there, and finds it worrisome that she can't see him, nor his shadow. She could call out for him if need be. But why is she afraid? It's just Teddy.

"You can't move in here. It wouldn't look right, whether you own the house or not. Or we can move out. Gross and I and Alfred. And you can move here. But if you stay at the Knickerbocker, you can visit. As much as you like."

His face is stupid with inebriation. He looks like he might cry.

"You should go now, Mr. Wharton. Take a taxi to the Knickerbocker Club. Sleep. That's what you need."

He bites his lip.

"You're wearing my locket," he says. His voice is so broken, so childish, it's wounding to hear. She reaches for the soft oval. Her clothes always cover it. But tonight the wrapper has displayed it to him. Her secret. She feels her cheeks burn. She might tell him she wears it always. That she cherishes it above all other personal treasures. But wouldn't that be the worst thing?

"It was a very kind present," she says. "Come. White can help you find a taxi."

"White!" she calls out. She knows her voice belies the panic she's feeling.

White comes soon enough for her to recognize that he was standing nearby all along.

"Come now, Mr. Wharton," he says. He escorts Teddy out to the street. She pulls aside the curtain and watches White standing in the street, a hero in shirtsleeves, waving down a taxi, gently helping Teddy in. She cannot calculate her relief as the hansom drives off in the direction of the Knickerbocker Club.

Should she call Dr. Kinnicut? He must be back in town. Maybe if she asks his opinion, expresses her concern for Teddy. It's Edith's place to do so, not Anna's. Yet how can she bother Edith when she's finally enjoying herself so much in England? So she writes the doctor and awaits his answer.

"I'm worried about him," she tells Gross.

"He certainly seems attached to you," Catherine says.

"I'm sympathetic to him. That's all."

Catherine flashes a dubious look.

"Should I tell Edith? Should I? And ruin the only happiness she's had in a while?"

Gross shrugs her shoulders and with a downturned mouth and cocked brows, she leaves the room.

The doctor writes back that he will hunt down Mr. Wharton at the Knickerbocker Club—being a member himself—and talk to him casually, then report back. And so Anna waits.

A few nights later, no word from the doctor, she is lying in bed thinking of Thomas. She can almost conjure his face, which seems to fade more each day like an unfixed photograph. If only she *had* a photograph of Thomas. Would he look old to her? Would his smile seem kind or forced? For the last month, she has found it painful to think of him at all. Even with all the good moments they shared. Oh! the time they had walking dusty Cretan roads hand in hand to rumored ruins in empty fields. They'd scan the expanses, see nothing at all. And then the surprises would reveal themselves. A fallen column in the grass. A handful of potsherds amidst the clay. In Greece, so warm and dry, Anna's knee didn't ache at all, felt like a new joint: young and strong and uncomplaining. She could crouch in the field and gather bits of stamped Roman redware in the basket of her outspread skirt, colorful painted shards of Cycladian amphorae, matte pieces of glass bubbled and effervescent like soda water. Thomas would hunt too, patiently weighing his pockets with treasures. Once he found a ring, the shank golden and no longer round, set with a tiny stone the color of dusk. Glass? A gem? Neither knew. He gave it to her: took her hand and slipped it on her finger. He looked so proud as he viewed it there, turning her hand this way and that in the sun.

At night, Anna and Thomas would spread their treasures out on the table between their wineglasses, commenting on them, trading them. When the night aged enough that the men began to dance on the tables, they would slide the whole stash into Anna's drawstring bag. In her room on the yacht, she had a dresser-top covered with their shared loot.

During the day, they'd pause to watch women returning from town wells, peasant blouses pulled low, balancing tall slender vases of water on their golden shoulders. How graceful they looked in their labor—living tableaus of the sort that inspired romantic paintings over middle-class American spinets. She and Thomas were happy together then.

Until he told her about his daughter. Until she realized it wasn't love he was after. Or was it? It all felt clear to her back then: that he had other reasons for being drawn to Anna. But now nothing is clear at all.

She is tossing in bed, invoking the night that Thomas grabbed her hands and pulled her up from her chair begging her to dance with him. The music—the pear-shaped bouzoukis, the hourglass-shaped *doumbek* drums—set down a beat no one could resist. She danced in Thomas's arms like a rag doll. Completely unsure where to put her feet or how to use the music. He whirled her around until she was dizzy. But she was exhilarated, stunned by a sense of juice, of *life*, flowing through her. Her main thought was, "I have never felt this way before. I will never feel this way again." Was it that night he told her about his daughter, Tabita? Was it that night that everything came crashing down?

She is jolted from her reverie by the doorbell.

Anna hears Alfred pulling open the creaking front door, talking. She gets up and pads to the staircase to hear better.

"It's far too late to see her. She's gone to bed."

Teddy again. Who else could it be? She descends a step or two so she can hear more, barefoot, in her nightgown. The stairwell is cold, filling with air from the open door.

"I'll just wait in the living room," Teddy insists.

"She won't be up until morning."

"I said I'll wait here." She can hear the agitation in his voice.

"But sir. It's past midnight. And we all want to go to bed."

"I don't care," Teddy says.

Anna doesn't know what to do. If she goes to bed, she knows she'll toss and turn, unsettled by his presence in the room beneath hers. If she goes down now, Teddy will begin to think that he's welcome at all hours. Or maybe he already does. And then she sees Albert climbing the stairs toward her. He doesn't seem to notice the state of her undress.

"He's downstairs again, isn't he?" she asks.

"He is," Albert says.

"Should I go down to him?"

Albert sets his hands on her shoulders, looks into her eyes. "He's drunk. Let him sleep it off." Anna can sense how much he wants to protect her.

"In a chair? He can't spend the night in a chair!"

"Miss Bahlmann. . . . Anna." Anna doesn't think White has ever spoken her Christian name before. "He shouldn't be here at all. Maybe if he's miserable all night . . ."

He doesn't have to finish. She understands.

"Yes, you're right."

"Good night, then," Albert says.

He passes her on the staircase, and she follows him. Anna finds her bed in the dark room, glad for the warmth of her hot-water bottle, her comforter. But even settled beneath the sheets, even trying to think of Greece again, sleep is a distant land.

In the morning, she finds Teddy sprawled on the sofa, his shoes still on his feet (and no doubt soiling the cushions—her cushions! Her sofa from her apartment long ago.) His mouth is open, his coat is still buttoned. Anna thinks she might cry. Teddy has never been a dignified man. That would be an erroneous description of who he is. And yet she has never seen him look more foolish. She decides she must let him wake on his own.

An hour later when she returns to the parlor, he is gone, a ghost of his form still denting the cushions.

With Howard Sturgis and the Babe in tow, Edith finds herself at last at the Vanderbilt apartment. She had been looking forward to arriving back in Paris, to settling into the rooms she has come to consider her spiritual home. But how unexpectedly sad she feels wandering its elegant halls. For this was where she and Morton first fell in love. Where he brought her a box of pastel macarons. Where she would come back from a day in his arms, thrilled and aglow. Was it love? Or maybe it was just love on her part. Since arriving in London months earlier, she has been sleeping beautifully. And writing better than ever. Having requested back the pages she sent in of *The Custom of the Country*, she is rewriting it. So much better than before, she thinks. The words seem to fall from her pen. But now, staring out at the empty echoing Rue de Varenne, she feels unsteady again. And the nights loom long.

She remembers something Henry told her the last time she saw him at Lamb House. "I can't deny it any longer. Morton is weighed down by an evil which only he can reveal to you. I urge you to ask him. Insist he tell you. It's the only way you'll discover the truth."

Henry has a tendency to be dramatic: he overstates most things. Evil? She can't imagine. But one day, while Howard and the Babe have gone to see a play she's already seen (and found overwrought), she scribbles off a petit bleu:

> *There is one question I must clear up. Is it possible for you and I to meet tonight?*

In the very next post, he proposes a café and time.

He is smiling when she walks in. A great improvement over their last meeting. And his eyes seem to twinkle as they used to.

"Wonderful to see you," he says.

"Is it?" she asks.

"Absolutely. Especially seeing you looking so well. What have you done to look so . . . so healthy, so rested?"

She can't help being pleased to see herself through his eyes as improved.

"Good travel. Good writing," she says. "England was a wonderful place to begin my year."

He leans forward. "I've missed you," he says. 'You are exceptionally special to me, you know."

She would like to feel outraged, after all he's put her through. But God knows she's pined for him. She hasn't felt so brimming with life since last spring.

With menus to shield them from each other, they order dinner, and she peers around at the other diners. Mostly couples, huddling over their candles. Some laughing. Most talking.

He doesn't ask her what it is she wanted to ask him. Just like him to have so little curiosity. At last, she knows she's the one who must broach the subject.

"Henry says I must ask you to tell me . . ." How can she put it? "He says an 'evil' is weighing you down, and that I must insist you tell me what it is."

Morton smiles faintly, says, "Oh."

"Perhaps he shouldn't have told me. But I've felt there was something you've been hiding for a long time. If you just could tell me . . . Will you? Please."

He nods. She shivers, wondering suddenly whether she indeed wants to be enlightened.

The waiter comes between them with a basket of bread, fills their water glasses. Morton waits until he has crossed the room toward the kitchen.

"Don't tell me later that you wish I'd never said a word," Morton says.

"I won't."

"I'm . . ." Morton leans forward and whispers. "You won't like this, and . . . I'm not proud of it."

"Say it, Morton."

"I'm being blackmailed."

Edith expels a lungful of air all at once, and finds it hard to form any words. Morton doesn't speak. He does nonchalantly nod at someone across the room, however.

"Who is blackmailing you?" she asks at last.

"My landlady."

"And why would your landlady try to . . . extort money from you?" Extort somehow seems a less odious word to Edith.

"I owe her rent," Morton says. He's not blushing. Not looking embarrassed. He almost looks proud. It ripples the hair on the back of her neck.

"And what is she holding as ransom?"

"She has letters of mine."

"Letters?"

"Personal letters."

"I didn't think they were business letters," Edith says huffily. "Why are they so . . . valuable?"

"Valuable to no one but the people who wrote them. I want you to understand they're old letters from two people. . . . Both are, I guess

you'd say, *public figures*. One is something of a *royal* figure. A *royal mar-*
ried figure. The other . . . a . . . politician."

"Go on. Who? You may as well tell me."

"And if I told you who they are, what would prevent me from tattling
about you with others? My affairs are my affairs. And best kept to myself.
All of this happened a long time ago. . . ."

"I see," she says, though still fails to see, and now is uncomfortably
curious.

"It's why I was uneasy when I saw you before Christmas. My landlady
said that she was watching me then. I do believe sometimes she was following me. You're becoming well known too, Edith. I didn't want her to
hunt for *your* letters. She's away right now. Down in Nice."

"And you're still living in her house?"

Morton nods.

"But why don't you move out, for heaven's sakes?"

"She'd retaliate. Besides, I . . . she's not a bad person, per se."

Suddenly Edith knows. Knows more than she wants to know.

"You've been intimate with them all, haven't you? The two who
wrote you letters. They're love letters. *And* this landlady. You've had a
relation with her as well?"

Morton looks into his wineglass, then takes a large swig, as if for
courage.

"You can think what you like."

Edith knows precisely what to think. If any woman lived life with the
sexual abandon of Morton Fullerton, what name would they attach to
her? She's heard Fullerton called a "boulevardier" by Anna de Noailles.
She's heard rumors from Eliot. But she never imagined his conquests
were so haphazard. Or so incautious. She realizes that one of the authors
of the love letters, the politician, must be a man. Maybe the royal figure
as well. What would a letter revealing *that* do to a public figure? What
did it do to Oscar Wilde?

"Are you still *romantically* involved with the landlady?"

Morton shakes his head. "Not at the moment."

"No, at the moment you're sitting in a café. . . . And the letter
writers?"

"Heavens, no. I have no idea where they are anymore. Either of them."

Impetuously, she reaches out and grabs his hand.

"Let me help you, then," she says.

"Help me? How?"

"What do you owe her? I have money. If we could lift this terrible weight off your shoulders, things might be different." Between us, she can't help thinking. But why, oh, why, does she want him so, when every word out of his mouth reveals him to be a cad? If only the heart weren't so capricious, so unable to absorb logic!

Morton stares at the tablecloth for a moment, traces the jacquard pattern with his finger. When he looks up, his face has reddened.

"I am perhaps not the most honorable of men, Edith. But I don't think I'd stoop so low as to take your money."

Edith feels relieved at his words but presses on.

"Why not?"

"Because then I'd be beholden to you. I'd be trading one trap for another."

Edith finds herself aghast, half-standing with outrage. "That's the most odious thing you've ever said to me!"

"I didn't mean that. It just came out wrong. Sit. Sit down. I'm not saying you're trying to trap me. I can see that's what you might have thought I meant. I just don't want to feel that our relationship is based on my owing you money, that's all. I'm already struggling with the very same situation."

"It's *not the very same situation*," Edith says, venom in her voice. Edith wonders—could he possibly see her as no better, no more desirable, than his landlady? A lonely woman who is turning to him for pleasure. She feels sick to her stomach. A burning has begun in her throat. Oh, the irony that she, a woman who has always detested surprises, swerves in the path, has chosen as her only lover a man who delivers nothing but bolts of lightning. She shakes her head, turns toward the door.

"I have places to be," she says.

"We haven't eaten."

"That's never stopped *you* from leaving a meal."

His eyes become childlike, pleading. He grabs her hand. His silken touch shakes her. "Sit down, dearest. Won't you?"

She does. She doesn't know why. He has an undeniable power over her.

"Is this . . . this *situation* why you didn't write me this summer?" she asked.

"Yes. I was in much worse shape in the middle of the summer. I've paid off some of my debt to her now. I thought if I stopped writing you, you might stop writing me. I didn't want her to get hold of your letters."

"But why didn't you just tell me? If you'd explained . . ."

He shrugs. "Perhaps I should have."

"Yes. You should have."

"Ah, but what would you have thought of me?"

"It was what I thought of myself when you didn't write that hurt so much."

The meal comes and she can barely swallow for the aching in her throat. She has wanted to know for months and months what mystery has separated him from her. But hearing all that he's told her, she thinks the mystery is far more complicated than she imagined. What sort of man would get involved in such a scandal? Walter, for instance, would never have allowed such a thing to happen.

But how different Walter is from Morton. Brilliant Morton. Childish Morton. In some ways, he is hardly more than an adolescent. A creature so beautiful that persons of all sorts wish to possess him: men, women. Who could resist him?

Against her will, as she shreds the *blanquette de veau* with the tines of her fork, she is suddenly in that chestnut-shadowed room in the inn, wearing only her bloomers, or cradled by the moss beneath the lilacs, entirely naked. These memories are so visceral. So real! How dangerous he seems to her at the moment. And the hurt she's had to bear from him is too fresh. Yet she can't help wondering, can't help praying that their *affaire de coeur* isn't over. Over before it's barely begun.

"The thing is," he says, "I don't know when I can clear things up. I really have no idea how to find that sort of money."

Edith forces herself out of the delicious lost memories and into the noisy café again. "Did you *never* pay her rent? How long have you lived there?"

"For years."

"And for years you didn't pay rent?"

"She didn't ask me to." She stares into his guileless eyes and is disturbed by what she sees.

"Ah . . ."

He sets down his fork, looking satisfied and full. The bill lies between them, fluttering in a breeze from the door.

"I need to go," she says suddenly. "I have guests staying with me."

He makes no move to lay out money, to pay.

"This one's yours, Morton," she says, standing up. "I wouldn't want you to feel trapped by my generosity."

"Edith . . ."

"I take it you have a *few* francs in that wallet of yours," she says.

He nods guiltily.

Then she pulls her wraps crisply and leaves the restaurant without looking back.

"Miss Bahlmann, let me put it plainly." Dr. Kinnicut has finally telephoned. And Anna has risen from the dinner table to speak to him. "Very simply, he's fallen into melancholy again, a serious depression. And he's starting to have the old problem with his teeth. And the pain in his head as well. He's barely been out of his room, which is why it took me so long to see him. I finally knocked on his door."

"But what are we to do?" Anna asks. "We're to leave in just a week's time for France. The whole household."

"Yes, he told me. And I think you should all go. A change may do him good. He wants to go. I've given him some medicine. I rather doubt it will do much but keep him rather numb. Alleviate some of the pain. He never did go back to Hot Springs again, did he?"

"No."

"He should have."

"Should I insist he go now? I don't know that he would listen if I urged him to go."

"He wants to be with his wife. He said so. Even though he's not keen on Paris. He also told me he wants you nearby. You seem to make him feel secure. He spoke of you continually."

"I'll be traveling with him," Anna says, feeling the shock of the doctor's words to her fingertips.

"Well, as much as possible, keep an eye on him."

"Yes, sir. I'll be sure to do that."

"And whatever you do, Miss Bahlmann, don't let him wander out on the deck alone. Many a hurting soul has given in to the lure of the sea."

Dr. Kinnicut's words make her stomach tighten.

"No, sir. Good advice."

"Have you warned Mrs. Wharton?"

"I was afraid to upset her. She seems to be so happy right now. . . ."

"No. Don't disturb her. Pull her aside when you arrive and explain what I said. The poor woman's suffered enough through his ups and downs. Last I saw her, it was taking a toll on her."

"I'm afraid so."

"Is she sleeping better?"

"She writes that she is."

"Between you and me, I fear Mr. Wharton is a very sick man. When he had his episode last year, and then the cure in Hot Springs, well, I felt it was an isolated incident. Now, seeing him like this two years running is very disturbing indeed."

It is a terrible crossing. Winter crossings are always the worst. Iceberg warnings. Large waves. No need to worry about Teddy wandering the deck when the air is so frigid and the winds so intolerable. Anna visits him every day in his cabin, as do Gross and White. They take turns, even draw up a schedule so he's rarely alone. He won't come to the dining room, feeling so ill. So they make sure food is delivered. And flowers. And sweets. Nothing seems to alter his dark mood. And with the high waves, even intrepid Anna isn't feeling quite herself. She can only pick at the food when it's set before her in the dining room. I must be unerschütterlich! she tells herself. Thomas would expect it of me! She thinks longingly of their dinners together on the *Amerika*, sharing Wiener schnitzel and Moselle wine. How the whole upper class dining room watched the two of them and wondered. That crossing feels like years ago.

"Just sit here and talk to me, Anna," Teddy tells her when she visits his cabin with Nicette in her arms, hoping that the little dog will cheer him up. "Talk in the old way. About the things we both care about." She settles the Pekinese in her lap, and Teddy reaches out and pets the golden creature's delicate turtle-shaped head, then lets his hand fall with exhaustion.

Anna prattles about how happy the dogs will be to see Edith again. "As will you," she says. She reminds Teddy about the horses he bought near the end of the summer.

"You can ride them next summer," she tells him. "Just imagine you're on one of those leafy paths that lead to town. There you are on your horse, warm breezes just *kissing* your face. Perhaps you and I can have a sumptuous picnic on Laurel Lake. We'll ride the horses there."

"But you don't ride."

"I haven't ridden since I was a child in Massachusetts. But you could teach me again. I imagine you're a very good teacher."

His mouth softens into a hazy smile. "I think I might be."

The man needs compliments, appreciation. And who has offered him any all these years?

"Will you teach me to ride? I would look forward to that. But you'd have to be patient, of course."

"Of course," he says.

It is comical to imagine herself on a horse. An old lady with gray hair doing something so foreign.

He reaches out and grabs her hand.

"Anna, hold me," he says.

"Mr. Wharton!"

"As a friend. As a friend! It would make me feel so much better. It's all I'm asking."

She sets Nicette down in her chair. The little dog curls up and yawns. Then she leans over Teddy, gray-faced and miserable, slumped in his bed, and she slips her arms about his shoulders. With a surprising violence, he clutches her to him so tightly she gasps. And then she understands he's sobbing against her. His whole body trembles in her arms.

"There, Mr. Wharton. No need for that."

"Hold me," he calls out.

"I won't let go," she tells him.

When he sobs himself to exhaustion, she finally lays him back on his pillow.

With his eyes closed, tears splaying his pale lashes, his voice just a whisper, he says, "If I die, Anna, you can tell everyone that you were the only one who made me want to live."

SEVENTEEN

SPRING 1909

"It's the season from hell," Edith writes Walter. "Teddy has arrived in worse shape than ever. And if it wasn't for dear Anna, I swear I'd go mad. She somehow can tolerate him, sits at his bedside and talks to him of the most inane things. I have come to realize that I am not, by nature, a tolerant person."

Edith had imagined that the arrival of the household in Paris would bring one difficult task: to apologize to Anna, or in any case to repair the fence that has sprung up between them. Instead, Teddy has pilfered all the focus. He barely could manage the steps up to the Vanderbilts' apartment. His face was the color of a hospital corridor.

"Dear God. What's happened to you . . . ?" Edith said, seeing him for the first time in the entry hall.

Anna, coming up the steps behind him, grabbed Edith's elbow and pulled her aside while White helped Teddy to his bed.

"He's as bad as he was last winter. Gout or melancholia, whatever it is. Dr. Kinnicut says . . ."

"You spoke to Dr. Kinnicut?"

"I was so worried . . . I had to see what he recommended. And he was so kind. He went to visit Mr. Wharton at the Knickerbocker Club. As a friend. As a member of the club. He did it at my behest. I don't think Mr. Wharton suspected . . ."

"You never said a word to me. . . ."

"You seemed so happy. I didn't want to worry you."

Edith looked into Anna's eyes.

"Bless you," she said. "I didn't know I was leaving you with such a heavy burden."

"I didn't mind," Anna told her.

So days pass and Edith has yet to take Anna aside and apologize to her, reassure her. They are back to being good friends and helpmates. Is there any point in bringing up the last miserable year at all? Edith's fresh writing pages are lifted from her doorway every morning and returned in the afternoon, neat and edited for typos. Anna always asks good questions: "Edith, I just have a few . . . queries," she might say, standing in the hall looking even smaller than usual.

"Yes."

"On page 91 here, would Peter Van Degen really say that? It sounds like something Ralph Marvell would say instead. And here. I thought the child was in the room. What happened to him?" Edith is grateful to have Anna as her first reader, thankful that they seem to be back into the old rhythm. Fannie Thayer had done a good job in Anna's absence. But she wasn't dear, thoughtful Anna. The only sign that anything is amiss emerges when Fullerton's name is spoken, and then Edith notes the subtle hitch of Anna's fragile shoulders, the pressing of her lips. All so restrained that no one but Edith could detect it. Still, Edith appreciates her restraint. These days, in truth, the thought of Fullerton makes her own shoulders hitch. Blackmail. Lovers. She is still absorbing it all. An indigestible meal that doesn't want to go down.

One night, lying in bed, Edith realizes she's never even taken a moment to ask Anna about her trip, about the mysterious detour to Greece and with whom she traveled. "I'll bring it up tomorrow," she resolves. She has so firmly imagined that it must be another maiden lady endowed with family money, traveling for "adventure," that Edith has even named her: Imogene. Imogene with a felt hat and men's shoes, a tweed jacket with leather pockets. And a voice like a parrot. But when morning comes, Edith's resolve to find out more about Anna's summer is as cold as ashes. Other urgent matters push their way to the top: a short story idea that crystallized while she slept, a need to answer a letter from

Walter, the desire to leave the house early so she doesn't have to spend too much time with the ailing, impossible Teddy.

Edith doesn't see Morton much that spring. At first, he writes, "Can we be together this Saturday?" and she pneus him back to say she's got plans. He stops by without warning, gifting her with the same Ladurée macarons that pleased her so last year, and she sets the box in the entryway, doesn't even ask for the treats to be laid out on a plate for him; if he wants them so badly let him buy a box for himself! She finds herself cold, inarticulate, the impossible woman he wooed last year. Later, she feels guilty, writes to apologize, but oh, how she hates the war that ensues inside her: she wants him and she fears him. Wouldn't it be better—safer!—if they were close friends like they were before he became so much more. She is comfortable as the older woman, sharing her experience, her counsel. Morton, whose desire to charm endows him with a chameleon's ability to read cues, to shape-shift, begins to consult her about his blackmailer, implores her to give advice. How easy and right it feels to write back about how he should handle this woman, "a person you believe to be half-mad." It is easy to forget that "this person" might not be so different from herself. Oh, she would never blackmail, but the desire for any leverage to maneuver a man as recalcitrant as Morton certainly has its dark appeal.

"Then listen to me, dear, when I say don't go on Saturday. Why should you be ordered about in that way?" she writes. Or, "When the interview does take place, why should it not take place before witnesses? Have you not a friend who would go with you? Or could you not take an *homme d'affaires* if there are business matters to be settled?"

One March night, when they unexpectedly meet at Rosa's salon, he is seated next to her, and beneath the table, he grasps her hand, resting his on her thigh. She can hardly bear the sensation: it enters her. It eddies and sings and sparks in a spot just above her pubic bone, a holy nexus that just last year she didn't know existed. She can't bear the ecstasy. The way it whips up her long-stored desire like a windstorm excites every particle of dust on a desert street. She rises in the middle of a conversation and rushes into the red drawing room to sit a while, to catch her breath. Later, she tells Rosa it was a touch of asthma, and Rosa doesn't question it. But Morton, smiling quizzically at her before he leaves, appears unsettled. Let him remain so, she decides, turning her face away. The next day, he writes another letter, begging her advice, flattering her.

"You always tell me the right things to do. I listen to you because you see so clearly what I cannot see." She smiles but keeps her distance. For the moment, it is the only safe thing to do.

Sharing her cautious mood, the season arrives slowly. Buds huddle in knots on the trees for weeks before opening. The lawn of Les Invalides waits to awake, a faded, straw-colored carpet. And she is heartsick much of the time, for last spring her life did indeed *spring* open like a jack-in-the-box after a lifetime of a metallic, insistent melody. But this year, she is wracked with doubt. Morton Fullerton was her whole world. And now she thinks she was just one of many to him. Nothing he does or says seems quite sincere.

But when Frederick Macmillan contacts her to say he thinks she may be the perfect person to write a book about Paris for the American market—how wonderful her motor-flight book was!—she has an idea. She'll recommend Morton. Who better to compose a book about Paris than a man who has lived beneath its lights for eighteen years? A journalist. A man who knows the city inside and out. If she can get Morton to agree, Macmillan can give him an advance to help wipe away his debt to his landlady! He'll be liberated. She'll be a hero! The thought electrifies her. She can't even wait for a pneu to reach him. She calls his bureau.

"I have a solution for you," she says, not even announcing herself. "At last, dear. A perfect solution."

She expects to be scolded, frozen out. He doesn't like to be called during his workday. But who can turn down a *solution*?

When she shares her plan, she hears his voice change from heavy, serious, formal, to excited, open.

"But do you think they'll accept me as the author instead of you? You're world-famous, whereas I . . ."

"I'll recommend you," she insists. "Say that you're the only one I know so qualified for the spot. Mr. Macmillan is in New York. He'll have to take my word. . . . No, I have a better idea. I'll recommend you, and ask Macmillan to write to HJ. HJ will support you one hundred percent."

"And what if I am not qualified?" he asks softly.

"Morton, how can you suggest such a thing? Of course you are. Of course you're perfectly, brilliantly qualified. Think of all you've taught me about Paris. How well you know the city. And you're Harvard edu-cated. You're so extraordinarily bright, so sensitive."

Flattery. She's flattering him now. They have exchanged roles. And it feels dazzling!

"Yes," he says. "Put me up for the job. God knows I need it."

"You mustn't be afraid of the work. It's nothing. It will be second nature to you."

When she hangs up, she knows there's one more thing to do: not only will she have to suggest that Macmillan hire Morton, but she'll have to supplement the advance. Fred Macmillan would never pay an untried writer like Morton enough to free him from his blackmailer. And Edith certainly doesn't want Morton—who says he's too proud to take money from her—to know the money is lifted from her own pocket.

She'll work it all out with Henry! She'll have the money sent to Henry's account in Rye. Then he can tell Macmillan he believes so much in Morton that he's offered to help pay extra toward the advance. (He wants to help the young fellow have enough to live on so he'll write more.) Henry will like the solidity, the financial stability the offer would convey to Macmillan. Morton will have the money he needs to extricate him from his landlady's spider web. Henry will have the standing he's been longing for. And she'll be the anonymous savior, reveling in the results rather than the gratitude. It's the perfect plot. It belongs in a book! But better than a book, because the repercussions will have a real and lasting effect! Oh, if only every day could turn out so satisfying!

Anna is extraordinarily relieved to be back in Edith's good graces. She has returned to her beautiful room at the top of the house. She enjoys her walks through the Faubourg, even when her knee aches from the damp French weather. And she doesn't mind the hours she spends keep-ing Teddy's head above water.

But when a letter arrives from Thomas, she feels much less certain.

Dearest Anna,

I am hoping that you are reading this letter. It is the third I've sent and all have returned sealed. But at last I have discovered how to reach your famous Mrs. Wharton and have sent this letter in care of her and pray that you have it in your hands wherever you may be.

I have thought much about how we said good-bye, and have come to the conclusion that you misread my intentions. If you are in Europe, mightn't I come see you? I am not afraid of travel, and the things I wish to say can't be spoken in a letter.

In haste and kindness,
Thomas Schultze

Anna touches the ornate handwriting on the front of the letter. An old-fashioned German hand not unlike the one gracing the yellowed letters her father penned her mother. She sets the letter on her bedside table, not sure how to answer him. Could she have misread his intentions? And if so, would it really make a difference?

Greece is a memory so warm and beautiful; in the cold embrace of Paris there are days Anna cannot envision herself as the main character of those reminiscences. Surely it is something she read instead of lived: a wealthy man, a yacht, good food, fine wine, *attention*. How tenuous she felt, moored off the coast of Crete with these gifts all around her. Sitting on the sand on a beach in Corfu with a picnic laid out before her. Never once had she ever imagined such a life could be hers. And how odd she found those offerings difficult to bear, feeling too often like an actor in the wrong play.

And then one night, Thomas said he wanted to make the arrangement permanent. They were on the deck of the yacht. A storm was blowing up and they were waiting for the captain to row them to shore so they could take hotel rooms and wait out the weather. But even with the storm gathering, the air was so warm and sweet, it felt like a love potion.

Thomas took her hand and looked at her. He often spoke without letting his eyes rest on her, dreamily looking out toward some future that didn't include her. But now he gazed at her frankly.

"I want to ask you to marry me," he said. As though he were going by script. As though it was all planned out. "But before I say the words, I must tell you something. You know I have three daughters, Anna. But I haven't told you about Tabita. It's time to tell you about my daughter . . . because this trip, this respite, is for me just a prelude for what I wish to happen for us."

"What about Tabita?" Anna asked.

"Unfortunately . . ." He cleared his throat. "She will be a girl all her life."

"I don't understand."

"My other daughters, Baldegunde, Sabinchen, haven't married, but I suspect they will. Though they are taking their time. . . ."

"I'm sure they will," Anna says encouragingly.

"But you see, Tabita . . ." He opens his wallet and pulls out a small photo. The girl in the photo is clutching a doll to her chest so ferociously it is the first thing Anna notes about her. Because from what Thomas said, she is a teenager. And then Anna peers more carefully, at a moon face beneath pale curls. At eyes with an epicanthic fold that reads as Asian, and a mouth that is sweet and smiling but slack in its way, open.

"She's . . . she's a mongoloid," Anna says, using the English word, not knowing how to say it in German.

"Yes, a *Mongoloider Krueppel*. You know about children like this?" Thomas asks.

"I knew a child like her once when I was young. I tried to help her learn to read."

When Anna was living at Aunt Charlotte's, there was a girl who lived down the street named Alissa with the same odd features and slack, happy smile.

"What's wrong with her?" Anna had asked Aunt Charlotte after they passed her for the first time on the street and she had said, "Hello, Mrs. Bahlmann," in a sloppy, soft voice.

"Oh, Alissa? She's a mongoloid idiot," Charlotte told her. Anna found the description perplexing. Charlotte was not a woman who called others names.

"Why do you call her an idiot?" Anna was indignant.

But Charlotte patiently explained. "*I* don't call her that. That's what the world calls people with her malady. Mostly, I just think of her as poor Alissa."

Anna liked tiny Alissa, who was eager to learn and addressed everyone openly and without fear of looking foolish. Anna would try to find books in Aunt Charlotte's library to show her. Together they sat on the steps of Alissa's house, Anna pointing at pictures and the words beneath them. Alissa loved the books, and in time learned to identify the letters, and with a great deal of repetition began to sound them out. She loved Anna, wanted to follow her everywhere. It breaks Anna's heart realizing that since Aunt Charlotte died, she's rarely thought of Alissa at all.

"Can Tabita read?" Anna asks.

"I think if someone were kind and patient . . . as you are. We didn't know if Tabita would live through childhood. But she has . . . ," Thomas says gravely. "She outlived Agnes. I never thought that would happen. Miss Bahlmann, you've never met a sweeter child. And you, having been a governess . . . well, you seem the perfect person to help her. To be there for her when I'm not."

"So you really want me as a governess, then? Not a wife . . . ?"

Anna shivers at the memory of that moment. She has no objection at the thought of helping the little girl in the photo. But the disappointment was dizzying. All along she imagined that Thomas might be falling in love with her, had chosen her for some unfathomable reason. But at that moment she knew with a chill what he really wanted.

How could she have believed that Thomas was falling in love with *her*? An old maid with gray hair and a tired knee. Not that he was a romantic hero. Aging. A bit stiff. He wrapped his napkin around his neck when he ate anything he feared might spatter. He rarely looked her in the eye. But for a few honeyed weeks, she had believed the stars had wheeled around in the sky and at last had dealt her a fate too good to be true. She should have known that stars can't spin so far from their natural orbits.

"I am going to ask something difficult of you, Tonni. And I hope you won't be angry about it. But you must take Teddy back," Edith says.

"You're the only one I can trust to cross with him. Dr. Kinnicut says there are new treatments he'd like to try. Some serums. And Teddy's getting worse by the day, don't you think? I am at wit's end."

"You want me to travel alone with him?" Anna asks.

"We'll send White, of course. You'll need help. White's strong and Teddy trusts him. I'm sorry to ask this of you, but Teddy wouldn't even consider going without you."

Anna thinks: why can't *you* come along? Why must *you* stay in Paris? Fullerton is a rare visitor. She hardly hears his name anymore. So why can't Edith start her summer when the Vanderbilt apartment is handed over in April instead of moving into Harry's or the Hotel Crillon and flouncing to the salons and chatty lunches?

"But do you think Mr. Wharton can bear being away from you?" Anna asks.

"Me? You're the only one who can settle him down these days. He's angry at me. Or haven't you noticed?"

Anna is baffled. She agrees that Teddy is sinking faster than she could have imagined. He hardly makes sense some days. She hasn't told anyone, but more than once he's called her other names: Nanny, his sister's name. And a few times Pussy. And there have been a few violent episodes, such as the day he threw his food tray across the room right toward the little housemaid with the red hair who quit in a flurry of French, saying she couldn't work for a madman. Or the evening he wandered into the salon while Edith was hosting an elegant old Faubourg clan—the Hermès family—and screamed at them that he couldn't stand to hear another *frog* word from their lips.

"Your voices are the voices from *hell*! With your jabbering French! Get out of this apartment immediately!" Except for the youngest Hermès, they didn't speak a word of English and had no idea what he said. But that was the last time Edith felt safe to invite people over.

"I need to stay in Paris," Edith says. "I've already arranged to scout for an apartment of our own. A place I can lease so we can stay year-round. You, me, all of us. In the Faubourg, preferably. I've already leased The Mount out for the summer. We had a particularly good offer. And how could Teddy spend the summer there in *his* state?"

"But he loves it there. He'll be crushed if he hears . . ."

"I've already told him and he didn't say a word."

"Are you sure he heard you?"

"He may be unstable. He's not deaf."

Anna is bereft. Who will look in to see fat Lawton in the pig house? Or stroll the beautiful new paths? Who will whisper to the horses and feed them sugar lumps and take them out on the trails? Strangers. The notion gives her an unsettled feeling, a pain in her ears. She can't soothe Teddy anymore with tales about how they'll ride together or visit the animals. What can he look forward to? His wife, whom he adores, can hardly bear him. He's lost the one sanctuary that made him giddily happy.

"Don't look at me that way, Tonni. I have no choice but to send you with him."

"I don't mind going with him."

"Then what? What are you thinking? After all you and I have been through, it's best you tell me. There have been enough misunderstandings between us."

Misunderstandings? Is that what Edith thinks they were?

"I'm worried about him, that's all. And, I'm worried about you."

"About me? Why should you be? Without the burden of Teddy, I'm just fine."

"That's what worries me. It's that you think you can just ship him off and be *fine*! I've never thought of you as cavalier! He's your husband. In sickness and in health. Aren't those the words?"

Edith's face burns with anger. Her nostrils flare.

"And what could you possibly know about those words, *Miss* Bahlmann?"

Anna looks down at the floor. Edith's right. What could she know?

But Edith has paled. She sighs. "I don't want to be angry with you, Tonni. Why must you bait me?"

"I wasn't baiting you. It just feels wrong."

"You're not my governess anymore. Right and wrong are concepts I create for myself."

"Right and wrong are concepts *you* create?" Anna says, but so softly that Edith says, "What?"

There is so much Anna could say. But she knows she can't change her old student at this point, or even her point of view.

"When will Mr. Wharton and I travel?" she asks.

"White will make arrangements. We'll let you know."

Anna nods and turns to leave the room, but Edith goes on.

"Sometimes . . . sometimes things become just too much. Sometimes we don't do the things we think we should. We do the things we *must*."

Anna turns to her.

"You've told him that he's going back? You've warned him you're sending him away?"

"I have. Or I think I have. You can reiterate it."

"Edith . . ."

"Yes."

"I don't want us to be at odds either. . . ."

"Then stop taking Teddy's side."

"There are no sides," Anna says, leaving the room. "He's not acting this way on purpose. He's in pain. He's *ill*."

"I know that. I'm not good at helping him. You know I'm not. You are. I'm turning him over to you."

Anna wonders if turning Teddy over to her strikes Edith as a compliment.

"I understand," Anna says, leaving Edith, now sitting at her desk, eyes closed, head down, as penitent as Anna's ever seen her.

Anna writes to Thomas that they cannot meet in Europe, that she is due to sail back to America with her ailing employer's husband and doesn't know when she'll return. She worries that Thomas will think she's avoiding him, or even escaping him. So she adds at the bottom of the letter.

> *Please understand that I would be happy to see you again and hear what you have to say. Perhaps I will be back in Paris by summer. I will be sad to miss the spring here which I consider very beautiful.*

She thinks to sign the letter "Anna Bahlmann" but stops at merely "Anna."

EIGHTEEN

Even without Teddy in Paris, Edith is at loose ends. Living at the Crillon with no secretary at all to sort out the burgeoning pages of *Custom*, she's set it down and turned to writing poetry and short stories. She wants closure and they provide it. She needs something to show for the hours she's spent with a pen in her hand, and they are much more easily tied up with a bow. Besides, sharing herself with Undine Spragg was taking its toll. Undine has far too clear a sense of entitlement, often seems too big for the page, when Edith herself feels that she owns nothing: her passion for Morton is folded up in tissue paper. She is walking away from the house she built to hold all her dreams. (How those dreams have fallen to pieces!) And now she doesn't even have the ease of the Vanderbilt apartment.

The afternoons and evenings she spackles over with gay lunches and teas. And salon dinners. And long walks just to repress the sense of restlessness that has again arisen. I'm icing a very badly formed cake, she thinks. A smear of gaiety over crumbling uncertainty. She looks at apartments to lease, but hasn't found one to her liking.

Morton will occasionally stop by unannounced, a book or box of sweets in his hand. He has finally signed the contract with Macmillan agreeing to write the Paris guide and has pocketed the money and ostensibly given it to his blackmailer, though somehow she still lingers on the sidelines, tormenting him.

"Have you begun to outline the book?" she asks.

"All in good time," he says.

"You've been given an advance. They won't wait forever."

He shakes his head and smiles at her.

"Yes, Mother." Often, he tries to kiss her lips when they part, taking her by the shoulders, drawing her against his chest. And she pulls away with a pained smile. She doesn't trust him. She doesn't know what he wants from her. She doesn't want to be just one of many women who find him irresistible.

"Not now," she says. "Please, not now."

Come May, Edith decides to return to England, where she found happiness the previous fall. She knows she will encounter overlit rooms (Oh, those sparkling just-washed chandeliers of London!), gaiety and spontaneity. Also an air of reticence and even untruth. Ah, the English! But truth is not what she wants or needs right now. What she longs for is pastel-colored distraction. Wit!

When she tells Morton she's crossing in late May, he asks that she wait until the beginning of June. He's had word that his father, the Reverend Fullerton, is ill, and he's booked passage from Southampton to America.

"We'll cross together. We can see Henry, then I'll catch my ship." She can't help feeling sorry for him. He looks worried and worn. Desperation molds his mouth, his brow. The June liner is the first reservation Morton can find at his price, now that his money is funneling to his landlady.

Edith debates. Should she go ahead of him? Since withdrawing her affections, he has grown more insistent, more interested. The game of cat and mouse irritates and stimulates her all at once. A struggle for power that she's never known before. The worry about his father makes him more vulnerable, more reachable. More desirable.

So plans are made to travel in June. Cook will drive. They'll cross on the ferry. She doesn't speculate what will happen.

The crossing is brutal.

"A green crossing," she tells Fullerton, for they all feel bilious being tossed about by the waves. Though it is rainy and cold, the two of them climb the stairs to the deck where at least they can see the horizon and settle their inner ears. Gross has spent the entire crossing vomiting into a spittoon in their suite. Cook has disappeared, perhaps enduring the same fate.

Standing in the dark gray mist on deck, shivering, at least they feel less seasick.

"I'm afraid to go home," Morton tells her after a while, throwing his cigarette into the waves. "I've rebelled against my father my whole life, Edith. If he dies, I know I'll feel unmoored."

She looks at him, hunched over the rail, pale and miserable, rain caught in his lashes.

"When my mother died, I felt free," she tells him. "And terribly guilty about it. I couldn't discuss it with anyone. Dying is so sacrosanct. But when she was alive, she stepped on me. Made me feel less than I was. Perhaps your father does the same?"

Morton closes his eyes.

"Actually, once, he was my champion. He always said I was the brightest in the family. Now I'm his biggest disappointment. The last time I saw him, he called me selfish and amoral. Undisiciplined."

He is, Edith thinks, but feels for him, longs to take him in her arms, press her face against his. There is no one else on deck, and who on this miserable afternoon would mind? But the nausea shoving up under her throat is too strong. And Morton looks like he wants to endure his misery alone, the way he hunches, folds his shoulders inward.

"Perhaps," she says, "when you see him, you can tell him how much it pains you to have disappointed him. Ask what he wishes for you. Tell him you will try to be what he wants you to be."

"A reverend. That's what he wishes me to be. Or a monk. A dried out scholar . . ."

"I doubt he wishes any of that," she says.

"Have I given you something of value?" he asks suddenly.

"I don't understand. . . ."

"Has our . . . our friendship touched you, mattered to you, been of *value* to you?"

"I . . . of course. You know it has."

"Then I am not as useless as he says I am. I give people pleasure. I soothe people. I understand what people need. . . ."

"That you do," Edith agrees. She reaches over and gently takes his arm into her hand. Feeling his biceps beneath the coat, she remembers the pleasures of his flesh. Her longing for him rises. Unwraps itself. Against her will.

"God, when is this journey going to be *over?*" he cries out.

"This crossing? Or your journey?"

"Either. Both."

"I know," she says. "Soon."

Arriving in the sodden dark in Folkstone, they all feel so dismal, they only want to sleep. Edith is glad they planned to stay there by the ferry rather than travel up to London.

"Sleep well," she whispers to Morton in the hall as he enters his room and turns to shut the door.

"As though I can," he says. Her room is just down the hall. And a few times in the night, she wonders if he will knock at the door. She wakes thinking she hears him. But it's just the wind shuddering the window-panes.

The next day the sun is shining again as they head up to London, where Morton can catch the train to Southampton. He's booked a hotel for himself a few blocks from Edith's. A sooty, redbrick and terra cotta pile right above the train station, Victorian, haunted looking, with trains running directly beneath.

"It's all I can afford," he tells her when they drop him off. "I've stayed here before. It's serviceable."

"I'm sure it will be fine," she assures him, wondering.

Henry, coming up to town from Rye for dinner, has arranged to meet them at Peppers, a restaurant half a block from the entrance to his club.

Henry's gained weight in just the months since Edith's seen him. He's added an extra chin, his skin is looking hepatic, but when he sees Morton he breaks into a joyous smile.

"My dearest friends. Together again. This is a marvelous occasion." He hugs Morton like a drunk might clutch a bottle of whiskey.

They argue. They dine. Morton orders plate after plate as though he is sure he's having his last supper.

"I will have to lend you my clothes after this supper, young man," Henry tells him.

After she puts Morton on his train in the morning, Edith will spend a few days in London, then a week or two with Henry. She has so looked forward to that part of her journey. But, laughing at the table with the two of them, she's sad to think that Morton won't be part of the company.

Not wanting Cook to have waited while they dined, they walk Henry to his hotel. He holds Morton in his arms for a long while before he goes in.

"Have courage, my boy," he says. He has never sounded more avuncular. "I'll see you soon, my dear," he tells Edith.

And then Edith and Morton step into the street to wave down a cab.

"Will you come to my hotel with me tonight? Say you'll be with me tonight," Morton says.

She turns to him in the streetlight. She has never seen him look more serious. More sincere.

"What are you asking?"

"You *know*," he says, taking her hand. "Please. I am desperate to hold you. To have you. It's been too long. And I know I've disappointed you. In so many ways. But if you only would. If you only would say you're willing. I can make some of it up to you. Show how I feel about you."

Show how I feel about you. The words have special resonance for her.

When the cab is secured, and they step inside, she merely says, "Yes."

Morton's room is small and dark with a tarnished brass bed, a soiled chintz spread over a hammocked mattress, an armchair whose cushion shows the impression of too many weary travelers. He lights the single lamp, a small mushroom of ruby glass whose glow is like a steady jeweled eye. The trains move beneath their window, howling into the spring night.

It is not the room she would ever have chosen for lovemaking. Nothing like the pristine inn laced in chestnuts. Nor the bower of lilacs where she knelt before him naked and thrilled. But when Morton takes her face into his hands and presses his lips to hers, she doesn't care where they are, wonders why she has resisted all spring. The sweetness of his mouth sends shockwaves through her. His touch, his presence make her giddy, but not too giddy to take it all in. He helps her with her wraps, and without words, begins to unbutton her dress.

"Morton . . ."

"Hush. We don't need to speak. We need each other, my love. We need each other."

She sees the two of them in the old-fashioned looking glass by the wall. A slender woman, a smallish man. They could be any age. But their passion, their desire to touch is undeniable. How many lovers have spent a moment captured in that glass? How many lovers, escaping crushing lives, marriage, sadness, have found peace in this threadbare room? Have allowed passion to rise and wash their miserable existences away? Morton moves behind her and, turning her toward the mirror, draws her dress from her shoulders.

"Look how beautiful you are," he says. "How I've missed seeing you!"

In the soft red light, she is transformed, her lips full and flushed, her breasts creamy and plump above her corset. He loosens the laces, kissing the back of her neck, sending hot and cold thrills all through her.

"Look in the glass. See that woman. I have wanted that woman more than I can say."

The heat of passion is more than Edith can bear, seems more urgent than she has ever imagined. Tearing off the bedspread, he lays her down onto the sheets and undresses before her, showing off his body to her hungry eyes, his taut chest, his boyish hips. He lifts his swollen manhood for her to approve, reaches for her hand, inviting her to take him into it.

"See how much I want you?" he says, pressing his own hands around hers. He slides down next to her on the bed, holding her and kissing her throat. The trains below rattle the bed, cry out into the night, allowing her to call out too with the pleasure of his exploring, his touching. How sweet it is to release the deliciousness, the agony of her ardor into a sound like a song. There is so much fondling, kissing, teasing, it must be an hour before he slides inside her, a sensation she knows she will relive again and again. Keen as a freshly honed knife, opening her petal by petal, a blooming flower. And even then, he takes his time, beckoning her to the brink, stopping just when she wants more, hurrying when she wants him to slow. Maddening her with his control, his understanding of her needs. Denying them. And then giving her all she could want. And when that dizzying spinning thrill comes to her again, she allows it to become her. Tonight, she doesn't care who hears. She calls out full-voiced along with the howl of the trains. And calls and calls as the night spins around them, pulling them both into a pool of dark silence.

In the morning, there is little to say, but little needs saying. Edith feels so utterly happy with Morton, satisfied, connected. When a dozen paisley roses arrive at her own hotel room later in the morning, she takes them into her arms. Not feeling the thorns which nick her wrists and palms, she lowers her face into the silky blooms and breathes in last night's musk. If only this ecstasy could linger, could permeate her life. If only.

Within just a few weeks, Dr. Kinnicut's new serum treatments have done Teddy a world of good. His teeth are no longer tormenting him. His headaches seem to have evaporated. But what has raised Teddy's spirits more is that he has managed to track down and telephone the proposed renters of The Mount to tell them that the property is no longer for rent. No discussion with Edith. He doesn't even let her know. Anna has to write Edith to warn her: Teddy *will* be in residence at The Mount this summer. And Anna and White will be there as well.

Anna can't help but be pleased, but there's much to do. She and White have to interview and hire a new housekeeper since Gross is traveling with Edith. And with an untried housekeeper at the helm, it's also their responsibility to engage new maids and footmen. "You should hire a ladies' maid for yourself," Teddy tells Anna. "I would happily pay for you to have one."

Anna laughs, baffled. "What would I do with a ladies' maid, Mr. Wharton?"

"She could do your hair. Take care of your clothes. Rub your back?"

"No one's ever looked after me in my life," she tells him. "I doubt it's a good idea for me to start."

He holds up his brandy glass in toast. "You, my dear, are an independent! It tickles me."

It is strange to be at The Mount without Edith. Watching the gardeners clear the weeds out of the flower beds gives her a sad pang when she realizes Edith will never see the blooms. Walking the new paths alone some afternoons—happy, truly happy!—Anna feels ashamed that she should take such joy in the dark green bushes, the wildflowers, the sunshine, when Edith is missing out on the beauty she helped to create.

Teddy insists Anna take dinner with him every night in the dining room. The first night, she is shy. She can never remember sitting at a table with Teddy without Edith there as well. He seems to think it's the most natural arrangement in the world.

"My dear," he says, seating her and pushing in her chair. He takes the seat across from her, tucks in his napkins, and launches right into describing his plans for expanding the staff quarters.

"Perhaps," he says, "you should move to one of the guest rooms. I don't like the idea of you climbing to the third floor and sharing a bathroom with the servants."

"I don't mind," she tells him. "It's what I'm used to."

"You deserve better." he says.

She raises her face and looks at him. She has a sick feeling in her stomach. He wants to make her what she's not. An equal. What might the servants think? Alfred lives out in one of the outbuildings. He wouldn't mind one way or the other. But what about the maids? The cook? The new housekeeper? Would they think she was taking over? Putting on airs?

But Teddy moves on to other subjects before she has a chance to comment, rattles on about the chickens. Describes in detail his day, and wants to know about hers. He is in good spirits again. Changed entirely since the dark days of Paris. She feels so light in his shiny new presence.

He asks her to join him in the drawing room afterward, insists on pouring her a sherry and says he'd be very happy if she'd stay with him until he goes to bed. And so it goes every night after. Often there is little to say, so they sit quietly, with the doors open to the terrace and gardens, the pine breezes wafting in lemony and cooling, the hoot of a wayward owl sometimes breaking the silence. Then she and Teddy will look up and smile at each other. Mostly she does her darning, or writes letters to Kansas City or London on a lapboard. Or she reads poetry in German. He reads his animal husbandry books, occasionally reciting a fact that takes his fancy. They might be an old married couple: happy in each other's presence but with no need to constantly communicate. Once, saying good night, he calls her "my darling."

The Mount's summers have always been peopled by a rolling list of guests: writers, painters, scientists, all invitees of Edith. There are no guests now. And Anna is happy. Happy to see Teddy thriving. Happy to immerse herself in the natural beauty of the place Edith created and once so dearly loved with no distractions.

Once, passing the scullery, she hears one of the new maids speaking to another.

"It's odd, *him* having *her* around him all the time like that. You'd think the lady of the house might be miffed if she knew."

"She's just a companion. They're old. Why should the mistress care? Though I hear the Missus is gallivantin' all over Europe. Most likely, she don't care one way or t'other."

Anna watches the mail, hoping that a letter might arrive sometime from Thomas, acknowledging that he hopes to see her when she returns to Paris. But the letters with her name on them come from Aennchen or her brother or sometimes Kate Thorogood or Fannie Thayer. And from Gross, who tells her of the whirling time Edith's having: whipping from Windsor to Rye to London to Gloucestershire. All through that part of Edith's trip, while Gross was along, there were short, breezy letters, then suddenly none. And none at all from Edith to Teddy.

Edith is enjoying England immensely, eating well, sleeping well, and at peace with herself. She hates to break the spell and return to France, but she simply must get back and look for an apartment before the season, or she'll have nowhere to stay at all. Having told George Vanderbilt she had no intention of taking his apartment for the winter, he's already leased it to someone else. So she prepares herself: thinks of her beloved Paris, its blur of lights and food and laughter, and books tickets for her departure.

But at the last minute, she receives a note from Henry asking if she'd be so kind as to return to Lamb House before she crosses the Channel. Edith can't help but worry. Henry's health has been spotty. And he's not one to ask her for help unless it's important. Arriving in the early evening, she's shown to her room to wash up before she sees him. She chooses a green frock he's always liked. And pins up her hair with more artifice than usual. But when she steps toward the drawing room, washed and kitted out as if for a formal London dinner, she hears someone speaking to Henry. And, knocking lightly, she opens the door to see a dark-haired man leaning on the mantel, his back to her.

"Henry, so sorry to interrupt . . . ," she says.

"Ah. At last! The firebird has alighted," Henry exclaims, his voice full of merriment. "Step right in, my dear. I have a little surprise for you." The man at the mantel turns slowly and rests his blue eyes on her. It is Morton. Henry chuckles like Old St. Nick himself, having brought his favorite little girl the one gift she's longed for most.

When the whole house is seemingly asleep, Edith hears an almost imperceptible rap on her door. She sits up, her heart thrumming. Without an answer, Morton opens it and slips in.

"Are you awake?" he whispers.

"As though I could possibly sleep knowing you're here," she says.

"Perfect! Warm me up!" he begs, climbing into her bed. "How could it possibly be so cold in July? Aren't my feet like ice?" It is past midnight. The Rye night is thick and sooty. Absent the streetlit glow of London, she can barely see him. But his eyes twinkle like starlight.

"It's the coldest summer I've ever spent," she tells him. "It's rained every day since you left. I do believe I am growing moss on my left side."

"That is not a romantic thought," he says drily.

"Sorry."

"Don't worry. It doesn't dampen my enthusiasm an iota. There. Do you feel my enthusiasm?"

"Yes. I don't think I've ever felt more enthusiasm."

He laughs softly, and then his lips brush her ear, "All through my time in Massachusetts, I thought of you. When things were bad with my father, I thought of you."

"Oh . . ."

"But if my father had the least idea exactly *what* I thought about you, it would surely have killed him!"

"You are terrible."

"I am terrible, aren't I? And to prove it, I'm going to do things to you you've never dreamed of," he tells her. "Terrible things."

"Oh, do expand my worldview," she tells him. "I dare you."

"You oughtn't dare me. That could be dangerous."

With Henry up front with Cook, she and Fullerton in the back (How fortuitous that she sent Gross off to Alsace to see her cousins as though she guessed Henry's surprise!), they motor all through Essex, hunting down quaint little inns, traversing beautiful towns. Every night, after a full meal and good laughter, she and Morton find each other. In her bed. In his. It hardly matters. They want each other equally. Their pleasure seems endless, like a magic bottle that refills every time a glass is poured. Never in Edith's life has she guessed that her body could give her such unceasing pleasure. With Henry as their buffer and chaperone, they don't argue. There is no tussle for power. She cannot remember ever being happier. If she were to die tomorrow, she knows she's tasted the sweetest morsels life could offer.

Having had Dr. Kinnicut's second round of serum treatments, Teddy grows jollier by the day. One morning he leaves in the carriage and returns with a new car. Sitting behind the wheel, he swerves into the forecourt, spitting stones, screeching the tires, stopping just before the front door. The car is as shiny red as a candied apple. The roof is coal black stitched in crimson. And the steering wheel sports a sewn leather cover with tiny holes in it just like golf gloves. But what really captures Anna's attention is that the car has a face. Its headlights are cats' eyes. Its grille, an angry mouth. She has never seen a car that looks so feral.

The entire household crowds the front door to ooh and aah over the new vehicle.

"When did you learn to drive yourself?" Anna asks him.

"An idiot can do it, I tell you. You cannot possibly imagine how fast this little filly can go. You will swoon when I drive you at that speed."

"I think I'd rather take your word for it," she says.

She doesn't like the idea of Teddy driving himself. Cars are for people with experience, experts like Cook. And Teddy is no expert. Lately, his happiness has again become giddy. Sometimes she hears him in his library laughing to himself as though he is too full of hilarity to contain it. He has begun to boast at dinner how his investing has netted the household a pretty penny. Soon Edith will have to acknowledge that when it comes to money, he is simply brilliant. "I may have quadrupled the money by summer's end," he declared just the night before last.

"White, what say we pull a bottle of the best champagne out of the cellar," Teddy proposes now. "I want the whole household to toast our newest arrival." He gives the fender a jaunty tap.

"The whole household, sir?" Albert says, his mouth barely opening.

"As I said."

Anna senses the maids' excitement. They skitter behind her, breathing through their teeth.

"I've never had champagne in my life," one of them whispers. "Wait until I write and tell my mother!"

Later that night, White stops Anna as she climbs the stairs to her room.

"Are you still here, Albert? I thought you'd gone home."

"Anna, I'm worried about him. Worried sick."

She nods.

"He's gotten a bit . . . a bit . . . out of control. And driving about by himself. Do you think we should tell Mrs. Wharton?"

"I don't know," Anna says. "Maybe we should keep an eye on him."

"I'm afraid he'll kill someone . . . or himself."

"Even Mrs. Wharton wouldn't be able to stop him from driving if that's what he's a mind to do."

"I'm afraid you're right," White says. "I don't think I'll sleep a wink tonight. Or maybe ever again."

When the motor trip around Essex has come to an end, and Henry is dropped at Lamb House, Cook is sent ahead to Paris, and Edith and Morton cross the Channel alone, arriving in Boulogne in the early evening. There are many things to see in Boulogne, but there is nothing that can compete with the pleasures of a hotel room. Signed into the Hôtel des Fleurs as Mr. and Mrs. Lawrence Selden—Morton's idea, making Edith nearly choke with laughter when the bellman insists on taking "Mrs. Selden's effects up to the room"—they bathe together in the giant cast-iron bathtub, eat cross-legged on the bed, lifting the silver domes of the dishes, trying to guess what's beneath each, and lie naked in each other's arms all night. When she blinks herself awake in the morning, the sun is pouring onto their skin as thick as honey. Morton has kicked off the covers, still asleep. She lets her eyes trace the landscape of his unclothed body: the hirsute expanse of his chest, the sharp blue knots of his shoulders, the sensual rise of his hip, the lazy slant of his penis. She knows she must imprint this moment on her memory like a painting seen at auction but bought by someone else.

She leans back into the pillows, sated and happy nevertheless. The room is peppered with the entwined aromas of sexual union and sweat. She has never breathed a sweeter perfume. She wakes him after a while to make love one more time before they must return to Paris. The only thing one can count on when it comes to Morton is that he is insatiable.

Teddy has started making regular trips to Boston, often not coming home at all. No one knows what to expect of him anymore. He may be gone two, three days, yet doesn't call The Mount to warn anyone. No one knows what he will do on any given day. The cook prepares a meal each evening, but a good part of it goes uneaten.

"Is he visiting his mother, do you think?" Anna asks White. "When he goes and doesn't return?"

White shrugs. "He's never come back from visiting his mother nearly so jolly."

More often than not, Anna eats alone in the servants' dining room, late, because she wants to be available for Teddy if he does arrive. When he doesn't, she finds herself as irritated as a scorned wife. Was her company not enough for him? What is drawing Teddy away to Boston with such a siren song? She longs for those earlier summer evenings spent so companionably in the drawing room. She is ashamed that she misses how he made her feel, just for a shimmering moment, like the lady of the house.

During one five-day disappearance, Anna worries he's in the hospital, injured in a car accident. In a drawer at the Boston morgue. She pads about the house with growing unease, thinks to call the Boston police, Sally Norton, anyone who might have clues to find him. She sits down at the servants' table, and puts her head in her hands. What will she tell Edith?

"You could eat upstairs, Miss Bahlmann," Mrs. Cotton, the housekeeper, tells her, drifting into the dining room. "No one would mind serving you there."

"Oh." Anna raises her head. "I couldn't," she says. "It wouldn't feel right. It hardly feels right as it is, but Mr. Wharton insists on my company when he's around. . . ."

"Do you mind my joining you here?" Mrs. Cotton asks. "I ate already. But I was hoping to talk to you. Edna, bring Miss Bahlmann her supper."

The roast beef is brought, the mashed potatoes, the spinach. A pretty plate. Anyone would enjoy the meal. But with worry over Teddy, Anna has no idea how she will get it down.

"The thing is . . . I'm sorry to tell you this," Mrs. Cotton says, leaning forward, biting her lip. "And maybe I oughtn't say anything. But Lonnie, the parlor maid, had a day off yesterday. She went up to Boston to see her beau and they were in the Common. You know how young people like the Common. Well, I certainly did in my day. Such a romantic place for a stroll, right in the heart of a city, no less!"

Anna leans back and hears herself sigh impatiently. What does the woman want to tell her?

"And she says . . . well, she reported to me that she saw Mr. Wharton there . . . with . . . with a woman."

Anna sets her fork down, feeling herself blanch.

"Well, we don't know who that might have been . . . maybe his sister?" Anna's voice is very level. When others are in a panic, one must keeps one's wits. She learned this long ago in the days when Lucretia would fly off the handle at Mr. Wharton, and Anna would softly, sweetly draw Edith into another room.

"Maybe I shouldn't be telling you this. But I know you and Mr. White have been worried about him. Lonnie says they were making a bit of a spectacle of themselves, if you get my meaning. She sure weren't his sister! And she was not the sort of woman anyone would expect to see with a gentleman like Mr. Wharton."

Anna doesn't want to hear more, can't tolerate more complication in their already complicated world. Teddy with a questionable woman? And here Anna is again: in possession of information that will upset Edith. Why does this fly ash of disturbing information always land on her ears, forcing her to consider whether she must be the bearer of bad news? It's her curse!

Anna scrapes her chair from the table, having lost her appetite.

"I have things to attend to in my room," she says. "Excuse me."

"I've offended you," Mrs. Cotton says, rising, grabbing Anna's elbow. "Please. I debated all day whether I ought to tell you. I'm sorry. I should have waited until you were through with your supper at least."

Anna shakes her head. "I'm glad you told me, Mrs. Cotton. The thing is . . . I don't know what to do about it. He's not himself these days. And I feel it's my job to look after him. Mrs. Wharton *counts* on me to look after him."

"You have an elephant on your shoulders with *that* task," Mrs. Cotton says.

Anna feels tears welling in her eyes. Is she emotional because she is caught in a storm, no shelter in sight? Or is she hurt? It had all been too pleasant. Too easy. Everything she could have wished for, for a brief, extraordinary moment. She feels mortified, ashamed that she wanted that ease and intimacy with Teddy so much—something that will never truly belong to her.

Oh, but it's more. It's that Teddy Wharton has disappointed her profoundly. Her friend. A vulnerable man she has defended so unceasingly.

She believed in Teddy even when no one else did. She never expected it could come to this.

"I'm sorry," she whispers as she draws up her skirts, willing her tears to wait until she gets to her room.

Mrs. Cotton nods and lets Anna pass.

Edith lands on the perfect apartment at last. And to think it's just across the street from the Vanderbilts' on the Rue de Varenne. But bigger, and newer, with its own guest suite and servants' quarters and steam heat! Unheard of in Paris. And what makes it so extraordinary is that the rooms are luxuriously spacious and overlook a small but elegant garden. A garden! It's all she could want in space and light. Precisely in the part of the Faubourg she loves. Of course, it wants work. The walls and floor are worn, though it can't be more than a few years old. And since it is to be leased empty, there is so much to purchase to make it a home. Edith is thrilled to throw herself into the task of finding objects and furnishings that express her own taste. Because since their arrival back in Paris, having once enjoyed such a perilous, delicious, inimitable closeness with Morton, she has written him almost every day, and received little in return.

Except that every time he does see her, he tries to persuade her that their intimacy will die if they don't tend to it. Sometimes he suggests that if she won't be alone with him at the Crillon, then they should check into a small hotel for just a few hours. He has many small urban inns to recommend, most of them tucked away on back streets, most reasonably priced, all reminding her that Morton has been to each of them with someone else. She can't do it. Outside of Paris, it was different for her, almost acceptable. But in Paris, the thought of a few hours at a second-class hotel feels like a tawdry way to express their love. She wants long, thoughtful walks in the Tuileries, whispers, talks about poetry. She wants him to value their intellectual connection as much as their physical one. But he vanishes, answers fewer of her notes, doesn't always show up when he says he will. And when she asks if he has begun the book about Paris for Macmillan—if he only knew she's paid for it!—he merely laughs.

"Will you never learn to leave me alone about that?"

"But I've vouched for you. My name is at stake."

"Nothing whatever will happen to your precious name. I'll write it when I can."

Morton. Like a sunbeam she tried to catch in her hand: when she opens her fist, alas, he was only a trick of the light. Soon Teddy will arrive. And any moments with Morton, even long, thoughtful walks, will have to be stolen.

The new apartment is a blessed distraction, assuages the sting of loss. But to really conquer the task, she needs Anna. No one can turn chaos into harmony faster or with more aplomb. A wizardess at keeping receipts, calling tradesmen, filing everything away with ease. Edith has already picked out Anna's room. Not in the servants' quarters at all, but right next to Teddy's. In case he needs her. In case he calls for her. A lovely room with a view of the garden and plaster sprays of lilies of the valley lacing the edges of the ceiling. It will be Edith's gift to Anna, who has so loyally watched over Mr. Wharton at his worst.

So she is unsettled when she receives a letter on the same day from Anna and Dr. Kinnicut, reporting that Teddy is acting "in a distinctly exalted state" (Dr. Kinnicut), "the unpredictable, giddy way he did last summer" (Anna). Dr. Kinnicut says his greatest fear is that shipping Teddy off to Paris might "send the pendulum back in the other direction."

But what is Edith to do? She cannot return to the United States. She *will* not. She'd be trading his happiness for hers. This is the only place where she can breathe. Where she can write. Where she belongs. Teddy will simply have to come to Paris with Anna at the end of July, and then she'll judge his state for herself. Perhaps, she thinks wishfully, he will choose to return to New York in time. She can live on in Paris. And though still married, without scandal or malice, they can live perfectly cordial existences continents apart. Oh, life seems a fragrant day in spring when she thinks of it!

NINETEEN

LATE SUMMER 1909

Gathering up the wayward Teddy, and having White pack for him, since he can't seem to concentrate from one minute to the next, Anna gets him as far as New York, where they both check into the Waldorf on Fifth Avenue the day before their ship is to sail. But that night as she meets him for dinner—at last, a dinner with Teddy after weeks of hardly seeing him!—they stop at the desk and discover word has arrived from Teddy's sister, Nannie, that old Mrs. Wharton is very ill and may not live.

"I have to head back up to Boston," Teddy declares, looking happier than he should be to be attending his mother's deathbed. "I just wish I had the damn car."

White asks to travel with him.

"Don't be silly," Teddy replies. "Go tend to the Missus in Paris." And in a blink, he is off to Grand Central Station.

"We're doing the best we can with him," White tells Anna with a sigh, and excuses himself to follow through with his plan to visit some New York friends.

Perhaps, Anna worries, as she picks at her filet of sole alone in the echoing Waldorf dining room, ugly rumors about Teddy having a paramour have reached Teddy's mother, and are what has made her so gravely ill. The rumors certainly make Anna queasy. If she consults

Edith, she's afraid Edith will ask her to spy on Teddy, to check into a hotel in Boston and stick close by. So Anna doesn't tell Edith a thing. She wants nothing more than to escape Teddy's mania.

She can deal with his melancholia. Every time his spirits dropped, he reached out for her. But now, having been transformed into a mad, childish version of himself, he has pushed her away. What if Edith blames Anna for it? What if Edith is angry yet again at Anna for not caging him in? She'll have to risk it. Anna wants, she *needs*, to be in Paris with Edith.

All the way across the ocean she is despondent. No word from Thomas. Teddy gone mad. Edith always picking her out as the perfect scapegoat. Anna tells herself soothingly that if things don't work out, she'll become a teacher again. How much more reliable and satisfying children can be than adults! And there's always Kansas City. Jessie Toibin would allow Anna to work in the library with her two days a week if she asked. She's sure of it. On Sundays, she'd dine with Aennchen and William, Charles and the boys. These daydreams sweep her across the ocean just as surely as the rumbling ship's motor, the rudders and waves.

By the time Anna reaches Paris, word has come that old Mrs. Wharton has died, leaving Teddy an estate to clean up. Teddy writes Edith that he will stay on in Boston for a while with Nannie.

"Imagine that, Tonni," Edith says. "Teddy *agreeing* to spend time in Boston. The man hates the place. Perhaps he is becoming less agitated, after all. I think you and Dr. Kinnicut were crying wolf. He sounds perfectly normal."

Anna shakes her head. "I wish you were right," she says.

But Edith is not fretting over Teddy. She is absorbed entirely in readying the new apartment. Even though it's evening when Anna arrives, it's still light, and Edith insists they take a cab from the Crillon and tour the place.

"No matter how tired you are, it will cheer you to no end," Edith says.

Anna isn't just tired. She's soaked in a soporific relief at being near Edith again. I'm like a dog, she thinks, who has paced by the door all night but can now curl up by the fire because his owner has returned.

Anna is not saddened at all by viewing herself as a dog. There is nothing and no one Edith loves more than her dogs. In fact, Edith carries Nicette in her lap to the Rue de Varenne.

"See. Nicette has missed you! Watch how she snuggles against you."

Anna barely has the energy to reach out and touch the silky golden ears of the little dog.

Unlocking the heavy outer door, Edith reveals the apartment house's inner courtyard, with its Corinthian columns and glowing mahogany doors, the modern garages neatly arranged along the back of the court. Elegant and simple, the place couldn't suit Edith better. And while the apartment, endless room upon room, has none of the elegance of the Vanderbilt apartment, it is spacious and light. How Anna will miss the old servants' rooms at the top of 58, though. Perhaps she will cross the street sometimes to see her old friends.

"It's lovely," she says.

"It's going to need our touch, our vision," Edith says, generously including her. "And this, dear Tonni, is your room! I think it the best room in the whole apartment. Do tell me you like it." Anna glances over at Edith, who, having set Nicette down to wander the empty herring-boned expanses, stands with her hands together, incandescent with the pleasure of giving. She is a changed Edith. It has been just a few months since they saw one another. So much has passed. And time has worn away at each of them. Does Edith look at her just as critically? Anna wonders. For she can't help noting that Edith has aged visibly. Her eyes are deeper set. And her hair above her ears is sparked with silvery notes. But also there is a girlish sway to her walk these days. A deeper, inner glow that warms her cheeks and softens her jaw. Has Fullerton given this to her? If so, Anna is grateful to him. Grateful that Edith seems so happy.

Anna walks to the window of her new room and peers out at the garden. In the late day heat, rising in waves from the flower beds, the daylilies and lavender shimmer like jewels. The pear trees that run along the fencing rustle and glint as dark as tourmalines.

"Edith," is all she manages to say.

"You do like it, don't you?"

"You want me here? In what would be a guest room?"

"We have a guest suite all its own. I want you here in the front of the apartment. I want you happy, Tonni."

"Do you?" Anna asks. Is it the exhaustion? The relief? Or the fear that this warm moment will soon fade like late daylight when Teddy's truths are revealed. She has to wipe a tear from the corner of her eye.

"Don't you dare cry," Edith warns. "Or I shall too."

"When you were a little girl, you once told me that when a room overlooks a garden, its ceiling is painted with watercolors."

"Did I?"

"Look. It is." Anna points up at the ornately edged ceiling, awash with shifting clouds of color as the garden's leaves move and sway in the cooling breezes. Baby pinks, azures. Overlapping, breathing. Anna turns to press a kiss on Edith's cheek.

"Thank you," she whispers. "I couldn't ask for more."

"There will be endless things to do. We can go shopping together. We have to fill this empty place."

Anna nods. "We should begin as soon as possible," she says.

The other shoe—Teddy's shoe, Anna thinks—does not drop for a wonderfully long while. He holes up in Boston doing whatever it is he is doing, and Anna keeps her worries to herself. It is easy to bury them with all the arrangements that must be made for the new apartment. Edith disappears some afternoons, and Anna suspects she may be off with Fullerton, who scarcely makes an appearance. But what does it matter? Her distaste for Fullerton stemmed from her desire to protect Teddy. Now she wants the opposite. Let Edith have her pleasures!

And then Teddy arrives with Nannie, and they move into the Crillon too, Teddy just as full of himself as ever.

"You will soon be kissing my boots, Puss, when you see what I have done with our finances."

"I rather doubt it," Edith says drily, looking down at his feet.

"The fact is, I should have been a full-time businessman. Some men get satisfaction out of working and now I see why."

"He's a regular entrepreneur," Nannie says, patting her brother on the back.

Teddy and Nannie are a pair! They eat at restaurants all over Paris and complain about them.

"Why does no one have plain roast beef here? Everything I eat makes me bilious," Nannie declares one afternoon, fanning herself. Nannie is hot no matter how cool the hotel.

And then Anna sees that Teddy is sinking again. His mouth is drooping beneath his mustache. His eyes take on that dead look once more. He chooses a favorite chair by the fire in the Crillon suite, and even Nannie can't budge him out of it. But Anna no longer wishes to be his guardian, though now he has begun to call for her again.

"Come sit with me, my friend," he says to her one afternoon. "You are the only one who understands me.

"I'm sorry," Anna says. "Edith and I have an appointment with the drapier at the apartment."

"I do think you're avoiding me," he says wearily, asking her no more questions.

When Edith invites Teddy and Nannie to see the changes they are making in the apartment-to-be, they say they will visit on Wednesday. But they demur at the last moment.

"We can't count on either of them," Edith whispers to Anna. "Thank heavens we can count on each other."

Teddy and Nannie finally plan a trip to the Pyrenees together, with Cook at the wheel. As Edith and Anna watch the car disappear around the Place de la Concorde, Edith doesn't even attempt to hide her satisfaction.

"We could just stay in Paris and work away this time without the Whartons pulling us down . . . but I've been thinking . . . come with me to Germany, Anna. Let's have ourselves a whirl. You can show me all the things you know. I'll be your student again. We'll take the train."

Anna is dizzy with the thought of a trip for just the two of them.

"Just you and I?" she asks. "Now?"

"And why not? Don't we deserve it?" Together, they map it all out: Munich and Würzburg, Bruchsal and Karlsruhe. And the trip itself is better than Anna imagines. Armed with guidebooks and Goethe poetry, they track their favorite poet, reading quotes, touching old walls, breathing in the scent of a time long gone, staying at exquisite hotels, sharing a suite like sisters.

And except for thoughts of Thomas (should she call him, go see him?), Anna doesn't think she's ever been happier. Finding herself back in Edith's good graces is a gift. A prize. It soothes the brittle edges of her disappointment over Teddy. They travel as equals. There is so much to share. So much to laugh about. And despite their exquisite accommodations, they aren't too self-important to drink beer in beer halls.

"Imagine my British friends seeing me here!" Edith laughs as a loud band with a tuba plays music that makes even Anna long to get up and dance.

What a fine time Edith is having, steeping herself in German romanticism. Taking in the intricate beauty of towers and gables and frescoed walls. And all without having to worry about Teddy and Nannie, who annoy her so. Anna is enjoying the trip as well. Edith can see the joy in her eyes. And it is good to share it with her.

But Anna is a mostly silent partner. Nodding in agreement. Happy when Edith is happy. Edith can't help but long for Morton by her side, in her bed.

Unable to suppress her constant longing for him, she starts a postcard for him from Augsburg and ends up with a full letter. She has never been able to hide her feelings from him. She has never learned to dissemble.

> *How I've wanted you today in this absurdly picturesque place, which we have seen under a balmy blue sky, and the brightest sunshine. At every turn, I thought how we should feel it together, or how, for us, the sensation would be deepened and illuminated by your share in it—as a reflection is often infinitely more beautiful than the object it reflects.*

She describes the beauty of their trip, the thrill, the charm of everything they've seen. When she posts it, she allows Anna's eyes to gaze at the address. Why not be open with Anna? She knows.

"I miss him terribly," she tells her.

"I wish he could be here with you instead of me," Anna says. "I know it would be more for you with him."

Edith squeezes her arm. She doesn't want to lie. And how generous Anna can be.

"It's been splendid with you," she says, at ease with the truth.

One evening, in an elegant restaurant in Munich, Edith glances up and says, "I've been meaning to ask you forever, Tonni . . . with whom did you travel in Greece?"

"Oh . . ."

"I've often wondered. A yacht. So suddenly leaving Italy like that. I can't believe I've never asked."

Anna can't help but smile when she thinks of the Parthenon shimmering in the heat, the parched fields of the Peloponnese.

"With a man named Thomas Schultze."

"A man!" Edith shakes her head with wonder. "What sort of man? You just took off with a man, Tonni? You do astonish me!"

"We were shipmates coming over from New York. He's a very wealthy steel magnate, it seems."

"Really! And he asked you to travel with him?"

"You needn't be shocked. There were others on board."

"Did he have . . . *feelings* for you?"

Anna pauses for a long time before she answers, looking into Edith's green eyes, wondering what they're anticipating. And then she simply nods.

"He asked me to marry him."

"What!" Edith can't help but let her mouth fall open. "I'm stunned! And did you not like Mr. Schultze?"

"I liked him very much."

"But you did not love him."

"I might have loved him . . ."

Anna can't press back the wave of feeling that comes over her when she reflects on Thomas and their days together. Hamburg. Venice. Athens.

Edith is taking the news rather comically, pressing her hand over her mouth as though suppressing her amusement.

"Well, I'm not one to pry, but do tell, Tonni. Why on earth did you turn him down?"

"I told myself it was because he had a grown child who needed special care . . . and I feared he was only wooing me because he thought I was the one who might give it to her. I didn't want to marry to be an unpaid governess. . . ."

"But that wasn't the reason?"

"The reason, I guess . . . is so that I wouldn't miss . . . this," she gestures to the restaurant, to Germany, to the trip that has pleased her so. "So I wouldn't miss you, Edith. The fact is: I like our life."

Edith's eyes cloud over as though she's read a complex passage she doesn't quite comprehend. She doesn't say anything for a long time.

"Our life? Really?" she says. Anna is uneasy. Edith probably never thinks in terms of "our life." Edith's life is hers. And Anna, most of the time, is just a facilitator. Someone to help Edith's days grind along more smoothly. But Anna's words are released, pigeons sent to take wing where they may. She can't beckon them back.

"You turned him down because of me?" Edith whispers. "Dear Tonni." And suddenly Anna knows that Edith hasn't rejected the thought that they have an interlocked life. She's touched. "Do you know, my own mother wouldn't have turned down any gratification for my sake. I don't think she ever did." Edith's eyes are shimmering with tears.

"Maybe that's why, dear friend," Anna says, resting her eyes on Edith's oh-so-familiar face. "Maybe that's why I do it with pleasure."

The very night they return from Germany, Teddy, weepy, miserable, drunk, confesses to Edith that he has done something terrible. That she will never be able to forgive him. And that he's contemplating suicide.

"Can it be so dreadful?" she asks him drily. After such a lovely, floating trip, she is dismayed to have to entertain this tiresome man. She sits down wearily in the velvet bergère, crosses her arms and waits for him to enlighten her.

He nods, doesn't meet her eye.

She is annoyed. Will he make her drag it out of him?

"Just tell me, Teddy," she says. "What odious thing have you done?"

"I've pinched some of the money from your trust fund." He says it so softly, she wonders if she heard him right.

"Pinched it? Pinched my money? What do you mean?"

"I bought an apartment house in Boston."

"Without even discussing it?" Edith asks. "What on earth for? An investment? Do you wish to live in Boston?" She tingles at the thought. Maybe Teddy will go back to Boston, and she'll be free in Paris to do as she pleases!

"I've made some bad choices, Puss."

"Such as . . . ?"

"Such as taking up with someone you might not approve of. . . ."

"I . . . I don't understand."

"Her name . . . her name is Maisie."

Edith doesn't say anything for a long while, and when she does speak, it comes out crackling, her voice as deep as Teddy's, and far more thoughtful. "I see . . . ," she says.

"She's a pretty thing. I set her up in an apartment—in the house I bought. I wasn't myself this summer. . . ."

Edith tries not to gasp, or scream, both of which she would like to do. Does everyone in New York know what she doesn't know? Information flies so easily from Boston to New York. Does Nannie know? Edith shudders.

"And do you wish to marry this . . . Maisie?" Edith asks, trying to sound equanimous. But she is rocked. She always knew that Teddy must take his pleasures elsewhere, but she's rested for years and years on the notion that he is wise enough not to make a spectacle of himself. No one has *ever* found Teddy Wharton interesting enough to gossip about.

"No. I'm married to you! I'm in love with you. I was angry, I guess," he says.

"Angry at *me*?"

"You were always making me feel not up to your standards. And last year . . . when you took up with your . . . your *friend*," he says the word so distastefully, it raises the hair on Edith's arms, "Maisie made me feel . . . appreciated."

Edith tells herself to breathe, to wait, to sound solid even if she doesn't feel it.

"I'm sure she appreciated you if you bought her an apartment house."

"She makes her own money. She wasn't asking me to do it. She's a dancer in a show. She's practically famous. . . ."

"A famous dancer?"

"Well, not ballet or anything. The follies. I filled the rest of the house with her friends from the show. . . . Made a little money back." He looks momentarily proud, and then his shoulders inch up around his ears. "At least I did that. . . ."

Edith starts to laugh, can't help herself. Her throat opens and laughter coughs up like bile, no matter how she tries to suppress it.

"Couldn't you have been more original?" she says. Her voice is so icy it sends a claw up her own spine. "A chorus girl. Teddy . . . And did you parade little Miss Maisie all over Boston?"

"I wasn't myself, Puss. I didn't know what I was doing."

Edith puts her face in her hands for a moment, sick with the news.

"And how are you going to clean up this mess?"

"There's more," he says, his voice sepulchral. Edith thinks that there never were two more horrifying words.

"Yes?"

"I pinched . . . actually . . . I borrowed more of your money. . . . I invested . . . not as wisely as I thought. I was maybe a little *too confident.* I was, I guess, too confident about many things last summer."

Edith's mouth is now so dry she can't speak. She gets up and pours herself a glass of Teddy's brandy. She's never liked brandy. Can hardly stomach it. But if she ever needed it, she needs it now.

"How much money did you lose, Teddy?"

Teddy licks his lips before he speaks. Like a snake. He *is* a snake!

"On or about . . ."

"On or about?"

"Fifty thousand dollars . . ."

"*Fifty thousand dollars!*" Edith gulps the russet-colored fire, which burns all the way from her throat to her stomach.

"I wasn't myself, Puss. You know I wasn't. . . ." Teddy's voice is so small, he might be six years old.

"Please leave my room," she says.

"Maybe I should kill myself. I'm not fit to be married to you. I know it. I *do* know it."

"Please leave my room," she repeats.

"I . . . you can't know . . . I can't help it. I get these flights of fancy, these times when I think everything is going along swimmingly and then . . ." Tears are running down his red face and dripping off his mustache like rain off a roof.

"If you don't leave, I'll . . ." but Edith can't think of a thing with which to threaten him. What a fool she was to let him handle her money, even after she knew he wasn't acting himself! Kinnicut tried to warn her. Anna too. She knew if she took the responsibility for her money away from him, he'd be furious. And so she let him go on. Still, she should have cut him off months ago. It's her own fault. And that's the thing that aches inside her: she hasn't been paying attention. Hasn't wanted to believe that she was married to a madman. But could anyone but a madman have compiled such a list of outrageous actions at her expense?

This is her punishment for having loved Morton, she tells herself. For trying to live a fulfilled life at last.

Teddy lingers by the door, twisting anxiously like a homely debutante praying to be asked to dance. "Get out!" she yells at him. In all these years, she can't remember raising her voice to Teddy. "Get out!"

Without shutting the door, he skulks down the hotel hall. She slams it, then squeezes her eyes so tightly she sees pinpricks of violet light. When she opens them, she drinks down every last drop of the terrible burning brandy like poison. What she's feeling is a noxious mix of grief, bewilderment and, worst of all, a sense that it was all inevitable. That she has finally—and oh so neatly—met her just rewards.

"Did you know?" Edith asks Anna. "Did you know he was keeping a woman in Boston?" Anna feels the color drain from her face. She has feared this moment ever since arriving from America. I was lucky to have that time in Germany, these months without Edith knowing, she tells herself. She stands glued to the spot, staring at the floor, speech-less.

"Don't worry. I don't blame you, Tonni. Sit down. Tell me: what did you know?"

"Mrs. Cotton said one of the maids saw him in Boston with a woman. That's all I knew. I'm sorry I didn't say anything. I couldn't bear to spread what I hoped was just a rumor. Is it true then? There was a woman?"

Edith nods. Anna feels her stomach squeeze tight like a fist. She had called upon the gods to make it false gossip. To no avail.

"What will you do?"

"He's embezzled money from my trust fund as well, Tonni. A great deal."

"I . . . I didn't think him capable of such deceit."

Edith looks up at her, shakes her head. "Didn't you? No. You've been his greatest champion all these years."

How accusatory it sounds! Anna feels her chin quivering.

"I excused him, Herz, for the boasting and fast driving and staying out all night . . . because he's been sick. But I didn't think he would ever steal money . . . from *you*! You, who have been so generous to him all these years! I didn't know. I didn't know. I just knew he was bragging about his investments and terrorizing the pedestrians of Lenox."

Edith smiles sadly, looks off into a distance that Anna can't fathom.

"Generous, yes. But I suppose you know better than I that I haven't been loving to him for years. I've been like my mother was to my father. Disdainful. But unlike my mother, and no one can say otherwise . . . unlike my mother, I've been patient with Teddy."

"Will you divorce him?" Anna asks very softly.

Edith turns and looks at Anna, aghast.

"Divorce him?"

"Some women would."

"Yes, but to hear that from *you*, of all people. It's not how I've ever seen myself. Divorced Woman. It's such a shoddy title."

"I'm not saying you should. I would never say you should. . . ."

"I'm sending him back to Boston. He's inherited money from his mother. If he can work it out with his lawyers, he'll pay me back. I made him promise he'll stay with Nannie and nowhere else. They deserve each other, those two. . . . And as for Maisie . . . did you know she bills herself as Maisie Courvoisier. *Courvoisier!* It's so laughable. Teddy's brother has been to see her, and is working to 'comfortably settle her elsewhere.'"

The two women look at each other with dark amusement. And then Edith steps toward Anna. She takes her elbows into her hands.

"You're probably thinking I'm no different than Teddy. That my feelings for Morton are hardly better than his for Maisie. . . ."

"I've never thought that," Anna says.

"You see, that's the sad part, Tonni. I *have*."

Oh, the weariness that descends on Edith! There were to have been rooms of new furniture for 53, rue de Varenne. Fresh and French and perfect for a new life. Knowing that Teddy has compromised the trust, there is nothing to do but cancel the orders. Only the orders for new beds, the curtains that are nearly finished and a dining table remain. All the days Edith and Anna spent visiting showrooms, workshops, choosing the most audacious little bergère, the silkiest rug—for naught. Who knows when more money will be coming in? There is The Mount to care for, the new leasehold in Paris, servants for both places. Edith can't shake away the memory of her father's misery at discovering his money gone. The financial burden these days seems to sit squarely on Edith's pen.

So, feeling hard-nosed and sensible, she opts to sell 882 and 884 Park Avenue, and to bring the New York furniture and rugs to Paris. Her life in New York is over, and with it both a nostalgia tinged with bitterness, and relief. Just the thought of a trip to New York to manage the closing of the houses, the transfer of furniture, is anathema to Edith. She asks Anna to go in her stead. Upon hearing the news, Anna nods almost imperceptibly, her lips straight and pale.

"Of course," she says. Edith can see that she's shaken.

"What is it?" she asks

"I'm sad to say good-bye to New York," Anna says, and leaves the room hurriedly. Edith wonders if she has left to cry.

The new year is coming. Edith feels *old* for the first time in her life. She wonders what to look forward to. Morton is mostly absent these days. Once, meeting her for an hour's tea break at a little café, he tells her, "I expect you will see less of me now."

"Less than I'm already seeing you? That would mean not seeing you at all."

"My job consumes me more and more."

"I know it's partially because I don't want to go off to just any hotel with you," she says.

He glances up at her, removes the cigarette from his mouth. "I've never met anyone else like you, *chère*. But you want what I can't offer."

She grabs her cup of tea. "What is it you think I want? I've never made a claim on you." The tea is too hot, scalds her tongue.

"You want true love," he says with far too much amusement in his voice.

"Don't be absurd. I am too old to believe in fairy tales." There is, unhappily, very little that's true about his love, she reflects.

"You deserve better," he says. "You make me wish I could transform overnight into a solid sort of fellow."

She shakes her head. "I love you for who you are, Morton. I married a solid sort of fellow—well, he was once—and you know how that turned out."

He kisses her when they part. A sad kiss. She wonders when she'll see him next. She doesn't want to be like his landlady. Hanging out by his door, waiting for him to return. She has too much pride. But, despite all the misery he's put her through, oh, how he still moves her!

It is painful for Anna to unlock the door to 882 Park for her last visit. This house is the closest she has ever had to a real home of her own, filled with things she is happy to see again: the Virginia chest of drawers, her books, her postcards, Aunt Charlotte's sofa, all of which she plans to ship to Paris. But this house contains far more than gathered furniture. For her, it is spilling with memories of more peaceful times.

She lights the drawing room fire, reflecting back on all the evenings she sat and read by its reliable heat, knowing that Edith and Teddy were next door, Gross in the kitchen fixing a pot of tea, whatever maids were in service, rinsing their stockings and hanging them in the bathroom at the top of the house. How kind of Edith to give the staff a space of their own. To give *Anna* a space of her own; all these years, she has felt the house was truly hers.

She stoops to gather the pile of letters on the floor by the front door, which she stepped over when she entered, and begins to sort through them. There is a thin blue envelope with Miss ANNA BAHLMANN, 882 PARK written on it in a familiar childish scrawl. She notes the Boston postmark.

> *Dear Miss Anna,* [All these years and Teddy calls her this still—like one of her students]
>
> *Can you find it in your heart to forgive me? I know Puss has by now told you everything and that my actions have lowered your opinon of me. I can't blame you one single iota.*
>
> *Once we were the best of friends. Do you think you can see your way to ever being my friend again? If not, I'll understand.*
>
> *Edward R. Wharton*

At first, Anna wants to press the letter to her breast. To smell it. To cherish it. To answer it! All these years she has stood by him. Believed in him long after Edith gave up. She was certain that he was the kindest man she knew. Perhaps he was not an intellectual. But the way he cleaved to animals and nature touched her indescribably. She believed he had an inherent purity about him. Purity! How could she have been so wrong? Flaunting a showgirl on his arm! Stealing money from Edith! But worse, and there's no use denying it, what hurts Anna the most is that he turned his back on what was for her the happiest times of her life, those few special summer weeks when every night he shared the drawing room with her so contentedly, breathing in the mint of mountain air, aligned, allied. The thought of it now breaks her heart.

She walks to the fireplace and stands with her hand outstretched, the letter held out but not quite touching the fire she's just set. The breeze from the blaze makes the notepaper shudder, turns her fingers pink with heat. How easy it would be to lay his letter atop the crackling logs, to watch it singe and curl into ash and nothingness. But with a gasp, she pulls it back, and in the end, slides it into the lining of her smallest suitcase, where, she thinks, perhaps, it will remain forever.

TWENTY

JANUARY 1910

All the month of January, Paris rains and rains. Edith can't walk anywhere without a sodden umbrella thrust over her head. The streets are conduits for jets of water. Motorcars throw disastrous wakes at anyone in their paths. At night the windows shudder and drip. Edith even dreams of rain.

Still waiting for Anna to arrive with the furniture, she pays her bill at the Crillon and moves the household into 53, rue de Varenne. She has a new bed, as do Gross and Elsie, the most recent *bonne*. There are a few chairs she's bought in antique shops. And a fruitwood table as worn and smooth along its edges as a piece of driftwood. In a way, the austerity of her circumstance suits her solemn mood. It's better to be in her own apartment than at the Crillion. But even the tight modern windows and steam heat can't keep the damp out. It seeps into her bones. Gross says she's never ached more in her life.

As warned, Morton rarely answers her notes. I mustn't expect anything from him, she tells herself. Edith tries to work on short stories each morning, but the words tumble together and her thoughts feel as sodden as the streets. Teddy's brother writes that Teddy's claims of filling a house with showgirls were mere delusion. Except for the apartment where he did indeed keep his mistress, the rest of the house was empty. The mistress has been paid off somehow. (Why else would she want to be with

Teddy other than money?) The apartment house is on the market. The proceeds will go back into Edith's trust fund. And whatever else Teddy owes will come from his inheritance.

But the money was never the issue. The thought of spending the rest of her life with a delusional, miserable, child-man that she no longer loves, that she can't ever *remember* loving, twists Edith's heart. And Morton is withdrawing. The hopelessness of her life feels like it's rising around her.

And then, three days before her forty-eighth birthday, the waters of the Seine begin to rise as well. Winter floods are not so rare in Paris. But there's never been one like this. The Seine roils and roars and rises right up to the tops of the bridges. Water rushes through the streets. The public clocks all freeze at once. At 10:50 A.M., the power station that controls the clocks with compressed air is swamped with river water. The motionless clock hands all over the city remind everyone the exact moment for days and days. Electricity snuffs out from street to street with a sizzle and a pop. The telephone lines fail. The night feels claustrophobic. Nothing glows. Nothing twinkles. The City of Light huddles in darkness. And Edith discovers she hasn't a single lantern in the house. Gross scares up some candles from a box she's just unpacking. Fat, white kitchen candles. She fixes them inside drinking glasses with dabs of wax and they walk with them from room to room. At least the steam heat is working!

Edith peers out the front windows and down onto the Rue de Varenne. It is difficult to make out anything: a cloudy night with no streetlights. What is that moving? A single rowboat floating toward the Rue de Bac! Who would keep a rowboat in the city of Paris?

"Do we have enough food to last?" Edith asks Gross. There's just Gross and Elsie and herself to worry about. The new hired cook hadn't yet arrived when it began to flood. Who will feed them?

Gross comes to the rescue. She boils noodles and makes some kind of gravy to flavor them. She steams cabbage and carrots with vinegar and sugar, just as her mother did in Alsace. For dessert, they eat green apples. Sated, sitting in silence all together at the one table in the apartment, Edith can hear the street sloshing below. They might as well be in Venice.

And so it is for days. The Seine rises to record heights. Walkways are built over the larger streets. Edith hears the echo of hammering but can't tell from which direction the sound originates: it bounces off the buildings. The water doesn't go down. Cook arrives one afternoon, having used ramp after ramp to reach them, but he was forced to walk with water up to his thighs down the Rue de Varenne. In his knapsack, he carries fat chunks of cheese, a tin of crackers, jam, chocolates. And wine. Three bottles.

"I worried you had no food at all," he says. "And you mustn't drink the tap water until you boil it, you know. It could kill you, they say." He tells them that the flooding outside the Gare St. Lazare is almost up to the awnings. The tracks appear to be under six feet of water, but who could know? One would have to swim to find out! Edith wants to cable Anna to wait until the flood has gone down before she sails. No trains can arrive from Le Havre. But of course, the telegraph lines are inoperative as well. On Edith's birthday, an intrepid, gawky boy, a cap pulled down over his broken-nosed face, arrives soaked to his chest, thrusting forward what appears to be a cone of newspaper.

"Madame Wharton?" he asks.

"Oui. C'est moi."

Edith reaches for the little bundle and sees that it is a bunch of wilting, though still fragrant violets. She pulls off the damp note attached to them:

> *Dearest,*
>
> *These old violets were minding their business on the table at my favorite not-yet-flooded café. I surreptitiously wrapped them in the newspaper I was reading and by now the café owner has missed them and is no doubt cursing me, because there are surely no more to be had in all of Paris. Under the circumstances, it is the best I can do to wish you a Bonne Anniversaire. I hope you are surviving La Grande Inondation and staying très très seche.*
>
> *Yours, Morton.*

No present could have pleased Edith more.

It is almost a month before Anna can bring the furniture to Paris. She nervously pores over the *New York Times* each morning, hunting for the latest news of the floods. She is fairly certain that the letters she sends to Edith will never reach her and hopes she's not worried about the furniture's whereabouts. But surely Edith has more pressing things on her mind. Procuring food. Keeping dry. Keeping warm.

Anna wrangles permission from the new owners of 882 and 884 to stay longer than planned since neither the furniture nor Anna have anywhere to go. It is sad and unpleasant living among boxes and crates in what was once her home and now seems more like the baggage room of Grand Central.

While waiting, she thinks of Thomas. His silence all these months niggles at her. She had not thought him the sort of man who doesn't answer. He is a man who declares himself one way or the other. An organized man. These are things she admired about him. If he has found a better candidate to be his partner, surely he would write and tell her, wouldn't he? Unless she has simply thrown too many obstacles in his path. Unless he thinks she no longer cares. Either way, she needs to know.

So she unpacks the box that contains her old stationery, and, drawing a piece of blue paper from a box with 882 Park written up top, she writes a short note telling him that she will soon be back in Paris and would be happy to see him, if he could find the time to visit France. She tells him that there has been much turmoil and illness in the lives of her employers, which deeply saddens her. She writes about the Paris floods and her concern for Edith. And she ends up by recalling how pleased she was to see him in the lobby of her hotel in Venice. "Like a Venetian mirage, there you were, standing by the desk. I had to rub my eyes to believe it was you. It would be splendid to have that moment repeated, in Paris. I hope you will find the time." The last thing she does is include the Rue de Varenne address.

She seals the letter and presses it to her heart for a moment. What will he think when he receives it? Will a new wife turn it over in her hand, wondering who sent it? She presses a stamp on its corner and sends it off with the postman, trying to feel nothing, certainly not expectation—for Anna firmly believes it is better to expect nothing than to be disappointed.

❀

At last, the *New York Times* reports that the Parisian flood waters are receding, and that Paris is coming back to life. It isn't until Anna assures herself that the trains from Le Havre are once again running that she books passage, uncertain of the world she will find when she arrives and deeply saddened to be leaving the city of her birth, perhaps never to live on American soil again.

❀

It is a beautiful almost-spring day when Anna boards the train from Le Havre to the Gare St. Lazare, and all along the route she views muddy devastation. Fields sit in foamy cocoa puddles. Houses are painted half-way up to their roofs with brown scum. And Paris is a slippery, miserable mess, just shaking the mud off the cobbles, coming back to life. Like a general, she waited in Le Havre to direct the crates of furniture to be packed into a cargo train before she boarded her own train. She is exhausted now, bone weary, and painfully aware that she is not a young woman anymore.

The apartment house at 53, rue de Varenne looks more beautiful to her than she could have imagined. Climbing out of the motorcar into the courtyard, she breathes a sigh of relief. Cook helps her with her bags. All the way from the station, he'd caught her up about the flood. About how he brought the household food and how Gross cooked until the new cook was able to come. How the rowboats floated down the streets.

"Mrs. Wharton will be so happy to have the furniture at last," he says. "She said just yesterday that living in those empty rooms with the polished floors was like living in a ballet studio!"

"Did she think I'd absconded with it?"

"She said, 'Anna is doing the sensible thing and waiting. I'm sure of it.'"

Anna smiles to herself, pleased to be assured of Edith's trust.

At the door to the new apartment, she breathes a sigh of joy and relief. And when Edith hears the door open, Anna can hear her fly through the apartment to greet her.

"You are here!" she says. "At last, a normal life can begin again."

Anna can't fool herself into thinking that Edith is speaking just of her absence, and yet she knows there is a kernel of truth in that too. Edith embraces her like a soldier separated from a fellow combatant during battle.

"Our new life," she says. "Welcome to our new life!"

When Anna reaches her glorious new room, on the bed (there is not another thing in the room but the bed), a letter sits unopened. Anna lifts it and sees that it's from Germany. But instead of a man's handwriting, as she was hoping to see, the new address is penned in a flowery hand. Could it be from her cousin? she wonders.

> *Dear Miss Bahlmann,*
>
> *When we received your letter, we felt very sorry indeed that we didn't write you sooner, for Father spoke of you often in the last year, and we should have let you know. There is no way to soften this information, so I will simply tell you: Father died last July of a heart incident. We had no idea he had a problem with his heart. It was a very sudden death. He ate dinner with us one night as usual, and read a book in his favorite chair in the library. And then he called Baldegunde and said he didn't feel well and wanted to lie down, yet he was so weak, he could hardly move. The servants had to help us settle him into bed. The doctor was summoned, but it was too late.*
>
> *I know he cared a great deal for you. He told me once he hoped that you would soon become a part of our lives. We were so stunned by his death that we didn't do our duty in letting you know. And I hope you will forgive us.*
>
> *Someday, perhaps, you will come visit us in Essen and we can meet the woman our father was so taken with. We would*

all enjoy that, and perhaps you would be curious to meet us as well.

> *With great sorrow,*
> *Sabinchen Schultze*

Anna drops to the bed and stares at the spidery words. Her heart is bumping, and a weakness pours through her. She suddenly understands the meaning of the words "her blood ran cold," for indeed, she feels as though every pump of her heart is sending out icy ichor—too gelid and thin to keep her alive. When she tries to conjure Thomas, she can't see him. She will never look upon his face again. And she has no photograph to remind her. She is too empty and weak to cry. And so she sits. The sun drops behind the garden, and she doesn't even have the strength to turn on the light.

When the dinner hour comes, Edith knocks on her door, and receiving no response, she opens it.

"Aren't you joining me?" she asks, peering around the door. "This new cook is quite an improvement. . . . What are you doing in the dark?"

When Anna doesn't speak, Edith comes toward her.

"Whatever's wrong, Tonni?"

Rather than explain, Anna just hands over Sabinchen's letter. Edith finds the light switch and, standing by the bed, reads.

She sits down beside Anna and slips her arm around her shoulders.

"This was the man in Greece?"

Anna nods.

"Thomas, yes?"

"Thomas." Just saying his name releases the tears that have yet to come.

Anna feels foolish. For she is a sixty-year-old woman. A woman for whom no personal life was ever planned. She has spent a lifetime serving others. And it has been her choice. Her joy. But now she sees that her last opportunity for a life of her own is gone. She finds it almost impossible to breathe.

"What sort of man was he?" Edith asks.

"A formal man. But a kind one. He wasn't young. But he didn't look ill."

"Poor Anna. I wonder if you recall what you told me when my father died," Edith asks.

Anna shakes her head. It is hard to remember so far back. Edith was an uncertain young girl, not yet launched into society, when George Jones sickened suddenly from a stroke and shortly after died. The family had been on a long journey through Europe, a wonderful journey. They had to return to the United States abruptly. Anna came to help them, to calm Lucretia and set the house in order. Edith clung to Anna then, followed her about. Anna was the only person to whom Edith could express her sense of loss.

Edith slips her hand into Anna's now. "I remember it very well, Tonni. One day I cried to you about how I couldn't imagine going on without Father. And you said, 'Edith, your father will never really die as long as you can remember a single thing he gave you. Your love of books, for instance. Your patience. Your joy in flowers. Those things will live on in you.' Your words were the only thoughts that comforted me. Because I knew you were right. I could recall my father perfectly when I remembered what we shared. So if you can think of a single thing that your friend Thomas gave you, then I expect you'll feel the same way."

Anna closes her eyes and remembers the bright light in Thomas's eyes when he called her "*Unerschütterlich!*" She remembers the gentle sweetness of his kisses. "He gave me . . . he gave me a chance to believe for a moment that I was a woman."

Edith's mouth opens in surprise, and then Anna watches Edith's eyes well up, as though Anna's words have touched a nerve, shocked some similar truth inside of her. Edith stands.

"Join me for dinner when you're able. I'll wait," she says, her voice revealing its tremor. Anna watches her leave the room, wondering what she might be feeling.

In just a matter of days, the apartment at 53, rue de Varenne is plumped and softened and fitted out like a home, graced with Edith's linens and silver, familiar chairs and plush rugs. Anna works tirelessly, unpacking and washing, organizing, clearing. If her heart is broken, it isn't apparent to Edith. She seems renewed by the simple joy of cleaning, readying and organizing. She has never seemed more in her element.

Edith feels utterly happy to be making a real home in France at last. Since she was a child, she has always dreamed of being a real citizen of Paris. The thrill of saying, "I've taken a little apartment on the Rue de Varenne" loses none of its joy in reality. And without Teddy underfoot, she is truly, briefly happy.

Her world is glowingly perfect until she thinks of Morton. Morton, as he warned, has a full agenda of activities that don't include her. Foolishly, she telephones him, too often, probably. She can't seem to help herself. She has discovered that at around four P.M., he seems to accept a moment's break. Even if he doesn't stay on long, just hearing him satisfies her. And she has so many good things to report about the apartment. About her new life. Her joy has nowhere to go if she can't share it with him!

But at night, when Edith sleeps, her dreams are ragged with disturbing thoughts of Morton. In one dream, she returns from the theatre and encounters Anna, whose lips are white.

"*He's* in there," Anna says, twisting her hands together, pointing to the drawing room.

Rather than asking if she means Morton or Teddy, for these days, each could warrant the same ominous tone from Anna, Edith steps into the new parlor and there Morton sits: naked, cross-legged on the settee, wearing all of Edith's jewels—her collar of pearls, her diamond earrings, his fingers decked with her rings. In fact, six rings per finger. He is laughing and says, "They're mine now. You gave them to me. I have no intention of giving them back." In another dream, he tells her that now that she's moved to Paris for good, he's decided to leave. "I really can't bear to see you this often," he says. He looks at her out of the corner of his eye, as though he can't tolerate addressing her face to face. "And these telephone calls. I assure you, I loathe them." She weeps and tells him that he isn't worth her time or effort, that he's a cad and a disappointment. And that no matter what Anna de Noailles told her, love should not hurt so much. When she wakes, she is exhausted. Why, oh, why, can't she be happy at this happy time?

The dream reminds her to call Anna de Noailles. One afternoon, she takes la Comtesse through the new apartment, and afterward they sit and chat about love over tea laced with American whiskey, which the Comtesse has smuggled in by flask in her purse. How the woman can go on! Especially with the lubricant of alcohol. She speaks of her lover with a lush longing that Edith finds both unsettling and exciting. "Maurice? I torture him," she whispers to Edith. "Sometimes I am wild for him, insatiable. I use him until he's too exhausted to speak. And then I tell him I like him best when he is silent. He is a man of letters, so it drives him mad! Other times, dear Edith, I feign that I am bored. And of course, I often am. Men can be so boring, can't they? Their minds are like greedy children. And how is your lover?"

Edith shrugs.

"You love him still?" the Comtesse asks.

"Yes."

"Then make sure it is *you* making the choices, *mon amie*. What do they say in America: 'calling the shots'? I like that expression."

When de Noailles leaves, Edith, noting that it is past four, sits at the phone in the library and calls Morton, and to her surprise hears herself saying, "I want us to be together. *Together*. Just as you've often suggested." She tries to sound like de Noailles, lowering her voice, seductive. In control. She attempts to entwine a taste of the lascivious around her words. If the Comtesse can do it, why can't she?

"Together?" he asks. "Am I interpreting right?"

"I think you know exactly what I mean, dear," she tells him.

Morton's voice rises, sounds unsettled.

"I would like that . . . but here in the city, you understand. With the bureau breathing down my neck, I have no time these days to go out of town."

"In the city. But discreetly," she warns him.

"Leave it to me." She hears his chest puff like a robin's. Extraordinary that this should be audible. Later, she hates herself for having instigated something so unacceptable to her in the past. But it is too late to call him back, to call it off.

The small hotel that Morton chooses in Montmartre has a café that is reached through the lobby, so anyone seeing her enter might think she is heading for a cup of *thé* and a croissant. He was kind to think it through to this extent, at least. He is waiting for her in a chair by the front desk, smiling, impish. Just seeing him does lift her heart.

Somehow, the places they visited in the country felt different, sacred even. But the lobby of this hotel, with its smeary-looking travelers, salesmen and a few women of questionable morals, doesn't make her feel the least gleeful and she knows he senses it.

"Are you sure about this?" he asks.

She presses her lips together and nods.

When he procures the key, he hands it to her discreetly by taking her hand in his and settling the key into her palm.

"I will be there in a minute," he says. "Not a good idea to go up in the elevator together." How often has Morton traveled this elevator and sent a woman ahead?

The room is simple and clean, and one can see the Sacré-Coeur from the window. Edith doesn't know why it makes her feel so weary, so sad. He even knew which room to ask for. She sits on the edge of a bed, feeling out of her depth.

When he knocks on the door, his face is kind, though. And he is smiling.

"Will you hold me first for a while?" she asks, standing, coming to him.

"Dearest," he says, and pulls her close. He is a courtly lover. No one could ever accuse him otherwise. She drinks in the pressure of his compact body, the strength of his arms, the scent of lavender wrung from his clothes.

"We'll have to hurry. I can't be away from the bureau too long . . . ," he says.

She wonders if she could be anyone to him. A rough acquaintance, a prostitute. His blackmailing landlady. His blue eyes flash greedily as he unwraps her clothing. But she can see that he is merely doing what is expected of him. He is hardly with her at all. His eyes are distant. His passion is merely a bodily function. And even if he is good at it, his heart is wrapped in batting. Lying naked on the bed, she does all the things he's taught her to do. (He once told her she was a brilliant student of depravity—she laughed at the time, at his mordant choice of words.) But now, she feels nothing but the steady pound of her breaking heart. They are two separate hearts. Always will be. When he enters her, tears spill from her eyes and do not stop until he has satisfied himself.

"You didn't enjoy that, did you?" he says after a while, lighting a cigarette.

Edith says nothing, lies on the miserable, stiff bolster and traces a crack on the ceiling with her eyes.

She hears him sigh. "I don't know what to do for you. What would you have me do? Marry you? If that's what you want from me . . ."

"That's hardly what I want."

"Then what? You called. You wanted this."

"I want nothing from you but . . . for us to be of one mind."

"Oh," he says, his voice vibrating with irony. "Is that all?"

"We were once. We often have been. We are so much alike in thought. . . ."

"We are nothing alike," he says. His voice isn't cruel; in fact, it's almost sensible. "I am a creature of desire. And you . . ."

"A creature of intellect?" she offers.

"And yet you have the ability, the capacity to desire all that I do. You've been unafraid. You have an appetite for passion just as I do. It's been a revelation. And yet you cut it off. You bury it. I don't understand you."

"I'm tired," she says.

"Of me?" he asks, sounding almost hopeful. "Most people tire of me after a while." He wants her to be tired of him. He wants to move on.

"Of everything," she says. "Maybe it's best if we are just friends again."

"Ah."

"I have never known, since the very first day, what I am to you."

He blows a cloud of blue smoke and settles his wrist over his eyes. He looks as though he is about to answer her, but the bells of Sacré-Coeur ring out joyously, a full-hearted song of devotion, interrupting any attempt he might have made to speak. By the time they have completed their concert, if he was going to answer, he's forgotten.

He suggests she leave the hotel first, exiting via the café, and he lies still with his eyes closed as she dresses. She notes the purple hollows beneath the arc of his lashes. The pinch of exhaustion at the corners of his mouth. How she cares for him. Even when she's angry, or feels betrayed, it's unthinkable that she can ever stop loving this man. Before she steps into the hallway, she says, "We should be friends now. Nothing more. I'm convinced it's best that way."

He shrugs. Looks at her blandly.

Walking through the café, passing tables of relaxed friends, openly romantic lovers, she is flooded with a bitterness, realizing that she will never have the single thing she wants most in the world.

When Teddy returns with Nannie in tow, he is a frightening specimen. He stares glassily and doesn't ask questions. While in the States, he saw Dr. Kinnicut again, who wrote Edith a note of extreme caution. "Of course you will be careful about being alone with Ted with nobody within call. You cannot tell what mental tensions have been accumulating since you've seen him, nor how explosive they may be." She has thought many negative things about Teddy over the years, but never did she imagine he might actually be a danger to her. Still, shouldn't she have seen it when he raised that butter knife to Eliot at St. Cloud? Shouldn't she have expected this? *My punishment,* she thinks ten times a day. *I have brought this on.*

So, introducing him to the new apartment, she uses a kind and even tone as one might use to soothe an easily spooked and dangerous animal. It is the voice Tonni used with him when he was ill. She points out the things she thinks he'll like: how his room is near the library; how the light pours into the drawing room from the garden. Teddy's always loved houses, but she wonders what he can see or take in. At their first dinner together, he exhibits an empty stare like a man who has been given a sedative. He speaks only when spoken to. And then just a syllable or two, as though he is too weary to generate more. The primary sound at dinner is the clatter of silverware. He doesn't even answer the maid as she serves meat to his plate, asking him how much, and piles up the potatoes assuming he'll stop her when she's given him enough. And so his plate is groaning with food, which he barely touches. Afterward, Edith walks him out in the garden, which sparkles with pansies and late tulips all honeyed by the early evening light. Despite his love of gardens, he doesn't say a word.

And then, as she says good night to him at the door of his room, he starts to shake and his eyes light with malice.

"You make me a prisoner in this horrid place when I can only be happy fishing. Or with my animals. Why must I be here in Paris with *you*? I hate the very sight of you!" She shudders, sick that the neighbors might hear him. He's never spoken against her this way, even when he was at his worst. And to think he begged Dr. Kinnicut to let him make the journey to Paris because he missed her. Before, when he was soaked in melancholy, there was always Anna to soothe him. Now, Anna mostly keeps her distance. Nannie is no good at all, running from the room the moment Teddy raises his voice.

It's fallen to Edith now, and she doesn't like it at all. She doesn't know how to speak to Teddy. Maybe she never did. While she ponders what to say next, Teddy suddenly snatches his bedside lamp, a Limoges vase that Edith had converted to give him light to read by, and, yanking its cord from the wall, flings it at her. The beautiful vase with its hunting gentlemen and slender ladies slams against the door frame, exploding into a thousand pieces, celestial stars of china spewing from a single center. She feels the spray against her skirt, the shock against her ankle, and, lifting her hem, sees three small roses of blood blooming there. Panicked, she gathers herself and escapes down the hall.

"*No*, Puss. Don't go. I love you desperately. *Desperately*," he calls after her. "If only you loved me. Instead of that *bounder*."

She calls for White to go soothe him, warning him that Teddy has turned violent. One of the braver maids accompanies White to sweep up the mess. And Edith telephones the Paris doctor who diagnosed his ailment as gout in the head the previous year.

"He's gone mad, I think," Edith says. She gingerly touches her bandaged ankle. "He wants to hurt me."

The doctor arrives in less than an hour, his black leather bag banging against his leg. His hangdog face observing her with irritation, accusation.

"I did nothing to upset him," Edith feels the need to declare. She holds up her hands like the victim of a bank heist.

"Of course not, Madame," the doctor says, his lips pressing together with doubt. He enters Teddy's room with a nervous smile, and speaks to him in childlike English, asking questions that just seem to confuse him. How is he feeling? Is he very, *very* angry?

"I'm not angry. I'm *not* angry," he says.

"I hear you threw a lamp at your wife," the doctor offers.

"I didn't do that," Teddy says. "It's just not true."

"Ah, but you did! I see a piece right here." The doctor bends down and lifts a small shard from the floor that the maid must have missed and holds it out to him.

"I see there's no lamp by your bedside. Perhaps this is part of it?"

"It ain't true. I didn't do any such thing. They just want to make it look like I did. She makes me the villain, but it's not so. It's a setup." Edith shrinks back into the hallway, shaken.

Later, the doctor tells Edith he has theories, but no certainty. A brain malady, he declares. Perhaps a rest cure in Switzerland would help? Other than that, he is at a loss. The patient feels persecuted, misunderstood. The doctor wants to verify: did he really throw a lamp? Edith shows him her wounds, annoyed.

When Teddy is finally asleep—Oh, thank God, he is asleep!—she writes Morton, telling him of the impossibility of her life. She hates herself for turning to Morton. But even as unpredictable as he is, she feels he understands her. If he would just pen one line about feeling sorry for her. Or wish her relieved of such a painful burden! Or worry for her safety.

It should not surprise Edith that no response comes. Teddy grows rapidly worse, weeping, screaming, calling her names, sweeping things off tables. Thank heavens they are no longer at George Vanderbilt's. At least here, when Teddy breaks things, the items are hers and she can replace them.

Days pass. Weeks pass. Edith is tired and literally sick. Food won't go down. Sleep won't come. Just a word from Morton would be a salve. She writes again. And still receives no answer. When it comes to friendship, she tells herself, Morton is an eel, slipping away into the shallows at the first sign of a stir.

One night, with still no word from him, she paces her room. She locks her door at night now, leaving the key in the lock so Teddy can't jimmy his way in. As she walks from one side of the room to the other—such a beautiful room—she sees her life as the most ironic of stories. At last she has her foothold in Paris. After all these years, a dream realized. She has finally known what other women know. She has tasted passion. She has loved, truly loved! She should be ecstatic. Her days should be bursting with promise. Instead, her hopes lie near death, the weight of each breath almost too heavy to lift.

Morton. Once her solace, again her anguish. And everything she's feeling focuses on him. Her hopelessness, her frustration. Who is more dangerous to her: Morton or Teddy? Teddy is no longer in his right mind. She expects nothing of him. But Morton should be there to soothe her, to hold her, to care and worry. Even as a mere friend! Barefoot, shivering, for rain is singing coldly against every pane, she nervously unlocks the door and, listening for movement from Teddy's room, pads down the dark hall to the library, lights the lamp and finds a pen, a handful of paper, and begins to write. She inscribes the first line slowly.

I am sad and bewildered beyond words.

She runs her index finger across the sentiment, knowing this is where Morton has brought her. To a desert of wordlessness. A woman who has spent the best part of her life, against all odds, shaping a respectable living from words! She could stop now, crumple the paper and throw it away. Wait for him. Wait on and on for this mercurial man to come to her again. But she can't. She writes for two hours. Considering every line. It must be said. It must be shared. She is worth more than this pain. More than this disappointment.

I am sad and bewildered beyond words. And with all my other cares and bewilderments, I can't go on like this!

I seem not to exist for you. I don't understand if I could lean on some feeling in you—a good and loyal friendship, if there's nothing else!—then I could go on, bear things, write, and arrange my life.

I understand something of life, I judged you long ago, and accepted you as you are, admiring all your gifts and your great charm, and seeking only to give you the kind of affection that should help you most, and lay the least claim on you in return.

I have had a difficult year—but the pain within my pain, the last turn of the screw, has been the impossibility of knowing what you wanted of me, and what you felt for me—at a time when it seemed natural that, if you had any sincere feeling for me, you should see my need of an equable friendship—I don't say love because that is not made to order! But the kind of tried tenderness that old friends seek in each other in difficult moments of life.

My life was better before I knew you. That is, for me, the sad conclusion of this sad year. And it is a bitter thing to say to the one being one has ever loved d'amour!

She finds an envelope, seals and addresses the letter and sets it out on the table in the hall where White collects the mail each morning to hand to the postman. And then she goes to bed. Her sleep is instantaneous and dreamless.

In the night, as Anna is sleeping, there is a timid knock on her door. At first she wonders if she's dreamed it. She pulls on her wrapper and, moving close to the door, whispers, "Yes?"

"Miss Anna, let me in." Anna shivers at the sound of Teddy Wharton's voice.

"Are you all right, Mr. Wharton? Can't we speak in the morning?" Most nights, there is a nurse watching over him. Or White. Or someone. He's too unpredictable. Dangerous. Strange. And she has avoided him. He is no longer her charge. He is not the man she thought he was.

But tonight, his voice is sweet. A whisper.

"Dear Anna, please . . . I must speak to you."

What would it hurt to speak to him? she thinks. She cracks the door just enough to see him standing in his nightshirt, barefoot. The moonlight from a window paints his shadow long, allowing it to fill the entire hallway. Why hadn't he put on a robe, slippers? It's not like him.

"Are you ill, Mr. Wharton?" she asks. "Shall I call the doctor?"

"Why can't you forgive me?" he asks, his voice as innocent as a child's. "Why?"

Anna can smell the liquor on his breath. The servants have been told not to bring him liquor, to lock the cabinet and hide the key beneath Edith's blue hat in the front hall closet. The liquor only exacerbates his condition, roils the gout in his head, makes him impossible. But somehow, he has cadged a bottle. Brandy. She knows the scent.

"I think you've been drinking," she says. "You really should go back to bed."

But he doesn't budge. He leans close to her door, his words low and intimate. "You loved me once, Anna. You have no idea what it meant to me. When Puss gave up on me, you still stood by."

His voice is so inviting, it rocks her. She takes a deep breath, stalls. What can she say to him? Once she knew exactly how to soothe him, how to settle him. She wracks her mind for her next move. Yes, she did love him. But she doesn't now. Can't say it. Won't say it.

"We all . . ." She tries to be brave, steps into the hall. Taking his elbow, she hopes to direct him back to his room, just next to hers. "We all . . . just want to see you get better. Come, let me walk you back to bed."

"Will you lie with me there?" he asks. His voice is not sweet or child-like, but sly.

She looks at him sharply. "Certainly not."

"But you want to, don't you? You want to feel me against you. You've always wanted me."

Keep breathing, she tells herself.

"You're mistaken, Mr. Wharton."

"A man knows these things. I've always known. . . ."

"Go to bed!" she says. She uses the voice she reserves for recalcitrant children, but he doesn't seem to hear it.

"Say you love me."

"No, Mr. Wharton. Go to bed."

"Anna. Say it."

"No. I won't say it. And you need to go to bed!"

Suddenly, his voice is harsh, terrifying.

"Say you love me," he barks.

"I . . . I . . . don't love you. I care that you get well. . . . we all . . ."

But in the middle of her sentence, with no warning at all, he turns and grabs her wrists and pins her to the wall. She is so small. He is so much larger in every way. Pressing himself against her, she can feel his round belly, his massive chest.

"I want you," he says.

"No. Please," she begs. "You're hurting me. Let me go." She squirms. She kicks. Still, he holds her fast.

"Why should I? Isn't this what you want?"

She has never known the animal in herself. But her animal instincts emerge now. She twists wildly until her hand is free, and, reaching out, she claws at his face in one awful murderous swipe. He jumps back, touching the wound in horror. She sees the gash of red she's inflicted, and runs. Slipping into her room, she slams the door before he can stop her. Where is the key? Where is the key? She must lock it. *Where is her key???* But he isn't trying to open her door. She hears him in the hall. Weeping.

"Y . . . You loved me once," he is saying. "You bitch. You loved me once."

✦

She finds the key, but doesn't sleep all night. In the morning, she feels a quaking in the pit of her stomach that doesn't stop even after breakfast. When she hears from Catherine that Mr. Wharton got into a bottle of brandy last night and hurt himself—scratched his own face, imagine that!—she doesn't refute the story. How could she tell anyone what he said? What he did . . .

For the next two days, Anna washes and washes her hand. Tries to obliterate the feeling of his flesh beneath her fingernails. But the misery won't retreat.

Ever after, she won't walk into a room if Teddy is there alone. She wedges her dressing chair beneath the doorknob at night. She believed in Teddy, but now she can't help but see him as utterly and irreparably mad. And in her darkest moments, it is painful knowing that Edith, whom she loves more than herself, is the one that drove him there.

Weeks pass and still no answer from Morton. Edith is too numb to be hurt. Teddy is causing scenes almost every night. Morton is absent. Some mornings she can hardly bear to wake. At night, she falls into bed exhausted and hopeless.

Lately, she has taken to asking Anna to sit with Teddy and her in the parlor after dinner. At least they can speak to each other, for often Teddy is mute. Better he should be mute than raving!

One night, when Teddy finally goes off to bed, Edith looks up to see her old friend quietly, studiously knitting.

"At least there were no scenes tonight," she says.

"Yes. It's a relief."

"Dine with us tomorrow, Tonni," she begs. "Every night from now on, please. I swear I'll go mad if I have to have another silent meal with *my husband*." How sarcastically she says the words. Her husband. How is it that this man could be considered anything to her? This man who hates her. Who threatens her.

"You must send him away," Anna says. Her voice is so small, Edith must lean forward. She's stunned by what she hears.

"You've given up on him entirely?"

Anna nods.

Edith raises her eyebrows, looks into her face.

"But he's not well, Tonni. He doesn't know what he's doing."

"He knows. I knew he was ill. But now I think he's evil. He threatens you. Me as well."

Edith observes Anna, head down, her heart-shaped mouth set with bitterness, and sees something she does not expect: utter heartbreak.

"Has he threatened *you*?" Edith asks softly. "But you alone always believed in him."

Anna's lips quiver, though it is clear she is trying without success to look neutral. Her needles clack. Her eyes swim with unrestrained tears.

"Has he hurt you?" Edith asks, alarmed.

Anna doesn't speak. But her silence says everything.

"If he is dangerous even to you," Edith says, "my God, maybe there *is* no hope." How is it that Anna hasn't spoken a word of this? What has Teddy done to her? And yet, there she sits by Edith's side. Stalwart. Loyal. How ironic that a friendship so unwavering is the one most easily taken for granted.

Edith leans over and grabs Anna's tiny hand. "I'm so sorry," she says.

Anna drops her knitting but can't seem to meet Edith's eyes. Outside or through the walls, one can hear someone playing Chopin études. Beautifully, without a mistake. The piano arpeggios swoop and swing, exuding joyous simplicity. "Tonni . . ." Edith notes that her own voice is trembling. "I want you to know . . . that I blame myself for what's happened to Teddy. You think I've been blind, that I didn't care . . . but . . . I know that my . . . my friendship with Morton . . ." She shakes her head, can't go on.

Anna looks up, tears pouring now down her face. "I don't suppose you felt you had a choice, Herz. Or you wouldn't have done it."

Edith nods. How bitter she feels. In fiction, consequences are the results of missteps. Shattering, wrong choices. What was it that Morton said so long ago about Lily Bart? About the seductive glow of wrong options.

But in real life, despite what she wrote to Morton, she cannot truly believe that loving him *was* the wrong option. If she had turned him away the first time he kissed her, the first time he touched her, she would have gone on living an airless, antiseptic life, knowing nothing of desire, nothing of love, nothing of pleasure. She would have died never having lived. Wouldn't that too have been a tragedy? Perhaps there were no right options. Perhaps there never are.

For a long time the women are silent, both of them crying for something lost. With the étude complete, the clock ticks, the steam heat clanks, laughter rises from the Rue de Varenne.

"We'll keep each other company, Tonni. What do you think? Two old ladies with handwork and poetry, watching out for one another?"

Anna looks up, her eyes both sad and grateful.

"Yes," she says. "Just you and me. We'll keep each other company."

EPILOGUE

SUMMER 1916

Edith leans to one side in her chair by the window, more weary than she knew possible. By leaning, she can just see the little back garden—once her favorite aspect from this apartment—now choked with weeds. Ever since the war, she has refocused her life. No time for gardens, nor servants available to keep hers in order. Healthy men are at the front. And everyone else is entangled in the war effort.

"Do you write as a woman, about women, for women?" Anna de Noailles once asked her. Back then she felt defensive. She did not see herself like other women. She did not see herself as a champion of women. But Edith's greatest war effort has been for members of her own sex.

With saved money, Edith has founded workrooms so that French women whose husbands have left to fight, or died in battle, can sew and make an income for their hungry children. The goods are then sold to wealthy Americans shielded from the war, thereby raising more money to help more women.

She's opened hostels where refugees, mostly women and children and the elderly, can seek out food and shelter, shoes for their bare feet and comfort from people who care. She has taken in orphans from the bloody fields of Flanders and the pale, exhausted nuns who walked them for days on their journey to safety. Edith's money is being used for something irrefutably good. And it has mended her heart at last.

She rarely thinks of Morton these days, though when she does, she always feels a faint bruise on her soul. Still, she can't regret it. Morton helped her taste the best of life, if only for a moment. She risked, and reaped the reward of that risk. In the process, she was scarred. But scars are beautiful, she believes. They are the marks of having lived. Teddy, sadly, is the one who wears the most gaping wounds.

Three years earlier, she finally divorced him after more threats, more madness. When the papers were signed, what she felt most of all was a sense of failure, hopelessness, exhaustion. Last she heard, he was making a spectacle of himself in Boston, holding up his stockings with gold garters, escorting a fancy woman on each arm. Someone said he threatened a prostitute with a knife. She knows she could easily fritter away more years regretting all the time she wasted with him. And rue her part in his demise. Instead, the war has given her focus. Together, she and Anna have done so much, making a difference for thousands of people in a terrible time.

And what it has meant to have Anna stand by her side! From the very beginning of the war, Anna was furious at the Germans. There was such loyalty in the way she raged against her own people, pledged her loyalty to France and to Edith's causes. Knowing Anna, Edith would have expected no less.

Now she is gone. When Anna asked to travel to America, against all warnings, across a sea teeming with torpedoes, what could Edith say? She knew Anna's cancer was advancing.

"I'll give our speech in Kansas City," Anna said hopefully. "We'll get the good ladies of K.C. to reach into their pockets. Please let me go. The Captain and Aennchen want to see me one more time, and then I'll come back."

She packed her speech in her valise—the speech she gave again and again over the last year traveling from women's club to women's club throughout New England. Raising money for Edith's charities, calling on a bestilled and safe country to help people whose lives had been torn apart by a war thousands of miles away. American soldiers are yet to

fight. No one is certain if America will join the war. But Anna helped
them to *see* it. To feel it.

Little Anna, tinier than nearly every woman she encountered,
already in pain, her bones growing tumors all around them, but not saying a word about it, standing again and again before skeptical crowds,
speaking out like an orator. Heartfelt. Proud. A tear escapes Edith's eye,
thinking of those meetings, the officious women presidents. The call to
read the minutes of the last meeting. And then Anna stepping up to the
podium, smiling her heart-shaped smile. Speaking up for women so far
away. And she did it because Edith's cause had become her own.

Walter says Anna was the engine behind Edith. Even when Tonni
had gone nearly deaf, when her illness made her moody with pain.
When her typing had grown slow and sloppy and Edith didn't know
what to do, Walter says the charity couldn't have happened without
Anna. Because somehow, her kindness made everything work. She
soothed weeping workers whose husbands hadn't written for weeks.
She told orphans about her own childhood, and about her life, of which
she was quite proud. There was much to look forward to.

In the end, Edith frequently grew cross with her. She got in the way
too often. Anna wept because she felt herself useless.

"I've lived to be useful. And now this . . ." What could Edith say,
because at the very end, it was true: she was no longer effective.

Walter, a glass of wine in his hand, his voice low so Anna couldn't
hear, said, "Let her go to her family, Edith. She wants to see them. You
owe her that." And Edith acquiesced. These last few years, Walter has
been Edith's strength. Through the divorce she never imagined would
happen. Through years more difficult than she could have plotted in her
books. Teddy so dangerous the doctor told her he was a danger not just
to Edith but to society. Morton more unpredictable than ever. And the
war tearing apart her beloved France. While she wrote *Ethan Frome*,
back in the miserable summer of 1910, Walter read her pages every night.
Nodded with approval. And Anna wept when she typed the ending.
Together they held her up when Edith didn't think she could stand.

And when HJ died just this February, Anna was there to remember
the list Henry had made her jot down for his funeral when long ago he

had a mere cold. Black horses. No cars. They laughed together. And wept together.

"You come back," she whispered to Anna at the dock at Bordeaux.

"Of course," Anna promised. Her face was as diminutive as a child's. Had it grown smaller with pain and age? Edith settled her in her cabin, stayed at the dock and watched the SS *Espagna* sail out into treacherous seas.

Without Anna by her side, and her war charities straining forward, Edith has hired a new secretary, so much more efficient than a fading Anna. And she has found the perfect woman to help her run the Children of Flanders Rescue Committee, a woman who has become her dear friend. Another to run the hostels. But no one can read her face and mood as fluently as the quiet bystander who watched her grow from child to woman. It could be a burden sometimes to be seen so clearly as Tonni saw her. Yet no one has ever made her feel more beloved.

Then, just a month ago, on a night as soft as a cashmere blanket, Edith received the cable that Anna had slipped into a coma and died. Walter held her all night long. And she told herself it was best that Anna hadn't suffered. That she was with family. But what makes a true family? Wasn't Anna's true clan populated by Edith and Walter, Gross and Cook and White? She wrote to Anna's niece:

> Dear Mrs. Parker,
>
> The cable announcing Anna's death came last night, and you can imagine the shock it gave me. I was so reassured by your letter that I was looking forward to the possibility of seeing her here again as soon as it was safe for her to cross. I wrote her a long letter, telling her all my gratitude for the share I know she must have had in obtaining for the hostels a generous gift from the Kansas City Relief Fund.
>
> You know, to some degree at least, what Anna has been to me for so many years, what a friend and helper and companion, and you will understand how it adds to my sorrow that she should not have been with me when the end came. Yet I am glad for her sake and for yours and your father's that you were all together for the

last months of her life, after so many years of separation; and her letters show me how happy she was in this reunion, and how much your affection and your devoted care were appreciated by her. I let her go reluctantly only because of her insistence, and because I thought she might be right in thinking that the Paris winter climate aggravated her illness, and I was much worried at the idea of her undertaking so long a journey. But alas, I think for a long time the end had been inevitable and I can only be thankful that it came suddenly since I knew she foresaw and dreaded much suffering.

I shall never have a friend like her, so devoted, so unselfish, so sensitive and fine in every thought and feeling. I send you all my deepest sympathy, dear Mrs. Parker.

Yours very sincerely,
Edith Wharton

Every day since, she has thought of Tonni too often, bitter that their last few months together were strained, that maybe Tonni escaped because she no longer felt valuable.

But how stunning that Anna, in her last and pain-filled days, had still managed to raise so much money in Kansas City! Such a genuine outpouring of interest and support—who could have imagined it in a small Missouri city! When the money arrived in an envelope, Edith thought: Her speech must have been extraordinary. The stack of money was wrapped in a glued paper band with Anna's handwriting on it: "The Kansas City Relief Fund's donations for our charities, Herz."

Herz. Edith has always been Anna's heart. How lucky she was to have Anna's love all these years. When other loves failed her, Anna's was unbending.

And now this letter from Mrs. Parker today telling her the true source of the money. It has shaken Edith beyond words. Almost too tired to get up, she does, walks wearily to her desk, pulls out her desk chair and picks up her pen. Her hand is shaking. But she must write it, while the news still rattles her heart.

Dear Mrs. Parker,

I am deeply touched by what you tell me as to the origin of the sum from the imaginary "Kansas City Committee." I never dreamed that this was a gift from Anna, but I know nothing more characteristic than her sending me the money in this way.

Anna's own money. All she had in the world! Sent to fund the one thing Edith cares about most. Anonymously.

She seems to have had a premonition that the talk she was to give for the benefit of my work would never take place, and to have wished that the refugees, in whom she took so much interest, should not be the losers. It was a beautiful thought, and just like her.

She did it for me. The words echo in Edith's brain. *She would have done anything for me.* Edith is too tired to finish, as though her heart is squeezed, unable to pump out enough blood to sustain her. She sets down the pen and blindly finds her way to her bed.

In the morning she will have to dictate the words anew to her secretary. The letter in her own handwriting is too pocked by her weeping, and the only person capable of reading the crabbed and tearstained loops is forever gone.